PRAISE FOR TERMS OF RESTITUTION

'A rollicking roed loyalties and some very combine to produce one of the most satisfying gangland thrillers of the year' – *Irish Independent*

'A winning combination of (effing) fisticuffs and philosophy' – Mark Sanderson, *Times* and *Sunday Times* Crime Club

'Dark humour has helped to make his thrillers world famous' – Magnus Linklater, *The Times*

'Meyrick's breaking the mould with the latest offering straight out of the underworld of Paisley and the gritty streets of London' – *Sunday Post*

'This one isn't to be missed . . . it's brilliant!' – Waterstones, Falkirk

'Another corker from Mr Meyrick . . . brilliant, at times terrifying, story of ganglands, revenge, and how hard it is to escape the life of crime. As ever, superb characters and believable plots make this a must-read' – Waterstones, Horsham

'Addictive, beautifully constructed, and a wild and sometimes surprising ride through a gangland that is both believable and utterly gripping' – LiveAndDeadly

'An enjoyable and fast-paced thriller/crime novel that leaves its readers almost as breathless as it leaves many of its characters, though in a rather different way' – Undiscovered Scotland

Also by Denzil Meyrick

D.C.I. Daley thriller series
Whisky from Small Glasses ✓
The Last Witness
Dark Suits and Sad Songs
The Rat Stone Serenade ✓
Well of the Winds ✓
The Relentless Tide ✓
A Breath on Dying Embers
Jeremiah's Bell ✓
For Any Other Truth ✓

Tales from Kinloch
A Large Measure of Snow
A Toast to the Old Stones

Short stories
One Last Dram Before Midnight

For more information see
www.denzilmeyrick.com and
www.birlinn.co.uk

A note on the author

Denzil Meyrick was born in Glasgow and brought up in Campbeltown. After studying politics, he pursued a varied career including time spent as a police officer, freelance journalist and director of several companies in the leisure, engineering and marketing sectors. His DCI Daley thrillers – *Whisky from Small Glasses*, *The Last Witness*, *Dark Suits and Sad Songs*, *The Rat Stone Serenade*, *Well of the Winds*, *The Relentless Tide*, *A Breath on Dying Embers*, *Jeremiah's Bell* and *For Any Other Truth* – are global bestsellers. Denzil lives on Loch Lomond side with his wife, Fiona.

Terms of Restitution

Denzil Meyrick

First published in hardback in Great Britain in 2021 by Polygon.
This paperback edition published in 2022 by Polygon,
an imprint of Birlinn Ltd.

Birlinn Ltd
West Newington House
10 Newington Road
Edinburgh
EH9 1QS

www.polygonbooks.co.uk

1

ISBN 978 1 84697 602 5

British Library Cataloguing-in-Publication Data
A catalogue record for this book is available on request
from the British Library.

Typeset by 3bType, Edinburgh
Printed and bound in Great Britain by Clays Ltd, Elcograf S.p.A.

To the good folk of Paisley,
'buddies' one and all.

La vendetta è un piatto che va servito freddo.

Prologue

Two years earlier

Paisley

Most young guys would have approached a Saturday night out on the town differently. In order to save money, most young guys would have sat in the home of a friend or partner necking cheap supermarket booze or enjoying the balm of illegal drugs before hitting the nightspots. On the other hand, most young guys wouldn't be wearing a three-grand Italian suit.

Danny Finn wasn't 'most young guys'.

He swaggered towards the bar in New Street as though he owned Paisley, passing like a malevolent wraith through the regular crowd of smokers, who stepped back, anxious not to catch his eye or the blank gaze of his friends. When he pushed open the door, it could have been a scene from the Wild West. Of course, it was by sheer coincidence that the music faded at this moment. But the general hush that spread along the length of the pub was another matter entirely.

Danny and his youthful crew were notorious – especially on Saturdays. But nobody thought for one minute about asking them to leave; not even the owner, sitting in the corner with a friend, gave it a moment's consideration.

That was asking for trouble. Things were just the way they were. It was Saturday night in Paisley; it was their turn to play host.

Danny placed his drinks order politely, making sure the barmaid took twenty quid for her trouble. She smiled at him, though her hand trembled as she poured the first pint. Most of the men eyed her, each with their own version of a mocking smile. Apart from Danny, that was, who regarded the whole process with an air of relaxed detachment.

'Davie, get that pair off the table at the back,' he commanded, before taking his first sip of a pint of Italian lager. Danny liked to sit with his back to the wall, looking straight at the door. He'd learned this from the movies, and it was just one of the many things he did in order to make an impression. After all, his father ran the town. Almost every pub, club and many other businesses owed their existence to either the financial help he'd given them to start up or the money they paid to stay open. The heir to the empire had every right to demand whatever he desired – or so he reasoned.

Danny glanced to the table at the back of the bar as a pale young man tried desperately to pull his girlfriend away. She was pointing her finger in Davie's face, her partner holding his hands up in a gesture that said, 'What can I do?'

'Here, get those two a bottle of champagne,' said Danny.

The barmaid looked at him blankly. 'We just have prosecco.'

'Aye, okay, a bottle of that, then.' He raised his glass to the unseated couple as they stood awkwardly between two tables, drinks in hand, as the bottle in an ice bucket was delivered. The girl glared at her boyfriend as he wiped beads of sweat from his brow.

Soon all five of them were seated at the table, Danny in the middle, telling jokes, making them all laugh, like a medieval robber baron and his retinue.

The barmaid arrived to wipe down the table, using the opportunity to pass on a message. 'Mr Payne says the next round is on him.'

'Oh, cheers!' shouted Danny, to thank the proprietor for his kindness. His attention returned to the barmaid. 'Make it the next three rounds and Jamie here won't go and bust that ugly coupon of his.'

She nodded, finished with the cloth and hurried away, giving her boss a barely perceptible shrug of apology as she walked by.

As she served the third round of drinks to Danny and his crew, the bar was noticeably quieter. Even those who didn't know the rowdy young men at the top table sensed a charged, unpleasant atmosphere and had decided another establishment might be a better option for a relaxing drink.

'Hey, Mr Pain-in-the-Arse!' shouted Jamie. 'I think another round's in order, eh?'

Payne looked at Danny Finn, who stared back with a blank expression. He nodded to his barmaid, who started pouring more drinks.

'And some chasers this time. Five large vodkas with Coke!' said Danny.

'I like mine with fresh orange,' said Jamie.

'Okay, we'll have five vodkas with fresh orange, and five vodkas with Coke. That way we can all decide what we like best.' Danny's request sent his friends into another chorus of raucous laughter.

Through their mirth, they didn't see the door open. Two figures in hooded sweatshirts entered, rucksacks strapped to their backs. The barmaid was the first to scream as they advanced towards the end of the bar, removing automatic weapons from their backpacks.

Just as Danny Finn stood, a rattle of gunfire hit him in the temple, spraying blood, bone and brain against the wall behind, now pockmarked by bullets, splinters of wood and the puff of dislodged masonry. He slumped back, a perfect quarter of his head missing, almost as though it was a neatly cut portion of a cake.

Beside Danny's lifeless body his friends' shoulders rolled in a sedentary dance of death as bullets ripped through their bodies.

The killers turned and walked calmly back through the premises. One of them stopped at the table where sat the shocked proprietor. Only a short burst of gunfire ended Mr Payne's life.

As she rushed to bolt the door, the barmaid stood on a shard of broken glass that went right through the flimsy sole of her sneaker, making her scream in pain and hop the rest of the way.

She fumbled for her mobile phone in her pocket and pressed the emergency button on the screen.

Six men dead in a dead man's pub . . .

*

I'm sitting in the comfortable lounge I've come to know so well. The room is wood-panelled, with paintings on the walls but no photographs, something that has always puzzled me. Though he is a retired priest, none of these paintings are religious. They are mainly landscapes from his homeland in Calabria – the tip of the boot, as he always calls it.

Father Giordano is busy pouring whisky as I sit in misery. I feel like this because my son has gone – murdered.

'Here, drink this,' he says, his expression all sadness, compassion and concern. I've known this man since I was a child. I can trust him. I take the small glass and gulp down its contents. I need it.

'How long have we talked about this?' Suddenly, his voice has a harsh, accusatory tone that surprises me.

When I tell him I'm not here to talk about the past, he shakes his head. Again I notice he has become old. His hair isn't grey the way my grandfather's was, but white. It is in stark contrast with the cracked olive skin on his face. He sits down heavily on the old leather winged-back chair. He lets out a sigh, no doubt a quiet protest at the pain of his arthritic knees that I know trouble him.

'Yet it's the past that has brought you here.'

I shrug, placing the empty glass back on the old wooden chest that serves as his coffee table.

'You remember why I became a priest, don't you?'

'You wanted to be more than just a head doctor,' I reply less than graciously.

'That's true – psychiatry has its limitations. I only studied that as a pastime. But it is not the main reason.'

I'm always struck by the way he sounds as though he's just stepped straight off the boat from Italy. His accent is as strong as it was when I first remember him as a child. He hasn't picked up any Paisley inflection, not a hint that he has spent more than fifty years away from his homeland; this, aside from his annual holiday back to Italy. Something of which he never speaks.

'You only have two choices.'

'And they are?'

'You stay, fight and kill.'

'Or?'

'You leave, and all this will end.' He looks at me intently with his dark, almost black eyes. There's still youth there; when I meet his gaze I can see a hint of the young man he once was. 'If you stay, well, you know what happens. More parents like you, sitting in rooms like this, or bars, or at home alone with whisky or needles puncturing their skin. Whatever eases the pain in their souls. This is how it works. It is the way it will always be.'

I shake my head. I want to shout at him. I want to ask him, where is the compassion that I saw in his face when I arrived? I want to ask him why he's speaking to me like my father and not the curator of my spiritual wellbeing. But in my heart, I know.

As if he can read my thoughts, he replies, 'If you want, I can take your confession.' His face is blank now.

'But you don't want to, right?'

'What I want and don't want is unimportant. It is what God wants that matters. And, of course, you.'

'I don't know. That's my problem.'

'You are usually a man of action, decisive. Why has this changed?'

'You know.'

'Another death. You've seen plenty of those.'

'Why are you being like this?' I hear the faint tremor in my own voice.

He sits on the edge of his chair and holds out his hands. When I reach forward, he clamps my right hand in his strong grip. Yes, he's still strong for an old man.

'Sometimes it's better to go, to leave things behind. Often that is the only way to find yourself, to find salvation.'

He stares at me. I can see tears in those dark eyes. 'I can offer you penance, absolve your sins. But I know you don't believe that's in my gift. I talk to you as a friend now, Alexander. You go, you make peace with yourself. Do this in memory of your son. Do not repeat the sins of others. Do not make this world an even darker place. I know there is goodness in you. It is time to act on what is in your heart.'

'Why don't you back to Italy, Father? You're retired, after all.' It's a question I've wanted to ask him for a long time. I fear this may be my last chance.

'If I were to answer that, then I would have to lie. Do you want me to add to the sins of this world?'

'No.'

He nods at me and lets go of my hand.

'We should pray. Then you must follow your heart.'

I

The Present

Police Scotland HQ
The Detective Chief Inspector of Police Scotland's Organised Crime Unit Amelia Langley looked across her desk at the photo on the wall. Three rows of young police officers stood in a passing-out day group photograph. Langley barely recognised herself; but there was no doubt the fresh-faced young woman under the cap was indeed her.

The sight made her smile. But as she looked along the line of brand new police officers, the pinched face of Mary Green jumped out. Now her boss – an Assistant Chief Constable, no less – her rise had been meteoric. This woman was her nemesis – or so it felt. Now her smile turned into a scowl, a scowl because there was more, much more. It haunted Langley, but she had to live with it.

She had considered taking the photograph down, reasoning – quite reasonably – that she felt the same mix of emotions every time she looked at it. But Langley realised that removing ACC Mary Green from her office wall would certainly not have the same effect on her life. Green worked in a much larger office on the floor directly above her. Her presence would still loom over Langley, photo or no photo.

They had been the intake of 'bright young things', as

one instructor at the police college had sarcastically named them. All university graduates, they were promised a rapid rise through the ranks. This was a proper career in senior management, rather than an unpredictable trudge through the lower levels of 'the job'.

For many it had worked – she had certainly benefited from the Accelerated Promotion scheme. Others had fallen by the wayside. The tall young man to her right had quickly decided that the police service was not for him. He was now CEO of an oil company in Aberdeen. Langley guessed he had few regrets about ending his law enforcement career after only a few short weeks.

She knew that she should be happier with her lot. But Green, superior in rank – well above her, as she was physically in the building – would always be a source of her dissatisfaction. This notion was not merely the product of jealousy; it came from the genuine belief that Green had taken shortcuts. Langley knew she'd made all the right friends in the force's hierarchy, but she'd also moved far too freely among some of the people they were employed to bring to justice. Unfortunately, as far as the latter was concerned, she could prove nothing.

The thought also made her feel like a hypocrite.

A knock on the door shifted her thoughts from what might have been firmly into the here and now. DS Neil Dickie sat down heavily on the chair opposite.

'Well, what have you managed to find out, Neil?' Langley liked her right-hand man in the Organised Crime Unit, despite a nagging feeling he didn't relish having a female boss, and at times made that far too obvious.

'The Albanians are like that Japanese knotweed, ma'am. They're coming out of the woodwork.'

'Carving up more of Glasgow?'

'Aye, doing their best. Paisley is just about finished. Well, the Finns are, at least.'

Langley sat back in her chair. She should have been thinking about the rise to power of Eastern European organised crime in central Scotland. Instead, she could picture only one face: a man who had seemingly disappeared off the face of the earth when his son had been gunned down in a Paisley pub two years before.

Zander Finn.

London

As there were a few spaces in the Notting Hill street, he had been able to park reasonably close to Mrs Quinn's ground-floor flat. She and her husband had bought it in 1979 for fifty thousand; now it was worth over two million pounds.

She was of the old school – no airs, no graces. A straight-talking Londoner, originally from the East End.

'We'll just get you onto the ramp, Mrs Q,' he said, pushing her slowly past a Ferrari towards the patient transport ambulance.

'It's roast beef today down at the centre. A good old sing-song round the old Joanna, too. I love a Tuesday, me.'

'I could do with some roast beef myself,' he said.

'I thought you Jocks liked haggis.' She laughed at her own joke.

'Can't stand it, dear. I'm more of a caviar man, myself.' He smiled as she laughed heartily at the seemingly unlikely nature of this.

'You're always a tonic, son. Remind me a bit of my Jake, you do. He loved a laugh, did Jake.'

He positioned the wheelchair on a flat ramp, secured

the guard rail, pressed the button and watched Mrs Quinn ascend into the back of the ambulance.

'It's like Southend when I was a gal,' she chortled. 'Only thrill I get these days.'

'I'm sure you've still a few thrills left, dear.'

'Huh, the nearest I get is having a good piss in the morning. Trust me, son, you don't want to get old.'

As he made sure her wheelchair was secured in the back of the vehicle, the thought of getting old made him suddenly melancholy. Too many young people didn't make it. Though he tried, day after day, not to think of this vexed subject, nearly every morning he was reminded of the tragedy of it all when Capital news told of another young person who had lost their life to knife crime. Unprompted, the old sadness returned.

'That's you, Mrs Q,' he said, knowing she loved the rhyme.

'Thank you, son. If we get round there sharpish I'll get a space near the piano.'

As he closed the back door he heard a shout echoing down the street. It was a particular name that bounced from the high buildings, repeating as though he was in the mountains. Or maybe he just imagined that. It was, though, a name he wanted to forget.

'Zander! Hang on, big man.' A tall, heavy-set figure was making his way towards the ambulance at what could best be described as half-jogging, half-walking pace. By the time he reached the rear of the vehicle, his face was as red as his hair had once been. That hair had now faded, flecked with grey, as was his drooping moustache.

'Don't worry, I've a defibrillator on board, Malky.'

Struggling to get his breath back, Malky grinned. 'Two years and that's all you've got to say to me?'

'No, I want to know how the fuck you found me?'

'Come on, big man. I've known where you've been for over a year.'

Zander looked his best friend Malky Maloney straight in the eye with an expression that was, at first, hard to judge. Then a broad smile spread across his face and he embraced the man he'd known since he was three years old.

'Listen, we need to talk, Zander.'

'I need to get Mrs Quinn to the day centre or she'll miss her roast beef. We can talk when I've dropped her off.'

'What will I do – stand here like a numpty?'

'You can come with us. Get moving!'

As Zander Finn watched his friend struggle into the front passenger seat of the ambulance, he could tell that what he wanted to talk about could only be trouble. He wasn't surprised that Maloney knew where to find him. After all, they'd been tracking down people they wanted to 'speak' to for years together. What troubled him more was why Maloney had chosen now to make contact.

As Finn turned the key in the ignition he wished he'd gone to France, not London, to escape his past. But he was shit at languages and it had never been a real possibility. What would be would be, as his mother always said.

His mother; something else he'd tried not to think about for a long time.

'How are you doing, darling?' said Maloney.

'Oh, another Scotchman, how nice.' Her smile was brief. 'I think we'll have to make it quick, Sandy. Me bag's just about full.'

As the noisy diesel engine burst into life, Maloney leaned into his friend, now at the wheel. 'Her bag?'

'Stoma – colostomy bag, you know.'

Maloney took a few moments to process this information. 'Oh, for fuck's sake, Zander.'

'She can't help it. Hey, who knows how we'll end up?'

'It's not just that. I mean. *Sandy*, come on. Could you not have used more imagination?'

In the back of the ambulance, Mrs Quinn let rip with a loud belch. 'I am sorry, boys. Had some beans for tea last night. Leaves me like fucking Windy Miller.'

★

Maloney watched as Finn delivered his charge into the day centre. It looked like an old school, but now instead of children starting their lives, those nearing its end walked through the gates. 'Walked' wasn't even the right description: some in wheelchairs, others on sticks, crutches, walking frames, disability scooters. Only a few unaided.

He shuddered as Finn arrived back. He'd lost weight, that was obvious, not that he'd ever been fat. But it was clear to Malky Maloney that his old mate no longer did an hour a day in the gym. The grey streak in his otherwise dark hair that had appeared in his twenties was now even more pronounced.

'Can I have a fag in here?' asked Maloney.

'If you must. I'll drive for the next patient with the windows open.'

'Good man.' Maloney produced a cigarette and lit it with a gold lighter.

'Right, enough of the fucking about. Why are you here?'

'I'll come straight out with it, Zander.'

'Please do.'

'You need to come back.'

Finn looked at Maloney for a few seconds before bursting into laughter. 'Are you serious?'

'Aye, I am.'

'You think I can just come back, business as usual, after what happened to Danny?'

'It wasn't your fault. You know that.'

'I should have protected him!'

'He pissed people off everywhere he went, Zan.'

Silence for a few moments, then Finn spoke. 'Never say that to me again, Malky.' His green eyes were brimming with hatred and hurt.

'Okay, we'll not talk about that. Keep calm, eh?'

'So, tell me. Why would I come back?'

'To save the people you have left, that's why.'

'Gillian?'

'Aye, and Robbie, too.'

'Robbie's in Afghanistan.'

'No, he's not. He's in a rehab unit in Hertfordshire. He lost a leg, Zander. A landmine.'

Finn took a deep breath and gripped the steering wheel until his knuckles were white. 'Fuck!' he swore loudly. 'He was there as an advisor – non-combatant, that's what he said!'

'Guess he was unlucky.'

'I'm cursed – all of us are.'

Maloney caught him by the lapel of his blue uniform. 'Listen, you're the only man that can sort this.'

'What?'

'These Albanians, they're getting heavy. I mean *heavy*, big time.'

'Eh? There's only about a dozen of them.'

'That was when you left, Zan. There's a load of them now. We're all losing business.'

'I don't give a fuck about business. I'm happy doing what I'm doing.'

Maloney watched an old man lean against the railings of the centre to catch his breath, a slick of drool slipping down his grey stubbly chin. 'It's no' just about dosh. They've threatened families. Big Joe Mannion's oldest boy is in the hospital. He might not walk again.'

'My son is dead! Or had you forgotten that?'

'Aye, but Gillian and Robbie aren't. And don't forget Sandra.' He paused. 'There's been a direct threat – to them, I mean.'

'In what way?'

'The Albanians want to be the only suppliers. Not just at home, Glasgow too. They're not for giving up, either.'

'That's pish.'

'Tell that to Senga.'

'As in my *wife* Senga?'

'You've not slowed down any. Aye, your wife!'

'They've threatened her, too?'

'In a roundabout way, aye.'

'Why in a *roundabout way*?'

'She's been running things. Well, sort of. Since you left, I mean.'

'Fuck me . . .'

'Listen, she's gone in with Glasgow. We have to stick together to survive.'

'Ally myself to the bastards who killed my son. You must be out of your mind, Malky.'

'It's not as simple as that.'

'Why?'

'Mannion didn't kill Danny.'

'Who did then – Mickey fucking Mouse?'

'It was the Albanians. And if you don't come back and run things, they'll do the same with Robbie, Gillian, Sandra – with us all!' He hesitated for a few moments. 'Oh, and your mother's ill – dying, I hear.'

'She's been dying since 1973. And don't mention Sandra to me. You know why.' Zander Finn waved his hand dismissively.

2

Paisley

The old woman stood at the window of her flat in the tower block that overlooked the town she knew so well. Or at least had once known so well. Paisley used to be a thriving community, a mill town famous all over the world. Now, as her eyes took in the skyline, familiar sights were missing while other less appealing edifices had sprung up. She sighed, reflecting on the nature of change and getting old.

The room was misted with a grey haze of tobacco. She turned when she heard the lounge door slide open over the thick carpet.

'Gillian, I near shat myself!'

'I rang the door. You did give me a key, remember?'

'Aye, I suppose. When I'm gone you can just move in. This is a nice wee pad for a young person.'

'You think?'

'Well, it's a bastard when you get old. They lifts stink of piss, and there's all sorts cloaking about. Some shite tried to steal your Auntie Gwen's purse the last time she came to visit me.'

'Oh, that's terrible.'

Maggie Finn shrugged. 'You know oor Gwen. Just gave him a boot in the balls, so she did.'

'And you want me to live here?'

'You're as bad as your mother. Always the comments. How is Senga Corleone, by the way?'

'I haven't seen her for a few days.'

Maggie turned round to face her granddaughter. Though the girl had her mother's looks, she had her father's eyes – her eyes. Gillian was thinner than ever, her face drawn. It looked as though she could have cut glass with her high cheekbones, framed by her honey-blonde hair. This is where ambition got you – a walking skeleton, so desperate to tread the boards she'd go to any lengths at the Conservatoire, Scotland's premier school for music, dance and theatre.

Her other granddaughter, Sandra, was so different: robust, wilful and confident. But families were a mystery, and she didn't want to think about Sandra.

'Will you open a window, Gran? It's no wonder you're not well. This must be more unhealthy than living in Chernobyl.'

'Too late for me to worry about such things.'

Ignoring her grandmother's habitual intimations of imminent death, Gillian carried on. 'I'm going to see Robbie. My friend Kirsty is driving me down. I thought you might like to come with us.'

Maggie thought of her handsome grandsons: one dead, the other missing a leg. She'd spoken to him on the phone and he'd sounded broken. She dreaded the thought of seeing him face to face. She took a deep breath. 'When are you going?'

'Tomorrow. There's plenty room. Her dad's a doctor. He bought her a big SUV.'

'I get sick in the back.'

'Then you can sit in the front!'

'What kind of driver is this lassie? I know what you young folk are like – speeding, all they heartbreak turns.'

'I thought it was too late for you. What are you worried about?'

'Don't get cute. I'll think on it the night.'

'Well, you'll need to let me know. We're leaving at six.'

Maggie took a seat on her long, cream leather sofa. 'You say that as though I've never been up at six o'clock in my life. I'll have you know, my shifts at the mill used to start at five-thirty when I was your age.'

'At least I'm spared that.'

'You'd look healthier than you do now. You take the weight off your skin and bones and I'll away and get you something to eat. You know how much you like my egg, beans and chips. Real chips, none of that oven rubbish.'

'I'm a vegan now, Gran. Have been for over a month.'

'Aye, you're looking great on it.'

'It takes a while to adjust, that's all.'

'What do you want, then? I can boil an onion,' said Maggie, with more than a hint of sarcasm.

'I should be making you something. You're the one that's dying.'

'What if I leave off the egg?'

'What oil do you use – it's not that lard, is it?' A brief look of horror crossed Gillian's face.

'Oh, for fuck's sake. I use vegetable oil – have done ever since the doctor told me about my heart.'

'I guess that sounds good, if you leave off the egg.' Gillian shrugged, gazing out of the window through the haze of smoke.

'What's the real problem, here?'

'Eh?'

'You've got a face like a wet Monday in Greenock.'

Gillian thought for a few moments. She knew that her grandmother wouldn't take kindly to the news – well, she thought she wouldn't. But she also felt as though the family matriarch had the right to know.

'You're not pregnant, are you? Bugger me, that would fair ruin your acting career.'

'No, I'm not.'

'So, who is?' Maggie hesitated. 'Wait, not that mother of yours. My poor boy, likely a rickle of bones by now, while it's open house for all and sundry in his home. She'd be better with one of they revolving doors in the bedroom.'

'Gran!'

'Well, it's the truth.' Maggie lit another cigarette.

'Don't say that Dad's dead. I know he isn't.'

'You've one brother dead, one half dead, and a father that disappeared two years ago. Come on, lassie, what do you think? I'm not into mollycoddling weans, you know that fine.'

'I'm twenty, Gran.'

'That's still just a wean.'

'No mention of my sister. I'm sick of it!'

Maggie's green eyes blazed. 'I'll leave you to work out why that is, Gillian. For somebody that goes to a place I can't pronounce to learn to act, you're not so smart, eh?'

'Kevin didn't have anything to do with Danny's murder. Surely you can see that. And before you start' – her voice had slowly risen so that she was now shouting at the top of her voice – 'don't say that thing about Mickey Mouse.'

'She's dead to me – to all of us.'

'Has there not been enough death in this family, for fuck's sake?'

'That's my last word on the subject. And don't curse in my house.'

'You do it all the time.'

'I'm old and dying.'

Gillian shook her head with a long sigh. 'So you don't want to see your new great-grandson?'

Maggie looked at her granddaughter. 'Is it Kevin Mannion's baby?'

'Yes, of course, but it's Sandra's, too!'

'I don't want to hear another word on the subject.' Maggie Finn crossed her arms resolutely, staring Gillian out.

'Do you know, you're all the same – the lot of you! As soon as I graduate, I'm out of here.' Gillian picked up her large handbag and headed out of the room.

'I'll come tomorrow – aye, and what about your chips?'

The slamming of the door was the only response.

3

Though Maggie Finn hadn't heard from her granddaughter, she was as good as her word. A large silver SUV drew up outside the tower block under the sodium lights just after six. Maggie had packed an overnight bag, even though she had no idea if they would be staying.

She stubbed out a cigarette with the toe of her leopard-print high heels before Gillian had the chance to jump out of the passenger seat.

'What on earth are you wearing, Gran?'

'Eh? Do you think I'm going to go down and see your poor mutilated brother like some tinker? No way!' She looked Gillian up and down. 'You could have made an effort, too.'

'Gran, you look like a geriatric prostitute.'

'Right, that's it. I don't want to embarrass you.' Maggie turned on her high heel, hefted her bag and took a few steps towards the entrance to the flats.

'Don't be stupid, come on. If that's what you want to wear, good luck to you.'

'At least I'm no' the weight o' tissue paper, or one o' they poor folk from Biafra.'

'Where?'

'Never mind. They were poor folk that didn't get much to eat – before your time.'

Gillian smiled sweetly, despite the barb. 'This is Kirsty. The friend I told you about.'

Maggie clambered into the front seat of the car and held out her hand to the pretty black girl behind the wheel. 'Maggie Finn, her grandmother, though there's no much similarity, as you'll have noticed.'

'Oh gosh, you're just as funny as Gillian said.'

Maggie turned to her granddaughter, now in the back seat. 'So, what did you *say*?'

'We don't have time for this. It's a good five hours to Stanford Hall,' said Gillian.

'To where?'

'Stanford Hall – where Robbie's being treated. It's a brand new, state-of-the-art facility. At least he's in good hands.'

'His hands are fine; it's only having one foot that's the problem. Anyway, you're never in good hands with the medical profession.' Maggie turned to Kirsty. 'I'll spare you the horror of what they did with my piles, dear.'

'I am sorry . . . Mrs Finn?'

'Just call me Maggie, darling. Suffice it to say, they made a right arse of the whole thing.'

'Oh!' Kirsty looked startled, as Gillian snorted with laughter in the back seat.

They made their way down through the dark streets of Paisley, heading for the motorway.

'Are you warm enough, Maggie?' said Kirsty.

'Aye, I'm fine. You young folk always have everywhere too hot these days.'

'What she means is, aren't you getting a draught with having hardly any skirt on, Gran.'

'I'll ignore that. I can still show off my legs. Yours are

likely matchsticks, though I don't ever see them under they awful pantaloons you insist on wearing.'

'They're jeans, Gran.'

'I'll put on some music,' said Kirsty, sensing the tension.

'Good idea, but I'd be grateful if you refrained from any of that thumping stuff. It's the bane of my life. Every night these cars going past with all that thudding. It's bad enough on the seventeenth storey, I hate to think what the fuck it must be like in the car!'

'Excuse my grandmother's language, Kirsty.'

'I think it's kind of cool. The nearest my nana gets to swearing is the odd *Damn it!*'

'I am what I am, Kirsty. Not to everyone's taste, I daresay. But you should always be yourself, not try to be someone else.'

'That's kind of unfortunate, as we're both studying drama, Gran,' retorted Gillian.

'You've always got an answer, eh? Just like your bloody mother.'

Kirsty pressed a button on the steering wheel. 'How's this, Mrs Finn – I mean, Maggie.'

'The Beatles! Now you're talking. At least someone has taste.'

Dawn was just breaking above the rooftops as they made their way along the M8 towards Glasgow and beyond to the strains of 'Old Brown Shoe'.

London

Though Malky had booked flights back to Scotland, Zander Finn wasn't keen. He hated flying, for a start, but Glasgow airport was basically on Paisley's doorstep – and his reputation went before him. If he was going to return home, he would do so as quietly as possible. So Malky hired a car.

They'd spent the previous evening enjoying a bottle of whisky, doing as friends do, remembering the good old days. Now in the cold light of a grim Brixton morning those rosy tales of the past seemed somehow diminished. Finn wondered just why anyone had seen fit to build the ugly block of flats opposite. Gone, the headiness of the spirit that came in a glass, replaced by what existed in the space between the ears.

Nursing his second mug of tea, he looked across the grey rooftops as his old friend snored loudly on the sofa. There was so much to be considered, not least his life.

In a way, he felt ashamed. He closed his eyes tightly to banish the tears as he remembered the sleek black hearse that contained his son's coffin. The wreaths that spelled out 'Danny Boy', not quite obscuring the dark cocoon within which his child would lie for eternity, made him recoil in a way he'd never done before at death.

He should have taken revenge; he should have buried his son and taken a life for a life. But Finn was sick of death and destruction. He liked money, of that there was no doubt, but the murder of the heir he was grooming to take over the family 'business' cost his soul more than any fortune could replace.

As soon as the funeral cortege entered the gates of Paisley's Woodside Crematorium, he'd made up his mind to wash it all away, to leave, never to return.

Having a normal job had been strange. He hadn't worked since his days managing one of his father's pubs in the town's west end. Even then, he'd been the boss, so being told what to do was a new and at first somewhat unnerving experience.

But as power brought responsibility, the opposite was also true. Eventually, he enjoyed getting out of bed without a mental list of things to do. He even revelled in helping others. Basically, he drove the elderly and infirm to day centres, hospital appointments, doctors' surgeries and a long list of other destinations. With his natural bonhomie and the quick-fire banter he'd acquired on the streets of his home town, he soon found himself the most popular of all the drivers, the majority of whom found the whole thing deathly dull and did it only for the pittance of a wage that was their reward.

Yes, he had found it strange to live on so little, but he'd always enjoyed the security of the big bag of laundered cash he'd brought with him in case of a rainy day. Anyway, he had all he needed: somewhere to lay his head, enough to eat and the odd dram or two to enjoy. He didn't need a car in London; that was nothing but a hindrance. He went most places by bus, or occasionally the tube.

Of course, there were those who tried to mark their territory – even in the world of patient transport. For a short while Finn had ignored the barbs of the fat man with the shaven head and the National Front tattoos hidden under his uniform. But inevitably the man had gone too far. The joke had been about a dead black kid. It wasn't directed at him – unlike the undermining references to 'Hey, Jocko', or 'What have you got under that kilt, you Scotch bastard?' – but the tastelessness of it all had galvanised him to action.

Finn waited for the man outside the boozer his colleague frequented and took his eye out with a broken bottle.

As he left his erstwhile tormentor screaming in a side street the old rush had returned, but he soon managed to force the genie back into the bottle. One brief memory of the ruined body of his son disappearing into the crematoria flames was more than enough to banish the feeling.

'Hey, where's my tea, Zander?' said Malky Maloney, his voice still slurred by a mixture of sleep and residual alcohol.

'In the fucking teabag! What do you think this is, room service?'

'Nice to see you're back to your old self.'

'You think?'

Maloney shrugged. 'You'll need to be.'

Finn drained his mug of tea. 'Listen, I've had a change of mind, Malky.'

'Come on, Zander. You telling me you're going to abandon your family, friends – everybody?'

'Why shouldn't I? What have any of you done for me, apart from pocket the large sums of money I've deposited in your banks?'

Maloney looked suddenly hurt. 'Thanks,' he said with a sigh.

'I don't mean you.'

'So you mean Gillian, Robbie, Senga – Sandra? Aye, she does still exist, by the way.'

Finn looked at the man in his underpants on the sofa. 'We don't talk about that, remember?'

'Ach, catch a hold of yourself, man! She's your daughter. Is losing one son not enough?'

For a few moments Finn balled his fists, his face reddening with anger. But soon it passed. 'You're the only man that ever told me the truth, Malky.'

'Somebody has to.'

'I know.' He walked across the room to a small sink beside which sat a kettle. Finn filled it and clicked the switch.

'I never asked you about Dusky, Big Tam and the rest. I suppose they take their orders from my wife now, do they?'

'Aye, but they're not happy about it. I'm sure you can picture the scene.'

'I can. They won't respect me any more.'

'They will, Zander.' Maloney produced a stiletto knife from his sock, flicking the vicious-looking polished blade out. 'They'll respect you or they'll get this. In any case, they're all shit scared. You've no idea.'

'How can things change so quickly?'

'First off, we were all too busy fighting amongst ourselves.'

'Secondly?'

'There was nobody steering the ship.'

'I thought Senga had the wheel.'

'She has the cash . . .' Maloney gestured dismissively.

'Okay, I'll do it. But it's not a long-term arrangement. We see off these Albanians, and I get a settlement.'

'Whatever you say, boss.'

'And another thing.'

'What?'

'I want to go and see Robbie on the way up. Get your tea and get dressed. Time to go.'

As Malky Maloney padded across the floor towards the boiling kettle in his vest and pants, Zander Finn looked back out the window at the grey buildings and the greyer sky.

'Fuck this,' he said to himself.

4

Stanford Hall

There was the inevitable security check as they approached the entrance to the grand-looking building where Robbie was recuperating. Maggie Finn searched through her handbag for the driving licence she always carried these days. You could barely buy a cup of coffee now without some kind of photo ID. Soon, they were escorted to the car park and given passes on blue lanyards that read 'Visitor' in broad, bold letters.

Maggie hated hospitals. She'd watched her parents waste away with cancer in the old Beatson hospital in Glasgow, then endured the final moments of her brother Bobby's life in the Royal Alexandra in Paisley. As medical staff had tried to resuscitate him, she'd known it was over – his second heart attack in as many days.

He'd had enough time in-between to point out a nurse who had chastised him for letting his piss bottle overflow, soiling the sheets. Maggie had almost cried herself when her brother – a man who had terrified those who'd had the nerve to stand in his path – burst into tears and told her that the nurse had made him stand while she took her time to find new sheets and make his bed, making no secret of what had happened.

Most grieving siblings would have spent the moments after their brother's death in inconsolable misery, or at least quiet reflection on lives shared. Maggie, on the other hand, exacted natural justice by locating the nurse and breaking her nose with a head-butt.

Maggie Finn wasn't like most grieving siblings.

This time round, walking down the long corridors to see Robbie, a man named after his grandfather, she felt nothing but misery and bitter regret. The family – even his useless mother – had tried so hard to dissuade Robbie from joining the army. Quietly, she had admired her grandson's determination to do something good, but she reckoned she knew the reality of what he was about to face. At least he was still alive. She knew there were many others who'd stood proudly at passing-out parades but weren't so lucky.

'Good morning, ladies. I'm Captain Fairfield. I'm looking after Sergeant Finn.'

Maggie eyed up the impossibly young-looking man, as her granddaughter gushed over him. 'Would he not be better in the care of a doctor rather than a captain?' she said, waspishly.

Fairfield laughed nervously. 'Of course I am a doctor, too.'

'Well, why not just say that? If I need my boat steering, I'll find a captain. If my leg falls off, I'll need a doctor.'

'Gran!' exclaimed Gillian, looking embarrassed.

'I'm not that kind of captain, Mrs, erm—'

'Mrs Finn, captain – doctor, whatever you are. I'm Robbie's grandmother. This is his sister Gillian and her friend Chrissie.'

'Kirsty,' corrected Gillian.

Ignoring this, Maggie carried on. 'Well, ahoy then, or whatever it is we do. I want to see my boy.'

'Yes, of course – this way, please.' He led them down a corridor, the doors of some of the rooms closed, others open.

'This section is where most of our leg amputees are billeted.'

'Billited? Would "treated" no' be a better word?' said Maggie.

'Ha! You have the right of it there, Mrs Finn. Old habits, and all that.'

Gillian glared at her grandmother balefully.

'Here we are, two hundred and thirteen – Sergeant Finn's room.' He knocked gently at the door. A weak response sounded from within.

London

Once on the motorway, it didn't take Zander Finn and Malky Maloney long to leave the suburbs of London behind. Finn stared out at the scenery, happy to let Maloney drive, despite his sore head. His own mouth was dry, not prompted by the alcohol of the previous evening but the thought of visiting his remaining son.

They passed a large blue sign that simply read, 'The North'. It was as though ahead lay some strange foreign land. From what he'd experienced of London, that might be appropriate, he thought. There was little doubt that Paisley and London were further apart culturally and socially than they were in terms of mere miles.

But Paisley wasn't the first stop. The satnav blared out another instruction, sending them in the general direction of Loughborough.

'You okay, Zan?' said Maloney.

'Aye, I suppose I am.'

'There's services in about five miles. I could fair go a coffee – we've got loads of time, big man.'

'Okay, I'm parched myself, Malky.'

Maloney stared across at his old friend. He looked grey

in the face – older somehow. He remembered their youth: football, pubs, girls – in his opinion it had been an easier life back then. Nowadays kids were surrounded with shit they didn't need and served them only to lead more and more isolated lives. The world was a strange place. But he'd always known that.

'Got a hold of some great knock-off smartphones from a guy in Aberdeen, Zander.'

'Oh aye.' The reply distinctly lacked interest.

Maloney persevered. 'Come from Korea. They just look like real iPhones, but we get them for a tenner a whip and sell them for three hundred.'

'What happens when your unhappy customers return?'

'I'm not stupid. We punt them at car boot sales, markets. By the time they realise they've bought a load of shite our boys are back on the road. We use a real one to demonstrate, tell them the rest have to be charged up.'

'So you don't sell in Paisley?'

'You think I'm daft. Remember they tellies?'

For the first time Finn smiled. 'The ones we shrink-wrapped?'

'Aye, they'd nothing inside but a bit of concrete block wedged in at the bottom to give them some heft – classic.'

'Remember the guy from Well Street?'

'Aye! He brought his back round the pub and hit big Dusky over the head with it. Man, that was funny.'

'Just as well he'd taken the concrete out.'

'That head of Dusky's could stop a plane, Zander. Anyway, I doubt he ever returned any faulty goods again.'

Finn remembered the aftermath. Dusky had dragged the man the length of the street and pitched him into the White Cart. 'That was just before the curfew, mind?'

'Aye, I mind. If you were in a pub after nine you had to stay there or go home. You couldn't enter another licensed premises. We always locked the door at Jiggy's at eight, remember?'

'That was a good law.'

Maloney steered into the slow lane before the cut-off for the services.

Zander Finn felt buoyed by the memories. It hadn't all been bad: broken bones, slashed faces, gunshot wounds – and worse. But, he reflected, most people got what they deserved. *If you don't like the game, don't play it*, his father had always said. He'd been right. But people always wanted more, and some got more than they bargained for.

★

'Gran, how are you?' said Robbie Finn, trying to force himself up the bed with the aid of Doctor Fairfield.

'In the name of fuck, what have you done to my grandson?' Maggie looked at the wasted, pale figure lying in the specially adapted bed. Gone was the big lump of a boy she'd known, replaced by a shadow. His cheeks were hollowed, eyes sunken, seemingly lacking any hope.

'He's doing well, Mrs Finn. We're very proud of him,' said Fairfield, using a hand-held control to adjust the bed.

'What do the ones that's not doing so good look like, eh? Do you get fed, Robbie?'

'Aye, Gran, the scran's not too bad. Just I've not got much of an appetite right now. You know, what with everything and that.'

'Why's your eye twitching?'

'Gran, will you just shut up!' shouted Gillian. 'Robbie, it's great to see you.' She leaned across her brother and hugged him awkwardly. As she drew back, she realised she'd patted flat the place where his right leg should have been and apologised quietly.

'There's nearly bugger all to see! Here, captain, I want a word with you, my friend.' Maggie grabbed the doctor by the arm and ushered him back into the doorway. 'Why didn't you tell us Robbie was dying?' she whispered angrily.

'He isn't, Mrs Finn.' Fairfield paused. 'But he's still suffering from shock – that's why his eye is twitching. I'm sorry to say this, but you'll have to be gentler with him. He's going through a very important transition phase right now. Physically, he's well, but . . .' His voice tailed off.

'What are you saying – he's lost it?'

'No, not at all. He's just a bit fragile, that's all. What happened to him, well, it's a shock to the whole system, you must understand.'

'Aye, I understand fine. One minute you're standing on two legs, the next you can see one thirty feet away. I'm not bloody stupid!'

'Do your grandson a favour, Mrs Finn. Be good to him, yes?'

Something about his stern look gave Maggie Finn pause for thought. 'Aye, aye, captain – but you better not be steering for the rocks, you hear me?'

5

The Iron Horse, Glasgow

The bar in Glasgow's East End was busy for a Tuesday afternoon, but it was half price drinks day, so every Tuesday was the same. A bald man sat at a badly out-of-tune piano, murdering his version of 'Sweet Caroline', while another pair of elderly men squared up to each other over a game of cards.

At a table near the less-than-fragrant toilets sat three women of a certain age. Their glasses were full, not half empty, the opposite of their heads. They sang along merrily to the song as a man in a flat cap capered at their side, a half bottle of whisky sticking out of the pocket of his threadbare jacket. The barman looked bored as he rang the till then went back to watching the horse racing, the rolling news channel of choice in the Iron Horse.

'Here, Jenny,' said one of the old women to her companion sitting nearest the toilet door. 'You've had a wee accident, so you have. Aye, and your wig's at a fair cant.'

'What are you calling me, Ina, you old bitch?'

Ina raised her voice. 'I'm saying your wig's at a *cant* and, well – take a look under the table.'

Jenny attempted to straighten her wig, but went too far. Now it was skewed to the other side. She then peered blinkingly at the faded red linoleum that served as the pub's floor covering. 'Fuck me, I've pished myself!' she announced, much to the amusement of her friends.

The capering man knelt forward, swaying, hands on knees, to have a look at the floor underneath their table.

'You're a clatty old bugger, right enough, eh?' However, happy hour had taken its toll and, having leaned too far forward, he lost his balance, pitched forward, his head narrowly missing the bottom of the table but sliding right into the pool of warm urine on the lino. 'Oh, you bastard!' he exclaimed, as he tried to get back to his feet.

'Who's the clatty bastard now, Willie Pollock?' said Ina. 'If you were a woman of our age, we'd be swimming in piss. You can't laugh or blow your nose but you're in trouble, let me tell you.'

'You can say that again,' said Jenny.

'Here, Pavel, Jenny's had a wee accident, can you bring over the mop and bucket?'

'I should have stayed in Poland,' muttered Pavel to himself as he reached under the bar for a bucket.

'S-w-e-et C-a-r-o-l-i-n-e!' The man at the piano ended the song with an extended flourish. He looked round, but all he saw was Jenny McKay, a damp stain on her light skirt, being helped into the toilet by her friend, while Pavel the barman mopped under the table unenthusiastically. To his left, Tam Wheelan sent his mate Andy Clark flying off his chair with a neat right hook, cards and a cribbage board toppling onto the floor. 'Thon fucking Elton John doesn't suffer this shite – aye, and we're the same age,' he said to Pavel as he passed by with the bucket and mop. 'I might as well just play a tune and give my gums a rest.' He reached into his mouth and pulled out his bottom set of false teeth with a sigh of satisfaction.

'I hate this place,' said Pavel to nobody in particular, as he grabbed for the pine disinfectant.

Like a stage, all life played out here in the Iron Horse under two flickering strip lights and a dim glow of daylight through the high, frosted windows adorned on the outside by stout iron bars.

★

Joe Mannion watched all this on the bank of small screens sitting across from his large desk. He shook his head in his office above the bar. 'I'm telling you, this place gets fucking worse.' He was addressing the man opposite, Jock, who was tied to a chair, his face bloodied and beaten, a huge lump erupting under his right eye.

'Aye, you're right there, Mr Mannion,' said Jock, through swollen lips.

'Will I give him another wallop, boss?' Sammy Sloane loomed menacingly behind the trussed-up figure on the chair.

Mannion took the cigar from his mouth. 'Hold your horses, Sammy. What's Jock here going to tell his good lady when he arrives home with his face looking like an accident in the passata factory?'

Both men looked at him blankly, Jock through one eye.

'Is that the place they make they cars, Joe?' said Sammy.

'Aye, that's what I was thinking,' spluttered Jock. 'Just couldn't make the connection, like.'

'It's Italian tomatoes! They ... och, never mind.' Joe gave up on the metaphor. 'Put it like this. It's not a pretty sight, Jock – got it?'

'Aye, with you, Big Joe,' he said, then spat out part of a tooth.

'So, tell me, where did you get the gear?'

'They albinos will kill me if I tell you. Give me a break, eh?'

'They're Albanians! Aye, and I'll kill you first if you don't fucking tell me where they're dealing from.'

'Shite, this is thon rock-and-a-hard-place stuff that everybody bangs on about, isn't it?'

'Answer the fucking question, you halfwit,' said Sammy, administering a sharp slap to Jock's balding head.

'Okay, then, but I might as well cut my own throat, here. I meet them in the city centre.'

'Where?' said Joe.

'That wee lane just off Bath Street.'

'Bath Lane, you mean?'

'Aye, that's it, Joe. Fuck me, you're like one o' they London taxi drivers – know every nook and cranny, so you do.'

'It didn't involve any mental gymnastics, Jock.'

'Eh?'

'Never mind. Untie this arsehole and get him cleaned up, Sammy.'

'Hey, big chap. Any chance of subbing me a twenty spot? I'll get it back to you next week, I promise.'

Mannion picked up his cigar from the ashtray and began to laugh heartily. 'You're a fucking riot, do you know that?'

'Aye, I guess so,' he replied, the battered man laughing along with the gangland boss for the sake of it, despite having no idea what he was on about.

'Tell Pavel to give him a half bottle for the road, Sammy. Aye, and get this mess cleaned up when you're finished.'

'You're a gent, so you are, Mr Mannion,' said Jock.

Mannion relit his cigar as Sammy untied Jock's bonds and pushed him out of the office. The boss ran his hand across the grey stubble on his head as he looked again at CCTV pictures from the bar downstairs. An old woman emerged from the toilet in a buttoned-up long coat just as her friend hung a large pair of knickers, a skirt and a pair of tights over a radiator. He sighed as he poured a large measure of malt whisky into the crystal glass on his desk.

The phone rang. Mannion squinted at the number on the screen and clicked the call on with a smile. 'How are you, Tracy-Anne?'

'I'm not bad, Dad. Here, your wee granddaughter wants to thank you for her birthday present. I'll put her on.'

The muffled roar of excited youthful voices sounded for a moment, then a child spoke. 'Hi, Papa.'

'Chardonnay, how are you, pet? Happy birthday, by the way.' He flicked a piece of bloodied tooth from his desk as he spoke. 'Are you having a nice party?'

'Yes, Papa.'

'And you liked your present?'

'Yay!' she shouted, forcing Mannion to remove the phone from his ear.

'Me and your granny will be over to see you before you go to bed.'

'Okay, thanks Papa.' His granddaughter put the phone down unceremoniously as Sammy arrived back in the office with a mop and bucket.

'I'll just get this blood off the floor, chief.'

'Aye, you do that, and make sure you don't miss any teeth.' Mannion took a long draw of his cigar. 'Get some guys over to Bath Lane tonight. I want these motherless bastards to get the message, okay?'

'No bother,' said Sammy, wiping the floor with the mop. 'Mind you, it's just mad teenagers they use – wee fannies from the schemes.'

'I don't give a fuck. Just make sure they get the message!'

'Aye, I've got that, Joe.'

'As long as they do, that's fine. We're haemorrhaging dosh, here.' He curled his nose up. 'What the fuck is that smell?'

'Must be the cleaning fluid, chief. Got the bucket and that from Pavel down in the bar.'

'Smells like pish.'

Sammy Sloane shrugged his shoulders.

6

Zander Finn looked at the large edifice of the building in which his remaining son was being treated. He hated hospitals of any description, but this one looked more imposing than most, especially given the army guards on the gates.

'How the fuck are we going to get in there, Malky? Folk are showing ID. I've no passport or driving licence,' said Finn. He was sitting on the bonnet of the hire car, blowing clouds of vapour from his e-cigarette.

Maloney fished into his rucksack. 'Don't say I don't think of everything.' He handed over a passport.

Finn stared at it for a few moments. 'Why did you bring this? You didn't know we were going to see Robbie.'

'I didn't know you were going to come back with me, either. But I figured it would be better if you had your passport. You know, if you decided to stay in London or the like. I never go anywhere without mine – just in case I've to jump on a plane. I needn't tell you how it is, Zan.'

Finn smiled. Malky Maloney looked like a Neanderthal: furrowed brow, heavy boned, slow of speech. But in fact he had a good head on his shoulders, always had. Finn wondered why his friend hadn't taken the reins when he'd disappeared. Then he realised how difficult the dynamics of such a thing would have become, especially with his wife having a strong hold on 'business'. This didn't stem from some prescient genius, merely from the fact she knew where the bodies were buried – literally – and had access to all the accounts, at home and abroad, legitimate and otherwise, that powered their nefarious activities. But he sensed something else.

'So what would have happened if I hadn't come back, eh?'

Maloney gave him a look only old friends could understand. 'Under normal circumstances, what would you have done?'

'Got rid of her.'

Maloney shrugged. 'But, as you know fine, these are not normal circumstances.'

Finn detected a strange look pass across his friend's face. 'There's something you're not telling me, Malky.'

'Like what?'

'You tell me.'

'You disappeared – what were folk meant to think?'

'That I was dead.'

'Aye, exactly.' Maloney stroked his chin. 'I've known you a long time. Ever since we were kids. You've faced up to everything – jail, broken deals, death. We just assumed somebody had got to you.'

'The Albanians?'

'Aye, of course. Plus you left everything you'd normally have taken – like your passport.'

'I took some money.'

'Senga never let on.'

'Suited her to make it look as though I was dead.'

Maloney made a noncommittal nod of the head, looking out into the middle distance.

'Tell me!' The sudden rise in Finn's voice made Maloney start.

Glasgow

The small hotel was in the middle of a semi-circular terrace in Glasgow's East End. He'd used it for years as a safe house. Officially he had no connection with the business, and made sure that he always arrived out of sight of any CCTV cameras.

The room was far from palatial: a double bed, chest of drawers, small wardrobe on top of which was balanced an old TV. The only heat came from one radiator and an old electric fire that buzzed and sparked.

He admired the curve of her back as she arched it with pleasure, letting out a yell of climax at the same time. Her skin was smooth, tanned. Her hair fell in golden trusses down her back.

She eased herself off him and slumped at his side on the bed, her chest heaving as she caught her breath – a film of sweat making her breasts shine.

They sat in silence for a few moments as he lit two cigarettes and handed her one. She drew at the tobacco hungrily, like a starving man eating the steak he'd been dreaming about.

'I still can't understand it,' he said.

'Why I'm so good in bed?' She smiled.

'No, why anyone gave you that name.'

'What's wrong with my name?'

'Eh, you kidding?'

'No, why should I be?'

'Because you're beautiful, that's why.'

'It was more common back then.'

'To be beautiful?' He grinned and took a long draw of the cigarette.

'No, my name, dafty.' She leaned over and bit his nipple

just hard enough to make him yelp. 'Anyway, what about yours?'

'It's a good name – what's wrong with it?'

'It's common.'

'Good, because so am I!' He looked at his gold Swiss wristwatch. 'I'll need to be off.'

'Wham, bang, thank you, ma'am.' She folded her arms across her chest and looked away.

'I've got something to do – it's important.'

'More important than me, clearly.'

'Nobody's more important than you.' He paused. 'Well, just about.'

'I know who you mean. You're so predictable.'

'I know.' He heaved himself from the bed, found his underpants on the floor and began to dress, but not before revealing his wrinkled backside.

'Where are you parked?' she asked, looking at his physique. Despite being sixty he looked younger – apart from his arse, that was.

'Outside the chiropractor's surgery. I always go there, then out the back and in here. The guy's a friend of mine.'

'You mean he owes you money.' She watched him as he sat on the bed and pulled up his trousers.

'Can't I just have friends?'

'You? No.'

'You're right, of course. The bastard owes me about thirty grand, but he's good for it.'

'I'd chop off his bollocks, if I was you.'

'Aye, and while he's recovering in hospital, he's not fixing any backs. Good idea.'

'He must have other assets you can squeeze?'

'Aye, I daresay he has. But then how would I get in here without being seen. And he's paying now – with interest. Anyway, if we go with your idea and chop off his bollocks, we'll have nothing to squeeze.'

'I can't be bothered with that petty stuff. A pound here, a tenner there.'

'There won't even be that soon.'

She shrugged and stubbed out her cigarette.

'Don't worry, I'll handle it.' Now dressed, he bent down and kissed her on the cheek.

'How?'

'In my own way.'

'Good luck with that, then.'

'I have got to go.'

'You'll miss the jelly.'

He smiled and left the room. So parted Joe Mannion and Senga Finn.

Stanford Hall
Zander Finn walked along the corridors with Maloney at his side. The hospital wasn't as bad as he'd thought. Mind you, he was used to the Royal Alexandra in Paisley. This place was new, nicely decorated – tasteful, with framed photographs and bright paintings. Had it not been for the bustle of medical staff, the odd machine in the corridor and the inevitable smell, they could have been in a hotel.

'Here we are,' said the nurse who'd led the way. 'Sounds like Robbie already has company.' She knocked gently on the door then opened it.

There was a pregnant pause while those inside the room took in the scene in the corridor and vice versa.

'Gillian, Robbie!' said Finn.

'Dad!' they replied almost in unison.

'How's it going?' said Malky Maloney.

'For fuck's sake,' said Maggie Finn.

'What's going on?' said Kirsty, looking at the nurse, who just shrugged her shoulders.

7

Stanford Hall

Maggie's expression was hard to read. As Gillian embraced Zander Finn, her head buried in his chest, she regarded the son she thought she'd lost as he stood in the doorway.

In his bed, Robbie's eyes filled with tears. 'Hiya, Dad. I'm sorry about all this. I can't believe it's you.'

'You're sorry? You've nothing to apologise for, son.' He kissed Gillian on the head and led her by the hand to her brother's bed, where he held both of his children close.

'Well, isn't this nice, eh?' said Maggie sarcastically.

'Hello, Mother,' said Zander. 'You're looking well.'

'Is that all you have to say? You've put these kids – aye, and me –through hell over the last two years, and you come out with that?' She shook her head, arms folded firmly across her chest.

'You off to the dancing, Mrs F?' asked Malky Maloney, eyeing her attire with a grin.

'And I don't want to hear anything from you, Malcolm Maloney. I suppose you've known where this one was all along?'

'No, not *all* along, no.'

As Maggie opened her mouth to reply, two nurses pushing a trolley groaning with screens and wires entered the room. The senior of the two – she wore a darker uniform

– looked round the room. 'You'll have to give us some space, please.'

'How much space do you need?' said Maggie.

'As in, please vacate the room. We have to test the patient on a regular basis, so if you don't mind. You can all take a seat in the corridor; we shouldn't be too long.'

As they shuffled out, Maggie stopped by the senior nurse. 'His name is Robbie Finn, not *the patient*. Got it, darling?' She tottered out on her high heels to join the rest of the visitors.

They were sitting on a couple of sofas and some chairs placed in the broad corridor. A thin man with two burly male nurses on either side struggled down the corridor on crutches, the metallic shine from his prosthetic limb at odds with the blue training shoe placed over its artificial foot.

Maggie watched him go, a look of pity in her eyes. 'This is it, this is what's ahead for our Robbie.'

'That's it, Mother, just you keep things cheery.'

'This is my dad, Kirsty,' said Gillian, still cuddled into her father's side.

'Pleased to meet you, Mr Finn.' She paused. 'Have you been away?'

He nodded. 'I've been in London for a couple of years. Nice to meet you, Kirsty.'

'We go to college together,' said Gillian.

'And how's that going? You can't have long to do now?'

'Still another year.'

'Oh.'

'I took some time out when – well, you know when.'

'Fucking happy days,' said Maggie. 'Here we all are, a family reunion on the Long John Silver Ward. Aye, just the ticket.'

'You've lost none of your charm, then, Mrs F,' said Malky. 'And you can shut the fuck up,' she replied.

*

Senga Finn drove her Range Rover up the hill that overlooked Semple Loch, about ten miles from Paisley. Her home was large, palatial; maybe even gaudy to some. But she didn't care. Though the on-going problems with the Albanians worried her, she was sure that Joe could fix it.

For once in her life she was happy. Despite the loss of a son and an estranged husband, and all the rest of the turmoil that surrounded her family, she felt as though at last her life was going in the right direction. No more was she the unseen baby machine, the stay-at-home mother. These tasks had stolen her life from her late teenage years right through to her thirties. Now she had power of her own. Senga could do as she pleased, in the firm knowledge her new lover would be more than up to the task of fixing their collective difficulties with the men from the East. Then life would be plain sailing.

Of course she felt a bitter loss in her heart, the way a mother would for any lost child. But life had taken her to a place where mute acceptance seemed much more attractive than wailing grief. In any case, what was the point in her wasting her life? Her dead son wouldn't thank her for that, of this she was sure.

She had brokered the alliance, and it had been a clever move. The crime barons in Glasgow, Joe Mannion at their head, united with her Paisley crew. No more petty squabbles, senseless death, lost business. Now – once they were rid of the Albanians – they could all sit and count the money, happy in the knowledge that everyone had their piece of the pie.

Had Senga been a wiser woman, she would have wondered why her income was reducing on a weekly basis. Had she been in possession of more acute animal instincts she might have doubted Joe Mannion's explanation as to her son's murder, seemingly a sickening crime perpetrated by the Albanians to create a turf war between rival families.

But these doubts evaded her. There was nothing she could do about her dead son. Nothing she could do about her depressed daughter. Nothing she wanted to do about her missing husband. She had two allies, and their lives were inextricably linked.

Then her phone pinged.

Senga Finn read the message from Gillian and for a moment stopped breathing. When she exhaled, her chest began to heave and she let out a scream and punched the window of the car until her knuckles bled.

She thought for a moment, then dialled up her contact list on her smartphone.

*

Joe Mannion was reading to his granddaughter. The room, lit only by a dim bedside light, was making this process a difficult one, but he could see Chardonnay's eyes blinking with sleep, so he persevered. 'And then the bear took the little boy to the cave he lived in and gave him honey . . .' The buzz from his mobile phone was enough to widen the blue eyes of his granddaughter.

'Your phone's ringing, Papa,' she exclaimed.

'Aye, it is, pet lamb. I'll just need to talk to somebody. I promise I won't be a minute, then we can carry on with your story.' He picked the phone from his pocket, noted who the call was from, then cleared his throat. 'Hi, Jamie, how are you?'

'Aw, are you still in the bosom of your family, Joe? How nice.' Senga's tone was mocking, with a distinct hint of jealousy.

'Yes, Jamie, that's right.' He smiled at Chardonnay. 'What can I do for you?'

'You can start worrying, that's what you can do.'

'Oh, how so?'

'Because my husband – at this very moment – is on his way back to Paisley.'

Mannion swallowed hard. 'You've made a mistake, Jamie.'

'Fuck off, Joe!'

Before he could reply the line went dead.

'Is Jamie a girl, Papa?'

'Eh?' he said distractedly.

'Jamie is a girl, I heard her voice.'

He regarded the little girl with a sad smile. 'No, dear. He just has a very high voice.' He began to read from the picture book again.

8

The light rain was like a shimmer under the sodium lights at either end of Bath Lane. The noise of the city was all around: car horns sounded, revellers chatted and laughed as they perused the delights on offer in Glasgow's city centre on a damp, cold Wednesday night. Their footsteps were hurried, anxious not to linger in the soaking smir.

The lane itself was darker, lit only dimly by a couple of security lights above fire escape doors that opened out into the lane from two restaurants that backed onto it. One of these doors lay open, a man in chefs' whites smoking quickly, only the tip of his cigarette truly outside in the elements. He took one last look around then closed the doors shut with a metallic clunk.

The lane reeked of rotting food left in a large plastic skip, a blocked drain at one end and a point at the other where late night drinkers ducked into the shadows to relieve themselves against a handy wall. Just beside this impromptu toilet, in the gloom, a pair of white shoes swung rhythmically in mid-air, as though of their own volition. A closer inspection would reveal an earnest young man thrusting at a woman whose back was against the wall. Her filthy mock fur coat was open, revealing her breasts as her stage squeals were silently lost in the shoulders of her grunting lover.

Suddenly, the motion of his bare buttocks slowed as his eyes rolled back in their sockets and he let out a long groan of relief. Over his shoulder the eyes of his partner were dead, lifeless almost. She pushed him away and hurriedly gathered the folds of her coat around her.

'You're not a bad ride for an old bird,' he said, as he pulled his trousers from his ankles and buckled them around his skinny waist.

'And you're a cheeky bastard. Just give me the stuff and cut the shit.' She eyed him as though he may just be the vilest creature alive, not her erstwhile lover of only moments before.

He smiled to himself. *Cut the shit*? he thought. It was already cut with any number of unlikely substances, from talcum powder to chalk, with a hint of rat poison. But what did he care?'

He handed over the small plastic sachet, then reached into the pocket of his jacket for a pack of cigarettes.

He watched as she hurried away, huddled into the dirty coat. She emerged into the light and took a mobile phone from her small clasp bag, where it had been nestling alongside a tight roll of money and some hastily pre-prepared joints. She leaned against the plate glass of a shop as she typed a short message into her phone before hurrying off into the night and the fix she'd just earned.

Back in the lane he smiled to himself, just out of the rain in the recess of the fire escape. He always gave the prostitutes the worst drugs he could find. It had been a cheap form of release – an erotic tea break. Now, it was time to start making more money.

Peter Anderson saw a shadow move about ten yards away.

'Ditri, is that you, man?' The name sounded strange on his Glasgow tongue.

Silence.

'C'mon, man, don't mess about, you arsehole.'

No sooner had the words escaped his lips than he felt a sharp pain in his side. He turned round to see a large man grinning down at him. 'Fuck!' He swore loudly before the pain set in and he opened his mouth to scream.

The tall man clamped his hand over his victim's mouth, while at the same time twisting the knife in the drug dealer's side.

'This is from Big Joe, Petesie. He's not keen on his men going out on free transfers.' Behind the attacker's paw of a hand, Peter Anderson's yell of agony was muffled. He tried to speak, but the gloved hand was now tight against his mouth, forcing him to breathe heavily through his nose as the knife twisted again in his side.

'Aye, and don't think you'll just slip away, Petesie. I've got you just in the right bit, more pain, more gain. You'll die eventually, but more like a slow bleed-out than a quick end. We're into sending a message to your new friends, know what I mean?'

Anderson felt faint now; only the agony of the knife in his side was keeping him conscious. He went limp in his attacker's arms. 'Gus, please,' he whispered as he fell back against the doors, his strength ebbing away.

Gus pinned him against the door and pulled the knife from Anderson's side. 'Now I can get a wee bit artistic, eh?' He held the blade just under Anderson's right eye, his other hand again clamped back over the stricken man's mouth.

Despite his pain, Anderson looked wildly at the flash of the bloodied blade now so close to his eye. He tried desperately to shake his head behind his tormentor's tight grip, his pleas for mercy still muffled.

Then he felt himself falling backward. All of a sudden there was a bright light and a tumble of bodies. He could feel himself being pulled one way then the other, no longer in Gus's grip. He hit a smooth cement floor with a gasp that forced the air from his lungs, leaving him to try and struggle to his feet, one hand on his injured side as he desperately tried to make sense of what was happening.

Then strong arms pulled him from the cold concrete.

'Are you okay?' The voice was low, slow and heavily accented.

'Ditri! Thank fuck, man.' Peter Anderson squinted in the bright lights of the bare corridor. The fire doors were now closed. In front of him, two large men were holding the limp figure of Gus Lee, the attacker who had been about to take his eye.

'You take this,' said Ditri, handing him a long-bladed hunting knife.

'What for, big man?'

'Cut his throat!'

'Wait, I'm not heavy like that. You know me, I'm just a dealer, man.'

'This piece of shit was about to kill you – suddenly you are guilty?'

'Nah . . . but this isn't my thing.'

'It is now. Do it!' Ditri pulled a phone from his pocket, clicked on the screen a couple of times and directed a bright light into Gus Lee's face. 'Now! Or you go first.'

There was a look in the Albanian's eyes that told Anderson he was serious. He walked over to where Gus Lee was pinned between two bulky men in thick leather jackets. Both of them looked as though they had no necks, the larger of the two had pulled back Lee's head, exposing his white, stubbly neck.

'Now, your last chance!' roared Ditri, holding the phone out in front of him.

Peter Anderson placed the knife at Lee's exposed throat, shut his eyes tight and pushed. He felt something warm and wet hit him in the face as he backed away from the sounds of the struggle, the muffled screams of Gus Lee and the grunts of his captors.

Only when it fell silent did he dare open his eyes again.

He felt a hand on his shoulder. 'You did well, Peter. Now we must get you treated, no?'

Ditri's words were lost on Peter Anderson as he stared down at the crumpled body of Gus Lee, a large pool of dark blood spreading from the gash in his throat like a crimson halo against the cold concrete.

'You – you filmed me, you sick bastard!'

'Nobody can see your face, trust me. Now, we get you to the best Albanian surgeon in Glasgow.'

'What are you going to do with the body?' asked Anderson.

'It stays here.' Ditri dialled a number, then held the phone to his ear. 'Mr Mannion, I have a little film for you to watch. It's a horror, I hope you'll enjoy.'

9

Zander Finn looked across towards the silhouetted roofs and spires of Paisley as he and Malky Malone drove onto the bypass. On the left, the huge Chivas whisky warehouse stood out in the darkness, bathed in security lights. To their right, views across fields and buildings that all seemed so familiar, even in the velvet gloom.

Finn tried to remember if he'd ever thought of his home during the time he'd spent in London. The answer came quickly: no. He'd been too keen to banish thoughts of his murdered son from his mind to spend any time on idle nostalgia. Yes, he'd missed the rest of his family, friends – but resurrecting them in his mind always took him back to the cold light of the mortuary where he'd viewed the ruined body.

'You'd be better off in a hotel, Zan,' said Maloney, a cigarette planted in one fist as he gripped the steering wheel and peered into the darkness.

'It's my house!'

'Aye, true, but you know how these things work. And given the circumstances . . .' Maloney's voice tailed off.

'I'll deal with that.'

'Don't you be going Radio Rental, big man.'

'Easy seen it's a while since you walked down a high street. You'll be telling me not to buy a pick and mix from Woollies or a pram from Mothercare next.'

'Eh?'

'Never mind.'

They drove on in silence, past Johnstone. The traffic was surprisingly light, which meant that he'd be reunited with Senga sooner than he'd expected.

They were in the countryside now, passing the farms and villages that were rapidly turning into small towns as the sprawl of urban creep reached out from the Central Belt.

'Every bastard's looking for their own little idyll, eh?' said Finn absently.

'You're talking in riddles again,' replied Maloney.

'I mean, everyone wants to be out in the country – you know, out of the town. The way things are going, there won't be any countryside left.'

'Aye, right.'

'Do you never worry about the environment?'

'Are you kidding? I've got more worries than a worry factory on overtime, Zander. And anyhow, what the fuck can I do?' His face was set. 'Well, I've told Elaine I'll get off the fags – go onto the vaping, like.'

'That's fine, then. Our troubles are over. We'll just tell that wee Swedish lassie to go back to school.'

'Every little helps.' Maloney thought for a moment. 'What wee Swedish lassie?'

Ignoring this, Finn carried on. 'So when your grandchildren are choking to death with nothing to eat, you can happily turn round and tell them they can't blame you because you stopped the fags and hit the e-cigarettes.'

'The long hours in your house tonight will just fly by.' Maloney shook his big head.

Shortly, they left the road, heading up a single-track lane bordered by trees. The further up the hill they went, the better the roadway became, until they reached a pair of stout gates, behind which was a sprawling house at the end of a long driveway.

'Home sweet home,' said Maloney.

'You think?' Finn looked less than delighted at the prospect of seeing his domicile for the first time in more than two years.

'I don't suppose you have your gate fob thingy?' asked Maloney. Finn shook his head in response. 'I'll go and speak into the box.'

Finn watched his old friend get stiffly from the car and walk over to a small intercom on the gatepost. He cracked his window open to hear what was being said.

'Hello, Senga darlin', it's me.'

'Who's you?' Her voice sounded tinny over the intercom, but it was enough to make Finn raise an eyebrow at the absurdity of it all. Here he was outside his own home as his wife pretended not to know who was trying to get past the gate.

'It's me – Malky.'

'How do I know it's you? I can't be too careful these days. You know that, Malky.'

'See, you know it's me. What's the problem?'

'Aye, but you could be under duress of some kind.'

'What?'

'Some bastard could have you at the end of a gun.'

'Don't be stupid. Just let me in. I need to see you.'

Senga hesitated. 'I'm still not sure.'

'Come on, it's freezing!'

Finn recalled the last time he'd seen Malky Maloney argue with an inanimate object. It was at a drive-through McDonald's near Gallowhill in Paisley. He remembered it had been about the sudden and unexpected rise in the price of a McMuffin.

Finn got out of the car. Maloney held his hands in the air in a gesture of resigned surrender and stepped away from the intercom.

'Senga, it's me. Open these fucking gates or I'll just drive through the bloody things, right?'

'If it's not the master of the house, back from the dead.' The sarcasm was palpable even at this remove.

'Just open them!'

There was a bleeping noise from the gatepost and soon the heavy metal gates swung slowly apart.

Back in the car, Maloney looked at Finn. 'Thought we weren't going to get in there, Zan.' He hesitated. 'She didn't sound that surprised to hear your voice, by the way.'

'Are you kidding? Half of Paisley will know I'm back by now.'

'I can't see how.'

'First of all, there's my mother.'

'Oh aye.'

'Not to mention my son, daughter – and what you told me earlier.'

'Understood.'

'Listen, you drive me up to the house and get on your toes, Malky.'

Maloney eyed him doubtfully.

'It's my house and it's where I'm going to stay.'

Maloney shrugged his broad shoulders. 'Okay, you're the boss.'

'No, I'm not.'

'You will be again soon.'

'We'll see.'

They parked by the steps that led up to the entrance.

'I've always liked they doors, Zander. Like castle gates, so they are.'

'Aye, castle misery.'

'I'm just glad we didn't have to drive through the gates.'

'Are you getting soft?'

'No! I've got to take the hire car back.'

Zander Finn wished his friend goodnight and took the first steps back into his old life, all the time knowing that no such thing existed.

*

She still looked beautiful. That was one thing he could never deny. Her blonde hair was well cut – longer than he remembered. She was smoking a cigarette, enveloped in a large, white fluffy bathrobe.

'Say what you've come to say, then fuck off!' She blew smoke at him dismissively.

'I've got lots to say,' Finn replied. As he looked round the lounge he noticed that she'd decorated. His favourite paintings had disappeared to be replaced by the arty tat he'd always hated. For him, any semblance of comfort had been sacrificed in favour of a minimalist showroom.

'Well, get on with it.'

He took a seat on a sofa 'What happened to the Chesterfield?'

'It went – not long after you, actually.'

'And you replaced it with this?'

'Oh dear, is it not up to your standards, Zander? That mother of yours gave you false airs and graces.'

'She sends her regards, by the way.'

'Aye, coated in rat poison. Or worse still, one of her plates of mince and tatties.'

Only when he sat down did Finn notice the large photograph of his dead son. He was smiling broadly from the monochrome image – his mother's smile.

'We've got things to discuss, Senga.'

'Like what?'

'These Albanians – the guy's aren't happy.'

'Big Malky, you mean?'

'Aye, he's one of them.'

'He knows the score.'

'He knows the score, all right.'

'Huh! He thought when you disappeared he'd just step into your shoes. I'd get thrown a few scraps – get to keep the house, a nice wee allowance. Well, fuck that! I don't need a man to run the business. My father taught me all he knew.'

'He tried.'

'You fucking arsehole!' She stood over him, gesturing with the cigarette. 'You bloody men think that women can't live without you. You're in the dark ages – just like the *guys* you're so fond of. Here's news for you. I'm getting along just fine on my own.'

'But you're not on your own, are you?'

Senga stepped back. 'If you mean the alliance with Glasgow, it had to be done.'

Finn smiled. 'And what were the terms?'

'None of your business.'

'They're not working very well. Malky tells me that money is down across the board. We've lost clubs, taxi companies – half the take on the street. We're not even getting a fraction of the construction work from the councils.'

'Corrupt bastards.'

'And we're the ones that corrupted them.'

'It's temporary.'

'Everything is temporary.'

'Meaning?'

'Like you grieving for our son.'

She flew at him, long finger nails like claws trying to rip at his face. 'You bastard! You fucking bastard!'

Finn grabbed his estranged wife by the arms and pulled her close. 'So that's why you're fucking the man who killed him?'

'That's not true. He didn't kill him – what the fuck do you know?'

'I know you believe every word that comes out of that cunt's mouth!' He stared into her eyes. 'I'm back, and things are going to change.'

'Over my dead body.'

He smiled. 'If necessary, aye.'

She pulled herself back from his grip, arms flailing with the effort. Her left hand caught the edge of a large ornate vase that was perched on a side table. As if in slow motion, it wobbled for a moment then toppled onto the parquet floor, where it shattered into many pieces.

'That cost me over a grand!' she yelled.

'You broke it,' said Zander Finn.

10

The Organised Crime Unit in Police Scotland's Gartcosh Campus had been quiet. Now it was buzzing, as more detectives arrived.

DCI Amelia Langley searched the faces of her staff as they took their seats in the large meeting room. They were a mix of old, dyed-in-the-wool cops and the new intake of smart young things, most of them with a university education. As head of the OCU, it was just how she'd planned it.

'Okay, settle down, guys,' she shouted above the hum of voices. 'Sorry to have brought you in at short notice, but we've another gang-related incident on our hands.' Deftly she flicked a switch on a remote control. The face of a thick-set man in his late twenties appeared on a large screen behind her. The image had been taken in a police office somewhere. His hair was tousled, expression grim – an arrest photograph.

'Most of you will recognise Angus Lee – "the enforcer", as he's known in the shite belly of Glasgow crime.' This elicited a thin laugh.

'I arrested him when he was fourteen. He was a bad bastard even then. One of Mannion's team,' said a grizzled detective sitting in the front row.

'Well, you won't be arresting him again, Ally. He was discovered in the fire escape of a restaurant which leads onto Bath Lane – oh, about an hour ago,' she said, glancing at her watch.

'Big Joe won't be happy. That's one of his up-and-coming guys,' said the same detective. 'Though I can't say I'm feeling any personal grief.'

'At least we don't have to worry about him any more,' said Langley.

'But isn't that a concern in itself, ma'am?' asked a young detective at the back of the room.

'Yup, sure is,' replied Langley.

Again from the back of the room, 'The Albanians?'

Amelia tapped the small remote off the bottom of her chin, staring at the screen deep in thought. 'Would you bet against it?' To this there was a general murmur of agreement. 'Yes, I thought you'd agree.' Langley turned to face the room. 'But there's more.' She clicked the remote again.

On the screen was a grainy image of two men. One of them was sitting on the bonnet of a car, while another man appeared to be gesticulating in front of him. Langley clicked the remote again. This brought a gasp from some, a groan from others.

'Taken earlier today outside a military hospital down south. It was flagged up via the Met's face recognition software. They collaborate with the MOD cops. Just as well, I'd say.'

Another click and the scene shifted to a hospital corridor.

'I'll be fucked! Pardon me, ma'am,' said another one of the older cops.

'Don't apologise, Neil. There we have it, proof of the afterlife, if proof you so require. Malky Maloney, number two in the Paisley mob, and beside him a man who needs no introduction.'

'Zander Finn.' The reply came from a few in the room.

'The very man.' Langley picked up an iPad. 'Last seen a few days after his son's funeral in Paisley. We thought our friends from Eastern Europe had dealt with him, too. But it would appear we were wrong.'

'Ma'am, how come it's taken until now to pick him out?' asked Detective Constable Shona Main from the back row.

'Good question. All I can say is that this technology isn't as widespread as people think. He entered an MOD establishment, so it was naturally flagged up.'

'But he must have known he'd be exposed when he went in there, ma'am,' said DS Neil Dickie. 'He might be a complete bastard, but he's a clever one.'

'Indeed. I think we can take it from this image that he isn't in hiding any longer – he's certainly not dead. In fact, here he is again, or the car he and Maloney were travelling in. A hire vehicle from London, it would appear. This image was snapped by cameras at the Johnstone bypass – about two hours ago.'

'Do you think he's involved with Lee's death?' asked Dickie.

'If he is, this car doesn't show up anywhere near the city centre. And given the time he left the hospital in England and the shot taken on the bypass on the A717, he'd have been going some.'

'Coincidence?' Dickie's expression was that of the unconvinced.

'That, Neil, we will have to establish.' Langley clicked off the screen. 'Now, we have to get our heads together. It's been bad enough over the last couple of years. But the return of Zander Finn can only make things worse. Do we all agree?'

A groan of weary resignation came from the assembled police officers.

Langley watched them trudge out, feeling a mix of emotions.

*

It was odd for Finn, bedding down in the large, well-appointed room after the time he'd spent in London in a cramped, damp flat. The conditions hadn't bothered him; he'd grown up in worse. But to be back in his own home was a bit of a shock to the system.

When he'd agreed to come back with Malky Maloney, he knew that his feelings of regret and remorse over Danny's death would be amplified. He'd done his best to steel himself against it, but it was still hard – just as hard as he'd imagined.

He and Senga might be sharing the same house, but they certainly weren't sharing the same bed – not even the same floor. He realised that ship had sailed, certainly now that she was shacked up with Mannion – metaphorically, at least. Finn's marriage had been over for some years. He'd hardly been a paragon of virtue, so it would have been hypocritical to question his wife's morals. Rather, it was her choice of partner that infuriated him. She seemed convinced that he had nothing to do with the death of her son.

Finn's instinct told him otherwise. And he always trusted his instincts.

They had parted as he had expected: her screaming at him to leave, while he refused. All of this amidst the wreckage of the expensive vase – symbolic of their union, he reasoned. Now she was in the master bedroom of their mini mansion, while he occupied a mere guest room. But this room alone was larger than his whole flat back in London.

He knew this situation could not prevail, but he was determined that his wife wouldn't swan around in this house while he slummed it somewhere else. No, they'd do what every other married couple in this situation were forced to do: either one buy the other out, or sell the house and share the proceeds.

Of course, his wife would resist this vehemently, but he knew she'd be forced to agree in the end. She had no other choice.

As far as business was concerned he would meet with his main men tomorrow. These were the guys who – in most cases – had been with him from the beginning, his lieutenants since before his father had died. He'd turned a few nightclubs and a couple of brothels into one of the best businesses in Scotland. But there were no awards for endeavour or innovation in his line of work. Yes, his wife had been running things since he bolted, but he sensed that her hold on power was a tenuous one. Probably – and he could only guess at this until he met the rest tomorrow – it was Malky Maloney who stood in the way of Senga being cast aside, or worse. That and her new relationship with Glasgow's self-appointed crime lord Joe Mannion, of course.

He knew the route he wanted to take, but Finn realised that he had a lot of making up to do. He wasn't even sure if he would be accepted back into the fold, far less take charge again. But the fact that Maloney had come to London to seek him out rather flew in the face of this reasoning.

The room was warm, the mattress was soft. He took a sip of water, set the alarm on his mobile phone and was asleep in moments. After all, it had been a tiring, emotional day.

In his dreams, though, Zander Finn stood between his son Danny and the bullets that killed him. The same dream he'd had night after night for more than two years.

11

'Why the fuck did you send him on his own?'

Though Sammy Sloane was bigger, younger and stronger than Joe Mannion, the former knew that any resistance would signal the end of his life.

'You know big Gus, boss. He's a loner – likes to do his own thing, so he does.'

'I fucking *knew* him, past tense!' Mannion, a vain bulging on his forehead, thrust his mobile in Sloane's face. 'Have you seen this?'

'Naw.'

'Well, now's your big opportunity.' Mannion held the phone up as the footage of the murder of Gus Lee played across the screen. Sammy Sloane's face screwed up in disgust at the sight.

'That's fucking disgusting, big man.'

'Fucking disgusting? That's what you say when some arsehole spews in your car or a bastard steals you granny's knickers off the washing line. Not when you've just seen one of our best men knifed in the throat by these bloody Albanians!'

'We can go after them, so we can.'

'How? Have we managed to find any of them yet?'

'Not really, boss.'

'What do you mean, *not really*?'

'Well, we have had some information, like.'

'What, when?'

'A few days – a week ago, something like that.'

Mannion sat heavily in the big chair behind his desk and massaged his temples. 'And why the fuck didn't you tell me about this?'

Sloane shrugged. 'I thought you'd have known.'

'I spend my life in this fucking place these days, or haven't you noticed? Your job is to get out there and do the business – be a shield so that the cops can't pin any fucking thing on me. We said at the time: delegate, manage, make sure our hands are as clean as possible – keep your ear to the ground!'

'I have been doing that, boss.' Sloane was indignant.

'That's why I'm just about to hear something you knew about a week ago.'

Again, a shrug from Sammy Sloane. 'Aye, I guess so.'

'You *suppose so*, not *guess*. We're not living in Utah.'

'That's up near Twechar, isn't it?'

'No, it isn't near fucking Twechar. It's in the USA, where they say *I guess so* instead of *I suppose* fucking *so*. You say that again in here and I'll personally cut off your bollocks and post them to your good lady.'

'That's a bit harsh, Mr Mannion.'

Mannion lay back in his chair. 'I'm not actually going to do that – it was an expression. Fuck, if I kill you, the way things are going it will just be me left.'

'Naw, loads of good guys about, so there are.'

'I was joking.'

'Oh, right.' Sloane smiled weakly.

'Do you know, I picked you out because I thought you were smart – clever, you know. Didn't you go to college?'

'Aye, so I did.'

'Which one?'

'The Food Tech. I was studying to be a chef and that.'

'Superb.' Mannion stared into the middle distance, a look of defeat on his face. 'Did you get the lasagne wrong and they booted you out?'

'Naw, I stabbed the lecturer. Mind, I was up in the High Court? Sure I got off because he was banging that wee lassie in the class. She was only sixteen, so she was.'

Mannion sighed again and looked right at Sloane. 'Okay, time to tell me what you know.'

'About that bastard I stabbed?'

'No, about the fucking Albanians!'

'Right, of course. Okay, so this lad was on the batter out in big Jamie's bar.'

'The one in Shawlands?'

'The very one, boss. Anyhow, he's got a good charge, this boy. Been on the snow and the bevvy. Big Jamie knew he was a stranger, like – because of his accent and that.'

'An Albanian?'

'Naw, the big guy thought he was from Aberdeen, or maybe Dundee. But this arsehole was so wrecked he told him he was from Albania. And that's not all.' Sloane had a *wait-till-I-tell-you-this* look on his face.

'Please, please tell what the fuck you're going to say before one of us dies.'

Though his expression had changed to one of surprise, Sloane carried on. 'This Albino tells Jamie that he was with their crew. If he has any trouble – in the pub, or that – just to come to him. Says he sorted out Danny Finn.'

'And you're just telling me this.'

'Aye.' Sloane shrugged.

Mannion thought for a moment, then spoke calmly. 'Right, find out where this bastard hangs out – better still, where he lives. You'll have heard that Zander is back, eh?'

'Aye, shock to the system, man.'

'Well, this could be our chance to keep him on-side. Because you know what that awkward bastard is like. And how much he wants to find the folk who killed his boy.'

Sammy looked confused. 'I thought his missus was running it over there now?'

'Now he's back, how long do you think that will last?'

'You'll know better than me.'

'What does that mean?'

'Just that you know more about things than me. I couldn't even peel an artichoke.' He laughed nervously.

Though he was making a joke of it, Joe Mannion knew that Sloane knew he was at the madam. So the guys knew that he was shagging Senga Finn – so what? 'Just you find out what I want to know, got it?'

'Aye, boss, I'm right on it.' Sloane turned on his heels.

'Hold up.'

'Aye, anything else?'

'Albanians and Albinos aren't the same thing.'

Sloane considered this new piece of information. 'It's kind of strange, though, eh?'

'Why is it strange?'

'That they'd have countries with nearly the same names.'

'Sammy, you've lost me.'

'Like, Albania and Albinio. Fucking weird.'

Mannion was about to explain just how wrong Sammy Sloane was but soon lost the will to do so. 'Aye, it's weird, right enough. Just you get going.'

As he sat back and lit a cigar he heard Sloane's heavy footsteps on the stair. Joe Mannion cursed stupid people – all of them.

12

The big workshop was on the edge of Paisley, not far from the M8. The steady rush of traffic from the White Cart flyover played like a familiar soundtrack, as Zander Finn left his car. He was happy to be reunited with his red Maserati. At least something comforting had been awaiting his return. When he thought about it, he was surprised Senga hadn't sold the car; she'd never liked it. It was too fast for a nervous driver like her. She preferred the raised driving position and the feeling of security afforded by an SUV; he loved its lines, the feel of luxury, smell of the leather seats, the roar of the engine. To Finn, it fitted like a glove.

The big roller shutter door was almost fully open, helping to ventilate those busy within. Finn was careful to shade his eyes from the flash of a welding torch, as the employees toiled away, crafting security doors, fences, gates, panels – all manner of things – out of metal.

As he walked towards the door that led to the offices, a few nodded to him and he heard shouts of 'Okay, big man!' Many, though, kept their nose to the grindstone – in some cases, literally. They'd all have heard by now that their missing boss had returned, but more than a few would be wondering as to the consequences for them.

He smiled to the men and women in the main office: three clerks and an office manager. Though they too would have gossiped about his apparent return from the dead, their welcome was more fulsome.

'Have you missed me?'

'Not really,' said Stephanie, the office junior, with a grin. Finn smiled back. He'd played football with her father and knew the young woman well. He'd taken her on after the death of her father. He had been murdered when some of Joe Mannion's men decided to play football with his head.

'Here.' He handed Stephanie a small curl of notes. 'Get yourselves out for a drink tonight, on me, by way of celebration. The wicked witch isn't dead, after all, eh?'

Leaving the office, he hesitated at the foot of the stairs that would take him to his old office, boardroom and the few other executive nooks and crannies of Chancellor Fabrications Limited. It was a company he'd inherited from his father and was a useful income stream, as well as furnishing him with the veneer of legitimacy.

Why he hesitated, he didn't know. What he did know was that he'd walked up these steps thousands of times. Most of the men awaiting his arrival upstairs he'd known since childhood. But still the voice of Father Giordano sounded loud in his head.

More death.

Finn drew in a deep breath and took the steps two at a time.

He knew they wouldn't be in his big office, or the even larger boardroom. Sure enough, he could hear the murmur of voices coming from behind the door that had, in his father's day, been a canteen and now served as a very private club with only a dozen or so members.

They fell silent when he entered. Malky Maloney, as was his wont, stood behind the small bar they'd had installed.

He served more drinks in this room than ever he did in the six pubs and two nightclubs he owned. Finn supposed it was a proprietorial thing.

'And there he is!' Maloney walked out from behind the bar and put his big arm around Finn's shoulders. 'Back from the dead – well, at least a shite flat in Brixton. Worse than being dead, if you ask me.' He laughed.

Finn studied them one by one, these men: his inner circle. It felt as though the world had slowed to the speed of a penalty kick replay: Big Dusky was lounging on a broad sofa, a large glass of something in his hand. His features belied his name, for he was neither swarthy nor dark-haired. He'd been christened 'Dusky' by Finn's mother because of his propensity not to get out of bed until the afternoon. In a Scottish winter, this meant he would be rising just as it was getting dark. He was tall, painfully thin, with a sparse thatch of what had once been auburn curls, now slicked back off his forehead. He looked at Finn with no sign of emotion on his pale face, just a questioning look.

Big Tam Skillen was six feet tall but because he was so broad he looked shorter. He had a solid presence, something substantial – like a wall. His ruddy, square face was crowned by spiked peroxide hair, a style he'd sported since the eighties, alongside a tan that once upon a time came from a sunbed but was now more likely the product of a tanning spray booth. It was said that he'd once punched a guy clean through a door. But these and other apocryphal tales abounded in the murky depths of Paisley's underbelly; though everyone who met him was more than convinced at first meeting they didn't want to be on the wrong end of one of his huge fists. He was beaming at Finn; they'd always been close.

Across the table from him was a small, rat-like figure. Davie 'Pockets' Kelly knew the streets like the back of his hand. He was quicker with a knife than a pen but had the mind of an accountant. He didn't need a notebook to know what a dealer owed. He ran the drugs operation with ruthless efficiency; in another life he'd have made a brilliant CEO of a blue-chip multinational. But the men in this room had been handed no opportunity to use their natural talents in the accepted sense. They grew up on the street and now lived off it. It was the way things were.

Donald Paton squinted at Finn over a pair of half-moon specs. He was a relic of Finn's father's time. Solid, dependable, he ran all the legitimate businesses, including the metalworks in which they now met. He was wearing a green cardigan over a checked shirt. His face was wrinkled, brow furrowed below a balding pate. Wearing a pair of roomy red corduroy trousers to match the rest of his attire, he would not have been out of place heading for a game of 'doms' at the local community centre, but of all the men in this room Finn trusted his counsel most. Paton nodded at the son of the man with whom he'd been so close; indeed, he was Finn's godfather.

They were all well dressed, save for Peter McKinlay. He looked as though he'd just jumped out of bed. There was fat, then there was Peter. The blue jogging bottoms he wore were bursting at the seams, his belly pendulous through a white jumper. His mousey hair stuck up in salt and pepper tufts, his pallid complexion broken up by untidy stubble. 'The king of the castle,' he said, as he clapped his bloated hands together. Finn couldn't help remembering the fabulous footballer he'd been twenty-five years and twelve stones ago. But the chain of bookmakers he ran on Finn's behalf brought in plenty.

There was only one young man in the room: Lonesome Dove. Sandy Hamilton had been called that since his parents died in a helicopter crash when he was sixteen. Of middle height, he was lean and strong. His father had come from Jamaica in the Fifties, making Paisley his home. Sandy spent a lot of time in the gym he owned; Finn was pleased to note he hadn't let this slip. His mother had been Zander's second cousin and, like a real family, despite the wind-ups and banter, they'd taken Sandy to their hearts when he lost his parents. He had a team of young men under him that Finn knew he could use to sort out just about any problem. Though he'd failed in his task of steering Finn's dead son Danny in the right direction, despite his best efforts. 'How's it going, Zander?' he said, meekly.

'We need a change round here,' said Finn. They looked at him questioningly. 'No women!'

'What do you mean?' replied Dusky. 'I know you've been away, Zan. But remember, the boss is a woman, so she is.' He stared at Finn with barely disguised irritation.

'I'm the boss. You know that, Dusky.'

'Not for the last two years, you've not been.'

'Come on,' interjected Malky Maloney. 'The man's just back in the fucking door. Can't you give him a break?'

'Listen – and I'm saying this to you all,' said Finn, raising his voice. 'Senga is out and I'm back, okay?' He looked around the men in the room. He knew they could tell him where to go, but he was still working on the assumption they needed him. Plus, judging by Dusky's reaction, Senga's rule had been as unpopular as he'd imagined.

'And what about Mannion?' asked Big Tam.

Finn thought for a moment before answering. 'You all know what I think of Joe Mannion. That will never change. This ridiculous alliance my wife has entered into ends now!'

Dusky snorted a laugh. 'Which alliance are you on about? What we do, or her jumping into bed with him in that shite hotel in Glasgow at every opportunity.'

Finn turned to Maloney. 'What hotel?'

'I'll fill you in later.'

He knew he'd have to do something, but Finn had no idea how he was going to be received. He walked across to the sofa on which Dusky was spread out. 'Get up,' said Finn.

'What for?'

'I said get fucking up!' Finn grabbed the thin man by the collar of his jacket and pulled him to his feet. Nobody else in the room moved. There was absolute silence.

'Hey, watch my jacket,' shouted Dusky.

Finn was tall, but he still had to angle his head up to stare in the face. Finn's green eyes met the pale blue of Dusky's. 'You listen to me. Everything that makes you money is mine, right!'

Dusky nodded, as much as he could in Finn's grip.

'If you want to take this outside, I'm happy to do that. I'll kick the fuck out of you, then feed you your own withered cock. Never speak to me like I'm a piece of shite again!' He thrust his knee into Dusky's groin, making him yelp and double over in pain. Finn caught Dusky with a jab to the chin, sending him flying backward, a sofa breaking his fall. 'Anybody else?' said Finn, looking round the room.

There were no takers.

Paton sighed. 'Right. We don't need to do things this way. We shouldn't be knocking lumps out of each other.'

'Who then – the Albanians?' Finn asked.

Paton shrugged. 'That's up to you to decide.'

'So you don't trust this "pact" my wife entered into?'

The older man shrugged. 'Do you?'

Before Finn could reply, Big Tam spoke. 'I've had a message. From Mannion, I mean.'

'Saying what? Welcome home?'

'Naw. He had information. At least, Sammy Sloane had.'

'About what?' said Finn.

Tam lowered his head. 'About Danny.'

'Tell me!' Finn's face was red, his eyes suddenly wild.

'An Albanian boy – knocks about the Southside. He's been saying he was one of the guys who did Danny.'

'And we're just hearing this?'

'Sloane says they've just found out themselves.'

Finn looked around. Dusky was still sulking on the couch, one hand covering his face, as though shading his eyes from the sun. The rest of them either failed to meet his gaze or shook their heads.

'Could be a gesture. You know, with you back, Zan,' said Maloney.

'That bastard Sloane killed my father,' said Sandy.

Finn flicked his eyes towards the bar. 'Somebody get me a drink, eh?'

Maloney was quick with a large glass of whisky. He handed it to his old friend, who sat down heavily on a leather recliner, accepting it gratefully. Finn looked round the room. After a few moments, he could see them getting restless.

'If you're going to say something, you should say it, Zan,' said Maloney.

'This Albanian. We go with Mannion's tip-off. I want to know all he knows, okay? I don't care how you do it, just make sure it gets done. Organise this yourselves. No doubt I'll be the centre of attention of our wonderful Scottish Constabulary for the next few weeks.'

'They've missed you, big man,' said Davie Kelly, his yellowed teeth showing rodent-like over his bottom lip as he smiled.

'I'm sure they have.' Finn took a gulp of his whisky.

13

Maggie Finn stared at the mobile phone on her kitchen table. She desperately wanted to reach out and make the call to her eldest granddaughter. But something was stopping her. She knew it was pride, the unseen force that kept her loyal to Danny, the grandson who had been the apple of her eye.

Her son's return from the dead was as much of a curse as it was a blessing. Trouble followed him wherever he went – it always had. Somehow – most of the time, at least – he seemed to profit, to get stronger through all the turmoil. She reasoned that Danny's murder had been the first true setback he'd experienced; at least, the first one that had hurt him. She worried about the consequences, now he was back.

She didn't know if Zander knew about the baby his eldest daughter was about to have with Mannion's youngest son. Would it create a bond between the two families? She doubted it. But she wasn't in the thrall of her newly returned son. It was up to her to mend as many bridges as she could.

But now thoughts of Danny crossed her mind. It was the same black cloud she'd been fighting for so long. She closed her eyes tight and tried to think it away, but his face haunted her in dreams of the night and day.

She picked up the phone. Maggie prided herself on her ability to use new technology. When the mill had closed, she'd ended up working in her husband's business. Maggie had taught herself to type, to send telexes, to read balance sheets – the list went on. So mobile telephones and computers, regardless of their 'user friendly' complexity, presented no problem. Not that she'd been in receipt of much gratitude for her trouble.

She scrolled down her contact list and found Sandra. Her finger wavered over the name, but she clicked on it, then the number.

The phone rang in her ear and she nearly ended the call and switched off her phone. But Maggie bit her lip; she would do what should be done. After all, nobody else would.

'Gran?' It was so long since she'd talked to Sandra her voice sounded strange. Like looking at the face of somebody you'd known well, aged after a break of a few years.

'Aye, it's me.'

The tone of her granddaughter's voice changed. 'If you've phoned just to give me a hard time, you can piss off.'

'Charming!'

'Well, it's not as though I've heard much from you in the last two years.'

'You're pregnant.'

'Gillian.' The reply sounded weary.

'Aye, Gillian, and don't bother giving her a hard time because of it. She's just being a good sister.'

'Huh, what's left of her.'

'She's lost a wee bit weight, aye.'

'Gran, you don't know the half of it.'

'Why don't you enlighten me?'

'Why don't you come and see me?' Maggie could sense hesitation on the other end of the line. She shook her head as she reached for her cigarettes. 'Do you think we're going to pitch you out the window?'

'I don't know. Everything's quiet, now this.'

'Your father's back, you know that, don't you?'

'What?' Sandra sounded genuinely surprised.

'Didn't Big Joe tell you? Because he knows.'

'Gran, we don't see Kevin's dad. How many times!'

'Well, when are you coming up to see me?'

'I don't know. I should tell Kevin.'

'He better come, too – no show without Punch. Anyway, it's me, your gran. I'll make egg, chips and beans? I've started using thon sunflower oil.'

'I'll think about it. Listen, I'll call you tomorrow.'

Maggie was left listening to the dialling tone. She shrugged. It didn't seem as though egg, chips and beans were as popular with her family as they'd once been.

*

The young man was stocky, with a pale, round face. He was wearing a black leather jacket and a roll-neck jumper. He whistled as he crossed the car park from the bakery to his elderly Mercedes, salivating at the thought of the coffee and the steak bake. He jumped into the driver's seat, closed the door and, removing the lid from the coffee, took a sip of the hot beverage. He was addicted to a growing list of drugs, but coffee still shouted loud when he'd gone a couple of hours without one.

Distantly, he heard the screech of tyres but thought nothing of it. This was the Southside, probably some young guy showing off to his girlfriend in a pimped-up old banger. He heard it every day. He laughed at the thought.

But as he took another sip, the sound grew louder.

In a flash, a car pulled up so close to the passenger side that it knocked off the wing mirror with a thud.

'You bastard!' he swore, locating the mug holder and reaching for the door handle. But before he could leave his car, another vehicle crashed into the other side, scraping to a halt. A van drew up behind. He was trapped.

He watched, eyes wide in terror, as men streamed from the cars either side of him. He turned round, as the back window of the saloon was smashed in by a sledgehammer.

The scene was chaos: shouting, a man kneeling on the bonnet of his car, a gun pointed at him. Though his English was reasonably good, so many voices alongside the panic that gripped him made what they were saying unintelligible. He'd spilled the hot coffee on his trousers, where it mixed with urine as he pissed himself in fear.

Then a gunshot. The man on the bonnet of the car fired in the air, then directed the weapon back at him. Though his ears were ringing, there was now only one voice to contend with, so he understood what was being said.

'Tell me what the fuck you know about what happened to Danny Finn!' The man's face was distorted, bitter hatred beneath a balding head, his teeth bared as he pushed the barrel of the gun against the windscreen.

Suddenly he felt his world collapse. He remembered trying to chat up the pretty girl behind a bar. He knew how some of his countrymen had become notorious gangsters in the city, and he was only trying to impress her with some borrowed cachet. 'I'm a plumber, you have wrong man!' he said, knowing that the sentence wasn't right but desperate to relate what he had to say to his tormentors.

'Okay, one last time, arsehole. Tell me what you know about what happened to Danny Finn!'

'I know nothing. I was speaking shit. You have to believe me.'

For a moment, he thought he'd got away with it. The bald man slid from the bonnet of the car and walked away, stashing the handgun in the back of his jeans. But then he remembered the others at the back of his car.

In the rear-view mirror he saw a flash of flame, then the crump of an explosion filled his head as a fireball ripped through the car. His last memory was of trying desperately to open the passenger door and escape this hell. But there was no escape.

As quickly as the flames spread through the Mercedes and the two cars and the old van wedged against it, men fled the scene in all directions.

A young woman who had served the foreigner in the leather jacket only minutes before emerged from the bakery doorway, a mobile phone to her ear. Only wild, agonised screams could be heard above the noise of the flames. All she could see was a writhing figure, black behind the wheel, disappearing amidst a crackling inferno. As flames consumed the dark shadow of the man's body, the screaming stopped.

Just as the call to the emergency services connected, she was knocked off her feet as the petrol tanks of all three cars exploded. Ears ringing, she felt the sting as tiny pieces of flying glass embedded themselves in her back. When a flying hot mutton pie hit her squarely in the face, she dropped her phone and screamed.

14

Father Giordano had three great pleasures left in his life: good books, better wine and the wireless. Though officially retired, he spent three days every week visiting members of his old flock, now mainly in hospitals or retirement homes. From time to time he filled in for the priest who had taken his place, though he felt that this final service to the Lord would soon come to an end. Old age, creaking knees and an apathetic congregation would see to that.

In his time, the Roman Catholic Church had seen so much pain, so many changes. In truth, even though he still wore a dog collar and his faith in God was as strong as it had ever been, he had little hope left for his church. Though he knew Pope Francis was fighting for reform, he wondered how one man could effect sufficient change in order to stop the whole ship from sinking. Maybe it would be like previous times, with alternative pontiffs springing up in other parts of the world to save the Holy Church. Maybe in South America, Africa perhaps – places where people, untainted by the tin gods of technology and greed, still believed.

As he leaned over to the table at his side, he shook his head at the perilous state of the world. The planet being destroyed: wars and rumours of wars; the young rising up, not against their parents but to try and rescue some kind of future. Is this how it would all end?

If Christ was to return to save the world, now would be a good time. But would Christ want anything to do with the hearts and minds of so many people lost to sin? But, of course, no one was without sin. He knew that. Maybe that was the point of it all.

His mind was still wrestling with these vexing subjects when the old radio crackled into life. He knew he should buy a new one, but this wireless had been his companion for so many years he felt it would be like turning his back on an old friend if he were to replace it.

He listened, absently at first, then more intently to the second item of news on the bulletin. He turned up the volume.

Police in Glasgow are investigating what they believe could be a targeted gangland killing in the Southside of the city earlier today. A car was attacked by a male assailant in a car park outside a bakery in Eastwood at around eight-thirty. Witnesses say shots were fired, then a man trapped in a car burned to death when his vehicle was set on fire.

Though we have, as yet, no official response from Police Scotland, it is believed the victim was of Eastern European origin. His murder would seem likely to be connected to the ongoing turf war between local organised crime groups and Albanian gangs. This dispute is thought to be the cause of a number of brutal deaths throughout the city in the last two years.

Though also unconfirmed and unconnected, rumours of the reappearance of Paisley crime boss Alexander Finn have emerged. The alleged gangland kingpin was last seen two years ago at the funeral of his son, Danny Finn, gunned down along with five friends in a Paisley bar. Though no one has ever been arrested for the murders, sources in the underworld told the BBC that Eastern European criminals were the likely perpetrators.

We'll have more on this in later bulletins.

Father Giordano switched off the radio and sat back in his chair, closing his eyes in silent prayer. The wood-panelled room cosseted him like a warm bed, insulating the old priest from the world outside. Now he was alone with God and his memories. Though he hoped his pleas for peace would be heard, his mind soon drifted back in time, as though this was the direction in which his Lord wanted to take him.

Five decades earlier

He could see the young woman through the grille of the confessional booth. Her light hair glowed and the scent of her cheap perfume filled the small space. Somehow, though, it didn't smell cheap on her. She was younger than him, only nineteen years old, but already it seemed as though she had the weight of the world on her shoulders.

'What troubles you, my child?' The words sounded strange on his tongue. Though his English was now good, he still found himself thinking and dreaming in his native Italian.

'Forgive me, Father, I have sinned.' Her voice was light, lilting despite the harshness of the accent.

It had taken him time, but he could not now merely understand the people, his flock, but identify with them. There wasn't so much difference between the people of Calabria and those of his new home in Paisley. Both had suffered war, destruction, death and poverty. They struggled to put food on the table, to put clothes on backs. Yet there was still warmth, kindness and human decency in abundance.

But studying the girl through the grille, he could easily make out a large bruise and lump under her right eye, despite her best efforts to disguise it with make-up.

'What is your sin, my child?'

'Theft. I have stolen, Father.' Her voice was quieter now; he could hear the shame.

'What did you steal, my child?'

She hesitated, as though considering the magnitude of her sin. 'A pan loaf – breed – I mean bread, Father.' She paused. 'Now I know I promised that I wouldn't be at the stealing again – you know, after that incident with the butcher's tongue – but we was hungry, you know?'

He fought hard to keep the smile from his face, but reminded himself he had a solemn duty to perform. 'You paid a heavy price for stealing the meat from your employer, no?'

She sighed. 'Aye, auld Jimmy Law – that's the butcher, Father – well, he wasn't very happy.'

'You lost your job, I think?'

'Aye, and the bastard kicked me up the fucking arse. I mean, he wasn't very nice about it,' she said, remembering where she was and regaining her best Sunday accent.

'Who hit you in the face, my child?' The question was direct, and he knew the answer. But he wanted her to know what he could plainly see.

'I-I'd rather not say, Father.'

'I see.' It was his turn to pause. 'How long is it since I married you?'

'It's not my man!' The denial was instant and defensive.

'Yet. He has caused much pain in the past, I believe – and to many others.'

'It wasn't him,' she said again, determinedly.

'You have sinned, but you have also been sinned against.'

'Aye – if you say so.'

'We will pray . . .'

*

He remembered that day so long ago, as he was transported back to the study, the musty smell of age and the ticking of the grandfather clock. He remembered the incident vividly for so many reasons. Most of all because he knew it was the day he'd first realised the truth.

15

The Tannahill Bar was quiet. It was only mid-afternoon, but still. There would have been a buzz about the place at this time of day back when he'd been a regular customer. He marvelled at how little it had changed. Of course, it'd had a lick of paint here and there, with a few new tables, bar stools. But he could still picture his younger self standing at the bar with a slim version of Malky Maloney, replete with a feather-cut mullet. He smiled at the memory. How ridiculous they'd looked back then: pixie boots, button-down collars, sleeves rolled up.

The man behind the bar seemed oblivious to his presence. Finn was pretty sure the lad had no idea who he was. He was from Australia, working his way round the world. He would know little of Paisley and its criminal hierarchy, and that suited Zander Finn nicely.

You only met people on neutral turf – in public – if there was likely to be a problem. And there was most certainly a problem. As he took a sip of his pint, the slight tremble of his hands made him realise how furious he was. The old saying was true – if you wanted something done, you were best to do it yourself. But Finn knew that the spotlight was firmly on him, and there was no way he could operate as he once had. For the time being, at least.

As always, he was early. He liked to be early. If you were late for something, you were always playing catch-up, trying to collect your thoughts, become accustomed to your surroundings, say the right things. Father Giordano had taught him the importance of good timekeeping – he had taught him so much.

Finn looked up from his drink when the door swung open. It was Dusky and another man he vaguely recognised but didn't really know.

'Where's Malky?' said Finn sharply.

Dusky shrugged. 'Dunno. He knew we were meeting here. I spoke to him last night.'

'Who's your friend?'

'This is my man Davey.'

Though Dusky was about to introduce his companion, Finn cut the conversation short. 'Do one, Davey,' he said casually, not looking at the other man.

'Eh?' Davey looked at Dusky.

'Fuck off,' said Finn calmly. 'And you don't need to look at him for confirmation. If I tell you to do one, you do one. If I tell you to jump into the Cart, you jump into the fucking Cart, understand?'

For a moment the younger man looked flushed with anger. His face reddened and he balled one fist. Dusky grabbed him by the arm. 'Just do what the man says, eh?' Davey turned on his heel and left the bar.

'Who the fuck was that?' asked Finn, nodding to a chair upon which Dusky sat down heavily.

'I'm grooming him.'

'What? To fuck him?'

'No! As my successor. You know, take the shit while I'm in Spain. Stuff like that.'

'Oh right. In Spain – lucky you.'

'You know I've got a place out there.'

'Aye, I do. Just as well, really. I hope you've brought your passport with you?'

'Why the fuck would I bring my passport?'

'Because you're going to have to fuck off, that's why.'

Before Dusky could reply, the door opened again and Malky Maloney appeared, looking red-faced and flustered. 'See that fucking Renfrew Road! It's like trying to navigate around Bogotá, so it is.'

'Where?' said Dusky.

'Never mind,' said Finn. 'Just know it's a nightmare to drive in.' He held the bald man's gaze.

Maloney took a seat. 'Here, there's a right wide-looking cunt standing outside. He gave me the eyeball when I came in, Zan.'

'Don't worry, it's Dusky's man. He's grooming him.'

'What? Have you jumped the fence, Dusk?'

'To be my right-hand man,' replied Dusky, wearily.

'He looks like a right piece of shit,' said Maloney.

Dusky stood. 'You know, fuck this. I'm not here to take shite from you pair in a hyena court.'

'It's a kangaroo,' said Maloney.

'What?' Dusky looked even more irritated.

'It's a kangaroo court, not a fucking hyena.'

'Sit down!' demanded Finn. 'It's not a kangaroo court you've got to worry about, it's the real thing, the High Court.'

'Why?' said Dusky, now back in his seat.

'Because you were clocked on camera yesterday torching that plumber.' Finn's voice was low.

'Nah, no way, Zander. Every camera in that row of shops was off. We own the security firm that runs them, remember?'

'Oh aye, they were off. But no' the camera on the phone of the wee lassie that worked behind the bakery counter. Hers was most definitely on. I had word from our man in Gartcosh last night. They haven't identified you yet, but they will, trust me.'

'And she's got bad burns into the bargain,' said Maloney.

'No way! She was nowhere near the fire. We made sure of that. Not a soul in the street. It was perfect, man.'

'She got walloped in the face by a steak pie just out the microwave.'

'It was a mutton pie,' said Finn, correcting Maloney. 'Happened when the petrol tanks went up.'

Dusky shrugged. 'So what? Some wee hairy gets a pie in the coupon. Who the fuck cares?'

'I do,' said Finn. 'I care about the whole fucking thing. Here's me, just back, and plumbers are getting toasted in their motors and a wee shop girl gets scarred for life with jumbo sausage. How do you think that looks? Not to mention the charcoal brick.'

'Aye, just about to go and fit a new lavvy, so he was.'

Finn turned to Maloney. 'How the fuck do you know that?'

'Just heard.' Maloney shrugged apologetically. 'Think it was in *The Sun*.'

Finn shook his head. 'I wanted you to find out if there was any truth in the shit that Mannion had given us about the guy. I didn't expect you to torch him on spec.'

'You told us that we should handle it.'

'And what did you discover? Our pal at Police Scotland tells me that he's legit – a plumber, nothing more. Meanwhile, I'm on the news in connection with the whole thing and I wasn't even there.' Finn leaned across the table.

'I don't care how you get there – I don't even care where you go – just fuck off until we sort this out.'

'Aye, if we can,' added Maloney.

Dusky looked between the pair, beads of sweat obvious on his balding head. 'So this is the way things are, eh?'

'You torch a guy in public, and yes, this is the way things are.'

'We don't even know if the polis will clock me.'

'We can't take the risk,' said Finn.

'If you're worried in case this lassie in the shop can ID me, I can soon sort that out.'

'She's still picking mince out of her hair,' said Maloney.

'Leave her alone,' said Finn. 'You've made a big enough fuck-up of things as they are. Get going – now!'

'And what about business, who's going to run that?'

'What about your groom dug out there?'

'Fuck off, Malky,' said Dusky.

'We'll deal with that, don't worry. You can take your boy and groom him in the sun. Maybe you'll both get a tan.' Finn sat back, arms folded to signal the end of the conversation.

'And I thought Senga was a pain in the arse when she was in charge,' spat Dusky. No more said, he stormed out of the bar and off into the grey Paisley day.

'He could be a problem, Zander. He was a pain in the arse when you was away, man.'

Finn nodded. 'Maybe Spain's too hot for him just now, eh?'

'Can't see that, big man. It's the end of October. It should be just nice there now – you know, about sixty-five degrees or so. Maybe in the seventies.'

Finn said nothing, just stared blankly at his old friend. 'Take a swatch at this.'

Finn removed a thin brown envelope from his pocket and handed it to Maloney, who removed its contents. 'Fuck!' he said, looking at the image of Dusky shaking Joe Mannion's hand outside the Glasgow pub that was his HQ. 'Are you sure, Zan? I had no idea.'

'Aye, I'm sure. You know how bad things were when my dear wife was at the helm. Can't blame him, in a way. But I can't trust him now, can I?'

'He's been around for a long time.'

'Aye, so has herpes.'

Malky Maloney shrugged. 'Never thought it would come to this.'

'We're swimming to survive, here. Why do you think Mannion chucked us that shite?'

'No idea.'

'Because it's like I've said all along, Malky. There's something we're not seeing.'

'I'm pretty sure he's not in with they Albanians, Zan.'

'No?'

'I suppose I've got things to do, then.'

'Yup. But first you can buy me another pint.'

Begrudgingly, Maloney headed for the bar. He stopped in his tracks and turned back to Finn. 'That Davey guy. There's something familiar about him.'

'Some shite from the schemes, likely. I thought I knew his face, too.'

Maloney nodded and carried on to the bar.

16

Chief Inspector Amelia Langley was scrolling through the images of the Eastwood attack frame by frame on her laptop. DS Neil Dickie was at her back, studying the footage over her shoulder.

'Nothing from the recognition software, Neil?'

'No. The image quality isn't good enough. They tell me it's poor resolution – older phone, plus it's taken through the shop window.'

'Shit! Every teenager in Glasgow is running about with the latest tech in their pocket apart from our girl, eh?'

Dickie shrugged. 'To be fair, she was only working part-time at a bakery counter. That phone shit costs a fortune now.'

'I've lost track. The job pays for mine.' Langley sighed. She paused the footage at the point the assailant had clambered down from the bonnet of the car. For a fleeting second, he half turned his head. She gazed at the figure then zoomed in on the image. 'I know who that is.'

'Who?'

'Big Dusky from Paisley.'

Dickie leaned closer to the screen. 'You think?'

'You don't, obviously.'

The detective shook his head. 'I can see what you mean. But even if it is him, the PF is never going to swallow that as evidence.'

'Doesn't stop us from bringing him in.'

'No, true.'

'And the security cameras on that row of shops just happen not to be working, of course.'

'No. Nor were some of the traffic CCTV cameras on the routes leading to the parade. Two of them were burnt out the night before.'

'How convenient. Who owns the cameras?'

'DME Security Services. I've looked them up, registered on the Isle of Man. Need I go any further?'

She sighed. 'No, you don't have to say any more. But one thing's for sure, this is no small-time drug hit. Whoever did this knew what they were at, so that narrows things down significantly, doesn't it?'

'Paisley, Glasgow, or the Albanians.'

'And this bastard looks like one of Paisley's finest.'

'It can't hurt to try, ma'am.'

'Bring him in, Neil.'

'Okay, will do. Now the fun begins.'

'Begins? It never ends, you know that.'

DS Neil Dickie left the room, leaving Amelia Langley staring blankly at the computer screen, deep in thought. She flicked off the footage of the attack and brought up another file.

Alexander 'Zander' Finn's face stared out at her from undercover surveillance footage. He was smiling at someone out of shot, his brown eyes flashing with bonhomie, arm outstretched in mid-handshake. His dark hair was neatly cut, perfectly framing his sallow face. To the uninitiated he could have been an on-the-stump politician; that he was charming she knew only too well.

Langley pondered a while on the paradox of the

criminal mind. This man was clever; he had a sharp brain, sharper suits, charisma and drive – all that was required to become successful at the top of many professions. Yet he had chosen crime. She could never fathom why.

Langley flicked back through his file, a snapshot of his life on a flickering screen. In context, she supposed, it all made more sense. From a poverty-stricken home in Paisley's Gallowhill, his circumstances had improved in line with his father's rise in the underworld. First, just muscle, then a small workshop making gates and railings. A twisted arm here, a bribe there and William Finn was soon fulfilling big contracts for councils the length and breadth of Scotland. By this time the family were in a much nicer home in Renfrew.

As his rise through the Paisley mob continued, William Finn inherited betting shops, pubs, clubs – you name it. In fact, much of what went on in the town bore his unseen mark. But he'd made enemies.

She scrolled down. Not such a pretty picture. William Finn lying dead in an alleyway in Glasgow, a large part of his chest bloodied by the blade that killed him. He was a murder victim, seemingly random, and never solved. But that was the way of things in the world of Scotland's organised crime.

She supposed that all Finn senior had so rapidly gained could have been just as quickly lost. But that hadn't been the case. His only son, Zander Finn, had stepped into the breach and, despite his tender age, not only had he held on to what his father had created, but he'd built on it, too – massively.

With only a handful of minor convictions, his own rise had been seamless until the day his son was gunned down.

Like grandfather, like grandson, she thought. When Zander Finn had disappeared, Scotland's law enforcement community had publicly treated him as an official 'missing person'. In private, though, many a glass was raised; the assumption being that he too had been taken out, albeit in a less public fashion.

Amelia Langley hadn't joined the celebrations. For her, Finn, though a crook to his bones, vicious and ruthless when required, was manageable. She knew foreign gangs were on their way, and they didn't have any qualms about the safety of those not involved in the dangerous game of organised crime. She'd been proven right, too. The murder rate in the Central Belt was soaring and the number of recognised organised crime groups had more than doubled.

Could Finn coming back from the dead prove to be a good thing? The thought lingered for a moment, then disappeared as she flicked the screen onto the charred remains of an Albanian plumber.

17

Maggie Finn was in her friend's car. They'd been for lunch in Glasgow and were now back in Paisley.

Sitting in the passenger seat, Maggie again found herself becoming nostalgic. She'd been doing this more and more recently, something she attributed to advancing years and the proximity of the end.

Maggie looked absently at a piece of waste ground. It took a few moments for her to realise that this was where her first marital home had once stood. A tiny flat in Incle Street, now gone, lost to the demolition ball, as had been so much of the town. She and her husband had lived in the flat for two years until Zander was born and they qualified for a council house in the rarefied surroundings of Gallowhill.

Zander: she thought about him and the events surrounding his birth. This was something Maggie normally kept to the back of her mind. But something was telling her things were going to change. She baulked at the thought.

She forced herself back to her main train of thought. Maggie had loved it in Gallowhill: a proper wee community. She got on well with her neighbours and she had a small back garden, three bedrooms, and for the first time in her life could be proud of her home. Not many could say that.

She remembered the detached house in Renfrew. It was to be the first home they'd owned – any of her family had ever owned, as far as she knew. And while her husband Willie loved it, she hated the place. She was marooned from her own kind, to endure life among the aspirational middle classes.

At first she'd done her best to make friends, but it hadn't taken long for her new neighbours to realise that Mrs Finn at number twenty wasn't all she seemed. Years of misery had disappeared in an instant when her husband was killed. It was wicked to think it, but it was true.

Sitting at the traffic lights just about where the close to her old flat in Incle Street would have been, she felt no nostalgia, nor pity for the husband she'd lost. Maggie knew this wasn't normal. A sin, no doubt. But she had promised always to be honest with herself, even though circumstances often dictated she couldn't be so with others.

The plain truth was she'd hated her husband. He was unfaithful, cruel and uncaring. She thought about the word 'unfaithful'. Maggie knew the meaning in that context, but to her faith was something different entirely. The faith she kept in her heart was one she would, could, never reveal.

'Mind that wee dance studio, Maggie?' said her friend Jenny, pointing across the road. 'We did thon line dancing in there.'

'Remember? Sure, I fell over and broke my ankle on the third night.'

'Oh, aye. Not so much "take your partners" as "take me to A&E".' Jenny laughed.

'Huh, I was in the RAH for three days – not so funny.'

'Baked potato city, they're calling it now.'

'What for?'

'Because everything you get to eat comes with a baked potato, that's how.'

'Better calling it the mortuary. I'm telling you, most of the folk that go in there come out in a box.'

Ignoring this declaration of doom, Jenny continued. 'See my wee niece Beyonce.'

'Beyonce? Oh aye, Charlie's wee lassie?'

'Aye. Well, when she was getting a D&C they ran out of dinners. All they could offer her was a bowl of custard and a baked potato.'

'Together?'

'Naw, on two separate plates.'

'I was going to say.'

'She ended up with chits for her dinner.'

'What was in them?'

Jenny looked at her friend in the passenger seat. 'How the fuck should I know?'

Maggie shrugged as the hole where the Incle Street flats had once stood flashed by the car window.

*

Home again, Maggie made her way wearily from the lift. She was momentarily shocked to find her door unlocked, but when she heard a familiar voice from within she returned the stiletto knife into the recesses of her large handbag and hurried inside.

'Gillian, dear. How—' The question remained unasked. Sitting beside her granddaughter was a young man, and at his side was Sandra, her eldest grandchild.

'Well, a "hello, Sandra" would be nice,' said Gillian.

'Aye, hello, Sandra.' Maggie looked at the young man. Her voice stiffened. 'Kevin, how are you?'

'Aye, fine, Mrs Finn. Fine and dandy.' The sandy-haired

man reached out and gripped his girlfriend's hand. 'We hope you can be as happy as we are.'

Maggie sat down heavily on her recliner. 'Aye, I'm happy for you both. But I can't promise everyone will feel the same.'

As she watched the pair gaze into each other's eyes, she saw nothing but trouble. 'We'll need to change our name to Catapult.'

'Eh? What the fuck are you on about, Gran?' said Sandra.

'She means Capulet – you know, from *Romeo and Juliet*.'

'How do you know that?' asked Maggie. 'A catapult will be of more use to you than Shakespeare when your father finds out.'

'Right, we're going!' Sandra stood up to leave, while Gillian looked at her grandmother with a pleading expression.

'Sit down and take the weight off that great belly of yours. Fuck me, you're the size of a single end.'

'What a nice thing to say, Gran,' said Sandra, her smile forced.

'Right, egg, chips and beans for three, is it?'

Gillian looked at her pregnant sister. 'Don't worry, she's using the oil now. No egg for me, Gran.'

'Oh well, that's all right then,' said Sandra. She sighed. 'Okay, egg and chips it is. But no salt, thanks.'

Maggie trotted through to her kitchen, as happy as she'd been for a long time. She muttered to herself. 'No eggs, no salt – what's the world coming to?'

Then she remembered her son.

18

Dusky lived in a converted farmhouse near Bishopton. His wife had left him years ago, so apart from visits from his daughter and the odd one-night stand, he lived alone. The arrangement suited him.

As he pottered about in the kitchen, Pink Floyd blared from the lounge. 'Shine On You Crazy Diamond'. The song made him think of Zander Finn, and that was the last thing he wanted to do.

'Fucker,' he swore under his breath, as he patted down the sandwich he was making. His big, wheeled suitcase was sitting by the kitchen table. He took a bite and thought about things. At first he'd been angry. Finn had just breezed back in and taken over, as though it was his feudal right. Then again, Senga had been a nightmare, and there was more to it all than he would ever reveal to Malky Maloney, or especially Zander Finn.

The mobile phone rang in the pocket of his jeans. He clocked the number and answered immediately. 'Aye, what's up?' Dusky listened to the short reply. 'Fuck! Okay, message received and understood. Give me ten minutes, eh? Then I'll be out of your hair.'

Ending the call, he took another bite of the sandwich and shrugged on his leather jacket. He made sure he had his passport, bank cards and some cash. He took a quick look round the kitchen. Everything was switched off. The note to his cleaner was pinned to the fridge. He was all set.

He hurried through the dining room and into the lounge. The remote control for the Bose sound system was on the coffee table. He clicked off Pink Floyd just as Dave Gilmour was reaching the exquisite peak of his guitar solo. Suddenly the room felt cold and empty.

Dusky lifted his car keys from the hall table opened the front door and strode out onto the front step.

As he pulled the door to make sure it was locked tight, he felt a blow to his chest that knocked him over. He stared down as a dark red stain spread across his white T-shirt. His world began to swim before disappearing forever.

*

Finn had always hated the high flats in which his mother had chosen to live. What was it about phone boxes and lifts that encouraged the male of the species to relieve themselves on the spot? As usual, the lift stank of piss. What a way to welcome your guests, he thought: take a halting ride in an elevator that reeks of urine, is covered in graffiti and strewn with rubbish, the odd used condom thrown in for good measure.

As the red numbers slowly ascended, guilt set in. He should have told his mother he was safe and well during his time in London. She'd just lost her grandson; he had been thoughtless.

Before he could become maudlin about this, the lift pinged. He had reached the seventeenth floor. Finn stepped out of the lift and placed the bouquet of flowers under his nose, savouring the pleasant scent. Anything to take the edge off the piss-ridden lift. As he walked to her door, he made a mental note to try again to persuade her to leave this place.

He smiled as the neat 'welcome' doormat and the miserable-looking garden gnome that sat beside it came into view. He remembered Senga gifting the gnome to Maggie one Christmas. She'd bought it online, thought it a great idea to buy a gnome fashioned to look like his mother, but he was sure Maggie had never spotted the resemblance. It was a running joke in the family.

He knocked sharply on the door.

*

'Right, that's yours, son, with eggs and salt. Sandra, that's yours, no salt. Give me a second, Gillian, and I'll get your plate.'

As Maggie turned on her heel, she heard a knock on the door. 'Here, Gillian, will you get that? If it's that bastard selling fake watches again, tell him I'll boot him right in the haw-maws.'

Raising her eyebrows, Gillian answered the door.

'Close your mouth, you look like a fish,' said Finn. He eased his way past his youngest daughter, the large bouquet almost obscuring his face. 'I take it your gran's about?'

'Dad, can you hold on a minute, please?'

'Why? Is my mother parading about in her knickers? Now, that's an image.'

'No, Dad, wait!'

Despite his daughter's protestations, Finn carried on through to the lounge, but he stopped in the doorway.

Sandra had a chip impaled on a fork at her open mouth. Her partner, Kevin, dropped the knife on his plate with a clatter.

Maggie appeared from the kitchen with a plate of chips and beans. She looked her son up and down. 'Nice flowers, Alexander.' She thrust the plate towards him. 'See this, it's what your youngest daughter calls a meal. She'll not even take an egg.'

Finn took in the scene. Sandra was pregnant – very pregnant. Beside her, the young man was unmistakable.

'This is a set-up, isn't it, Gran?' Sandra snarled. 'You did this on purpose. I'll never forgive you!' Trying her best to bend forward, she placed her plate of food on the carpet in order to get up.

'How come? I didn't know you were all coming today. Fuck me, I sit here week after week without seeing a soul. It's like buses. You wait for an hour, then they all come at once.' She turned to her son. 'Aye, that's Joe Mannion's son. He's about to be the father of your grandchild. You'll have to like it or lump it. Now, do you want some egg, chips and beans?'

Unfazed by the situation, Maggie grabbed the bouquet from her son and bustled off into the kitchen. 'Lovely flowers, son. Thanks again. Your father always brought me a bunch like that when he'd been away shagging some tart.'

'Dad, it is what it is. You've been away – we all thought you were dead. You've no right to make any comment.' Sandra grabbed Kevin's hand tightly, all the while looking defiantly up at her father.

Relieved of the bouquet, Zander Finn walked slowly towards the sofa on which Sandra and Kevin Mannion were sitting.

'If you try to hurt him, you'll have to kill me first.' Awkwardly, Sandra tried to clamber on her boyfriend's knee, hindered by her swollen belly. All the while Kevin Mannion looked as though he was trying to shrink into the fabric of the sofa, desperate to disappear.

'Will you sit down, Sandra. Your gran will kill you if your waters break all over her carpet. You know how much she loves it,' said Finn, staring unblinkingly at the young man.

'No! Not until you leave, Dad.'

Finn pulled his hand from the pocket of his coat, making everyone in the room flinch. 'I'm Sandra's dad, but you probably have worked that out by now. Pleased to meet you, Kevin.'

Before taking his hand, Kevin Mannion glanced at Sandra, who nodded almost imperceptibly. Hesitatingly, he took the hand of his father's most bitter enemy.

'I was just saying, it's like they Catapults,' said Maggie Finn, arriving with a plate of steaming hot egg, chips and beans.

'Capulets!' said Gillian, standing stock-still in the doorway.

19

The gangster's body was in plain sight on his own doorstep when Neil Dickie and DC Peter Hynds arrived at the house outside Bishopton. The blood was black through his shirt, revealing Dusky's ruined chest. A small calibre bullet hole in the centre of his forehead marked this out as a gangland execution.

'Fuck!' said Dickie, as he regarded the scene. 'Get assistance, Peter. I'll give the gaffer a bell.' He pulled the mobile phone from his pocket, took a picture, then sent it to Langley. He waited a few moments before his phone rang. 'Yes, ma'am,' he said, wearily.

'How could they possibly have known we were moving for him?' Amelia Langley's voice was strained, more than a hint of anger obvious.

'I have no idea, boss. By the look of things, they've only just got him.'

'Finn is back for a few days and this starts up. One dead plumber and now Dusky.'

'There was always going to be a reckoning.' Dickie hesitated.

'What?'

'Who knows what happened while your man was away. But I was just wondering, ma'am, are we assuming too much here?'

'Like what?'

'Well, this might not be the work of Zander Finn.'

'You mean, it might be retaliation for the plumber?'

'Yes, absolutely.'

'Why on earth would the Albanians want to avenge the death of a guy who fixes toilets?'

'Might be connected in some way: family, friend – who knows?'

Langley thought for a moment. 'It's possible, I suppose.'

'Might even be Mannion, eh?'

She thought for a moment. 'Could be. A kind of line in the sand to Finn – a warning?'

'Aye. You know that Dusky was one of his top guys.'

The more Langley thought about this, the more it made sense. 'Okay, SOCO are on their way. Sit tight, Neil. I'll be out as soon as I can.'

As DS Neil Dickie slid his phone back into his jacket pocket, he stared at the gangster's corpse. 'Fucking idiot,' he said under his breath.

He shouted to Hynds, who had just finished his own work on the phone. 'Go get us a coffee from somewhere, would you? We'll be here for the duration when the cavalry arrives.'

Hynds looked between his superior and the murdered man.

'What are you worried about? That he might jump to his feet and strangle me?'

The younger man shrugged. 'It's not procedure, is it?'

'What if some old dear out walking her dog had found him? Probably no mobile in her pocket, in the middle of nowhere, has to go and sound the alarm from home? Work it out, son. They teach marching about and a lot of shit at that police college. You'll get your real education here with me. Now, fuck off and get the coffees. For your impertinence, you can pay.'

He watched Hynds slope off, tail between his legs. 'Young cops!' he said, with a snort and a shake of the head.

Dickie walked towards the body. He pulled a pair of surgical gloves from the pocket of his trousers. Stretching them on like a surgeon, he kneeled over Dusky's body. He slipped his hand into the inside pocket of the dead gangster's jacket. 'Bingo, first time!' He looked at the mobile phone he'd just found, switched it off and placed it quietly beside his own, all the time looking to see he hadn't been observed.

Dickie looked down at the man he'd seen on so many mug shots and had first arrested more than twenty years before. His eyes stared sightlessly ahead, with nothing to see. 'You always were a useless bastard,' he said to nobody.

In the distance, he could hear the wail of sirens.

*

Langley looked at the whiteboard on the wall of her office. There were three headings: Mannion, Finn and 'The Albanians'. She was dismayed at how little she knew about the structure of the foreign organisation. People just seemed to come and go, disappearing as soon as they arrived, leaving a trail of death and destruction in their wake.

The locals OCGs were a different matter.

Joe Mannion stared from the image straight at her. He looked like a solid door, no emotion, no pity, just seemingly immovable. She'd known him for a long time. Their first encounter had been when she'd worked in Strathclyde's old 'D' division. She was young and wet behind the ears. In a new, sharp uniform, Langley walked into a bar on a routine check. Three men were sitting at a table at the back of the smoky room. A few other customers, either elderly, addled by drink, or both, eyed her with distaste. It was fair to say that in this part of Glasgow the police force was not the most respected organisation.

Langley gritted her teeth as the memory played out behind her eyes. He'd called her over: younger then, streaks of dark hair slicked back on his head.

'Yes, sir,' she'd said. 'Can I help you?'

'Aye, you can, as a matter of fact.' Mannion was grinning broadly.

She remembered taking her notebook out.

'What are you doing?' said Mannion with feigned surprise, his companions smirking by his side. 'I want you to get your tits out, never mind your fucking notebook.' They all laughed, as did the straggle of customers in the bar.

She remembered reaching for her radio.

'What are you going to do? Call for your mates? What for?' He looked round the table. 'Did you hear me welcoming this fine young police officer to the neighbourhood, Sammy?'

'Aye, you were right polite, Mr Mannion, so you were,' replied a large, young man to Mannion's left.

'See. No crime here, lassie.' He'd taken a long draw on his cigar, then snarled, 'If I was you, I'd get back to London Road and tell old McCutcheon I'm asking for him.'

'Inspector McCutcheon?' She remembered just blurting this out for something to say, all the time conscious of the blush spreading across her face.

'Tony Two Tickets.'

'Why do you call him that?

'Use your powers of detection to work it out. Now, if you don't mind, I'm a busy man. Fuck off!'

She remembered the shame of it all. She'd turned on her heel and left the pub as quickly as her feet would carry her. She stumbled down the street for a few yards until happening upon a close doorway. She shirked inside and leaned against the wall, desperate to catch her breath.

As Amelia Langley stared at Mannion's image, these memories were as clear as the day they had happened. She'd experienced many more harrowing times as a police officer since. But only one of them stuck in her mind the way that encounter had. As it turned out, Tommy 'Two Tickets' McCutcheon was so named because two was the number of seats Mannion bought him for every home game at Ibrox.

She turned her thoughts to Finn. Good-looking – darkly handsome, they'd have said a few years ago. Still did, probably. He was charming, funny, but ruthless. She shuddered at the crimes this man had committed. But still she couldn't help liking him. There was something alluring about his politeness, his grin. He would never have behaved towards her the way Mannion did.

She remembered the night he'd saved her.

A young cop had been first on the scene the night Finn's son had been murdered. The woman reminded her of herself twenty years before. She'd walked into carnage: blood, bone and death. Langley had done her best to comfort her youthful colleague.

She could see Finn's face when he arrived at the pub in New Street. The acrid smell of spent cordite still in the air, mixed with blood, death and powdered masonry. They'd had to keep him back, but he'd broken through far enough to take in the horrific sight. He looked utterly bereft, all of the swaggering arrogance gone. It was replaced by the devastation felt by a grieving, broken parent.

The next morning she'd heard about the huge bouquet of flowers that had arrived at the police office in Paisley addressed to the young PC who had been first at the scene.

I'm so sorry you had to witness what you did last night. Thank you for doing your job. Alexander Finn.

It was an act of kindness that had cost him nothing. But to Amelia Langley it revealed the human behind the mask she'd known had been there for so long. The flowers had long since withered away – gifted to a hospital ward at the Royal Alexandra Hospital in Paisley. But she knew that the man who cared enough through his own grief to think of another human being was still there. If she were to succeed, Amelia Langley knew she must somehow reach that person.

20

He looks older. I'm surprised by it. I don't know why. Two years have passed, so why wouldn't an old man look older?

The clock is ticking in the familiar room. It smells the same, looks the same, but something has changed. He just stares at me.

'Are you going to say nothing?' I ask.

He sighs and lowers his head. 'What do you want me to say?'

'"Hello" would be nice.'

'Hello.' This is flat. His face remains expressionless.

'I thought I should come and let you know I'm back.'

'I already know. I only have to switch on the news to see that.'

I know he's disappointed, angry with me. But he doesn't understand.

'If I hadn't come back, things would be worse.'

He laughs, the first time a smile has crossed his face since I arrived.

'In your mind, things are always better when you are in control, yes?' The very question is a condemnation.

Suddenly I don't know what to say to the man I've known for so long. The bond I thought we had seems broken. I know he knows about my life. I know he knows about the things I've done. I suspect he knows more than

I think. But he's always been there for me; like the angel on the shoulder of the boy in the cartoon I read when I was a boy. I decide to leave, but he gestures to me to sit back down in that peculiarly dismissive Italian manner, a command rather than a request.

'You should never have returned. Now you are damned. Do you realise this?'

I decide to fight back. 'So, I'm damned for protecting my family, my friends?'

'Yes, how is that going?'

I'm surprised by the way this modern phrase sounds coming from his old cracked lips. 'I don't know yet,' I reply.

'Maybe ask Dusky. He is a friend of yours, yes?'

Though his eyes bore into my soul, I give nothing away, though I am surprised.

'May I tell you about a man I once knew?

I nod my head. I know he's going to tell me, regardless.

He sits back on his chair and closes his eyes. 'He was young, but like you he had great responsibility placed upon his shoulders, despite his tender years . . .'

Sixty-one years earlier

Calabria, Italy

The street in the small village is in ruins. Shop windows have been smashed, rubble and glass strewn on the parched ground like hard tears. Young children cry, a stray dog howls, though none of them can know what has happened this day.

An old woman in widow's weeds wills herself up off the dusty road. Her face is pinpricked by dots of red blood where grit and glass have cut deep into her skin. Tears fall down her wrinkled brown cheeks. She's lived through many summers, but not one like this.

The car is in the middle of the road. Until a few moments ago it was polished to a black silk-shining splendour. Now smoke and flames have eaten away at the paintwork; the explosion has removed the roof, blown twenty feet in the air, landing twice that length away down the cluttered calamity of the cobbled road.

The widow was flung on her back when the car carrying Don Alessandro was destroyed. Her heart is breaking, not just because of the shock of it all but because she knows how her life will change. All life will change. Every one of those who live in the village and miles around will share suffering as it sweeps through their community like a scythe through summer grass. The baker who bakes the best bread you will ever taste, brown-crusted and so soft inside; the butcher who proffers fine fleshy cuts and his beautifully cured ham and sausages; the suntanned woodsman who cuts the logs to keep the chill of the winter's night at bay; the fishmonger who drives his narrow winding way to the port every morning, long before the cock crows, to buy the best of the catch; the fat, fabled hotelier with his white shirt and tails. Oh yes, he has tales that spring from his loose lips as the striped waistcoat stretches across his ample belly. Dino in the café, who stays open longer than he should to chat to the old men who reminisce over the sweet red wine that runs like frothing fresh blood from the old oak casks he keeps in the cellar; the mother with her baby held tight to her breast, the child searching out her nipple, not for food but comfort. The men idling in the sun do so no more, for they too know. Their chairs are cast aside, eyes blank with fear. Now there is no thought of a good hand of cards, or the cleft between the breasts of Maria, who serves them beer on the warmest days. All talk of football and tales of war are out of their heads, banished by the aching pain in their hearts. For this is worse than war. This they know.

The mayor looks out of the wide waste of his window and faints away. He knows that life for him can never be the same. His home, his friends, the fine food on his flush table, his lush, languid life of ease and plenty; this is now as nothing. All gone in an instant of flash, thunder and flame. Like the wrath of a vengeful deity who has, for reasons known only to infinite wisdom, abandoned them.

A young man, dark robes of the seminary flying behind him like wretched withered wings, sweeps round the corner, as would a whisper on a warm wind. He stops; the scene before him is like a still life. It will remain in his head, just like this, painted in something more lasting than ink and oil, for the rest of his life.

Those standing in the street eye him sadly. The men remove their threadbare, sun-bleached caps, while the women lower their heads and feel the sap of a mother's musing rising in their chests; for each one, young and old, would mother this dark-clad youngster now.

He falls to his knees as a carrion crow caws in the distance. He cries out, not in the prayer one might expect but in despair. Despair and prayer, they sound so alike, for they are brothers.

If seconds change lives, then an instant can last an eternity.

★

As I listen I try to gauge what he means. What has this tale, well told, to do with me? I ask him and he shrugs.

'Take from it what you will. I would have hoped the meaning would be self-evident, no?'

'The man in the car – it's me, isn't it?'

He shrugs again. 'Only if you want it to be.'

'The boy – the young priest – what happens to him?'

'I don't know.'

'Oh.'

'When does life's story play out to its end? When can a tale be told?'

The atmosphere, the story, all this has confused me. My head is addled enough by worry over my children, irritation at my wife, troubled times, my mother's obsession with egg, chips and beans. I came here expecting guidance, a listening ear. Instead, all that I face in the wood-panelled room is cold detachment and riddles.

'If I die the way the Don does . . . Well, I've deserved it for being stupid or careless. In any case, your church has been pardoning men like him – like me – for hundreds of years. All of our sins washed away by penitence. You know that.'

Again, the Latin shrug, but he holds my eye. 'And see how much the world has gained from it, all this penitence.'

'So you don't believe what you've been telling me all this time? Great!'

'*When I was a child, I spoke like a child, I understood as a child, I thought as a child: but when I became a man, I put away childish things.*'

'First epistle to the Corinthians.' I remember it from nowhere.

'I'm pleased you were listening all that time ago. The question is, did you really understand?'

As always, I shake his hand warmly. But I leave with more questions than answers. Is this the way it's always been? I'm not sure. But the story he told has unsettled me. I know he's a wise and clever man, but was this some kind of warning?

21

The Waterstones in Glasgow's Argyll Street was busy. For some reason, this surprised Joe Mannion. He supposed it was because he thought the delights of the Internet – gaming, and streaming movies and TV shows – would have taken the place of the printed word. But the bustle in the store was proving him wrong.

He browsed the shelves of children's fiction. He didn't have a clue what to choose for his granddaughter, but when he saw the picture book about a cat on a small island he felt that would be something she'd like. He was determined that she would have a better start in life than he'd had. He was equally determined that his grandchildren, unlike his children, would do something with their lives – go places, get away from Glasgow. He'd been too caught up with climbing the ranks of the city's criminal underworld to oversee the upbringing of his offspring, and that disturbed him.

As he took a seat in the store's café, he was pleasantly surprised to see so many young people. Beside him a fresh-faced father was reading a book to his daughter. Despite the distractions all around, the little girl looked absolutely wrapped up in the story. He felt more than a twinge of guilt.

Then he looked up to see Sammy Sloane weaving his

way through the bibliophiles. If Mannion felt out of place in this palace of words, Sammy looked it. In fact, by the expression on his face, his henchman could just have landed on another planet. His mouth was agape, as he gazed with great puzzlement at the bookshelves and those staring at them.

'Over here!' Mannion called, in tones he wouldn't have deployed in the Iron Horse.

Sammy waved his hand and wound his way through the tables in the direction of his boss. Sloane was behind a young woman with a pushchair. She was desperately trying to negotiate the small spaces between seats, tables, bags and other obstacles, in order to find solace in a rest and a cup of coffee. She looked stressed, no doubt worn out by the ordeal of shopping in the city centre with a baby. The rush to buy for Christmas had arrived, and her story was doubtlessly being repeated across the world.

'Give the lassie a hand!' Mannion shouted. At first Sloane looked confused, until he realised that he was supposed to help the woman with the pushchair. So, noisily, he began to clear her way to an empty table. He achieved this by pushing at chairs and flicking at bags with his large right foot.

'Hey,' said one middle-aged man when Sloane unceremoniously booted his large rucksack under his table. 'Watch what you're doing!'

The big gangster leaned across the table and replied quietly. 'Shut the fuck up, or I'll ram that rucksack as far up your arse as it will go, right?'

The man blanched at this, placing his book firmly in front of his face, between himself and Sloane like a shield.

'There you go, darling,' said Sloane, sliding a chair way from a table to allow the young mother to take a seat.

'Thank you,' she said with a smile, as she fussed over the child, who stared up at the tall Sloane with wide eyes.

'How's it going?' He waggled his fingers at the baby in an approximation of what he felt children might appreciate. To his dismay, the baby's face crinkled and she burst into floods of tears.

With a grimace, Sammy Sloane decided to move on, heading to where Mannion was seated.

'Top marks there, Sammy. Easy seen you've no weans.'

'Me and Denise, well, she's got a deformed womb . . .'

'Do I look like a gynaecologist? I'm trying to relax, here.'

'Aye, on that subject, why here, gaffer?'

Mannion lowered his voice. 'The spotlight's on us, Sammy. Who knows who's listening to what? Let's be honest. This is the last place anyone would think to find you and me.'

'We're safe back at the Horse, surely?'

Mannion shrugged. 'Are you sure? You know what they bastard cops are into now. They could have a satellite tracing us, for all we know. Bugs in the wall, all sorts.'

Sammy Sloane raised his eyes heavenwards. 'Are you taking the piss, big man?'

'Naw! You see it all the time. Have you never watched *CSI Miami*?'

'Nope. We're having a lot of bother with our dish right now. Aye, and you can't get Sky to answer the bloody phone, neither.'

Mannion was going to point out the irony, but realised it would be lost on Sloane.

'So, what's the scoop, boss?'

'You heard about our buddy, yes?'

'Aye, tragic, so it was. He wasn't the worst, big Dusky, man. I hate they Albinos!'

'Try and keep this as abstract as you can, Sammy.' Mannion moved his eyes to and fro to remind his companion that they were in public.

'Aye, right, boss. No, it's a right tragedy, so it is. See they workplace injuries and that. Worst ever, so they are.'

Mannion sighed. 'And what makes you think it was our friends from the east, eh?'

Sloane looked confused, as he narrowed his eyes at Mannion. 'The Edinburgh mob? Nah, they've got enough on their plate over there without worrying about us, Joe.'

'Further east,' said Mannion, showing his displeasure.

Sloane thought for a moment. 'Oh, you mean the Albinos.' He hesitated. 'Who else would it be?'

Mannion leaned forward and lowered his voice. 'First off, they're Albanians – how many times? Secondly, take a wild guess.'

A waitress arrived at the table with a small notepad in her hand. 'What would yous like?'

'Just a flat white for me, dear,' said Mannion.

Sloane licked his lips. 'Can I get a large chocca mocca, aye with a big swirl o' thon cream, darlin'.'

Mannion raised his eyes as the waitress took the order and bustled off. 'Your man knows,' he said pointedly.

'What man?'

'Our man from the mill town.'

'Eh?'

'The man that's just come back from his holidays!' Mannion's face was taking on a red hue now.

The tip of Sloane's tongue appeared between his lips,

as he scrunched his eyes, deep in concentration. 'Any more clues, boss?'

'Oh, for fuck's sake,' said Mannion under his breath. 'Who do we know who's just come back after being away for a while?' He nodded, hoping this would jog Sloane's memory.

Suddenly, the penny dropped. 'Got it! Big Zander.' Sloane smiled broadly.

'See, if I'd wanted to tell half of Glasgow, I'd have put it on a billboard, Sammy.'

'Sorry. Ach, you know me – I'm a man of action, not good at this secret service stuff.'

'Well, now we've established what's going on, we'll have to do something about it. The plumber thing was a mistake, he had nothing to do with the young man's death, you know what I mean.' Again Mannion nodded to try and get the message through.

But it seemed that Sloane was picking up the idea of this covert banter. 'Nah, he never blew Danny away. He was fitting toilets. Likely just shouting his mouth off to impress that lassie in the bar.'

Mannion held his head in his hands. 'Aye, and now he's a toasted sandwich. Listen, our man in Paisley means business. He won't stop at Dusky. However, he knows about our deal with his ex-pal, trust me. We have to make a gesture to dissuade him from going any further. And it has to be a big gesture. Be ready, I've got a lot of thinking to do. Get a team together – do you know what I mean?'

'Aye, of course, I get it. Do you think I'm thick?'

Before Mannion could reply, their order arrived.

'Hey, well done with the cream, hen.' Sloane took in the huge swirl on top of his drink.

'Get it done – today!' said Mannion when the waitress had gone. 'I'll be in touch later.'

Sloane nodded, a dollop of cream now on the tip of his nose.

22

Zander Finn had been able to persuade his wife to let him see 'the books'. These were lists of numbers no accountant would understand; however, to the initiated they transmitted the same idea: a basic understanding of where they were in terms of money in, money out, and profit. As an organisation the results were calamitous. He'd no idea things could have become so bad in such a short time.

'You can take that look off your face, Zander,' said Senga, cigarette smoke billowing from her mouth as she spoke. 'Everyone did their best under the circumstances. Remember, I was grieving.' She glared at him with undisguised loathing.

'I was having a ball.' He didn't look at her but carried on reading. 'The slot machines in the Southside. What happened to that?'

'That was Dusky's thing.'

'And what we were getting going with Manchester – you know.'

'Dusky took that on when you went. How was I supposed to know what to do about having weans take shit up on the bus to Ullapool?'

Finn smiled. 'But I bet your boyfriend knows how to do it.'

'Fuck off!'

'You knew, didn't you?'

'Knew about what?'

'About Dusky and Joe Mannion. You knew that he was playing both sides of the fence.'

'It's an alliance!'

'Between you and him – not the rest of the guys. That's what you said. Anyway, an alliance is supposed to go both ways. From what I can see, this is one-way traffic!'

'Well, how was I supposed to know what every bastard was up to? Everyone thought you were dead.'

'Well, I'm not.'

'So you say.'

'Do you think anyone liked the way you were running things? Shagging old Joe was just the last straw.'

'Huh! Didn't stop other folk jumping into bed with him.'

'You're into metaphors now.'

'What?'

'Never mind.' He closed the jotter and walked across the lounge towards her.

'Don't you dare lay a finger on me!' Senga backed away.

'In all of our marriage have I ever hit you?' His face was now in hers.

'No. But don't think you can start now.'

'I wouldn't waste my time. But know this, from now on you have no say over anything, understand?'

'You don't know what's been going on. You can't stop me!'

'Oh, you can do what you want with that old man. I don't care. But you're with him now. And I want you out of here.'

'Fuck off! We've discussed this. This house is as much mine as yours.'

Finn laughed. He walked back to the plush leather sofa and took a seat. 'Big Joe, he's a right family man, isn't he?'

'I'm not interested in your mind games.'

'See these wee cameras you get now, brilliant, so they are.'

'What are you talking about?' Senga accentuated each word as though she was trying to make herself understood to someone who didn't speak English.

Finn reached into a briefcase at his feet and pulled out an A4 envelope. 'This is what I mean.' He skimmed the envelope across the room at his wife. It landed at her feet.

With a puzzled look, she leaned forward then opened it. It contained large images of her and Joe Mannion in bed. 'You bastard!'

'It's you that's having the affair!'

She ripped at the images, one of her false nails coming off in the process and landing on the thick carpet.

'You're not daft enough to think I don't have the originals, are you?'

'I fucking hate you!'

'I'll give you until tomorrow to move out. You can take the car, and I know you've got plenty of dosh stashed away.'

'Do you really think these will bother Joe?' She gestured at the torn pictures on the floor.

'No, he'll probably get a semi looking at them, if he can manage that at his age. But his dear wife and those lovely kids of his won't like it at all.' Finn grinned. 'Make sure you're out by five tomorrow. Oh, and take what you want. I'm not interested in your tasteless tat.' He got up, lifted his briefcase and walked towards the lounge door. 'And another thing: if I was you, I'd stay away from hotels for a while. Especially those fleapits in the West End – bad for your health.'

'Wait! These photographs were taken before you came back.'

'Did you really think that someone wasn't looking after my interests when I was away?'

Zander Finn slammed the door behind him as he left the room.

Senga was breathing heavily. She reached into her bag and fetched out her mobile.

*

The chiropractor was pinned over the examination table in his consulting room, with Malky Maloney's powerful hands round his throat. He yelled out in pain as his back was forced further back over the edge of the table.

'Now, we've found you a nice new place to work from. Right in the centre of Paisley. A great wee spot. You'll have loads of customers.'

'There's fuck all left in the centre of Paisley,' said the stricken man, despite his perilous position.

'This is our version of town centre regeneration. See me, I'm right sad every time I clock empty shops and that. Used to be a great wee cobbler just off Espedair Street, he's gone and I've nae bugger tae fix my good boots. Arnotts, gone too. Even the Piazza's away now. No, something has to be done to make Paisley great again.'

'Aye, okay. But you'll break my back!'

'Just as well you'll know how to fix it, eh?' Maloney released his grip on the man's throat. The chiropractor hauled himself back into a seated position.

'This new place, how much will it cost?'

'How much are you paying here?'

'I'd have to look to get you an exact figure.'

'Well, whatever that is, we'll double it. Sound fair?'

'Fuck off!'

Maloney made to grab the chiropractor's throat again.

'Right, okay. Whatever.' He caught his breath for a moment, then sniffed the air. 'What's that smell? It's burning!'

'I wouldn't worry. It's just the hotel next door on fire. It was a fucking eyesore, anyway. Damn near a knocking shop, eh?'

'Do you know who owns that place?

'Aye, I do.' Maloney burst into laughter. 'And you know how fire spreads, and you just next door. Here, me and the boys will give you a hand with your kit.'

'Shit!' The chiropractor flung himself off the treatment table and dashed around the office desperately filling boxes and bags.

'That's the spirit,' said Maloney just as his phone rang. 'What's up?' He listened for a moment, then ended the call. 'That's the fire on your roof now. You'd better get a move on!' He smiled. 'It'll be great to see the old town busy again.'

★

'Now, this is about a wee cat that lives on an island. He looks funny, doesn't he?'

'I don't like they books, Papa. Can I not get my iPad?'

'Now, come on, Chardonnay,' said Joe Mannion. 'It's important that you like books.'

'It's shite. I don't like it!'

'Now, what would the author say if he heard you? He'd probably take you to court. Just read the book with Papa. And shite's not a nice thing to say. Wee girls shouldn't be speaking like that.'

'My mammy says it all the time. Aye, and fuck all will stop her neither, so Daddy says.'

Mannion's mouth gaped. 'Tracy-Anne, get up here!' He heard her feet padding up the stairs.

'What's up? Is there a fire?'

'Have you heard the words this wean knows?'

Tracy-Anne shrugged. 'What can I do about that? She's clever, picks things up right quick, so she does.'

Mannion was about to reply when his phone rang. 'Fucking shite!' he said, as he ended the call.

'There's a fire, I need to go!' He kissed his granddaughter on the cheek and rushed to the door.

Chardonnay watched him leave, a frown on her tiny face. 'Papa shouldn't be saying these words, should he, Mammy?'

23

Gramoz Makur liked Scotland. He liked it so much he'd purchased quite a lot of it. From a small estate in Aberdeenshire to a large mansion in North Ayrshire, he had invested heavily. Gramoz liked the place, liked the scenery, liked the people, but most of all he loved the money he could make.

It was simple for him: here there were fewer problems. He liked the rule of law in the UK. You could be reasonably comforted by the fact that if one of your enemies were to move against you, they would have to factor in the police – even the intelligence services. Back home in Albania, well, that was another matter entirely. Since the fall of the ultra authoritarian communist government, Albania had become one of the most lawless places on the planet. He couldn't sleep at night for worry. Whole families were wiped out in an instant; the perpetrators faced few, if any, legal repercussions.

Here, everything was so well arranged. As long as you oversaw things from a distance, nobody appeared to care. As far as anyone who knew him was concerned, he was a man from the east who made millions from renewable energy. A Russian, maybe – who knew, who cared? The Scottish government had even given him a nice fat grant to help with 'research'. Though, apart from a largely empty factory – also government-funded, manned by a handful of misfits he'd picked up from the list of the unemployed, for which he was also very well remunerated – very little research went on. In fact, he would shortly pull the plug on this feeble operation, pleading financial meltdown, and happily start up again somewhere else with nice fat grants that spilled from the public coffers like wine from the fountain in the village in which he grew up.

He thought about home. On festival days there, the young men would stand under the fountain, mouths open, their shirts drenched red by the cheapest fruit of the vine. He smiled at the memory. His smile faded when he thought of his father. The man had been cruel and brutal, blighting his young life. But, as it turned out, he was not invincible. Makur shied away from the memory.

He also liked Scotland for another reason: he had red hair. This was unusual in Albania, and he'd been bullied for it as a small child. But, he surmised, very little happened for no reason, and he'd soon learned to fight back, learned he was good at it, too. He learned he was better than everybody else. This, and a long spell in the army, had made him. An intelligent mother, weighed down by the grind of domestic chores, fear of a brutal husband and poor health, made sure that, as a small boy, her son read. And he read prodigiously. He hadn't realised from whence these books had come, back then. Later, he discovered his mother's brother, his uncle, was a professor at Padua University in Italy. Somehow, he managed to have everything from Stendhal to Steinbeck smuggled in for his bookworm nephew.

In stature, he was short. In his bare feet, he barely reached five foot seven inches. But to compensate for this, he was strong, his shoulders broad, his knotted muscles rippling across his squat frame. He'd learned that it didn't really matter how tall, short, strong or physically weak you were. It was your desire that took you places – the lengths you were prepared to go to, to get what you wanted. And Gramoz Makur wanted a lot – he wanted it all.

He loved marching down the grand old wooden stairway in the morning. The smell of oak and opulence, the magnificent collection of paintings he'd assembled, the tick of the antique grandfather clock in the wide reception hall. He'd first read about grandfather clocks as a young child in Albania. For a little boy, in a country where very few people even had watches, this seemed to be the height of decadence. Now he had a beautiful example, made by the legendary Wilhelm Baur of Vienna in 1895. It was solid and elegant, the pendulum swinging to and fro, quite as hypnotic as the loud tick that echoed round the ground floor of the mansion.

The man waiting for him beside the clock was dressed casually, but his head was bowed in old-fashioned deference. As though he wasn't there, Makur opened the clock's casement and brought out a large key, with which he began to wind the antique slowly and carefully. Only after the last turn of the key did he address the man.

'So, you have found out what I wanted to know, Jotir?

'Yes, sir.' He almost bowed when answering the question. Makur had been his colonel in the army, he'd saved his life, and there was no greater bond between two men than that. He owed Makur everything, right unto death.

'And what did you discover?'

'As we thought, Finn is slowly taking control. He has replaced his wife, assassinated one of his men. He thought he was working with Mannion.'

'Was he?'

'Yes, it is almost certain that he was. This bastard did something else. The dead man, I mean.'

'The murder of your cousin.'

Jotir hesitated. 'He was my mother's cousin, sir.'

'Still, family, nevertheless. And you think Finn ordered it?'

'I know he did.'

Makur was now using his handkerchief to polish one side of the clock. 'This place for dust, it's everywhere. I don't know where it all comes from.'

'I read that it was mainly old skin.'

'Then the previous owners must have been walking skeletons, no?' Makur laughed heartily, slapping Jotir on the back. He wiped his eyes dry with the same hanky he'd used to dust the clock. 'Something has to be done. Everything has been going so well, we can't take backward steps now. This Finn, he is smarter than Mannion, I think. Though the old man is cunning, of that there is no doubt.'

'I would like to kill Finn, sir.'

'Would you? Why not Mannion?'

'Because Finn was responsible for the death of my cousin.'

'But you don't know why he had this cousin of yours killed?'

Jotir shrugged. 'To get back at us somehow – retaliation?'

'Does Zander Finn sound to you like a man who would make such a mistake?'

'No, but he was responsible for this. I know he was.'

'Mannion passed on information to Finn. He told him that your cousin was one of those who killed his son.'

Jotir looked puzzled. 'And Finn believed him?'

'Yes. The death of his son is his weakness, even now. If he'd thought about this, he would have been more careful. But he had his men kill someone they didn't know was responsible for the crime.'

'Maybe they fucked up, yes? Maybe Finn didn't want my cousin to die.'

Makur shrugged. 'Yes, maybe so, it is possible. But, in that case, he hasn't regained true control of his people.'

'Then he is weak.'

'Yes, Jotir, then he is weak. But a man like him, he will soon build his strength. He is no . . .' He searched for the word.

'*Budalla?*'

'Ha! Yes, idiot. It is strange how many words in English I cannot remember.'

'Why don't we speak Albanian?'

'Because we learn, and to learn is important – it is good for business here in this country. We must make sure that their words cannot be our masters.'

'So, what do we do with Finn?'

Makur watched the clock's pendulum swing to and fro. 'He is dangerous, yes. But he knows about business, he is clever.' He nodded to Jotir. 'Despite this terrible thing that happened to your cousin.'

'This goes unpunished, then?'

'No, it does not. But we have to consider our next step carefully. Come, we have coffee. It always helps me think.'

*

The café in Paisley's Moss Street was busy. The narrow space was mostly cluttered with those desiring really good coffee but without the time to sit and enjoy it, so Finn found a table easily.

He scrolled through his phone, checking the door every now and then. He'd just finished writing a quick email to his legitimate accountant when she entered. The sight of the thin, young woman made him catch his breath. He'd held her when they'd been reunited at Robbie's hospital bed, seen her at his mother's even. He supposed that the worry over seeing his son like that and the distraction of Kevin Mannion at Maggie's was why he hadn't really noticed then.

'Dad, hi.' She slid onto the chair easily.

'Hello, Gillian. What do you want?' He was determined that she eat something. His daughter was painfully thin.

'No, this is my treat. I said, remember?'

'I'm honoured! I want some cake – coffee cake. You used to love that when you were a wee girl.'

'I'm not hungry, Dad.' Her smile disappeared.

'You're not eating.'

'Fuck, you sound like Gran.'

'Oh, don't say that.' Finn grimaced.

'I don't understand why you don't get on – you're too similar, that's the reason.'

'That's even worse! She's a bad-tempered old bastard.'

Gillian laughed. 'Why do you think I met you here?'

Finn shrugged. 'I dunno. Why?'

'The Grumpy Monkey.'

'I see. Okay, you win. I'll have an espresso, a cheese and ham toastie and a slice of coffee cake.'

'You're an expensive date!'

'You offered.'

He watched as his daughter walked to the counter and

placed the order. Of all his children, she most resembled Danny in looks, but her character was the polar opposite. She'd always been a sweet, happy child, while his dead son had been turbulent and difficult from birth.

She sat back down. 'I heard something on the news, Dad.'

'Oh, yes?' said Finn, pretending not to know what she was about to say.

'Dusky. He got shot. He's dead.'

'I know, it's really sad. But you know the life he led.'

'Like yours, you mean?'

'No, not like mine.' He shook his head. 'You know that I'm not part of that any more. Now I know why you wanted to meet me in public, not the house.'

Gillian looked unconvinced. 'That's not the reason.' She held out her hand and grabbed his. 'Well, maybe in a way it is.'

Finn looked into her green eyes. It was like a mirror, sometimes comforting, now disconcerting. 'If it's about your mother, I'll make sure she's okay. She's already at the house in Howwood. It's been empty for two months, apparently.'

'I'm not worried about her.' Suddenly Gillian looked disgusted.

'She's your mum, remember. Whatever happens between her and I, that won't change.'

She gripped his hand more tightly. 'I know what she's been doing, Dad. Her affairs. It's disgusting.'

'She thought I was dead.'

'She was at it long before you left. I'm not stupid.'

He sighed. 'Our marriage has been over for a long time. Don't blame her. The thing with Danny hit us all hard. It gets to you in different ways, you know?'

'I guess so.' She paused. 'I need to tell you something.' Her face was now pale and serious.

All of a sudden the bottom fell out of Zander Finn's world. It was the same feeling he'd had when he'd been told about Danny's murder. 'You're sick. I knew it! Look, there's nothing of you.'

'I'm not ill, just a bit stressed with the course. I should eat more.'

'Yes, you should!' he agreed enthusiastically.

'I have something to tell you. Please don't make a fuss.'

Finn stared at his daughter. 'Well, go on. Let's get this over with.'

'I'm seeing someone.'

Finn sat back in his chair. 'Not another one of Mannion's sons! Don't tell me that.'

'No, but you've met this person.'

Finn thought hard. 'If it's one of Danny's old pals, I wouldn't recommend it.'

'The ones that aren't dead, you mean?' She stopped. 'I'm sorry, I shouldn't have said that.'

'No, it's true.' Finn swallowed back the emotion.

'I'm seeing Kirsty. You met her when we were with Robbie.'

It took Finn a moment to process this information. 'So, you're gay?'

'I don't know.' She pushed her hair back off her brow.

'Well, you're either gay or you're not. If you're seeing a girl – like that, I mean – it's pretty straightforward, no?'

'I still fancy boys.'

'That'll be your mother in you.' He laughed.

She stared at him. 'You mean, you're not bothered about it?'

He leaned across the table and touched her face. 'Of course not! What do you think I am? I just want you to be happy. Life is for living. Just be yourself, whatever that is.'

At this, their order arrived.

'Dad, you never stop surprising me, do you know that?'

'I'm not sure how your Uncle Malky would have reacted if it was Jenny.'

'Oh, I dread to think.' She laughed.

'Right, if that's the big revelation over, I want you to eat half of this toastie.'

'You know, I'm actually quite hungry now.' She reached over to his plate.

'I don't suppose you've told your gran.'

'No, I was kind of hoping you would.'

'Oh great, egg, chips and beans for two and a flea in my ear into the bargain.' Father and daughter laughed together.

Outside, the sky was getting darker.

24

Malky Maloney had woken in a bad mood. His night had been restless, plagued by dreams of Dusky.

Dusky was impetuous, that he knew. He'd always been the one most likely to land them in trouble. But he was also a fine man to have at your back. On more than one occasion, especially in their youth, Dusky had saved him from a beating, or a knife in the ribs.

Zander had ordered it, so it had to be done. But the results still sickened him.

For a moment, he wondered if he'd made the right decision in bringing his old friend back from 'dead'. But under the circumstances he knew he'd had little choice. They were slowly being enveloped by Glasgow; consumed, as though by some terrible wasting disease prompted by a host parasite. But he was still in an awkward position. After all, everyone had to swim to survive. He'd seen that shit on nature documentaries. In turn, Mannion's empire was being eaten away by the faceless Albanians. It was the law of the jungle.

Malky Maloney couldn't think about Joe Mannion now. Though he knew for a fact that Dusky had become involved with the man. It was Senga who had driven him away – she'd driven everyone away.

Maloney knew the nature of his best friend, Zander Finn.

When he thought about it, he'd always known there would be a reckoning, on his return. And he knew it wouldn't end with Dusky's death. There was more to come, of that he was sure.

'Mandy! Where's they scants I like?'

He listened to his wife's distant reply and located his underpants in the appropriate drawer. He pulled on his jeans, sucking in his stomach in order to get them buttoned below his waist, pulled on a heavy jumper, thick socks and then his boots. It was cold, and the man who'd once worn a T-shirt to show off his muscles in all weather now hid his middle-age spread under as many layers as he could.

Dressed, he thudded down the stairs, almost trampling over their cleaner, who was bent over the vacuum, wrestling with an over-full bag.

'Murder they things, eh, Dina?'

'They sure are. Especially this bastard!'

'I'll get Mandy. She used to work in the Hoover factory before we got married.

'That's before all this went space-aged, Malky.'

'It's near before they invented the fucking wheel!'

He left his cleaner laughing as he went in search of his wife. He found Mandy in their big kitchen, baking furiously.

'That's enough to feed an army. Have you started your own catering company?'

'It's for these poor weans in Africa – Gambia, you know?'

Maloney scratched his head. 'It's rice and stuff they need, dear, not cupcakes.'

'Aye, that's me baking cupcakes to send over to the starving children. I thought they'd like a treat.'

Maloney shrugged. 'You've always had a big heart, darlin'.'

'It's for a coffee morning down the community centre tomorrow! Do you really think I'm going to send these off to Gambia? We're raising money for the kids.' She raised her eyes. 'Sometimes I wonder if you're living in the same world as the rest of us.'

'Ach, you never make yourself clear enough. It's like fighting a snake in the dark.'

'I'll snake you!' She chased him round the kitchen with a handful of flour.

Malky grabbed her round the waist. 'Listen, I need to go. Do you need me to bring anything back later, shopping or whatever?'

She looked into his pale blue eyes for a moment, the expression on her face suddenly serious.

'What's up?'

'I've been thinking about what happened to Dusky.'

Maloney hugged her, whispering into her ear. 'You know what the big fella was like. He was careless, hot-headed. You mind he was never out of the jail when we was kids.'

'He didn't deserve two bullets.'

'Listen, I don't know. I've not seen much of him recently.' Though Maloney was determined not to show it, his feelings of guilt were beginning to constrict his throat.

'And what about your lord and master, eh? I hear he flung Senga out of the palace.'

'She's hardly on the bones of her arse, is she? That house in Howwood is big enough for a family of twelve.'

'Still and all, he comes back, out of the blue, and everything starts to happen. No coincidence, is it?'

Malky kissed her on the forehead. 'You know how things are now. We're into the pubs and clubs. It's all legitimate – has been for yonks. In fact, I'm off to meet some guy that wants to sell me a hotel in Dumbarton. What do you think of that? Us in the hotel business, eh?'

'Okay, Rocco Forte. If you can, bring home some steak from Tulloch's and we'll have it for dinner. You can't beat their sirloin, so you can't.'

'A wee bottle of red to wash it down, eh?' He fluttered his eyelashes teasingly.

'Huh! I'll be too knackered after all this baking for any bedroom gymnastics, you bugger!' She rubbed flour in his face.

'Only on my birthday these days, honey.'

'Aye, if you're lucky.' She wiped the flour from his face and kissed him on the cheek. 'Good luck with the hotel.'

'We'll see. I've never heard of this guy, so I don't know how it will go. Could be a pig in a poke.' He heard loud music burst into life upstairs. 'What's m'lady up to today?'

'Jenny? What do you think? Lying in her bed all day listening to that racket, or sitting glued to thon Netflix. Then she's off out tonight – again!'

'She's young. You know what we was like, Mandy.'

'We had jobs – well, you sort of had.'

'Hey, have I not brought you riches beyond the dreams of avarice?'

'Aye, so you have.'

'Listen, if this hotel thing comes off, I'll get her in there. You know, get some bugger to show her the ropes then she can manage the place, like.'

'Good luck with that!'

'I'd rather she was a healthy, happy lassie than cloaking about like Gillian Finn. She's like the walking dead. I got a shock when I saw her.'

'You need to be thin to be an actress, Malky.'

'She could do with some of those cupcakes.' He looked at his watch. 'Here, I better get going.'

As he was leaving the kitchen, she called to him. 'Maybe get a bottle of red, right enough.' Mandy winked.

'Yes, on a promise!' He smiled. 'After last night, I just had a feeling today was going to be a good one.' Maloney hurried off.

When he pulled the front door of his home he stopped, looking across at the view of Kelburne Cricket Club's ground. The air was cold but sweet. Though he could no longer smell the smoke from thousands of fireplaces, winter was certainly in the air; his favourite time of year. This day did feel different. Bit like the day you were off on holiday, he thought.

*

The Marston hotel looked in reasonably good nick. The windows were boarded up, but roof looked sound enough to Maloney's untrained eye. Though he could see some water damage from broken guttering down one gable end. A dark stain was slathered down the white walls. But that was minor stuff.

When he walked round the front of the building the view was, to say the least, impressive. To his right, Dumbarton Rock loomed. It still guarded the estuary to the Firth of Clyde and the city of Glasgow beyond. He remembered the history he'd been taught in school: everyone from the Romans and ancient Britons to the Vikings had occupied the fortress on the rock at one time or other.

He could hear the broad Clyde make its way to the sea. Seagulls squawked overhead, and the tang on the air made him feel even more like going on holiday. This was a great spot. Depending what he found inside, this could make for a superb location to do something special.

'Mr Maloney?' He heard a woman's voice and turned towards it. She was tall, dark-haired and well turned out. A typical estate agent, he reasoned. Now for the hard sell, he thought.

'I'm Grace Turner, pleased to meet you.' She held out a delicate hand and shook his.

'How are you doing? I'm Malky Maloney.' He turned back to face the Clyde. 'Brillant place to have a hotel, eh?'

'Oh yes, just beautiful. You can imagine how lovely it is on a nice day in the summer.'

'What happened to the previous owners? Be hard not to make something of this.'

'Oh, they are over-extended at the bank, I think. Took on too much. I suppose you'll know all about that, having been in business for so long.'

'Aye, a fair bit about it, that's for sure. Folk think running bars, clubs and hotels is easy, especially if they've no experience in the game. They associate them with good times. You know, getting pissed and all that. It's not as easy as you think. Even in a place like this.'

'Right, then. Would you like to have a look inside?'

'Aye, sure, lead on. Hope you've got a torch!'

'I think they have temporary lighting in place. We should be okay.'

'Brilliant!'

Grace Turner produced a set of keys from her handbag and they headed towards the main entrance of the hotel.

It was dark. Despite Grace's continued attempts to find the emergency lighting with the aid of the torch on Maloney's phone, she seemed to be making little progress.

'Listen, Mr Maloney, I'll need to go back out to the car. I've a big LED lantern there for just this kind of situation. I'll be back in two ticks. I'm so sorry about this. I'll call the owners if we can't get this temporary lighting on. You sometimes wonder what people expect from estate agents.'

'A hefty percentage, in my experience. No offence, like.'

'None taken.'

He watched her disappear in a shaft of light through the front door as he continued to look around by the dim light from his phone.

Maloney walked from the reception through swing doors into a much larger space. A bar, he supposed. Sure enough, to his right were beer fonts in front of a gantry, empty, save for a few bottles of spirits with dribbles of liquor in them.

The whole place smelled musty. But he'd been in many places like this. They always looked like lost causes until the workmen had been in; new paint on the walls and bright lights transformed them into small goldmines. If you knew what you were doing, that was.

Talking of light, he heard movement from behind and turned round, expecting to see Grace, the estate agent, back with the lantern. 'Let's get some light on the subject, eh?' said Maloney, though he couldn't see her. 'I'm in the bar, just through the swing doors.'

Two things happened at once. Suddenly a bright light shone in his eyes. He was about to protest when he was hit hard on the back of the head, sending him spiralling into darkness.

25

Zander Finn was in his office at Chancellor Fabrications. He'd arranged to meet Malky and Donald Paton to discuss contracts they were bidding for with Glasgow City Council. It was for fencing surrounding a park and, with the mark-up, would likely bring in a pretty penny, legitimate cash.

Paton was reading through their proposed method statement, making sure everything was in order before submitting the bid. 'I assume it's the usual arrangement?'

'What arrangement?' Finn replied.

'With MacConachie. He's still our man over at Darnick Street.'

'That's Malky's department. He was supposed to be here about half an hour ago.' Finn lifted the mobile phone to his ear.

'*This phone is switched off. Please try later, or send a text.*'

Finn threw his mobile onto a bundle of papers on his desk. 'Bugger's phone has been off for the last two hours.'

'Not like Malky. He spends half his life on that bloody thing.'

'Have you even got one yet?'

Paton raised his eyes to the ceiling. 'Yes, I have a mobile phone. But I use it for three things only.'

'Which are?'

'Phoning people, answering bloody emails and finding my way about in Glasgow.'

'Eh? Surely you know Glasgow like the back of your hand.'

'Did know it, you mean. When's the last time you were up in the Townhead?'

Finn shrugged. 'A good while ago. Why?'

'Well, get up there and tell me you have any idea where you're going. Nothing left of Parliamentary Road, never mind Swann Street.'

'Progress, Donnie.'

'So they say. My brother used to live up in the high flats in Kennedy Path, remember?'

'Aye, vaguely.'

'We used to go to the Hurdy Gurdy – opposite the Royal Infirmary.'

'That's ancient history.'

'Yes, but it was still a good boozer.'

'Things change, you know that.'

'Rarely for the better, in my opinion.' Paton turned his attention back to the proposal.

Finn was back on the phone. 'Hi, Mandy, how are you?'

'Well . . . a voice from the past,' Mandy Maloney replied. 'I haven't seen you since – well, since you came back.' She was going to say back from the dead, before remembering the last time she'd seen Finn was at Danny's funeral.

'We'll need to go out for a meal. Tell when you're free. Talking of free meals, have you any idea where that husband of yours is?'

Mandy paused, clearly puzzled. 'He was off to see some hotel in Dumbarton, last time I heard.'

'Hotel? He never mentioned it.'

'I think he just got the call about it yesterday. The place is closed. I think the owners are looking for a quick deal.'

'Aren't we all. Did he say which hotel?'

'Nope, I just know it was somewhere in Dumbarton.'

Finn thought for a moment. 'Listen, Mandy, if he appears, get him to give me a bell, please. His phone's switched off.'

'Ach, he's likely run out of battery. If it wasn't for me, the damn thing would never be charged up, but I'll tell him. He was up half the night pacing about on the damned thing. That's what will have happened to his battery. It's good to hear from you, Zander.'

'You, too. We'll catch up soon.'

When Finn ended the call, for some reason, he felt uneasy. Maloney spending half the night on the phone didn't sound right. But since his return, everything was unfamiliar. He banished the thought from his mind.

★

'Why are you doing this?' groaned Malky Maloney, his face battered and bloody. One of his eyes was already closed and the other wasn't far behind. He'd lost several teeth and his right cheek was swollen like a balloon. Maloney was tied to a chair in the boarded-up dining room of the hotel. He was trussed, hand and foot, and couldn't see his attackers because of the bright light shining in his eyes. The blows, and there had been many of them, rained down on him from nowhere. He'd fallen out of consciousness on a couple of occasions, but they'd brought him back with drenching buckets of ice-cold water.

Again, he was caught on the face by a blow that flashed between the blinding light and his failing vision.

'Listen. I've got money, if that's what you're after. I'll give you anything you want. Just fucking stop this!'

Another heavy blow, this time to the back of the head. Flashes of stars swept across his vision.

'I don't even know what it is yous want. Tell me, for fuck's sake!'

Now another shadow, but instead of an agonising impact he was aware of a figure between him and the light. The silhouette was that of a tall woman. She kneeled down in front of Maloney, her features indiscernible. He could smell her perfume, so at odds with his current plight.

'You want to know why we do this to you?' The voice was heavily accented, but light.

'Fucking scum!' Maloney shouted, with as much passion as he could muster.

'Scum?' The punch came right out of the light and broke Maloney's nose with a crack.

'Bastard,' he whispered through the pain. 'Tell me what the fuck you want. If you leave us to our own bit in Paisley, there's no problem. You can do what you want in Glasgow.' He spat out part of a tooth, hoping it would hit his tormentor.

'I don't want to know anything from you, Mr Maloney. You are here for one reason and one reason only.'

'Eh, what the fuck are you on about?' The shadow moved away, but Maloney kept shouting. 'You let me fucking go or you know what will happen, you fucking pieces of shite!'

The voice again, this time from behind. 'It wouldn't be good if we all knew what was in front of us, I think.'

Maloney opened his ruined mouth to reply just as the blade cut into his neck. The agonised scream was cut off to a grotesque gurgle. He struggled for a few moments against his bonds before his lifeless body went limp.

Finn was driving along St James Street in Paisley when he noticed the long parade of traffic at a standstill just before him. He banged his fists on the steering wheel in frustration. It had already been a hard day. Maloney hadn't appeared, so they'd had to delay submitting a proposal for the fencing contract. He was angry with his old friend. Now he just wanted to get home, pour a dram and relax in front of some shit on TV.

He turned off the Journey track he'd been listening to and switched over to BBC Radio Scotland. The traffic in front was showing no sign of movement. He listened for a few minutes before, right on cue, came Theresa with the travel news.

And now, Theresa, we've got big hold-ups either side of the Erskine Bridge, haven't we?

Yes, indeed we have. The bridge has been closed for the last hour or so because of what's being termed a 'police incident'. Though we don't know what's caused this, the upshot is that traffic is backing up all along Dumbarton Road and on the other side of the river at the St James Interchange.

Cursing, Finn reached for the mobile now ringing on the passenger seat of his Maserati.

'Mr Finn?'

The woman's voice was familiar, but, in his irritation, he couldn't place it. 'Aye, who's this?'

'Detective Chief Inspector Amelia Langley from Police Scotland.'

'Oh, great! See, instead of phoning me, why the fuck aren't you doing something about the bloody Erskine Bridge?'

'Are you near there?'

'Yes, I'm stuck in the biggest fucking traffic jam I've ever seen. So if you don't mind, I'd rather concentrate on this than pass the time of day with you. In fact, I'd rather stick needles in my own bollocks than pass the time of day with you, to be honest.'

'Still the same old charm, Zander.'

'Still the same old pish, Amelia.'

'Believe me, I take no pleasure in this.'

'Pleasure in what?' The tone of her voice made a cold shiver run down Finn's back. He'd heard police officers adopt that sympathetic tone before. Suddenly Danny's butchered face passed before his mind's eye.

26

It was dark now. Finn was on the River Clyde in an RIB belonging to Police Scotland's Diving and Marine Unit. He was kitted out with the requisite lifejacket and wet gear. At his side, Amelia Langley appeared pliant, almost sympathetic.

The lights of the city began to string out the further down the Clyde they sped. The RIB was hitting almost forty knots and, despite the relative calm of the river, this still made for a jolting passage.

Langley stared straight ahead. If she was right, Finn was about to experience another black day in his life. She watched him as he leaned his head back, taking in great gulps of air in preparation for what was to come.

'Are you okay?' she shouted, her hand on his arm.

'Aye, brand new,' said Finn. In truth, he was feeling sick, and not just because of the motion of the boat.

The Erskine Bridge loomed in the distance. From this angle, it looked massive; the nearer they got, the further he had to crane his neck back in order to see the complete structure. There were bright arc lights on the bridge and just near its apex across the river small lights seemed to hover in the air, like bees around a jam jar.

'What are those?' he shouted in Langley's ear.

'Drones. The lights are so they can get clear images, though some of them have night-vision cameras.'

The noise from the great inboard diesel engine lowered as the boat came to a stop, the police officer at the helm making sure they remained almost still in the middle of the Clyde by subtle use of the throttle.

Finn looked up. It was clear that something was hanging from the bridge, swaying to and fro under the bright white lights and pinpricks shining from the drones. He felt the bile rise in his throat.

Amelia Langley had something held in her hands, an iPad, cushioned and waterproofed in rubber. Her expression was grave. 'You don't have to do this, Zander,' she said, holding out the device to him.

With the engine now at a low purr, he could hear much better. 'What is it?'

'It's a visual feed from the drones.' She swallowed hard. 'We want to try and get an ID before we attempt to recover the body.'

'Why?'

'You did ask. Are you sure you want to know the answer?'

'I wouldn't have asked if I didn't want to know.'

She bit her lip then looked him straight in the face, brushing a strand of hair from over one eye. 'The body is in such bad shape, we're not sure if we can recover it intact.' Langley blinked as she gauged his response.

'Okay, give me the thing.'

'You can change your view by pressing here.' She pointed to an arrow on the screen of the tablet.

Finn took a deep gulp and held the iPad in front of his face. The first image was of something swaying in the wind like a grotesque pendulum of an old clock. He pressed the arrow. The image was closer now. At first he thought the face was made up like a clown's, until he realised that the great gaping 'smile' was a huge slash in the victim's neck, a vivid black under the lights.

Finn tried to calm the revulsion he felt at the pit of his stomach as he pressed the arrow again. The image was remarkably steady, pointing right into the face of the victim, moving with it as the body swung gently in the still night air.

The face was battered and bruised. One eye was already obscured, but where the other should have been there was a black hole, with trickles of dried blood streaming down the ruined face like black tears.

'Is it Maloney?' The question was laden with empathy, or so he felt.

Zander Finn clicked the screen again. This time it was easy to make out the face he'd known for most of his life, despite the mutilation. He could hear the sound of sirens carried on the wind from the Erskine Bridge. He felt his world begin to swim.

The last thing Finn remembered was replying with a weak 'Yes' to Langley's question before fainting away at the horror of it all.

★

Gillian Finn was in her room in the flat in Glasgow she shared with some other students. Connor, one of her flatmates, had just made them a dish he called 'vegafusion', but it tasted like a cross between vegetarian bolognese and a cauliflower curry. She had taken a few mouthfuls before excusing herself. She knew her friends were worried about her lack of appetite and recent weight loss, but she couldn't eat what she'd been given, despite its vegan credentials.

She lay back on her bed, listening to the sounds of the city through a slightly opened window. Gillian couldn't sleep in a sealed room; she always felt as though she would suffocate. Regardless of the chill outside, she would always have her window open, at least a crack, to let fresh air in.

Her hand lingered over the mobile phone at her side. She's been waiting for a message from Kirsty all day but had heard nothing. She reasoned that Kirsty, a year ahead of her at the Conservatoire, was busy in her preparations for the Christmas show they'd be staging. She knew what it was like trying to learn lines. You had to have peace and quiet. She was slightly hurt by the fact her girlfriend hadn't at least sent a text, though she reasoned that her lack of presence across her social media platforms spoke to the fact that she had her head down studying.

I should be doing that, thought Gillian, just as her phone burst into life. At first her heart soared, but that feeling was soon replaced by an emotion altogether more ambivalent when she saw who was on the other end of the line: Jenny Maloney.

Like many an offspring of best friends, she'd grown up with Jenny as her playmate largely by default. They'd had fun as kids, making holes in the large hedge at the bottom of the huge garden of the Finn residence, turning it into what approximated a secret house. There they played with dolls, before graduating to listening to music and discussing boys, fashion and the problems they shared as children of the kind of parents they had. But in their young teenage years they had begun to drift apart.

To Gillian, Jenny appeared dissolute, directionless. She loved partying and drugs. Gillian had often felt Jenny had more in common with her brother Danny. But she was aware youthful friendships often ended as children became adults and interests diverged.

'Hi, Jenny,' she said, trying her best to sound friendly. 'Hello?'

For a moment there was silence on the other end of the phone, then came Jenny's slurred voice. 'How are things at your posh acting school, Gildy?'

'Fine,' Gillian replied. She readied herself to listen to her childhood friend's long list of habitual lamentations about how badly the world was treating her.

'I fucking hate you, and I hate your fucking family. Especially that cunt of a father of yours!'

Gillian sat up in her bed. Jenny's voice seemed distorted by spite. 'What have you been on, Jenny? Why are you saying these things?'

'Oh, so you've not heard?'

'Heard what?'

'My father is dead! He's been murdered and it's all down to your fucking father, the great Zander Finn! Why the fuck didn't he just stay hidden away under whatever rock he'd found?'

Gillian's mind was in overdrive. Jenny was more than capable of talking shit when she was out of it, but this sounded different. 'Honestly, I have no idea what you're talking about, Gillian. What do you mean your father's dead?'

'Fuck off, and tell your shit of a father to do the same!'

With that last statement, the line went dead.

Gillian sat for a few moments. She wanted to go through to the lounge and talk to her friends, but what was the point? They hadn't lived the life of a child of gangsters, so how could they possibly understand? The person she really needed now was Kirsty.

Gillian did something she'd wanted to do all day. She scrolled Kirsty's name up on the screen and pressed the call button, but her phone was switched off. Gillian knew she sometimes did this when she was studying, so scrolled down to 'Kirsty Home', dialling her land-line number.

After a few rings, a man answered. He had a deep, resonant voice. Kirsty's father was unmistakable.

'Hi, Dr Campbell. I'm looking for Kirsty, is she in? It's Gillian.'

Dr Campbell cleared his throat. 'No, as a matter of fact, she's not here.'

'Oh,' said Gillian, momentarily off her stride. 'Do you know where I can get her?'

'I don't think she wants to talk to you, at the moment.'

'What?' Gillian felt sick.

'I believe you talked to your father about the "relationship" you and she have been having?'

'Yes.' Her reply was weak.

'Well, no doubt as you arranged together, Kirsty spoke with us.'

'I see.'

'Don't get me wrong, Gillian. We like you, and we have nothing against same-sex relationships.'

'But?'

'You're right to assume there is a "but".'

'Tell me!'

'I will not have my daughter throw her life, her future, away on someone with a background like yours. It's something her mother and I have worried about for some time. Now we know the true extent of this "attraction", we have decided it cannot continue.'

'I think Kirsty is old enough to make her own mind up about who she sees! This isn't the nineteenth century!'

'You don't understand, Gillian. Kirsty, faced with the facts, could see our reasoning. She has taken a sabbatical from the Conservatoire and is away at the moment.'

'I don't believe you!' This she shouted at the top of her voice.

'Whether you believe me or not is inconsequential. Things are as they are. Please don't try to contact my daughter. If you have the feelings for her you think you have, let her get back to a normal life. She won't tell you any different. The decision was mutual. And before you say it, it's nothing to do with you being white.'

The phone went dead.

Gillian sat motionless, the mobile phone still to her ear. She couldn't process what had just happened. In a few moments her world had been turned upside down. She thought about Malky Maloney; surely Jenny was just out of it, as usual. But Kirsty – Dr Campbell had always been so kind to her when she visited.

She lay back on the bed, silent tears streaming down her face. It wasn't her fault that her father was who he was. In that moment she too wished Zander Finn had stayed away.

Then she began to worry.

27

When Zander Finn awoke, he experienced a blissful moment when everything seemed right, the first waking moment before the world's problems crowd in. He was able to convince himself that the nagging feeling in the back of his mind was nothing more than the aftermath of a lingering nightmare. Soon, he realised that this was very wrong. His friend, his best friend and confidant, was dead; tortured and killed in the most brutal way.

To make matters worse, he had a hangover. He'd come home to the big empty house and encamped in the lounge with only loud music, a bottle of whisky and a blanket for company. Here he'd drunk himself to sleep in exactly the same way he'd done when Danny had been murdered.

He tried to mash some moisture back into his mouth but failed and went in search of something to drink of the non-alcoholic variety. As he stumbled across the hall and down the few steps to the sunken kitchen, all he could see was the dead, mutilated face of Malky Maloney.

Finn reached the big fridge and noticed to his dismay that it held precisely nothing to drink: no orange juice, no Coke – even the milk was sour. He slammed the heavy door shut with a rattle, then walked to the sink and grabbed a mug from the dish rack. As he filled it with cold water he squinted through the broad window into the distance. Down the long driveway, beyond the tall gates, he could see cars and people.

The press.

Amelia Langley had told him that they would confirm Maloney's death first thing in the morning, once his family had been informed. Finn looked at his watch. It was already after ten. The whole world would have known of Maloney's fate for at least two hours.

Making his way back to the lounge, he picked up his mobile and dialled. There were two rings before it was answered.

'Chancellor Fabrications, can I help you?'

'Is Donnie in yet?'

The voice on the other end was hesitant. 'Yes, Mr Finn. I'll put you through. And I'm sorry about Mr Maloney.'

'Thanks, honey,' he said. It was good to hear a friendly voice. Hold music sounded briefly in his ear, then the familiar voice of Donald Paton.

'I've been watching the news, Zander. You have my condolences.'

'You knew him, too – like me, since he was a boy.'

'Aye, I did that. Where are you?'

'At the house.'

'Okay, I'll come over. Give me half an hour.'

'It'll take you that time to get through the press at the gates.'

'I'll get some bodies over. We'll soon clear them.'

'Aye, I suppose.' Finn looked out of the big window again just in time to see a man with a camera slung around his neck scale the front gate and drop down onto the gravel driveway. 'Listen, Donnie, I need to go. You tell everyone to keep their heads down. Aye, and be careful. We don't know who did this.'

'We can guess, surely.'

'Mannion? Nah, he wouldn't go this far. A knife in the back? Aye, maybe. Something this high profile, no way. Anyway, we'll discuss it when you get over.'

'I'll stick on an auld boiler suit and come in one of the vans.'

'Good idea, see you soon.'

Finn ended the call, flung his phone on the sofa and pelted out of the room to the front door. As he opened it, he caught sight of a figure ducking round the side of the house. With no shoes on, the gravel dug into his bare feet, but he didn't care. In his mind's eye, all he could see was the swinging, broken body of Malky Maloney dangling high above from the Erskine Bridge. As he turned the corner, the man was crouched behind an oversized ornamental plant pot. A poor choice of hiding place.

Finn pulled him up by the lapels of his jacket. For a second, he stared at the photographer's frightened face, before propelling his head against the nose of the man from the press, hearing the satisfying crack and squeal as he did so.

'Fuck you!' said the photographer, as blood poured down his face.

'Your fault! You fucking fell over trying to break into my house.'

'No, I didn't! I'm in your garden.'

In a flash, Finn propelled the man to the floor with a punch to the solar plexus. As the man groaned on the gravel, Finn pulled the camera and its big, and doubtless expensive, lens from round his neck and dashed it against the plant pot, sending shards of glass, plastic and pottery showering over the gravel. He was about to stamp on the man's head when unseen hands grabbed him from behind.

'Enough!' shouted Langley. She was accompanied by a phalanx of uniformed police officers, two of whom had him by the arms. Another plain-clothed police officer stood beside her. Finn recognised DS Neil Dickie.

'I want this man charged with serious assault,' said the photographer, still holding his broken nose and being helped to his feet by another cop.

'Piss off, Jimmy. What did you expect? We saw you jumping over the gate.'

'Not in time to stop me getting a doing! Aye, and look at my kit.' He gestured to the broken camera and lens on the gravel.

'We came as quickly as we could.' Langley smiled. 'Reminds me of the time you and your squalid little paper were trying to accuse me of corruption when I first got promoted to the OCU, remember?'

Jimmy the photographer looked as sheepish as a man could with one hand clamped over a bleeding nose and a burgeoning bruise on his forehead.

'Save the shit for your wedding photographs clients.' She nodded to two constables. 'Please escort Mr Stein from the premises. And clear away his colleagues at the gate while you're at it. Neil, you go and talk to the press. Don't give them anything more, just a holding statement.' She turned her attention to Finn. 'Come on, you and I need to talk. In private.'

Finn shrugged off the grip of the police officers and walked back round to the front of his home and in through the open door.

In the lounge, Langley observed the empty whisky bottle and discarded blanket. 'Rough night, Zander? Don't blame you, to be honest.' Without being asked, she sat on a leather chair.

'I told you all I knew last night. That's it. Any other questions and you can either arrest me, or contact my solicitor.'

'That's not why I'm here.'

'Fuck, don't tell me someone else is swinging off a bridge with their throat cut and eyes gouged out?'

'She's fine, but I need you to listen. Sit down, Zander!'

It took him a second to register the word 'she'. But as reality dawned, he sat down on the sofa.

'It's Gillian.'

'Fuck, no!' Finn's face took on a desperate, horrified look.

'She's okay. But she took an overdose last night. Her flatmates found her in time and got her into the Queen Elizabeth. She's still there, but she's okay – Gillian's going to be fine.'

Finn looked about the floor for his shoes. 'I better go and see her.'

'She doesn't want to see you. I left her about an hour ago. Her mother's with her.' Langley changed her tone, quieter, trying to calm the man in whose home she was sitting. 'You need to take it easy for a while. And get someone to look at your feet – they're bleeding.'

Finn rubbed his face with one hand, an expression of disbelief spread across it. 'How has all this happened?'

'I don't know. But we're looking into it all.'

'What about my daughter?'

Amelia Langley shrugged. 'I'm sorry, I don't know. She wasn't saying a great deal earlier. Her mother asked us to leave.'

'Asked? Aye, I can just hear her "asking".'

'That's not important.' She got up and walked over to the gangster. Looking round to make sure they were alone, she knelt down and kissed him on the forehead. 'You should never have come back, Zan.' She cradled his chin in her hands, staring into his bright green eyes.

'I know, Amy. I know.'

She held the man that had saved her life close to her chest, all the time listening for the return of her colleagues. For what had passed between her and Zander Finn was a tale that never could be told.

28

Joe Mannion was still in bed when his wife woke him. 'You better see this,' she said, as she flung the newspaper at him.

'What the fuck are you on about? You know I had a late night. I just want to have a kip. I'll read the paper later.'

'Trust me, you'll want to read this.' With that, she turned on her heel and was gone.

Mannion had learned a lot in his life. Some of it proved to be useless information, much of it was handy; the rest, somewhere in-between. But of one thing he was sure: he trusted his wife's judgement. So, reaching on the nightstand for his glasses and trying to blink the sleep from his eyes, he grabbed the newspaper.

Gangster Tortured and Killed: The Macabre Slaying of Paisley Underworld Boss.

The headline and its subtext were plain enough. Mannion squinted at the blurry picture. Though the resolution was awful, he could make out an object hanging from the Erskine Bridge. He read on to discover the gruesome fate of Malky Maloney.

Having scanned all of the six pages on the murder covered in colour, including a short biography of the dead man, Mannion discarded the newspaper. He lay back in bed and sighed. He knew what would happen.

He lifted his mobile phone from the nightstand and dialled a number from memory. The call was answered quickly. 'Can I speak to Detective Chief Inspector Langley, please?' He listened to the reply intently. 'Oh, she'll want to speak to me, of that I'm sure. Tell her Joe Mannion is looking for her. I'm sure she has the number.'

★

Maggie Finn was sitting on her sofa, a large mug of tea in her hand. She was staring in disbelief at the screen of the big TV her family had bought her. The boy she'd watch become a man was plastered over not just the local but the national news too.

Traffic is now moving freely on both sides of the River Clyde following the brutal murder of Paisley gangster Malcolm Maloney. However, the area where his body was found is still cordoned off.

The reporter gestured over her shoulder at the bridge, then had the camera swing round to frame the roofs and spires of the town Maggie knew so well.

Forty-eight-year-old Maloney is thought to be one of the leading figures in organised crime in Paisley, second only to the recently returned Alexander 'The Taxman' Finn.

Maloney's body was found at around four o'clock yesterday afternoon hanging from the underside of the Erskine Bridge. Though the police have yet to confirm this, sources close to the gangster have said that he was tortured prior to his death.

This sickening murder comes just two years after the brutal attack on Alexander Finn's son Danny in a Paisley bar, where the nineteen-year-old was gunned down with a group of friends.

Recently, a young Albanian man was also found dead amidst a wreck of burnt-out cars in Eastwood in the Southside of the city.

This was followed by the murder of John 'Dusky' MacBride, found murdered on his own doorstep near Bishopton a few days ago. MacBride is thought to be another major Paisley gang figure.

It is believed that this spate of killings accelerated with the return of Alexander Finn. There is known to be an ongoing turf war between rival organised crime families in and around Glasgow, with added pressure from Eastern European criminals.

This horrific crime caused chaos in much of West Central Scotland yesterday, bringing traffic on both sides of the Clyde to . . .

Maggie could take no more. She used the remote control to click off the television, taking a last gulp of her now cold tea.

She sat back on the sofa and closed her eyes. Zander and Malky had been childhood friends – before school, even. She could picture them as children playing football in the garden of her old home in Renfrew. Could see them with their pimples and ridiculous haircuts and awful suits as they headed out for the night in the eighties. Watched them take a stranglehold of life in the town, as they had families of their own.

'So, it comes to this.' She shook her head, tears making her mascara run.

Taking time to correct this, Maggie Finn put on her coat, called for a taxi and left her flat high in the tower block. She could think of only one person to speak to – and it had been a while.

*

Gillian Finn was alone with her mother in the room in Glasgow's Queen Elizabeth University Hospital. Yet another nurse had been in to take blood samples and test her blood pressure.

Senga Finn was standing by the window, looking blankly out at the grey, smir-slathered scene outside. It was as though there was no colour left in the world, only drab monotone. Far below, buses jerked into life from bus stops; people scurried in all directions under hoods and umbrellas, as cars, vans – all manner of vehicles – stopped and started to the command of the only splashes of colour she could see, the controlling sequence of red, amber and green.

'You're father will want to see you. There's nothing I can do about it.' Senga turned to face her youngest daughter, who was lying on her back wired to a heart monitor, with a drip feeding into her left arm.

'I don't want to see him – or Gran.' Gillian's face was pale, but her manner was determined.

'Okay, but how long do you think you can keep your father from coming here, or not telling your gran? You know what they're like. You can imagine the fuss. And – well – with what happened to Malky yesterday, your father will be in full-on loss-of-control mode. You know what I mean?'

'This is a hospital, Mum. People can't just walk in and out as they please. There are rules, you know.'

'This is your father we're talking about.'

Gillian looked away, not at anything in particular, just staring at the ceiling. 'You know, all this time I've always told myself that Dad – and Uncle Malky – weren't what folk said they were. You know, kids at school, in the papers. All that shit.' She closed her eyes and swallowed hard, holding back tears. 'But in reality they're even worse. You live by the sword and you die by the sword, that's true, isn't it?' Gillian stared wearily back at her mother.

'Don't you worry about all that just now. Just concentrate on getting better. For the life of me, I cannot understand why you did this, Gillian.' Senga looked exasperated. 'Do you realise how close you came? I've already lost one son and nearly another – now you! How the fuck do you think I feel?'

'Of course, it's all about you, Mum, isn't it? Isn't it always?'

'So why did you want me here, not your father? He'll know about this, you know. He's got half they polis of Police Scotland in his pocket.'

'You make him sound more romantic than he is, Mother. He's just a fucking thug. Uncle Malky was no better.'

'So you forget all the things Malky bought you, eh? Toys, clothes – he even bought you a car when you got into that bloody college, which you gave to some lowlife bastard.'

'His name was Karim. He couldn't get into the halls and had to travel all the way from the Borders every day. I didn't need the car. I live just round the corner.'

'Oh, what a big heart you have.' Senga walked towards her daughter and leaned on the end of her hospital bed. 'You know the biggest mistake me and your father made?' There was an edge to her voice now.

'You mean apart from being born?'

'No, trying to make sure you had a better life than we had. Trying to make sure you didn't have to grow up like we did. If you think your granda Finn was a saint – well, think again. He used to wallop your gran and your father – aye, and not just a wee tap on the head neither.'

'I suppose that's why he ended up dead in an alley with a knife in his gut.'

'Do you think that's funny? He was murdered, for fuck's sake!'

'Yeah, just like my brother. Just like Uncle Malky and Uncle Dusky. This isn't a family, it's a butcher's shop!'

'I tried my best to keep you away from all that – so did your father. Well, if you can call anything he does "best".'

'I have to tell you something.'

'What now?' said Senga, throwing her arms up in the air.

'This isn't just about Uncle Malky.'

'What do you mean?'

'Just what I said. There's something you don't know.'

Senga held her hand to her forehead. 'Bugger this. I'm not sure I can take any more bad news.'

'I've been seeing somebody.'

'Oh fuck, don't tell me you did this because of some daft boy?'

'No, a daft girl, actually. I love her.'

Senga grabbed a chair and sat down at Gillian's side. 'And you're just telling me now?'

'I told Dad.'

'Eh?'

'The other day, I told him.'

'Fuck, that's brave. No wonder you took an overdose.'

'He was cool with it.'

'He was?'

'Yes, he was.'

'Well, you hear something new every day.'

Gillian made to sit up in bed. 'See, if he had a normal job – he wouldn't be like this. Did you know he drove a patient transport van for elderly people when he was away? He told me.'

'Aye, and I flew home from Tesco yesterday.'

'He did! If my dad, if Uncle Malky, was a welder, or bin man, accountant, teacher – anything – then everyone would still be alive.'

Though she made to speak, Senga knew this was hard to deny, so she decided to change the subject. 'What about this girl? Do I know her, even?'

'You've met her.'

Senga thought for a moment. 'Do you mean that Kirsty lassie?'

'Well done, Mum.'

'So, what happened?'

'She told her family the same time that I told Dad.'

'And they didn't like the fact their daughter was gay? Fucking dinosaurs.'

'No, it was nothing to do with that.'

'What, then?'

'They didn't like us – what we are – my family. That's what ruined everything!'

'But they're black!'

'Oh, for fuck's sake. You're calling them dinosaurs? They're right, that's the thing. Who on earth would want their child to get involved with us?'

'Campbell, that's her name, isn't it? Kirsty Campbell.'

'Don't bother looking for her. She's out of the country.'

Senga shrugged. 'I was just mentioning it, that's all.'

She got up and walked back to the window. This time there seemed to be more colour about the place. A woman's jacket looked red instead of a dull hue. A bright green car streaked past in the distance. Maybe there was a chink of sunshine on the grey day. Maybe Senga Finn was just really angry, seeing things in an enhanced Technicolor rage.

29

Maggie knocked on the door of the old house, noting that it was badly in need of a lick of paint. She heard shuffling feet, then the sound of a big key turning in a heavy lock. A man with white hair and a crinkled, sallow face blinked at her in the late morning light.

'Forgive me, Father. It's been twenty-two years since my last confession.'

Father Giordano smiled at her. 'You are forgiven. Come in, Margaret.' Gently, he took her hand in his and helped her up the two shallow stairs and into the hall.

As the front door clunked shut, she looked round. 'You've not lavished any money on interior decoration, then?'

'Why do this when I am happy with things the way they are?'

'For a wee change, maybe?'

'The world outside is changing too quickly for me as it is, without my adding to it. Come through. I know why you are here.'

'Into mind-reading too, eh?'

'I don't need to be able to do that to know what's troubling you. How long has it been?'

'Ten years, maybe more since I've been here.'

'You look good.'

'You look old. But then again you can't slap on the war-paint like I can.'

They walked into the familiar room. The clock ticked, the place smelled exactly the same: of old oak, good brandy, red wine, leather and mouldering books.

'Take a seat,' he said, before turning to note that she was already sitting where she always sat when she came here. It was as though it was only yesterday they had last met. Oh yes, and she'd been wrong. It was nearly twelve years since she'd been to this house. He knew and remembered it exactly. Though he had seen her at her grandson's funeral two years before. On that sad day, though, the pair hadn't spoken.

'Don't bother with coffee or anything,' said Maggie.

'I'm afraid I've nothing as fancy as green tea or soda. So many people now are giving up coffee; I couldn't live without it.'

'Och, I've not given it up. No, I need something stronger. Some of that brandy you're so fond of would go down a treat, right now.'

He poured her a large measure and handed it to her in a balloon glass.

'This is like a football.'

'It allows the spirit to breathe. Helps you to catch the aroma.'

'I'm going to drink it, not spray it under my oxters.'

As he laughed, he tried to remember the last time he had done so. Perhaps at a comedy on the wireless, or maybe something he'd read in a book. But Maggie Finn always made him laugh in a way nothing else could.

'No laughing for me today.' She stared into the glass like a fortune teller. 'In fact, I've not had much to laugh about for a while now.'

'I know life has been hard. But everything is sent to test us.'

'Aye, tell that to Malky Maloney's wife and wean. I'm quite sure they're not laughing either.'

'It is tragic.' He paused.

'But he deserved it. That's what you really think.'

'No one deserves this fate, whatever their sins. Sin breeds more sin. The world is weighed down by it all. But there is little we can do but pray and help where we can. We can live our lives under our Lord as purely and honestly as our existence permits. It is not for men – or women – to judge, to punish. That is the Lord's business.'

'So me and you will be up in the front of the queue when the big day come, eh?'

Father Giordano smiled. His past sins flashed before his mind's eye, like a film being played at high speed. The faces, people, places all spiralling into one great black pit of despair. It was strange, he thought, how this woman could awaken such emotion in him. These were feelings, memories he normally kept under control. But not with her; no, never with Margaret Finn. It was impossible.

'He's been here, I take it?' Maggie asked. 'Since he came back, I mean.'

'Yes, he has been here.'

'And?'

'What do you want me to say?'

'What do you think? Is he better or worse? I'm buggered if I can tell.'

'He is neither better nor worse; he is merely himself.'

'I'd forgotten about all the riddles. What on earth does that mean?'

'When he was persuaded to leave here, he became a different man – a better man. But now that he is back, his sins have multiplied. However, he is still the same man.

He – like us all – does what he thinks is best. I believe he came back for the right reasons. It's just these reasons have consequences – like everything in life.'

Maggie glugged back the brandy. It tasted good and already she felt more at ease. That could have been the mollifying effects of the alcohol, or just being in this place with this man – maybe a mixture of both. But she had sought solace and it had been found. 'Things are going to get worse. You know that. Especially after what has happened to Malky.'

'I told your son as much when he visited.'

'My son?'

For moments, they just stared at each other.

'I don't want to see Alexander hanging off a bridge somewhere. I've lost too much already.'

'No. None of us want to see this.'

'So, I shall leave it all in your capable hands?'

How long had it been? He realised now how much he still missed her. 'I will do my best for his soul, Maggie.'

'I know you'll do what's right, Father.' Maggie Finn downed what was left of the spirit in one gulp. 'Here, that was good, eh?'

'I'm pleased you liked it.'

She held out her glass. 'I wouldn't say no to a refill.'

'So you don't want to confess?'

'I will if you will,' Maggie replied, with a smile.

*

Donnie had gone, leaving Finn alone again. He had opened another bottle of whisky and already a quarter of its contents were gone.

He knew he had to think, to give himself time. Suddenly he felt tired, really tired.

He was lying on his bed now. It felt warm, the same brief feeling he'd experienced on wakening that morning. He felt light, as though all his cares, and sadness, had disappeared. His body was like a freed spirit. He moved easily from the bed across to the long wardrobe. Finn stood, staring at himself in its mirrored door. He was an old man. He saw grey hair and wrinkles he didn't recall noticing the last time he'd looked.

But there was something else. As he moved his face nearer the glass he could see the world reflected in his own eyes; first a round blue sphere with clouds scudding across its surface. Then he felt a sensation as though he was tumbling through the air, being pulled towards the earth. The rush roared in his ears, but he landed without sound, like a feather on stone.

An old man shuffled into sight. He was pulling a tartan shopping trolley, like something Finn's granny had used. The figure was walking away, a slow, deliberate, painful trudge, as though every step was a monumental effort. Finn could see that the bottom of the trolley had ripped open. Things – all this man owned, for all he knew – were tumbling onto the ground.

'Stop!' he shouted. And the old man did. He turned to face the voice that had called him to a halt.

Just as Finn was about to speak, the old man's face became visible; but it wasn't an elderly countenance, the features were young: pink cheeks and youthful stubble, his eyes alive with hope for the future. It was the face of someone unencumbered by thoughts of his own demise, a damnation that plagued everyone the older they became.

There were no visions of gravestones, pallbearers, cold earth or blazing funeral pyres. This was a face full of wonder, excitement at a world still to be explored, to be conquered.

Finn reached out to touch him, but in that instant the face began to spark and was soon lost behind a mask of flame. Like a match it flared, soon leaving behind nothing but a blackened oval, a mouth moving with nothing to say, all signs of youth and hope burned beyond recognition, extinguished.

The figure began to collapse on itself like a pile of black ash.

He felt a tug at his leg. Finn looked down. 'Sandra!' He recognised the little blue dress he'd bought for her sixth birthday.

'Come here, Daddy.' Her tiny voice was insistent as she pulled at his sleeve. He watched as Sandra put her shoulder to the sliding door, pushing for all she was worth.

'Darling, don't,' he heard himself say. But, as though she was pleased with her efforts, she stood and smiled, holding out her hand like someone welcoming a guest inside their home.

With a rush, the long door of the big wardrobe slid fully open. He stood silent, then let out a scream, a scream that made the glass of the windows shatter.

Looking at him was a corpse. His father was hanging from an oversized coat hanger, his face just as Finn remembered. The wooden hilt of a blade protruding from his stomach was slowly disappearing inside him. It was almost as though its blood-slathered length had been consumed by the very man who'd given him life.

'Look,' said the dead man, pointing.

Finn's gaze followed the direction of his dead father's finger. A young boy was keeping up a football. The boy stared at him and smiled. But before Finn could move towards him, his head fell forward. It was the head of his son, Danny, a neat quarter of his face missing, bouncing up and down off the boy's foot, as blood, brains and gore spread up his leg.

A figure fell in front of his vision. Malky Maloney swayed in the air, staring at him through empty black eye sockets, from which black blood streamed like newly tapped oil. He was speaking, but not through his mouth; his voice issued from the gaping slash in his throat.

'I'm glad you came back. This one's on me, Zan.'

Finn sat bolt upright, scattering the glass from his lap and knocking over the whisky bottle, which glugged out its contents over the parquet floor.

His phone was ringing.

Still gasping for breath, sweat lashing from his forehead, he reached into his pocket.

'Dad, it's me. I'm sorry about Malky. I'm so sorry about everything.'

'Gillian.' Zander Finn's voice was just a whisper. 'Why didn't you come to me? You wouldn't even let me come and see you. How are you? Why did you try to kill yourself?'

'Dad, I didn't know what you would do.'

'In what way?'

'In any way.'

'Listen, where are you? I'll get someone to pick you up. I want you here with me, Gillian.'

'I'm still in hospital but they're going to discharge me soon. I'm going home, I'll be fine.'

'No, I need you here. Please.'

Gillian wasn't used to hearing a tremble in her father's voice, but she heard it now. 'Okay. I'm at the Queen Elizabeth. If someone is here in an hour, it should be okay.'

'Thank you.'

Gillian was sure she could hear her father sob as he put the phone down. She stared at the device for a moment. Was everything she'd been so sure of just a lie, a façade?

At the moment, nothing made sense to Gillian Finn.

30

Paisley

William Finn was in the Wee Howff. He liked the tiny bar; it made him feel safe. In such a confined space, what could go wrong?'

Denny MacBride was prattling on as usual but, with the help of whisky and the thought of hard-earned cash in his pocket, all was right with his world. This feeling had grown in recent years, burgeoned like spring flowers. In the beginning it had all been much harder.

He'd worked at Chrysler for a while, been a bouncer at a few clubs; he'd even tried his hand at welding. But for Willie Finn, very little seemed to stick; he either became bored, or his fondness for drink led to summary dismissal for the days he'd been late or hadn't bothered to turn up at all.

It became apparent to him reasonably early on in adulthood that a normal life was not the way he would roll. The alternative was to go to Australia or Canada. He had family in both places. But the more he considered this, the less enamoured he became of the prospect. And in any case, he'd just take his old problems with him. After all, someone who liked a drink and kept late hours was hardly going to be changed by a new continent.

There was only one obvious way out: crime.

Willie was big, tall and broad-shouldered. In his early twenties, when most of the men his age still bore the flimsiness of youth, looking painfully thin, pale and mostly undernourished, he was the opposite. He'd always been told that a man didn't really become a man until he was thirty. Whatever the truth of this, he worked hard to make sure his ascent to manhood was accelerated.

The fact of his height was an accident of birth. Many of his peers were short. They were the product of generations of the hard work, poor living conditions and malnutrition suffered by working-class families across Scotland's big cities and towns. So, to be nearly six foot three by the time he was eighteen made him stand out. He'd augmented this with regular trips to a boxing gym. Subsequently, he'd broadened out, with arms like tree trunks, knotted with hard muscle.

Work on the doors of nightclubs in Paisley and Glasgow had brought him into contact with the criminal fraternity. First he was employed as an intimidating figure to go and collect money. Then he graduated to administering the odd hiding or two. Soon, he was supplied with a gun and became an armed robber.

He was lucky. He'd been arrested on numerous occasions, but charges never seemed to stick. Having a clever, if – in his opinion – overly pious wife, he'd managed to strike out into the world of legitimate business, though his main source of income was still derived from nefarious activities, despite his wife's protestations.

He'd started Chancellor Fabrications at Maggie's insistence, with a few welders, strays from the declining ship-building industry on the Clyde, and some old acquaintances.

Soon they were making garden fences, gates – even jobs for the council. He had a good man managing the place, and he was much better at being a boss than he had been a mere hombre. Though his wife kept nagging him to give up crime, the money was too good, and tax-free. What she didn't understand was that it wasn't all about the money, though that was a big draw. He liked the danger. Like any gambler, he was addicted to the thrill, whether it be battering somebody's face against a wall or pointing a gun into the chest of another.

They had a nice home in Renfrew, and his son was growing up to be a clever, if somewhat lippy, young man. That, he'd taken from his mother. He saw it in the boy's eyes the day he'd been born, and Willie Finn had been right.

'Come on,' said Denny MacBride. 'We'll get a chippie at Tottie's, then jump a cab to the Paddle Wheel. At least that way we'll be near enough home to stagger back. Mind, we got a lock-in the last time we was in.'

Willie Finn had to agree with this sentiment. They were already half pissed and he could feel the 'drink hunger' cloying at his empty stomach.

'Aye, come on, we'll neck these and get a fish supper and hit the Paddle Wheel. That was a wee cracker behind the bar, last week, eh?'

'Aye. But mind you're a married man, Willie. Maggie would have your balls as ornaments on the mantelpiece if you was to try it on with another bint.'

'Ach, I'm thirty-eight years old, man. I can think for myself. Anyway, not as though it's the first, eh?'

They drank up and said their goodbyes to the other drinkers: a slap on the back here, a friendly rub on the head there.

Walking out into the cool of a Paisley evening soon brought on the desperate need to pee in Willie Finn. 'Here, you go up and place the order. I'm going doon the lane here for a pish. Mind and get me a single pie as well as a fish supper.'

'You're a greedy bastard, Willie,' said MacBride, as he staggered further up the street.

'Aye, and don't forget to get plenty of salt and pepper, too.' He turned down a dark lane and was soon leaning somewhat unsteadily against a wall with one hand while a flow of urine splashed off the wall. Finished, he shook himself dry and sighed with relief. Nothing better than a good pee when you'd had a few drinks.

Willie Finn was zipping up his trousers when he heard movement further down the lane. 'Hey, MacBride, is that you?'

There was no reply. But all of a sudden the dark figure was upon him. The last thing he thought he saw was a flash of steel, before a blade was rammed into his stomach and jerked expertly upwards, scraping his ribcage.

The world soon spun before Willie Finn fell in a puddle of his own urine.

*

Zander Finn didn't know why he was thinking about his long-dead father so much these days. Perhaps it was just part of getting older. Tears came to his eyes when he recalled how badly Malky Maloney had taken his mother's death. Again he saw the gruesome face swing before his eyes on the small screen on the police launch in the Clyde.

His father had been cruel; he knew that. He was cruel to his mother, his employees, his family – just about anyone who crossed his path. But the blood was strong, he reasoned. Though, apart from his height, he and Willie Finn shared little in common. They could both do what had to be done, but for Zander it was a last resort. His father seemingly had taken great pleasure in dolling out a beating to one unfortunate or another.

Even as a child he'd wondered why his mother was so clumsy. She regularly had black eyes, where her face had connected with a cabinet or door. She seemed to break her wrists a lot, too. Looking back, he'd known about his father's brutality towards her long before he'd walked in on them when he was thirteen. He remembered desperately trying to pull his father off, hitting him as hard as he could on the back in the process. But it was like a wasp stinging a whale. His father carried on, as though his son wasn't there. Worse still, once he'd finished with his wife, Zander felt the force of his wrath, ending up with a broken nose for his pains.

In those days, only Father Giordano could soothe his troubled soul. He was wise and kind. But as the youthful Zander Finn sat in front of him with the huge plaster across his nose, placed there by the doctor to protect it after being reset, he saw something else in the Italian. There was more than just compassion; there was sorrow too behind his large brown eyes. He saw what he thought was real anger.

It was the first time he'd tasted brandy. His parish priest was a practical and pragmatic man. He'd calmed the panic and shame the young man in front of him felt by administering what was literally a medicinal measure.

'Drink is one of man's great pleasures, Alexander,' he remembered Father Giordano say. 'But it can easily turn into his worst affliction. Use it wisely.'

Though Finn hadn't adhered rigidly to this maxim, those words stayed with him.

Now, looking round the mess of broken glass and empty whisky bottles, he realised that he better tidy up before his daughter arrived. He rushed to shower, brush his teeth. He was determined to make himself presentable for Gillian, despite the banging in his head and the rock in his stomach.

After he towelled himself down and changed, he had a dash round with a large black bin liner. The place at least looked better, and he felt it.

His phone rang: Davie Kelly. If anyone could find out who had killed Malky, he could. 'Well?'

'Not Big Joe – at least, none of his men. Our friend over there confirmed that.'

'Can you trust him?'

'Oh, aye. He's shit scared since we poured that petrol over him the last time. Plus, I gave him a decent bung. It's a double incentive.'

'The Albanians.'

'Looks like it, Zander.'

'Retaliation?'

'For the guy that wasn't the guy?'

'Aye, the man with the toilets.'

'Could be. Can you think of anybody else?'

Finn thought for a moment. 'No, nobody. No other bastards would have the balls.'

'Exactly.'

'Right, tomorrow morning, bright and early, we meet

at the usual place. Use the fucking back door. You can juke in through the fence – you know the score.'

'Of course!'

'Make sure Lonesome is there.'

'He's a big boy now. He can handle this. If you and me is thinking along the same lines, that is?'

'No doubt we are.'

'When is the funeral?'

'How should I know? The polis will want to take him apart, won't they.'

'From what I hear that's been done for them, no?'

'Any more smart comments?'

'No. Sorry, Zan.'

'Just get everyone to keep their heads down – be careful. I said this to Malky. The polis are all over this. They'll be all over us, too.'

'Consider it done.'

'I'll have to rely more on you now, Davie. Especially since – you know.' He swallowed hard to keep the tears at bay.

'Aye, of course. Hey, we go back a long way all of us, don't we?'

'Yes. Problem is, you never know how long that will be going forward these days.' Finn heard the intercom buzz. 'Listen, see you tomorrow, just after eight. Make sure nobody's late.'

'Don't worry. The usual place, through the fence at the back.'

As the call clicked off, so did a digital recording device at Police Scotland's Organised Crime Unit.'

*

Gillian Finn stared at the huddle of journalists and photographers as the large gates protecting her father's house slowly slid open. She was momentarily blinded when a camera was thrust in front of her window and a bright flash filled the car.

'You okay?' said Mick, her driver.

'Yeah, just a shock, that's all.' She knew the man. The taxi firm belonged to her father, or one of his friends. She remembered Mick taking her to school once. He'd had a problem with a crossing attendant en route and, having brought the taxi to a screeching halt, was out beating the man with his lollipop seconds later. She had thought they were just clowning about at the time. Gillian and the little girl who shared the taxi with her laughed, imagining the whole episode as a sketch like they watched on children's TV. Now she knew that there had been nothing funny about it.

'Don't worry, hen. I'll have a word with him on my way out.'

'Oh, it's okay, Mick. These guys will get pictures anywhere.'

'Hey, still and all.'

As they drew up beside the steps at the front of the big door, her father was standing there. She rushed into his arms and he held her tight, slamming the door closed with one foot.

'I'm not going to ask anything, or make any comment, okay?'

'Okay.' She was looking straight into his face now.

'Just promise me one thing. Never do anything like that again.'

'Or what?' She smiled thinly.

'I'll kill you!'

The sadness they both felt was cut by their laughter. The ice was broken.

Inside the house, Gillian glanced out of the big window. At the gate, she could make out the taxi driver pushing a cameraman over a nearby bush.

31

The Paisley morning had dawned dark and miserable. A low smir of cloud hung over the observatory, not far from where the spectacles, hankie and the heart were picked out in the cobbles. This was a touching tribute to a workman who had lost his life falling from the spire of the nearby church. It was said that his still beating heart, his handkerchief and ruined eyeglasses were found together on the hard road. It had touched the people of this town, with the tough reputation concealing a soft heart, for there were few places in the world like Paisley. The unusual memorial had been fashioned by his workmates, and still nobody walked over it – not those in the know, at any rate.

Across the town, silent figures were lurking in the shadows of factories and small business units. Abercorn Street was a place of business and enterprise. Mechanics, architects, welders, platers, painters, lorry drivers, warehouse workers; all manner of folk plied their trade from the street.

Amelia Langley was in a van parked in the grounds of the college on Renfrew Road. It ran parallel with Abercorn Street but was higher up on the hill. The car park would soon be full of students ready for another hard day learning something that would lead to a job – hopefully.

Langley was irritated that DS Neil Dickie had called in sick that morning. Her detective sergeant was a pivotal member of the team and she needed him. But, as always, she accepted the inevitable.

'Langley to all units, are we in position?' She listened as various call signs replied in the affirmative. She knew they were probably early, but you couldn't rely on the old adage that gangsters were late risers, certainly not where Zander Finn was concerned.

She turned to the younger woman at her side. She was sporting a pair of headphones and monitoring a bank of screens in the back of the van. 'Okay, DS MacDonald, are you ready?'

Her colleague revealed one ear. 'Yes, ma'am, all ready to rock and roll.'

'I don't know if there will be much rock going on. But if we can nab Finn and his crew about to head off on some revenge mission – tooled up, even – heads will certainly roll.'

She thought about the newly returned criminal for a moment. She'd been surprised that the feelings she'd had for him had lasted the two years of his absence. He'd just looked so small in the big room. The big man was a little boy. She'd cradled his face, as tears spilled from his bright green eyes. The swipe of grey amidst the thick thatch of what was otherwise black hair caught in her memory.

It had been awkward – very awkward. But nothing was said. It was merely one human being comforting another – the most natural thing in the world. But when he'd looked into her eyes, she felt the same tingle down her spine. The most dangerous thing was that she knew he felt it too.

But Zander Finn wasn't one to let emotion get in the way of business, and neither was she. Why couldn't the world be different? Was it some celestial trick being played on humanity by the mischievous deities of old? Like Apollo tempting Agamemnon, or the conjuring up of Pan to coax Julius Caesar across the Rubicon? The perils of an education in the classics always haunted her. They were clever buggers, these Greeks and Romans. The circumstances may be entirely different, but she knew that defeat here for Finn would cast her in the role of Pyrrhus, and this car park would – for Ameila Langley, at least – forever be the fields of Asculum.

Langley often questioned why she'd become a police officer in the first place. She could be living the life of an academic now, publishing books and papers at her leisure. She always recoiled when she happened upon fellow students who had bagged gigs walking through ancient ruins, telling their tales on TV and radio. That could have been her.

Instead, Dr Amelia Langley was sitting in the back of a stuffy transit van waiting for a collection of gangsters – most of whom had half a brain – to appear for a war council arranged to wreak vengeance for the brutal murder of one of their own, Malky Maloney.

Again, her thoughts returned to Finn. He could easily have been a first-class student. They were both products of what life had thrown at them. She supposed it was the same for just about everyone.

Still, if she could bring him down, she would. Life was a game, of this she had no doubt.

She placed the airwave radio before her lips. 'Langley to all units: everyone moves on my signal and not before.'

*

Joe Mannion hated boats. It didn't matter if they were big, small, on a river, loch, or the open sea. He just hated them: from cruise ships to sailing boats. For him, they were beneath contempt, all of them.

These thoughts passed across his mind as he pulled on the wet-weather suit in order to board the RIB secured to the rickety-looking pier on a remote shore of Loch Lomond.

'Okay, sir, now if you zip that right up to your chin and put this on, please.' The young man in the suit that matched his in every way, apart from the size, was all business. Mannion placed what could best be described as a cross between a cycling helmet and a luminous hard hat on his head, then followed the man to the edge of the pier.

'And you're sure this bloody thing is safe?'

'Yes, safe as houses. Anyway, if we sink you don't have too far to get to the shore.' He laughed.

'What's your name, son?'

'Tim Tomely.'

Mannion raised his brows.

'Oh, I know, I sound like someone from a Dickens novel. The joys of having humorous parents, I'm afraid.'

'Can you not change it to something else? I'm fucking sure I would.'

'Oh, I don't know. I think it has grown on me the older I've become. And anyway, it sounds worse in the Scotch accent, you know. Like most things.'

'Watch your lip, son!'

'Sorry. I get so much stick for being English up here, I take revenge when I can.'

'Never mind revenge. First of all, get me aboard this bloody thing and over to this island.'

'We'll be there before you know it.'

'Aye, that's what I'm worried about. Drowning while looking like a sumo wrestler in this get-up.'

'You're safe with me.' Deftly, Tim Tomely jumped aboard the RIB and held his hand out to Joe Mannion.

*

It was just before eight, and already students were arriving at the college car park.

So much for 'bright and early', said Amelia Langley to herself. She watched the screens carefully, anxious not to be blindsided by Finn in some way.

'Ma'am, look!' said DS MacDonald, pointing to the screen.

Langley leaned across to make out what was going on. She could see an old white transit van driving past parking places towards the very rear of the space. 'That's them! They're heading for the fence!'

As she predicted, the van turned round the corner of a building and parked next to the fence backing on to Abercorn Street.

'What have we got on that?' asked Langley.

DS MacDonald stuck the tip of her tongue out between her lips, while fiddling with a keyboard. 'Actually, we don't have any visuals on that area, ma'am.'

'Fuck! Units two and three, attend the rear of the college at the fence, get eyes on a white transit van, over.' She waited as the conformation of this sounded over the radio.

'Here's another van, ma'am.'

This time a small, red and battered ex-Post Office van appeared and made for exactly the same spot, turning the corner just as Langley lifted the radio to her mouth. 'Two, three, do we have anything?'

'Yes, ma'am. Just getting a feed to you now, over.'

A screen at Langley's right burst into life. The smaller red van pulled up beside the transit by the fence.

'Two, three – all units, the focus is now on the back of the college. Leave your positions and locate at the bottom of the bank to the rear of Chancellor Fabrications.' Langley heard this order acknowledged by her various teams. She stared at the vans. There seemed to be absolutely no movement inside either, at least none that she could detect. She was tempted to have her men move in, but what would have been the point? If Finn's crew were armed and ready to take the fight to Maloney's killers, she might as well wait until they broke cover.

*

The short journey was enough to make Joe Mannion's stomach churn. Two suited figures were waiting by a small pontoon on the island. One leaned forward and helped him from the RIB with a strong arm.

'Hope you enjoyed your trip, sir,' said Tomely.

'Naw, I didn't.'

'I'll be waiting for you for the return journey.'

'My lucky day.' Mannion looked between the besuited men who obviously comprised his reception party. 'Right, where now?'

The taller of the two looked him up and down. 'You need to get out of that suit.' His voice was deep, with a foreign accent.

'Here, Tim Tom, or whatever the fuck your name is, help me out of this bloody thing.'

Mannion hated all the cloak-and-dagger stuff. He felt

exposed here on this island in the middle of Loch Lomond, without even Sammy Sloane for protection. But he'd had assurances, and his host was well aware that if he didn't return in two hours they had better be sure to have an army on the small island to fight off his men. He hoped it wouldn't come to that.

'You come with us.' The besuited men made their way off the pontoon, Mannion in their wake.

The track was rough and overgrown, and Mannion wished he'd worn stout boots rather than an expensive pair of loafers. 'Here, hang on. I'm not an Olympic athlete, you know.' He wheezed as the men held back, waiting for him.

'We don't have far to go.'

They were as good as their word. They reached the top of a rise and, a short distance away, surrounded by the black fingers of wintering trees, stood a well-appointed house. It was much bigger than he'd expected – three floors, with ornate brickwork. It seemed out of place on this tiny island.

'Right, lead on,' said Mannion, finally able to catch his breath.

*

Langley was breathing heavily now. The vans hadn't moved for twenty minutes. She began to doubt her judgement. Again, she cursed Dickie. She trusted his experience and would have liked him to be present to bounce ideas off. It was another character flaw, she reasoned. No faith in herself. Outwardly, she projected a super confidence. Inside, though, she was riven by doubts.

'Unit two to Langley, over.'

'Go ahead.'

'We have movement, ma'am. Just about to get you visuals.'

Langley held her breath as the image on the screen to her right changed. Now she could see the other side of the white transit, the driver's door, facing onto the back of the college.

'Roger, unit two, I have eyes on.' Just as the words left her mouth, the door began to slowly open.

32

Finn left the vehicle and looked about. The coast seemed clear, but then he'd expected nothing less. On his way to the rendezvous, his mind had worked overtime. He'd had a chance to collect his thoughts, and his reasoning was no longer pillowed in a fog of alcohol. He knew what he had to do and was ready to go to any lengths to achieve his goal.

For years there had been an uneasy peace between warring gangland factions in west central Scotland. Sure, there was always going to be the odd turf dispute involving minor players. But as long as the agreement between those in charge held, things could be resolved pretty quickly, normally by the swift application of money.

All that had changed when his son had been murdered – and now Malky Maloney.

He'd grieved in his own way for both of them. A loss of a son compared to that of a best friend was hard to define. In a way, he knew that he was closer to Maloney than he ever had been to his son Danny. Though his mother disagreed, he had seen the similarities between Danny and his dead father, William, from a young age. The same cock-sure arrogance, the disregard for the feelings of others, the inability to realise when enough was enough.

Zander Finn had always treated this matriarchal opinion with disdain. But, all too late, he realised that he should have acted much sooner to mitigate his son's many faults – many dangerous faults. He'd also – for the first time – begun to understand the deep loathing his mother felt for William Finn, or so he thought.

Though his father's murder had never been solved, neither by the police nor the many hidden resources of the underworld, he couldn't help wondering if she had been involved in some way. It was a fanciful notion, he was sure. However, occasionally, he caught a look in her eye when the subject came up – as rarely as that was – which he couldn't explain.

But he was aware that anything could be analysed to death. It wasn't the first time that ghosts had jumped from every darkened corner when he'd been assailed by troubles. Whether this was just human nature or some personal flaw, he wasn't sure. But he'd fought hard to resist the scream of paranoia, something that was part and parcel of the life he led.

He thought of Maloney. Not the grotesque corpse swinging from the Erskine Bridge, but the guy who'd been his friend and ally for most of his life. There was no better man to have at your back than Malky Maloney, period. He was a counsellor, friend – his right hand. Only Father Giordano could compare. And he didn't expect the octogenarian priest to tag along and address the many illicit problems that he now faced.

Money. There was that word again, twisting in his head like a spiralling spinning top. His greed for it sometimes abated; in his mind's eye, he could see the top begin to falter, the spin that kept it upright fail. Though, even in London it still tottered at the edge of his consciousness like a nagging reminder of the life he'd left behind.

As Finn breathed the heady fuel-slick fumes of a Renfrewshire morning, deep in thought, movement to his right caught his eye.

*

Mannion was walking through a large hallway. The walls were plain, unadorned by paintings or décor of any kind. Just plain white. He contrasted this with his own home; no less grand, but cluttered by tat that his wife had accumulated in the course of a lifetime. There was something refreshing about living without clutter and encumbrance; there was something refreshing about the notion of living without his wife.

As he was shown into a large room, his thoughts strayed momentarily to Senga Finn.

'You're smiling, Mr Mannion.' The woman's English was good, though her accent was strong. She was sitting on a burgundy leather couch. A small table, bearing cups and a large French Press coffee maker, sat in front of her on the polished wooden floor.

'Hello,' said Mannion, walking towards the woman. 'Joe Mannion. But you know that already.'

Without standing, she merely held out her hand limply, palm down. At first Mannion considered trying to grab it in an awkward handshake, but he quickly realised that the intention was that he should administer a kiss.

He leaned forward as far as his bad back would allow, still a few inches from her hand. 'You'll have to help me out here. I've got a touch of arthritis in the old back. You know how it is.'

'Fortunately, I don't.' She raised her hand to his lips and let Mannion brush them against her wrist. 'Take a seat,

Mr Mannion. Over there, I think.' She gestured to a deep leather armchair that matched the couch. 'Coffee?' she said, while gesturing with her eyes to the two men who had accompanied Mannion into the house.

'Aye, black with three sugars, please.' Mannion heard the door close quietly and looked around to notice the taciturn pair had gone.

'White, or brown?'

'No, just black, please.'

'The sugar, not the coffee.' She smiled mirthlessly.

'Ah, right. It's just that my wife has three stages of coffee. White's made with milk, black with no milk, and brown with milk poured in, if you know what I mean.'

'Fascinating,' she said, pouring the beverage into a small china cup on the table. 'My name is Ginerva, by the way.'

'Nice name. I'm not up with Albanian names, I'm afraid to say.'

'What makes you think I'm Albanian, Mr Mannion?'

'Oh. I just sort of assumed,' he stammered. A shaft of fear caught his heart, but he managed not to let it manifest itself as an expression.

'Not your fault. If I were you, I'd probably have reasoned that I was from that shithole, too.' The word sounded strange coming from her. She was so elegant. Probably of early middle age, in a well-cut, black trouser suit. Her dark hair was neatly bobbed, and though she was wearing make-up it was applied subtly, augmenting her sallow features rather than prettifying them. 'I hope you like the coffee.'

'Oh, aye, thank you.' Mannion lifted the delicate cup to his lips, worrying that, with his meaty fingers, he didn't have a proper grip of the fine handle. 'Aye, just the job,' he said after a slurp.

'Now, you mentioned Albanians. I believe that you've been experiencing a few difficulties with them of late?'

'Aye, well, you could say that. The buggers – I mean, they folk – just seem to appear out of the woodwork.'

'How apt. Yes, they do have a habit of that. I don't care for them myself,' she said, as though referencing a biscuit or a brand of cornflakes.

'Well, we agree on one thing, at least.'

'Oh, Mr Mannion, I'm sure we'll agree on many things.' Ginerva smiled enigmatically. 'Have you ever been to Italy?'

*

Before they managed to leave the vehicles, Langley ordered her units to intercept. In a matter of moments, the two vans at the back of the college car park were surrounded by police officers, some of them armed.

Langley jumped from the back of the observation van and hurried round the corner to assess the situation. If she was right, this was a major coup. Better still, should Finn and his associates be armed in any way she would be able to take down one of Scotland's most dangerous criminal gangs at a stroke.

Amelia Langley heard shouts of protest as she pushed her way through the throng of officers.

Five women, of what could best be described as being 'of a certain age', were gathered together, hands in the air. One of them looked defiantly at her under a pair of etched-on eyebrows.

'What the fuck is this all about?'

Langley hesitated. 'What are you doing here?'

'Huh! You tell me first, lassie. Me and the girls here have just come to pick up some items from a friend in the college.' Maggie Finn looked less than chuffed. 'I wasn't aware that constituted a crime these days, but obviously I was wrong.' She glared at Langley.

'Where's your son, Mrs Finn?'

'How the fuck should I know? He's a big boy now, or haven't you noticed? He's not in the habit of telling his mammy where he's going every time he leaves the house.'

Langley spoke into her airwave radio. 'All units in Abercorn Street, enter Chancellor Fabrications. I repeat, enter Chancellor Fabrications now, over.'

'Are you looking for some garden gates? The boys are great in there, do a fabulous job, so they do. Don't buy the double-glazing, though. The wind blows through mine. Right shoddy.' Maggie looked around the gathered police officers. 'You must be after a good few items, by the look of all these folk you've brought along. I'm sure they'd have delivered if you'd just asked.'

A small voice sounded, attracting both Finn and Langley's attention. 'Here, Maggie, can you ask these polis to let me go? All this carry on – well, I'm fair needing the toilet. A number two, if you get my drift.'

A pair of fire doors at the rear of the college opened up with a clatter and scrape. The gathered police officers, as they had been trained, swung their weapons to face what could well be an imminent threat.

'Oh, cool your jets,' said a man in a brown dustcoat. 'I'm just helping out some of our senior citizens. What the fuck is going on?'

'Helping them with what?' said Langley, irritably.

'Bits and pieces of furniture and the like – here, take

a look. The apprentices make them as part of the courses. We give them to charities, like the old biddies here.'

'Less of the old biddies, Jimmy Dow,' said Maggie.

'You can go and ask the principal, if you want. It's all above board, like.'

Langley heard a call on her radio. 'Langley, go ahead.'

'Unit one, over. No sign of any suspects at Chancellor Fabrications, ma'am. We've been right through the place, over.'

'Suspects? Are welders criminals now?' said Maggie. 'I mean, I know they're lazy bastards and that. But this is ridiculous.'

'Stand down,' Langley shouted into her radio. She turned to the elderly women, all still with their hands in the air. 'Where did you get the vans, eh?'

'My son sells second-hand cars and that,' said one of the women.

'Aye, you tell her, Betty,' said Maggie.

'Return to base,' Langley shouted.

'Thank fuck for that!' An old woman in a headscarf limped off in the direction of the fire doors. 'Here, let me in, Jimmy, before I shite myself.'

A group of students had gathered. Almost all of them were holding out mobile phones, on which they were filming this unexpected diversion.

'Classic, man,' said one tall, spotty youth with a laugh. 'This is going to go viral!'

33

'Come on in, boys,' said landlord Raymond Deans. 'It's all set up in the top room for you, as usual.'

Deans owned a pub in what had once been a sleepy Renfrewshire village but was now the size of a small town. Handy for commuting to Paisley, Glasgow and Ayr, one private housing estate after another had gone up over the previous ten years. Initially this had raised Deans' spirits; after all, more people surely meant more customers. But as was the way of things in the licensed trade these days, his new potential clientele were overextended by mortgages, car loans, credit card payments, mobile phone contracts and holidays, with their two point four children. They had no spare cash to fritter away on fags and booze the way the previous generation had with such abandon. The pub still had a few regulars, and the odd function, but in effect Raymond Deans was in semi-retirement.

Finn watched from the secluded cellar door of the bar as one by one his crew slithered down the bank from the house on the hill above. The owner was a friend, and he didn't mind a parade of gangsters parking in his driveway, tramping through his home and down the hill to their meeting. In any event, Finn made it worth his while every time this happened.

Tam Skillen was the first to arrive. He looked down as Finn shook his hand. 'Can't believe it, Zander.' His voice trembled with emotion.

'Nobody can,' said Finn.

Donald Paton was next, then Davie Kelly. They patted Finn on the shoulder before taking to the stair to the room above.

Lonesome Dove looked exactly as his nickname suggested. He was younger than the rest of them, and the sadness in his brown eyes blended in with the grey day. Sandy Hamilton looked at Finn with tears brimming onto his cheeks. 'Anything, Zan, you know that.' He shook his head in disbelief. 'Big Dusky was bad enough – but Malky.' He bounded up the steps two at a time.

'Just help yourself to drinks and that, Zander,' said Deans. 'There's nobody in the bar. The cleaner left about half an hour ago. I've laid out some grub. Nothing fancy, just the usual.'

'Cheers, big man. You know it's been a hard time, eh?' said Finn.

'Oh, aye. We all liked Malky – everybody.'

'And Big Dusky?'

The publican shrugged. 'He was what he was. Didn't deserve that, mind you.'

'No, you're right,' said Finn, not meaning it. 'I better get up there before McKinlay eats the lot.'

When Finn walked into the small function room, he saw the same faces that had greeted him in the 'canteen' at Chancellor Fabrications so recently. Though they were two down. He swallowed hard when he looked at the small bar, half expecting to see Malky standing there, ready to serve up the drinks.

They were sitting at a large round table with a battered copper top.

'Okay, King Arthur, what is your pleasure, my liege?' Davie Kelly hated sombre situations, and he was doing his best to lighten the load, the sadness they all felt.

'Dusky was playing for both sides,' said Finn, taking a seat, but leaning on the bar.

'I always thought it,' said Tam Skillen. 'I should have crushed that bald dome of his.'

'The guy changed. We all saw it,' McKinlay observed, as he lifted a pie to his bloated face.

'How come I never heard about it?' said Davie Kelly. 'Not much you can't find out from the shite on the streets my guys come into contact with.'

'Trust me,' replied Finn. 'He was at it – with Mannion. He jumped when I took some time out.'

'You left us, Zander.' Sandy Hamilton's voice was quiet, almost a whisper.

'It's in the past,' said Donnie Paton. 'He's back, and we're in the collective shit. You know the cops are pulling Chancellor apart, Zander, eh?'

'We knew they would. Langley will be pissed that we've outplayed her. It's just them puffing out their cheeks. We all remembered the code, I'm glad to say.'

'Aye, but what are we going to do, big man?' said Skillen. 'If we reckon it's they Albanians, then we have to hit back – aye, and quickly. This can't be left the way – well, you know what I mean, Zander.' He looked nervously at the bar.

'I agree.' Finn looked at Kelly. 'Have you done what I asked?'

'Aye, we know all the dealing sites. Wasn't that hard. I mean we used to have half of them.'

'Good, so we hit them where it hurts, in their pockets.'

'Look what happened to Mannion when he tried to disrupt the supply,' said McKinlay. 'His man didn't get very far. They was ready for him.'

Finn looked at Kelly again. 'We've worked that out. Tell them, Davie.'

Kelly cleared his throat. 'Right, we all know how they operate. Stick guys on near our dealers, then offer cheaper gear.'

'Better stuff, too,' said Sandy Hamilton.

'What are you, a heroin connoisseur?' Kelly stared at him and carried on. 'Every time we – or Mannion, come to that – have tried to push back, they've had feet on the ground in minutes.'

'Which means?' Skillen asked.

'Which means that every dealer they have on the street is protected. Aye, at close quarters, too.'

Finn was behind the bar now. He poured himself a large glass of whisky from an optic, emptying it three times before he was satisfied with the level of the spirit in the glass. 'They always use local junkies as dealers. These guys know nothing apart from where to pick up the shit, where to sell it and where to deposit the dosh. That's why these Albanians are like fucking ghosts. Nobody knows who they are, or where they are.'

'But now we've worked out how to flush them out,' said Kelly.

'Aye, keep us in suspense,' said Tam Skillen.

Finn smiled. 'Here's what we do. We have each dealer clocked. We create a diversion – just enough to bring the cavalry, you know. A wee skirmish here, a drunk guy getting aggressive there, another not wanting to pay up or, worse still, trying to pocket the take. Anything that brings out the minders.'

'Good idea, Zan,' said McKinlay, chewing hard on a slice of pizza.

'I'm glad you agree.' He looked at Skillen. 'Your boys are the diversion. They go in there, start whatever it is they need to do to get noticed.' He turned to Sandy Hamilton. Lonesome Dove was staring at the copper table. 'Sandy, when the Albanians show themselves, then you go in, okay?'

'How many guys do I need?'

'Thirty – forty – I'll leave that up to you. But the most important thing is that this all happens at the same time, on the same night. They won't know what's hit them.' He looked around the faces he knew so well. 'This won't be like Mannion's attempt to get back at them. When we're done, we should have a few bodies to be able to lead us to who is at the heart of this Albanian mob.'

'Make them speak, you mean?' Skillen asked.

'Aye. I'll leave that to you, Tam.'

'We'll lose people,' said Sandy Hamilton.

'Aye, we will. But if we don't do this now, we'll lose everybody. Just the way we lost Malky.'

There was silence in the room, broken only by the murmur of music coming from the bar downstairs. Finn recognised 'Thru And Thru' by the Rolling Stones.

'You'll be running it, Zander?' said Hamilton.

'No. I'll be at the theatre with my daughter. Donnie will run it, with Davie the street boss. He has all the logistics. Okay?'

Silence.

'It's that old thing: speak now, or forever hold your peace.'

'I'm ready,' said Lonesome Dove.

'Aye, me too,' Skillen added.

'Good, let's get a drink. Enjoy it, because it's the last one until we do this. No room for fuzzy heads.' Finn lined up a row of whiskies along the bar. One by one, they left their seats at the table and each lifted a glass. 'To Malky Maloney!' said Finn.

Those in the room echoed his toast.

*

Ginerva smiled at Mannion. 'You see, we too are no strangers to those who try and take our place. It happens all across the world. If it's not the cartels from South America, it's the Russians, or the Mexicans. We've faced Latvians, Albanians, Jihadists, white supremacists, black supremacists. Then we have the Yakuza, the Chinese. The list just goes on and on.'

Mannion looked puzzled. 'Wait, this isn't a big pie – in Glasgow, Paisley – Scotland, even. Why would somebody like you care about the small shit we do?'

'Because we want everything, Mr Mannion.'

'Oh great! So we just swap one foreigner for another. No disrespect, you understand, Ginerva.'

She stood and walked over to the large bay window that looked out across Loch Lomond. 'How is your history, Mr Mannion?'

'What, like Robert the Bruce and all that? Aye, I know as much as the next man.'

'Before then. Long before then, Mr Mannion.'

'Oh, right.' Mannion looked confused.

'Let me give you a little history lesson.' She turned to

face him, now a silhouette in front of the bright light from the window. 'My ancestors, the Romans, we ran the known world. And what we didn't know about wasn't worth knowing. But, more importantly, we only cared about discovering and conquering places that would bring us something.'

'Well, I think you'll find poor fare up here.'

'No, not in the slightest, Mr Mannion. You are an island. It is one of the biggest economies in the world. There are people all over this nation who will buy our drugs, use our other services.'

'Oh, aye.'

'But what we've lacked is a base here. Places like London, Manchester, Liverpool, they have strong organisations already at their heart. Here in Scotland, not so much.'

'We do our best.'

'County lines. From what I can glean, those running such projects are doing so from England. If a junkie in Stornoway buys a line of coke, it more likely comes from Liverpool than Glasgow, yes?'

Mannion shrugged. 'I don't do much business in Stornoway.'

'You don't do much business in London, either.'

'I'm sorry, Ginerva. But you've got to see my point of view. What's in it for me, apart from the pleasure of watching you use my old stamping ground as a base for your world domination?'

'Ah – this is where we come back to the Roman Empire, Mr Mannion.'

'Do we have to?'

'Oh, I think you'll like this bit.'

'Go on then, if you must,' he said wearily.

'When we conquered lands two thousand years ago, we had to hold it. To do that, we had to have help – co-operation. In this country, old tribal chiefs took off their war-paint and became rich. They swapped their wattle and daub huts for our villas, with hyper courses and hot baths. Togas replaced homespun tunics; wine filled glasses, instead of rough ale in horn mugs. We were good to those who co-operated with us. Do you see?'

Mannion was looking into space, picturing himself in an emperor's robes. 'Aye, I think so. Carry on.'

'Imagine a world where not only are there no Albanians but you have no competition at all: a world where you rule your little kingdom without hindrance. But this is a much bigger world than just Glasgow or the west of Scotland. You, taking money from London to Newcastle, from Edinburgh to Orkney.'

'All the time paying you a nice hefty cut.'

'Think of it as the Pax Romana, Mr Mannion.'

'You'll have to help me get rid of the Albanians first – aye, and the likes of Zander Finn.'

'Have you ever heard the expression "divide and rule"?'

'Aye, sure I have.'

'Well, just let me divide, while you rule, Mr Mannion.'

'If you say so.' Mannion shrugged.

'Think of it like this. You dominate your city and all of central Scotland. Any problems, and we step in. In the meantime, you are at the heart of our county lines operation. Together we will run drugs all across the UK. With us, you will become richer and more secure than you could possibly imagine.'

'And just who are "us"? I mean, who are you?'

'We're your friends from sunny Calabria.' Ginerva placed

her delicate cup back on its saucer. 'Now, Mr Mannion, can we shake on it?'

As Joe Mannion stood and took her slim hand in his, for some reason a chill went up his spine.

He put it down to having been on a boat.

34

It was a typical late autumn night across the west Central Belt of Scotland: cold, drab and wet. Those visiting pubs, clubs, restaurants and theatres did so huddled in their coats, or under umbrellas, hoods and scarves. As the rain beat down more heavily, even the odd plastic carrier bag became an impromptu hat.

In the dark places, the back streets and the alleys, lurked those with lots to do, or nothing to do at all. Prostitutes hoped the rain would ease off. Rain was always bad for business. Sheltering in doorways was an occupational hazard as much as it was a place to keep dry. If you couldn't be seen, who would stop to buy your wares?

Making a place to sleep under archways, bridges or in shop doorways, the legions of the city's homeless sought sanctuary from the night, the weather, and in some cases those who would inevitably try to torment, injure or, in the worst cases, kill them. Their crime was that of being vulnerable, mere entertainment for the cruel, drunk or bored. To insulate themselves against the penetrating damp and misery, they huddled under newspapers, old blankets, sleeping bags and cardboard boxes, many high or drunk. It was the only way to survive.

As in most cities, they were the problem that nobody wanted to talk about. Ignored or defiled, the homeless could rely only on the kindness of strangers for a bite of food, or a roof for the night from time to time.

As people poured out of big venues – the football stadiums, concert halls or cinemas – most did their best to avoid the desperate plight of the poor. Society had abandoned them; most seemed more than happy to treat their fellow citizens like dog dirt on their shoes. All the while, these same individuals were happy to recycle their rubbish, buy the latest smartphone or new car, preaching one political ideology or another, as the real problem stared them in the face.

Then there were the others who dwelt in the shadows. Those who dealt in misery of another kind: pay them to change your mind, pay them to lift your spirits, pay them to stop you shaking and feeling sick. It was the chemical equivalent of Disneyland, or a holiday in the sun. Forget all of your problems for thirty quid – forget everything for thirty more.

The dealers worked away, their business guaranteed, no matter the weather. The cloying desperation of addiction was enough to drive those in its grip out in the fiercest storm. With bony, shaking hands, they exchanged rolled-up notes or handfuls of change in return for an armful of glory and peace, a snort of pure joy. Then, the rain meant nothing. In their heads, it was spring. The deep cherishing warmth of the drug cossetted failing flesh from the fetid world.

Of course, for many it was the battle just to remain normal. The real addicts found little of the joy that had first turned them onto their drugs of choice. The chemicals – often cut with talcum powder, rat poison, a myriad of toxic concoctions – ate away at minds, souls and bodies.

To avoid the desperation of withdrawal, they would brave the rain and cold. They would brave almost anything just to find the peace of mind with which they were born.

It was on this night, into this dark world, that some new figures arrived. They too slunk in the shadows, but their purpose was an altogether different one. In Glasgow, Paisley and so many other communities they appeared, unheeded by the underbelly of life.

In a lane off Argyll Street, two young men rounded on a dealer. It began with abuse, then a punch and a kick. In an instant, two stout men came to his aid and chased off the dealer's tormentors. But as they turned to seek the comfort of a warm car, they were set upon by a fury of blows, followed by the slash and deadly puncturing of sleek blades.

In Paisley, hidden in the shadows at the corner of Underwood Lane, three men lay in the rain, neat gunshots in their foreheads. Their blood, diluted by the downpour, made for the nearest drain, as a queue of cars stopped on either side, halted by this roadblock of death. The line of cars was so long and tightly packed that Mrs Girvan had to walk all the way to the end of the street to gain access to her flat on the other side. She wasn't happy.

In Motherwell, Giffnock, the schemes of Glasgow, a country road that led to Loch Lomond – so many places – the story was the same. Dead men on wet roads or face down in the mud. Dead men ritually impaled on fences; dead men scattered like the outpourings of the wickedest storm.

*

Amelia Langley was watching this unfold in her office in Gartcosh as the reports came in. Big screens were feeding information and images from beat cops, detectives and the force helicopter. She watched this slumped forward on a desk with a cup of lukewarm coffee in her hand. Her mouth gaped, as report after report sounded over the system in the large room.

For a moment, she felt like a spider at the centre of a web. But this spider had lost all control over what was happening in her domain. She felt as though she was slipping into a void. For Amelia Langley knew what was happening, knew who was doing it. Just didn't know how she could stop it or, more importantly, prove it. They had been careful – very careful. The attacks took place away from the gaze of security cameras, of CCTV. But then this was where the purveyors of drugs did their trade, so for their attackers the work was done.

'That's another, ma'am, just hot off the press.' DS Neil Dickie handed her a sheet of paper. 'Three dead, only yards away from Glasgow's Sheriff Court.'

'Are we sure they're part of all this, Neil?'

'Aye, ma'am. Two Eastern Europeans, one local male – he's a known dealer, ma'am. He worked for Mannion for years. Looks like he changed sides.'

'Lucky him,' sighed Langley.

'Ma'am, we have another problem.'

'Go on.'

'Well, two problems, actually.'

'For fuck's sake, just spit it out, Neil!' Langley's brain was frazzled and she was in no mood for riddles.

'The press and the ACC. She wants to see you as soon as, ma'am. They're calling it the Glasgow massacre.'

'The Glasgow massacre? What about all the other places this is going on?'

'You know the hacks, ma'am, especially those from down south. To them anywhere within a sixty-mile radius of George Square is Glasgow.'

'Try telling that to folk in Ferguslie Park.'

Neil Dickie shrugged his shoulders. 'Interpol has also sent us this, ma'am.' This time Dickie held out an iPad to his boss. Pictured on it was a dark-haired woman, the image clearly taken from a CCTV screen grab.

'Who is she?'

'Her name is Ginerva de Lucca, ma'am. This image was captured at Heathrow, where she was waiting to board a flight to Glasgow about a week ago.'

'Very interesting, Neil, but why the fuck should this bother me now?' Langley gestured angrily to the large screens in front of them.

'Because she's underboss of the Calabrian Mafia, ma'am.'

'What?' Langley looked startled. 'You mean *the* Calabrian Mafia?'

'Yes, I do. She was being tailed by a Met OCU team who duly lost her in Glasgow airport when she went to the bog and never came out.'

'You have such a lovely turn of phrase, Neil.'

'Thank you, ma'am.'

'And why did nobody see fit to tell us?'

'They thought that she was planning to fly elsewhere. That is, that Glasgow was just a stop on the way.'

'To where?'

'They didn't say, ma'am.'

'You don't think she's involved with this, do you? We have enough to do, coping with the shite of our own.'

'And the Albanians, ma'am.'

'There doesn't appear to be many of them left, Neil.

Or hadn't you noticed?'

He shrugged. 'In any case, the ACC is waiting for you now, ma'am.'

'Mars, bringer of war! Or in your case, arse, bringer of gloom.'

'Sorry, ma'am?'

'Not a fan of Holst, Neil?'

'No, I prefer a good Scottish beer, ma'am.'

Langley sighed, as she picked up her phone and papers from the table in front of her. 'When I come back, I want to know why you missed the show at Abercorn Street.'

'Bit of a flop, I heard.'

'Glad you're so engaged.'

'Eh?'

With a look that plainly said 'fuck off', she strode off in the direction of the Assistant Chief Constable's office.

'You should have stuck with your classical Greek and ruins,' said Neil Dickie under his breath.

*

The crowd spilled out of Glasgow's Theatre Royal to the wail of police sirens. Zander Finn and his daughter Gillian were walking arm in arm down Hope Street as two police cars, blue lights flashing, sped past them.

'What's going on, Dad?' said Gillian, looking up at her father. The heavy rain had become a light drizzle, now no hardship to the hardy folk who lived in this part of the world.

'Who knows? The football on tonight, maybe?' said Zander.

'Huh, if football was on, you'd know about it.'

'My eye's been a bit off the beautiful game in the last wee while, dear.'

Gillian bit her lip. 'Sorry, I wasn't thinking.'

'That's exactly what I want you to do.'

'What?'

'Not think too much. You get that from your gran.'

'She just thinks about rubbish. She phoned me last night to complain about the storyline in *Coronation Street*. She says if I appear in it when I graduate she'll never talk to me again.'

'That sounds about right for her.'

Another police car roared past, this time in the other direction.

'At least I know they're not after you, Dad. You've been with me the entire time.'

'Yes,' Zander said with a smile.

'Be honest, did you enjoy *Gilgamesh*?'

'Yes. Long, but good.'

She giggled. 'And that was the short version. I can just see you as a Sumerian king who wants to rule the universe.'

'You can? Is that what it was about?'

'You mean, you didn't get it?'

He nudged her with his elbow. 'Of course I did.'

'Are you sure?'

'Well, I did have a wee look online yesterday.'

'Cheat!' said Gillian, in mock outrage.

'You know me.' Zander smiled broadly. 'Come on, let's catch a quick drink before we head back.'

'Okay, you've twisted my arm.'

A large van full of uniformed police officers was sitting at the lights.

'Something really bad must have happened. I hope it's not a big accident.' Gillian thought for a moment.

'What about a terrorist attack!' She pulled the mobile phone from her pocket, turning it back on after being in the theatre.

'Whatever it is, there's nothing we can do about it. Put that away, Gillian. We're out to cheer ourselves up, have a good time. Come on, this bar looks okay.'

'It's a gay bar, Dad.' Gillian slid the phone back in her pocket.

'So?'

She looked at him doubtfully. 'Don't you dare try to set me up with somebody.'

'As if.' Zander Finn smiled at his youngest daughter as yet another police car screamed by.

35

Assistant Chief Constable Mary Green sat behind her desk, deliberately not taking her eyes from the papers laid out before her.

Amelia Langley was left standing like an errant schoolgirl in front of the headmistress. Here she was, her old classmate from the police college resplendent in her fancy uniform. The woman was notorious for her ambition – and her uncanny ability to make sure that whatever went wrong, her hands remained clean. But Langley knew that was far from the case. The trick was trying to prove it. Her desire to be the next Commissioner of the Met Police was well known and she was widely tipped for the job. Green was a slip of a woman. Beneath her short fringe was a thin, almost drawn face, pallid and lined.

'Take a seat, Langley.' Green had no time for rank – at least not for those who ranked under her. 'Let's just say, things haven't gone quite as well as we'd hoped recently, eh?'

'No, ma'am. But we were acting on the best intelligence.'

'No intelligence that pointed to what's happening tonight, though?'

'No, this has been – well, an unpleasant surprise.'

'Is that your best shot at describing this – this bloodbath?' Green's voice was raised now. She glared at Langley with barely disguised malice.

'Nobody could have predicted anything of this scale, ma'am. Nothing like it has happened before.'

'And yet we knew that there would be retaliation following the murder of Maloney and this Dusky fellow.'

'Yes, we suspected it. But have you ever experienced the likes of this?'

Green sat back in her chair, steepling her fingers in front of her face. 'I've been in this job for as long as you, you know.'

'Oh yes.'

'I worked my way up from being a cop on the beat to the position I currently occupy. You know how hard that was.'

'Yes,' said Langley, waiting for the story she'd heard so often.

'Men, that was the problem. They had girlie magazine pages pinned to the walls, made crude jokes – cruder remarks. I was expected to make the tea during our breaks, ordered to do so by an inspector, no less. One officer sexually assaulted me.'

'Oh, I'm so sorry. I know how bad things were.' Amelia Langley struggled for something to say.

'But you see my point, don't you?'

'That things have changed for the better?' Langley knew that this wasn't what she was about to be told but decided to play along for the hell of it.

'You think me getting where I am now is unfair. You think I'm beneath you because you're a doctor of whatever it is. You've always been the same.'

'I did my two years on the beat, ma'am.' Langley's hackles were up.

'With sojourns to the police college and holidays. Just how many weeks did that really add up to?'

Langley began to object but was stopped from doing so

by a gesture from Green that could have been used to halt traffic on the road outside.

'I never wanted you in this job. Not because I don't want women in senior positions in the service – quite the opposite, in fact. No, what I want is to see more women in the highest ranks of the police all over the country. We have come a long way since I was forced to brew up the tea. But incompetence such as you have displayed in the last few days, culminating in this bloodbath tonight, puts my good work, and the work of so many dedicated women in the job, in jeopardy.'

Amelia Langley stood and banged Green's desk with balled fists. 'I don't have to listen to this shit! If you want to suspend me, do so. But I'm here to do a job, not listen to your sanctimonious bullshit! We have multiple crimes out there – murders. All you can do is lecture me on my so-called failings. With the greatest of respect, *ma'am*, forgive me for saying that you're missing the big picture here! Don't forget, you're the woman in charge.'

'Sit down, Langley!' The order was plain.

Resuming her seat, face flushed with anger, Langley obeyed. But she glared at her superior defiantly.

'At last, a bit of spirit! Carry that spirit out of this room and bring me those who've done this.'

'Who do you have in mind?'

'Can't be that hard to work out, surely? Zander Finn has been back for a matter of weeks and people are being murdered left, right and centre. Bring him in now!'

'And what about evidence? Apart from the anecdotal, we have nothing. If you think that Zander Finn will just hold up his hands to all of this, you're much mistaken. He's too clever to leave any trace of his involvement.'

'Well, you are an admirer, aren't you?'

'Sorry?' Langley could feel her face redden again, this time not with anger but embarrassment.

'We have a source. He came to me, not you. Which I think speaks volumes.'

'What source?'

'You'll find out shortly. In the meantime, get ready to face the press. You will make the usual noises about having everything under control. You'll tell them that we are making arrests, and that we already have made a significant breakthrough as to the cause of this night of violence. You're on at seven in the morning. So if I were you, I'd make sure Finn is in custody, then get as much beauty sleep as you can. You'll be on the news across the world by tomorrow morning.'

'And will you be with me? You know, down with the sisterhood and all that.'

'You can leave now.'

Amelia Langley turned away, heading for the door. Just before she stopped to open it, she turned to face ACC Green. 'And what about Ginerva de Lucca?'

Green's attention was back on the papers in front of her. She signed something with a flourish, then moved on to the next document. 'Mere coincidence, nothing more.'

'So you think that the fact we have the senior lieutenant of the biggest criminal organisation in the world on our doorstep when there is chaos on the streets is just a coincidence? I've been thinking about it, and I'm not sure.'

'What have I just said?'

'All I can say is, *ma'am*, I hope your "source" is a good one. Zander Finn has caught us out already. I want it on the record that I'm against arresting him at the moment.'

'Duly noted.' Green carried on with her paperwork.

36

Langley was standing not far from the reporter who was giving her piece to camera in a very animated fashion, all arms and flying adjectives.

Despite Green's advice, she had been unable to grab as much as ten minutes' sleep. The shadows under her eyes bore testament to the fact. She'd just endured the press conference; now it was time to do a face-to-face interview. It was going to be difficult – very difficult. At that moment, the thought of her old friends at university who had appeared on television doing their best to add some lustre to history came to mind. Langley was inwardly cursing them all as the interviewer turned to face her.

'With me is Detective Chief Inspector Amelia Langley, head of Police Scotland's Organised Crime Unit. Chief Inspector, can you give the public any reassurance as to their safety after what can only be described as an unprecedented night of violence across central Scotland?'

Langley cleared her throat nervously. 'Not that it's any consolation, but it must be noted that all of those who were injured or who lost their lives last night were known to the police, either here or abroad.'

'So, are you saying you're not troubled by what happened to them because of previous criminal behaviour?' The dark-haired reporter was sharp as a tack as she probed Langley's defences.

'No, that's not what I'm saying at all. I'm merely pointing out that these are not random attacks perpetrated upon members of the public. Most certainly not terrorism, as I've seen reported in some news outlets.'

'But some of last night's twenty-one victims were foreign nationals. How can we be sure they weren't the subject of racially motivated attacks?'

'It's quite clear that these terrible crimes are part of an underworld turf war between rival factions in Glasgow and the surrounding area.' Langley was holding her own, or thought so, at any rate.

'I'm quite sure most of our viewers will have had no idea that organised crime has reached such levels. What is Police Scotland going to do about it?'

'Rest assured, we have a large team of officers working on this, both here in Scotland and abroad.' Langley was ready with the *coup de grâce*. 'In fact, a man we believe to be heavily involved with the incidents last night has been taken into custody.' She breathed a silent sigh of relief. This was bound to put the reporter off her stride, even if she doubted the wisdom of the arrest. Here was new information that hadn't been revealed in the press conference. Now she could relax: interview over.

The reporter consulted her notes. 'Yes, we have been contacted by the lawyer representing Alexander Finn, the man we believe you arrested in the early hours of this morning at his home in Renfrewshire.'

'I'm afraid I can't make comment on that at this time.' Langley was back in the mire.

'Are you aware that up until a short time ago Mr Finn was working full-time as a patient assistant and ambulance driver in London?'

'As I say, I cannot make any comment on these matters at this time.' Langley was now desperate for this torture to end. She should have realised that Finn would have been prepared.

'Does he really sound like a man who, in a few weeks, could plan and execute such a clearly co-ordinated attack here in Glasgow?'

'Again, I can make no comment on these matters now. All I can say is that our inquiries are ongoing.' Please let this end, thought Langley to herself.

The reporter half turned to the camera. 'Chief Inspector, we know how busy you are. But we'd be grateful if you could watch this short piece put together earlier this morning by our colleagues in London.'

'Really, I must be getting on . . .'

But this had no effect. Her attention was drawn to an image of an old woman in a wheelchair pictured on a monitor beside the camera that was filming them.

'With me is Phyllis Quinn, who lives here in Kensington. Good morning, and thank you for speaking to us today.' The man's voice was disembodied, the camera pulling in on the old lady's wrinkled face.

'That's my pleasure, son.'

'The man you know as "Sandy" has been arrested this morning in connection with a series of murders and other serious crimes in and around Glasgow last night. Can you tell us what you think of this, please?'

'A lot of bloody nonsense, if you ask me. He was a lovely man. His Scotch was sometimes hard to make out, but he was a gem. Made sure I was always comfortable, lit me fags for me. Even brought chocolate, or gave me a cupper from his flask when it was a bit nippy out. An absolute gent.'

'So, it would be fair to say that what you're hearing about him on the news this morning comes as a bit of a shock?'

'Me shocked by what the Old Bill gets up to? No, son. They fitted up my great-uncle in nineteen-forty-eight. They'll do anything to cover their arses, that lot.'

'Mrs Phyllis Quinn, thank you.'

The screen went blank and the reporter turned back to Langley.

'Can I ask you for a response to what you've just seen, please?'

'As I say, no comment at this time.' Langley's face was bright red.

'Thank you, Chief Inspector. With that, from Fi Hunter here at Police Scotland's Organised Crime Unit at Gartcosh, it's back to the studio.'

The reporter turned to thank Langley, but she was already striding back into her headquarters.

'Think we caught somebody by surprise there,' said Fi Hunter to her cameraman, with a smile.

*

Maggie Finn looked through the peephole in her front door before allowing access to the person standing on the landing outside.

'I am sorry to bother you, Mrs Finn.'

'You know it's Maggie, Father.'

The retired priest nodded, removed his black trilby hat and followed his long-time parishioner through into her lounge.

'Take a seat, Father.' She was unadorned by make-up or

eye shadow, and looked uncomfortable to be seen without this mask.

To the old man, the cosmetics were more than mere beautification or the desperate attempt to ward off old age. He knew that the face Maggie Finn presented to the world wasn't just a carapace but a shield. And she'd had plenty to fend off in her life, of that he was more than aware.

She held up the front page of the tabloid newspaper. 'You don't think he could have done this, do you?'

Father Giordano read the headline – *Gangland Slaughter!!* – and shrugged. 'All I know is what I see. It only makes the heart ache to speculate on things about which we cannot be sure.'

'But they've lifted him. My granddaughter said they appeared at just after four in the morning at the house.'

'She will be upset.'

'She's always upset about something. Just been chucked by her girlfriend, no less. I mean, girlfriend – I'm so sorry, Father. You must recoil at the sight of what my family has become.'

'You know that's not how I feel, Maggie.' He looked at her, his dark eyes saying so much without saying anything. 'Love is love. It is not for us on earth to question why God puts people together or pulls them apart. If we learned that we are but small parts of a greater whole, then our lives would improve immeasurably.'

'Aye, well, I'm sure you're right. It just shows you. It's circumstances that make people, not their blood – or whatever it is they call it now. That's what I think.'

'Genetics: much the same thing. But in the end, as eventually with DNA, we are all the same in God's eyes.'

'If you say so. How does this DNA thing sit with His Holiness?'

'With him? I don't think he cares. The Pope just wants what what's good for the world. I admire him. He is a pragmatist.'

'A bit like you.'

'I do what has to be done. We do not exist in a world where everyone lives as they should – rather the reverse, in fact. If we are to succeed in banishing sin, then we must meet it face to face, unflinchingly.'

'Noble words, Father. Can I get you something to drink? I don't have any fancy wine or brandy. But I've got a kettle, and there's a bottle of Smirnoff somewhere. I don't normally drink at home.'

'I need nothing, but I do need to speak with you. Please, sit here beside me.'

Maggie did as he asked. As she sat beside the priest on her sofa, he reached out and grabbed her hands in his.

'There has been much sin in my life.'

'We don't need to go there again. We've been through it for years.'

'There is something you must know. It is of great importance, and none of us are getting any younger.'

'Right cheery, then?'

'This is serious, Maggie.'

'Aye, right, I'm listening.'

Father Giordano cleared his throat and began his story.

37

Gillian Finn watched the TV with increasing despair. Though the news channel had made sure the reporting of the night of murder and mayhem that had washed over Glasgow, Paisley and many other places besides wasn't graphic, they couldn't hide the facts. Nine men lay dead. Two women and another eleven men were seriously injured. Scotland was the centre of press attention from across the world.

Having seen enough, Gillian closed the laptop and sank back on her bed in her father's house. She stared at the ceiling and spotted a spider making its way along a cornice. At this point she wished she were anywhere but here – wished she was anyone else but who she was.

They'd had such a good time watching the play. She and her father had stayed in the bar until a taxi picked them up at just after one in the morning.

Gillian had been asleep when she'd heard the frantic knocking and shouting at the front door. For a second, her heart had frozen. Were these people here to kill her father? But when she made out the call of 'Police!' another fear gripped her. Was her father responsible for what she'd seen all over the media in the last few hours? How could he be, she reasoned. He'd been with her since early evening. He'd laughed – been his usual self. Surely he couldn't have known what gruesome horrors were happening in his name without letting it show. She was tired, so closed her eyes, desperate to find the sleep she knew wouldn't come.

After a few minutes, just as she felt herself drifting off, her mobile phone rang. She'd been expecting one of two things: a call from the police to back up the alibi she could easily provide on her father's behalf, or journalists looking for any dirt they could on Zander Finn. Both part of the same thing, she reasoned.

When she saw the name on the screen, Gillian shot up in her bed. 'Kirsty!'

'Hi, how are you?' The voice was quiet, distant, but at that moment the sweetest sound Gillian could have hoped to hear.

'Kirsty, I don't know what to say. I mean, how are you?'

'Okay, I guess.' There was a pause. 'Listen, Gillian, I'm so sorry about everything.'

'I don't understand what happened. One minute we were okay, then you were – well, gone.'

'I know.'

'I spoke to your father.'

'Yes, I heard.'

'So he told you?'

Another silence.

'Kirsty?'

'No, I was there – when you spoke to him, I mean.'

'Oh.' Gillian felt something, but she wasn't sure just quite what it was. Hurt, anger, betrayal. She couldn't tell. But she knew the feeling was strong. 'Why the artifice?'

'Woo, listen to who goes to drama school!'

Gillian laughed. Kirsty always made her laugh – until recently, that was. 'It doesn't matter, we're speaking now.'

'Yes.' Kirsty sounded doubtful.

'What's wrong? You sound funny.'

'Gillian, you know I'll always love you. This was my father's idea. You don't really know him, but he's so ambitious – not just for himself, for us all.'

Gillian felt her heart soar as it began to slowly mend. She'd thought all along that Kirsty had been at the mercy of her father's opinions. She'd even spotted him once dismiss his daughter with no more than a wave of her hand. Doctor he may be, but Gillian was sure she didn't want to be one of his patients.

'That's why I'm phoning – you now, to tell you.'

'It doesn't matter! I always knew how you really felt. At least, I hoped I did.'

'Wait, I'm not saying this very well.'

Gillian felt her heart begin to falter. Like Icarus too near the sun, she felt her face flush and prickle, as though a thousand tiny pins were being thrust into it. 'I don't know what you mean. You're talking in riddles.'

On the other end of the line, Kirsty sighed. 'I just want you to understand.'

'Well, you're not doing a very good job of it.'

'I hated my father for splitting us up.'

'Don't hate him. He was just doing what he thought was right.'

'That's just it.'

'What?'

'I've been thinking – you know, about what he said.'

'And?'

'We're too different, you and me, too young to get involved in something so – so deep.'

'Eh?'

'I'm still like a child – so are you, Gillian. We pretend to be grown up, all sophisticated, going to drama school. But at heart we're just stupid teenage girls that haven't seen or experienced the world.'

'I just hear your father talking, Kirsty.'

Silence.

'Kirsty, are you still there?'

'Yes.' The reply was sheepish, but then everything came out in a rush. 'The truth is, well, what happened last night, that's your dad, isn't it?'

'What? No, no, it isn't!'

'That's not what everyone is saying on WhatsApp.'

'Oh, so that's where you find the truth, is it?'

'Your dad comes back, then everybody starts to get killed.'

'Fuck you! My father isn't involved. Anyway, your family isn't perfect!' Gillian was on the defensive now.

'Oh, you mean we're black?'

'No! I never mentioned anything like that. You know me, I hate the racism shit! But I do think your father is an arrogant prick, if you want the truth.' Gillian winced just as she said the words.

'Huh! And your father kills people. I know what I prefer, Gillian.'

'I'm sorry, but you brought family into it first.'

'See what I mean?'

'What?'

'We're just like kids in the playground. Big kids playing at being adults.'

Gillian was flailing now, crashing to the ground, falling fast. 'This isn't the way to do this, Kirsty! We need to meet – you chose the place.'

'It's too late, Gillian. I've read the news and watched the TV. It's not just WhatsApp. I don't want anything to do with a family like yours. It's over. Please, for both our sakes, don't try and contact me again, okay?'

'Kirsty, please . . . none of it's true. The stuff you're hearing, I mean. Kirsty?' Gillian listened, but the line was dead. She was dying inside.

★

Maggie Finn looked out of her window on the seventeenth floor, just in time to see the man in the black raincoat and trilby hat cross the car park and slip out of sight. He looked like a figure from another age, which is just what he was, she considered.

It took a lot to take Maggie Finn's breath away, but what Father Giordano had said had made her question just about everything she believed in. There was so much she hadn't known, so much that now made sense.

She felt the need of a lift, something to calm her frayed nerves. Maggie made for the kitchen. She'd been right – in the back of a cupboard was a bottle of vodka. She stood on her tiptoes and grabbed it. There was nothing in the fridge or cupboards to mix it with. Sometimes she had fresh orange juice when she was on one of her many health kicks, but today there was only milk and a bottle of mineral water she'd brought home from somewhere.

'Fuck it.' She poured a large measure into a glass and gulped half of it down. For a second, as it caught her throat, she thought she might be sick. But soon the spirit's burn became comforting warmth. She made her way back to the lounge and flopped on the sofa.

She knew her son was in custody. She now knew things she could never have suspected. But, she reasoned, she now knew much more than Zander did. And this knowledge could prove invaluable. It certainly changed things.

Maggie Finn took another gulp of straight vodka and reached for the phone on the coffee table in front of her. She ordered a taxi, finished the vodka and rushed off to put her mask back in place.

38

Ginerva de Lucca cast her eyes over the skyline of Glasgow through the blacked-out back windows of a large SUV as she was driven through the city. She was aware that – despite being free of any official investigation – the CCTV cameras would be turned in her direction the minute she broke cover. But she was well used to due diligence in this regard. Her philosophy was to give the authorities just enough knowledge of her whereabouts to keep them busy, then disappear.

Ginerva had stepped from the RIB and taken just a few steps up the tiny beach by the loch to where stood the SUV. She knew that there were no cameras where she was going. Her host had guaranteed that.

What a miserable place to live, she pondered. Low grey cloud hung over a slate grey landscape, populated by grey-faced people. She winced as an old man hawked the contents of his throat onto the pavement while the SUV stopped at a set of traffic lights. How could anyone live, love – exist – in such misery?

When she was young, Scotland had been a place of long-haired warriors in her mind – of bold, brave men in Highland garb, fighting their way from one rugged castle to another. The reality was hunched, pallid, unhealthy individuals fighting their way through rain and wind to the nearest off-licence, pub or club, or shooting up in parks or dingy alleyways.

Ginerva had watched a Visit Scotland ad on YouTube during her flight from Italy. The sky was bright blue, the sand a glistening white, as fresh-faced, invigorated young people gambolled by a blue, blue sea. Children played, gulls soared and legends were written in the ruins of craggy monuments to days gone by.

As she watched a dog squat to empty its bowels in the gutter, she wondered at the imagination of the people who had made the advert to attract people to Scotland. Certainly, judging by the reality in front of her, an Oscar would be poor reward.

But Ginerva had long-since ceased to be surprised be anything. Disappointment was hovering around every corner, no matter where she found herself. The human condition was a miserable one – even under the Calabrian sun. That's why people like her existed. She peddled sex in the shape of trafficked women from Eastern Europe; dreams in the form of the best cocaine and heroin money could buy; thrills and the promise of riches to all who participated in her illegal numbers rackets and casinos.

That such desires had been in the hearts of men since the beginning of time was proof positive that humanity was damned. She was merely a facilitator, a conduit to what people really wanted. It wasn't her fault mankind was so flawed.

She thought about 'mankind', for men were – in the main – those who put money in her burgeoning bank accounts located in the most secretive and customer-friendly places on the planet. From the Isle of Man to the Caymans, Switzerland to South America, she found clever people in smart suits more than happy to keep safe the money her organisation made from the worst instincts the world had on offer.

Her organisation. This was complicated; she was the 'under boss' – well, at least officially. She had been running things for ten years – the ten years since her father had occupied the same role. Ginerva had carte blanche to do what she wished. She knew that the chances of the only person who could gainsay her objecting to what she wanted to do were vanishingly small. In short, she was the biggest, richest, most successful criminal in the world.

She closed her eyes and her mind drifted to the beach on the Cayman Islands where she'd spent two blissful weeks recently, part business, but mostly for pleasure. She could feel the sun on her bronzed skin; see the palm trees swaying in the cooling breeze under the azure sky.

Then the SUV came to a halt outside a grey building with small, barred windows and those dreams drifted away.

★

'I mean, it's not what you expect when you're just watching the telly with your weans, is it?' The woman chewed gum aggressively in-between sentences.

Amelia Langley regarded her with a weariness she hadn't felt since having to cram for her finals at university. If it weren't for the fact she knew why she was so tired, she'd have been compelled to seek the advice of a doctor. Every part of her wanted to sleep; yet when she tried, sleep would not come. 'Tell us about last night, Mrs Maguire – in detail, I mean,' said Langley wearily.

'Well, he was away at the football. Partick Thistle, would you believe? I mean, I know fuck all about football, but even I know they're shite.'

'Yes, I'm sure.'

'Are you like me? Just can't be bothered with watching men chasing about a wee ball?'

'No, I'm not so keen. Anyway, back to last night. What made you look out of the window?'

'Nothing else to do, that's why. It was either his season ticket or Netflix. Guess what we bought?'

'The season ticket, by any chance?'

'I can see how you're a super inspector, or whatever.'

'Chief Inspector.'

'Aye, that's it. Right mouthful, eh?'

'So, you looked out the window . . . when?'

'Just after *EastEnders* finished.'

'And what time was that?'

'I dunno, half eight? You'd need to check the TV guide. Och, they have it on at all different times just now. I missed a couple of episodes a while ago because they was all over the place. It's a pain in the arse.'

'I can imagine. So, when you looked out of the window, what did you see?'

'Young Gemma Colville winching a wee ned from Dunmore Road. She's a right tart, so she is. Supposed to be engaged – engaged, my arse! That's a right nice boy she's cheating on, too. I was at the school with his uncle, so I was.'

For an instant, Langley pictured herself with her hands clamped around Mrs Maguire's neck, but did her best to banish this thought and carry on. 'When did you see the dealer?'

'He's always there. Every night from six until late. You can set your watch by him. He stands by that hedge at the side of the car park.'

'Right. He's by the hedge – what happens then?'

'Well, these guys come out of nowhere. Three of them, like.'

'Did you recognise them?'

'No, but Bianca down the close reckons one of them might have been a cousin of her friend's from the Drum.'

'Is she sure?'

'I wouldn't pay much heed to what she has to say. She told me that auld Jimmy next door to me was having it off with the dinner lady from Our Lady of the Rock primary school. Turned out to be pure shite, so it did.'

'Can you give me her address, just in case? We'd like to have a word with her.'

'No way, man! Me get the name for being a grass! You must be fucking joking. Anyhow, she wouldn't tell you lot fuck all.'

'Oh? Why?'

'Because one of your mob burst her man's nose when he was minding his own business one night a couple of weeks ago. The poor guy was just walking through a rammy. He'd a hold of that baseball bat because it was his son's birthday the next day. It was a present, you know what I mean?'

Langley's temper broke. 'Mrs Maguire, can we please stick to the matters in hand? Please remember, two men were killed outside your home last night. You can surely understand why I'm so anxious to find out what happened.'

'Okay, keep your wig on, man. If you ask me the right questions, I'll be able to give you an answer. All this shite about what's on the telly and Partick Thistle is putting me right off.'

Langley was about to remind the woman who was chewing her gum across the table that it was her who had brought up the subjects of football and *EastEnders*. However, she thought the better of it. 'These three guys start noising up the dealer. Then what?'

'They, like, started pushing him about. Nothing serious, just winding the bastard up, likely.'

'You didn't see any weapons at this point?'

'Naw, nothing.'

'And then?'

'Your man took this for a couple of minutes. Then a big black beamer comes shooting into the car park. Two of the biggest guys you've ever seen come boosting out of it. One of them had an axe in his hand, the other a steel bar or something. I can't be sure.'

'They approached the dealer and the men who were hassling him in a black BMW, right?'

'Aye, that's right.'

'What did these youths do?'

'What would you do? They got on their toes, quick smart, like. Flicking the Vicky at these two big guys. Cheeky wee zoomers, so they were.'

'The big guys – did they speak to the dealer?'

'Aye, they goes up tae him and have a fag and a wee chat. All relaxed and that.'

'Then?'

'So my wee lassie – Cologne, that's a lovely name, so it is – well, she starts roaring because her brother's left a shite in the bog without flushing it. He's a wee bastard for that. I don't know how many times I've had to tell him about it.'

'And when you looked out of the window again?'

'Oh right, aye. So, like, these two big guys is back in the motor, just pulling away. Next minute it's like fucking mayhem, man. Guns firing from all directions into their car.'

'Did you get a look at anyone?'

'Eh? Are you wrong in the head or what? I got away from the window as quick as I could. Me and the weans hid in the toilet until the noise stopped, which, by the way, was stinking because Lennon had left a big log floating in the lavvy.'

Langley looked at Neil Dickie, who was sitting to her left. He nodded.

'Okay, Mrs Maguire. We'll get what you've told us written up in a statement so that you can sign it as being a true representation of what you've told us. It won't take long.'

'It better not. Me and my bestie, big Morag, are away out on the bevvy tonight.' She chewed furiously for a few moments. 'Here, I won't have to go to court, will I? If yous ask me, I'll just say no, got it?'

'I don't think it'll come to that. It's not as though you can identify anyone. We just wanted to get a picture of what happened last night.'

'Aye well, picture away. Mind, I'll need a lift back home – aye, and no' in a marked motor neither. I don't want half the scheme thinking I run off to the polis at the least wee thing.'

Back in the corridor, Amelia Langley leaned back against a wall and rubbed her eyes. 'Cologne – can you imagine?'

'Aye, the poor wee bastard. Mind you, it's lucky she didn't call the boy for an aftershave. Brut, even.'

'Well, we know how they did it, at least. Well planned, eh?'

'Yes, ma'am. They get some wee shites to noise up the dealer and when cavalry arrives, the big boys pick them off. It's somebody who knows their business, that's for sure.'

She sighed. 'Okay, back to Finn. We can question him a bit longer. But we've got nothing on him, have we?'

'Nope. Everybody saw what happened, but nobody saw who did it. Come on, ma'am, if it was you, would you be rushing to give evidence?'

'No,' Langley sighed. 'Let's have another go at Finn.'

'Can I suggest something?'

'Yes, of course, Neil. You know I value your opinion.'

'You're not going to like it.'

'Oh, just spit it out!'

'We're not going to get anything out of Finn, you know that. Why don't we release him and see what he does next?'

'Tail him?'

'Aye, we're much more likely to get something that way. He has to have another move up his sleeve.'

'Okay. But you run it, Neil. Our best men, right?'

'No problem.'

'I know someone who won't be happy.'

'Green? Fuck her, what does she know about anything? She's just a desk jockey with gold braid.'

'Funny, that's just what she thinks about me.'

Langley watched DS Dickie head off to put their plan in place. She didn't really share his confidence that Zander Finn would fall so easily into such a trap, but they had to try something. Now all she had to do was go and tell her superior what was happening.

39

Ginerva de Lucca was like a Ming vase in a junk shop. She didn't look right walking past the old man rolling his cigarette with his clawed, nicotine-stained fingers, nor the plump young woman in strained leggings swearing at the fruit machine, onto which her pendulous belly was precariously balanced, as she fed more money in for another roll.

Every eye in the Iron Horse was on Ginerva. Not least those of Pavel the barman, who – for the first time since he'd taken the job – felt a twist of excitement. This feeling was somewhat tempered by the presence of two large men in suits and dark glasses who stood on each side of the dark-haired, beautifully dressed woman.

'You're like thon Sophia Loren, so you are,' said an old dear with no bottom set of falsers, gums tough-looking and shrunken. 'Like a fucking painting, so you are.'

Ginerva smiled at the compliment. 'You are so kind.' She turned to one of the men at her side. 'Buy this wonderful lady a drink – in fact, buy everyone a drink!' She said this loudly enough to initiate a stampede. Chairs scraped on the faded linoleum and a crowd soon gathered at the bar, all smiles and expressions of thanks.

'You are very generous,' said Pavel, as he went to work behind the bar. 'Some of these people haven't moved this quickly since the war.'

'Aye, and fuck you too,' said an elderly man. 'You'll be on your way back to Poland, the way things is heading. You should count yourself lucky we've made you welcome in our community.'

'Oh, it has been such a *pleasure*, Archie.' Pavel said the word with long vowels. 'How could I wish for a better place in which to live and work?'

A door opened and a large man with a scar down one cheek emerged behind the bar.

'How are yous all?' He took in Ginerva and her associates with a leery eye.

'We are very well. Mr Mannion, we come to see him.'

'Aye, I get that. He's just in the bog right now, but I'll take you up to his office. Follow me.' Sammy Sloane performed what could best be described as a cross between a bow and a curtsey for his new guests, a movement at odds with his bulky frame.

'Big Sammy, you're not at the dancing, you know,' exclaimed a man at the bar with brown tape around one arm of his spectacles.

Sloane leaned towards him and whispered in his ear. 'See they broken specs of yours. You know where they're going in just two minutes.' He turned to his guests. 'Up here, this way.'

As the party of Italians walked behind the bar, Ginerva received a ragged cheer from the clientele of the Iron Horse, to whom she had been so generous.

As they disappeared up the steep stair an old woman shook her head. 'Aye, she looks bonnie in they heels and those nice clothes. It's amazing what you can do with that, and some expensive make-up and a good haircut. See, once she gets home and slips into her leggings an' a big jumper, she'll no' be so bonny.'

This engendered a murmur of agreement in the room, as people drifted back to their newspapers, fruit machines and dominoes.

*

Senga Finn sat uncomfortably in her new home in Howwood. She was uncomfortable because she was with her mother-in-law, who was sitting on the chair opposite. They had always enjoyed a strained relationship, like two dogs circling each other in a backyard. But this silent war of dirty looks, off-hand remarks and raised brows was a cold war that had gone on for decades.

Zander had often maintained that his wife and mother could never get on because they were too alike. But Senga found it hard to see any of herself in the woman with the thin legs poking out of expensive shoes, who in turn was regarding her with equal distaste.

'Our Gillian opted to stay with her dad, then,' said Maggie Finn.

'So it would appear,' Senga replied defiantly. 'Though she wasn't so keen to see him when she was in the hospital. Oh no, when it came to her life being in danger, it was Mummy she wanted to be with.'

'I suppose she has to get to know you somehow.'

Senga took a large gulp of wine and tried to keep her temper. 'Are you sure I can't get you anything?'

'Bit early in the day, is it not?' Maggie felt no sense of hypocrisy saying this: even though she'd downed a large vodka before making her impromptu visit: she was using alcohol medicinally, while her daughter-in-law was a lush.

There was a clear difference in her mind. 'Anyway, I'm not staying long. The taxi's coming back in half an hour.'

'Half an hour! What the fuck are we going to talk about for all that time?'

'Your family.'

'Oh, *my* family, now! You've got nothing to do with it when things aren't going so well. It was the same when they were kids. If they did something good in school, Granny tramped up in her high heels and took all the credit. When there was spew, dirty nappies, broken hearts or skinned knees to be dealt with, Granny was elsewhere.'

'I did my fair share of that shite. That's what mothers do.'

'Huh, you only had the one – easy-peasy.'

'Oh, you think managing Zander and his father was easy? My arse, it was!'

'At least he's still alive.'

'Och, don't start that shit. You're banging the man that likely killed our Danny.'

Senga sat forward on her chair. 'I don't care whose mother you are, or what age you are either. You speak to me like that again and I'll come across there and snap one of they chicken legs of yours!'

'You'll need to lose some weight off they thighs of yours if you want to catch me.'

'What?'

Maggie sighed. 'I need you to listen to me. This isn't a game. For once we have to behave like adults. Your family – my family – are in danger.'

'So, what's changed? I'm down one and a half sons, or had you forgotten?'

'This is worse – much worse.'

'And how do you know? Been to that soothsayer, or whatever she is again?'

'She's an astrologist.'

'Aye, right, so I've got to burst into action because Mystic Meg tells you something. That will be shining bright.'

'It's not from her. I know things.'

'Well, why don't you tell your precious son? From what I hear, he's doing just fine in the "standing up for himself department", eh?'

'I can't tell him. And anyway, it would do no good. You know what he's like.'

'Aye.' Senga's eyes roamed around the room. 'That's why I'm here in this hen house, not in my own home.'

'Hen house? You've got six bedrooms. Aye, and I bet you've made use of all of them already.'

'Fuck you!' Senga returned to her glass of wine.

'Listen to me. I'm not saying this for badness. Joe Mannion isn't who you think he is.'

'Oh, change the record, Maggie. My marriage to your son is over, end of story. And I'll see anyone I like. When your precious Zander was pushing about OAPs in wheelchairs, I was holding things together, remember? And I couldn't have done it without Joe.'

'The trouble with they Albanians, you mean?'

'Aye, well spotted. I thought you just concerned yourself with bingo and the Darby and Joan Club.'

'If you mean our crib nights in the Tile Bar, why not?'

'For fuck's sake, it's like the Star Wars pub in there.'

'Enough!' Maggie stood up. 'Joe Mannion is plotting to wipe us out – all of us. And he has help.'

'Bollocks. You need to go see a doctor. You're just at the right age.'

'You're talking to me about age? Imagine, you and that old man – it's disgusting.'

'Mind your own business. Anyway, I heard you was having it away with wee Tam the baker from Causeyside Street. He wears a surgical support, everybody knows it.'

'Does he fuck!'

'Ha! Caught you. How would you know about that unless he'd been in about you?'

'I'm being serious. You can help save us. I don't care what you think about my son. Do you want Gillian or Sandra to go the same way as Danny?'

'The drama, it never ends.'

'You keep tabs on your decrepit boyfriend, you'll see.'

Senga drained her glass. 'Get the fuck out of my house.'

'Don't you mean get the fuck out of Zander's house?'

'Just go!' Senga flung the empty wine glass to the floor, where instead of breaking it just bounced off the thick pile carpet.

Maggie picked up her handbag. 'Same slapper you always were. But you'll be the sorry one in the end.' She shook her head at Senga. 'I'll see myself out.'

As Maggie stomped off, her daughter-in-law shouted in her wake, 'Aye, and don't find your way back in!'

Even so, once she heard the front door slam, Senga Finn bit her lip.

40

Ginerva de Lucca was sitting across the desk from Joe Mannion. Despite the unfamiliar surroundings, she looked relaxed, to the extent that she seemed more at home than the bald man who was facing her.

'Things are going well, no?' she said. 'We are definitely safe to speak?'

They were alone now. Sammy was in the room next door, with de Lucca's minders.

'Aye, don't worry about a thing. The polis – the police, that is – don't spend much time in this street, never mind trying to bug the place. I do my due diligence. We sweep it every morning. And have eyes everywhere.'

'So, your community is loyal. That is a good thing. It's the way we work in Italy.'

'Treat folk right, and they treat you right. That's always been my motto.'

'A very noble one, Mr Mannion.'

'Please, we've agreed, it's Joe.' He leaned across the desk and smiled broadly at her. 'You know, I was thinking. I don't know how long you're here for – in Scotland, I mean. I thought maybe we could take some time out. I could show you the sights.'

Ginerva smiled back. 'I've already sampled some of your "sights": junkies and dogs shitting in the streets. It makes Napoli look like Disneyland.'

'Oh, come on. You must admit, where you are on Loch Lomond is lovely. I can show you lots of great places. I've got a wee place on Mull. It's a beautiful island. We could take a couple of days out, go up there and relax. There's nothing like the view across Tobermory Bay on a nice night. My house is up on the hill.'

'I can think of one problem with the view, Mr Mannion.'

'What?'

'You'd be in it.'

'Charming.'

'Our arrangement is strictly business. Do you really think you're my type?'

'You can't blame a man for trying. If you don't ask, you don't get.'

'Do yourself a favour: stop asking. I'm not Senga Finn.' She glared at him for a moment. 'Such an ugly name.'

'That's my business.'

'This is where you are wrong. As we have proved, you might think you have her where you want her, but she still has loyalties to her husband.'

'She hates him!'

'They have much in common – a family, for instance.'

'Some family.'

'Never underestimate the bonds of a family, Mr Mannion. Take the warning. Do something about it.'

Mannion shrugged. He knew he had a great deal to gain. Was the loss of Senga Finn a price worth paying? He considered it and decided, yes.

'Everything else is going as we planned. Mr Finn obliged in every way.'

'He did a good job. I'm quite impressed.'

'It was on a plate for him. It was easy. The good thing is

that now he thinks he is the big cheese – the *grand fromage*, as you'd say, eh?'

'That's French.'

'Aye, right enough. But not far away, eh? You still understood it.'

Ginerva looked away and sighed.

'One thing bothers me, though,' said Mannion.

'What?'

'Okay, Zander got the men on the street. He didn't get the big boss. No bugger knows who is in charge of the Albanians.'

'I do.'

'Oh.'

'And I'm addressing that problem, as we speak. But we mustn't make things too easy for Mr Finn. I have a plan. You will do as I say.'

Mannion sat back in his chair. 'And what if I don't want to play ball?'

'Then your balls will be saying goodbye to the rest of you.'

'Aye, fair enough.' Mannion reached for a cigar. He hated being talked down to – especially by a woman, and a foreign one at that. But where there was money to be made, and lots of it, it paid to be pragmatic. His time would come.

'Finn has taken all the risks and rid us of the Albanians on the ground. I don't know why you found it so hard to do this yourself.'

'The time wasn't right,' Mannion muttered.

'I see. Well, Zander Finn succeeded where you failed.'

'Thanks very much.' Mannion's tone was sarcastic. 'If you're that keen on Zander Finn, how come we're sitting here discussing our partnership, eh?'

'*Partnership*.' Ginerva said the word slowly, as though savouring the sound on her tongue. 'You're right, of course, this is a partnership.'

'Aye, too right.'

'But you are very much the junior partner. I'm not sure Mr Finn could ever operate in such circumstances.'

Mannion's mouth gaped and his cigar fell onto the desk. He wiped away the small flurry of burning ash and placed it firmly back between his teeth, staring at the woman opposite.

'Before you have another cigar failure, I'll answer the question you're about to ask. Yes, we did consider working with Zander Finn instead of you and your *organisation*.'

'Gee, thanks for the vote of confidence. If you're into boosting someone's ego, it ain't working, my dear.'

'You are wise enough to know that we could have taken our pick from a handful of your crime gangs here in Scotland. We chose yours.'

'And not Finn – why?'

'It's complicated. All you have to know is that the first phase of our work is done. Now, we take over.'

Mannion stared into her dark eyes. He'd made as much as he could of the fact that Finn had been overlooked – feigned surprise, even. But he knew that the Italians would have been thorough when looking for a partner in the UK. He knew he had to be pliant and subservient at times – so what? As Ginerva de Lucca used Glasgow as a base to take over the UK's county lines drugs trade, he would become richer by the day. In any case, it was time he took a back seat. Everything was perfect.

Then Ginerva spoke again.

Finn blinked into the low sun as he stepped out of the custody suite at Gartcosh. Amelia Langley was at his side.

'Nice to have a wee send-off, thank you.'

'You're not as clever as you think, Zander.'

He shrugged. 'I don't think I'm clever at all. In fact, I've been the most stupid man on the planet in my time. But I'm making up for that – or trying to, at least.

'Don't leave the country.'

'How could I? You've got my passport.'

'How stupid do you think I am?'

'I'm not going anywhere, don't worry.'

'She'll do anything to break you, Zan. And remember, that's my job too.'

'Green? Piece of shit. Why you let her get away with setting you up, I'll never know.'

'I'll never know how my saviour arrived.'

Finn looked her up and down. 'Things happen. You must know about most of the arseholes in my world. They can't keep their mouths shut.'

'And you listened – why?'

'Would you rather I hadn't?'

Amelia Langley smiled. 'See you soon, Zander.' She watched Finn walk away. But a memory returned like a horror story.

'Langley, you're on five beat tonight.' The order was terse. There was no acknowledgement that the woman handing out the instruction knew the constable to whom she was allotting a nightshift beat.

'Yes, sergeant,' she said, wondering why she'd been removed from her usual beat. 'Who's my neighbour?'

'Up there? You don't need one.'

'Hey, Langley,' whispered one of her male colleagues sitting beside her in the muster room. 'It's all old warehouses and demolished houses. Easy night.'

As they broke up, each heading out into Glasgow's East End, Constable Amelia Langley stared at Green. Almost exactly two years after their probation was over, she now wore a sergeant's stripes. The pair who'd joined the Accelerated Promotion scheme together, now separated by rank.

Langley swallowed hard at the memory. It always left her feeling cold. She noticed her right hand was shaking, as she watched Finn climb into a taxi.

She'd heard nothing, not the pad of a footstep or the grind of rough ground under four pairs of stout boots. The first sensation was one of surprise as she was grabbed around the neck and pulled through an old doorway into a disused warehouse.

She kicked, punched, tried to scream. But her attackers were stronger. Almost immediately a gloved hand was clamped over her mouth, making her breathe desperately through her nose.

The rough floor hit her like a truck in the back, winding her, making her groan for air. Even in the half light of the warehouse, she could see the man in the mask as he forced himself on her, a heavy weight pressing down, almost crushing her.

Still she struggled.

Finn's taxi was pulling away now.

He'd loosened his grip on her, as he'd tried to force up her skirt. She made a grasp for the balaclava. It was a face she could never forget. She recognised it from the run-down bar, from so many mug shots.

Joe Mannion pulled off his disguise and punched her in the face. 'So, you recognise me. Who cares? Where you're going, folk don't come back to tell tales.'

A bright light flashed in her eyes. For a moment, Langley thought she was dead.

'Get off her!' The voice was that of a young man, she remembered thinking.

'Eh?' Her attacker forced his crushing weight from her as he stood up.

Her head was still spinning from the blow and the shock of the attack. Langley tried to stand, but couldn't.

'You little shit. Who the fuck do you think you are? You're dead, man!' shouted Mannion.

'Fuck off! Now! Before I change my mind.'

More words were exchanged; she couldn't make them out.

Footsteps. Cursing. A figure leaned over her in the light of a bright torch. She recoiled, tried to shuffle away on the rough, damp floor.

'It's okay.' Gently, he helped her to her feet. 'You've been set up. Don't trust anyone – and certainly not your colleagues.'

Amelia Langley remembered the first time she'd set eyes on Zander Finn. He was the man who'd saved her life . . .

*

High above, from her window on the top floor, ACC Green looked down. A scowl spread across her face. She took a sip of coffee as she stared into the middle distance. As Zander Finn disappeared into the taxi, she turned round and faced the man sitting on the other side of her large desk.

'Nice view?' said Donald Paton.

'Not really. But it gives me time to think,' said Green.

'Not good for you, that. Thinking is overrated.'

'Maybe, for once Langley is right. Who knows what Mr Finn will get up to next?'

'You let people die. I told you what was happening, but you just let it go ahead.'

'Why should I care if a significant number of very dangerous foreign criminals are taken off the streets?'

'Innocent people could have been killed.'

'Mr Paton, in your long years involved in organised crime, when did you ever worry about "innocent people"?'

'I've always worked in a legitimate business. I never got my hands dirty that way, ever!'

'But not so keen on paying your taxes.'

Paton shrugged and turned away from her gaze.

'I could have you put away for a very long time, you know that. How fortunate that we struck up this little relationship last year. Before Zander Finn even reappeared. I'm so glad our paths crossed.'

'I'm not.'

'Well, you should be. I let you live in your nice house, with your lovely wife. I even let you go on holiday.'

'To Devon. Very big of you.'

'We couldn't have you popping off abroad then deciding not to come back, could we? Anyway, your friends would have been suspicious if you hadn't had a break. You know what you criminal types are like. It's all about appearances.'

'Yes,' he replied wearily.

'Anyway, you know what to do. I suggest you just go and do it.'

'And what if Zander gets suspicious? He's not stupid, you know. His father was, but he's a very different person.'

'Then you'll just have to do what you've been doing all these years.'

'What?'

'Keep your head down, listen and learn, then hope for the best. Good day, Mr Paton.'

41

Zander Finn was experiencing the usual feeling when someone died at his hands: guilt.

He looked absently out of the window of the taxi he owned as it sped through the outskirts of Glasgow. He was back to protect his family, he kept telling himself, but this return had come at a cost. His best friend was already dead, and now he'd had to unleash murder and mayhem on the streets where he lived.

Murder and mayhem was never good for business, that he knew. But he'd had to act and the time had been right. The information he'd needed had fallen into his hands at just the right time.

For some reason, this thought began to trouble him.

Just at the right time.

The more Finn thought about it, the more convenient the revelation appeared. The red mist of revenge had consumed his attention. Now, though, everything seemed too convenient. But it had come from a trusted source, and he knew his blood had been running high following the death of Malky Maloney. Vengeance was the order of the day, and he had acted accordingly. After all, these were the men who might have killed Danny.

'Drop me here,' he said to the driver.

The car pulled up in a space on Glasgow's Hope Street.

Finn got out and tipped the man at the wheel. He needed head space, time to think, away from everyone.

He walked a few paces up the street and turned into a small bar. The sweet, warm waft of alcohol hit him as he opened the door. The place was quiet, apart from two young men who were noisily bantering at the far end of the long room. For a moment, Finn thought of finding somewhere else but reasoned that there would be few places to sit and have a quiet drink in this city without such annoyances. He nodded to the barmaid and ordered a large single malt.

The place was pleasantly old-fashioned. No blaring music, just quiet crooners and a rack of the day's newspapers. He made to reach for one, then remembered that he knew exactly what would be in it. Instead, Finn sought out the solitude of a table by the window.

Pubs in Glasgow had – in the main – eschewed the dark windows, or no windows at all, that had once so marked out their presence on a street. Now, especially in the modern city centre, it was no longer an offence to the eye to look from the street upon people consuming alcohol. Likewise, customers inside could sit and people-watch. Finn had enjoyed people-watching all his life.

He looked at a smart man in a business suit and wondered what constituted his life, loves and loathing. Two teenage girls passed by the window arm-in-arm, high on nothing other than life and the joy of being young. The contrast between them and the old woman in the filthy, tattered raincoat tied with blue string could not have been more marked. The girls strode past her unconcerned, as she rummaged in a bin, fishing out a half-eaten burger bun.

He sighed at the sight. Life was unfair – unjust. That could just as easily have been his mother – himself, even. While the massacre of a few Albanian gangsters settled uneasily on his heart, the sight of the elderly woman now tucking into a meal served from a street bin really dragged him down.

He swallowed his whisky in one, then walked back to the bar for another. The barmaid was middle-aged, efficient and friendly, with dark, bobbed hair and a big smile.

'You needed a drink, eh?'

'Aye, you could say that. Another of the same, please,' he said, as a heavy lorry thundered along Hope Street.

'Listen, if you're having a few, just give me a nod and I'll bring them to your table. It'll give me something to do. It's always quiet at this time of day during the week. Apart from that pair.' She gestured to the two youths at the end of the bar. One had spilled a drink down his shirt; both were the worse for wear.

'Throw them out,' said Finn.

'I'd love to. But they're friendly with the owner's son. I need to keep this job, even though it's shite.' She served Finn the drink.

He walked back to his table and again stared idly out at passers-by. In a few moments he ceased to see individuals, just the hypnotic movement of people. Their ebb and flow made him think. He pictured his estranged wife, his troubled daughter, his dead son; the list went on. Though Finn tried hard to lift his spirits, no release would come.

A rumpus at the bar caught his attention. The barmaid had refused to serve the young men and they weren't happy.

'Fuck you, you old whore. I'm phoning Bradley. He'll fucking sort this, that's for sure.' He spat the words across the bar at her, his face twisted with anger.

'You can phone who you like. You're drunk, and I'm not serving you any more. I'd be grateful if you left the bar, please – both of you.'

Finn admired her pluck. The barmaid was by no means a big woman, and both of her truculent customers were well over six feet tall, their aggression spurred on by alcohol.

'Just do what the woman asks, eh?' said Finn, his voice raised, though he was still looking blankly out of the window.

'Oi, stripey heid, mind your own fucking business.' The pair laughed at the Mallen streak in Finn's hair.

Finn snorted a dismissive laugh. 'Just get to fuck, you spotty bastard. Don't you know lager is bad for your complexion? Take my advice and away and find some Germolene and a glass of water.'

In a split second, they were at his table. The more aggressive of the two had blond hair and a gold ring through his nose. 'We'll give you two minutes to get to fuck, stripey.' He pushed the table into Finn's midriff.

'Okay, keep the head,' said Finn. He stood up, his hands in the air in mock surrender. 'I'm out of here.' He winked at the barmaid, as he walked from behind the table.

The blond stuck his face into Finn's. They were around the same height. 'Aye, fuck off, you fucking oddity, man.' Flecks of his saliva showered the gangster's face.

In one quick movement, Finn hooked his right index finger through the nose ring and pulled hard, sending the youth screaming to the floor, blood pouring down his face. His friend produced a knife from his pocket but was too slow. Finn cracked his whisky glass off the table, then jabbed it into the boy's cheek, where it left a large gash. The youth staggered back and fell over a table.

Finn leaned over him, his foot on the younger man's throat. 'You should listen to people who know better than you, arsehole.' He continued pressing down with his boot on the wide-eyed youth's throat as the groans from his companion filled the room. 'And that means just about everybody.' Finn pulled back and walked away, leaving his erstwhile tormentor gasping for breath.

He threw a few large denomination notes onto the bar. 'For the damage, and your trouble. I apologise.'

'No need to say sorry. I enjoyed every minute of that,' said the barmaid, with a smile.

Leaving the young men writhing on the floor, Finn walked back into the bustle and noise of the city street. A few yards away, the old woman in the tattered raincoat was trying her luck in another bin, passers-by looking on with distaste as she fumbled through the detritus of others in search of something – anything – to eat.

'Here, take this.' Finn handed her a wad of twenty-pound notes. 'Go and get some clothes and something to eat, love.'

The old tramp mashed her toothless mouth. 'God blesh you, son.'

As Finn walked away, he heard the words of Father Giordano in his head.

Money won't buy you a place in heaven, my son.

Finn was sure that nothing would buy him a place in heaven, never mind money. He continued down the road, noticing its name on the side of a building. 'Hope Street'. How ironic, he thought.

42

Gramoz Makur ended the call. At least Jotir was still safe, and on his way. His right-hand man knew exactly what to do in such circumstances. So did he. For Makur, planning was all, and he rarely left anything to chance. Of course, in his line of work, risks had to be taken, but they were normally calculated.

Though he'd lost the bulk of his men – good men – there was no shortage of eager and willing replacements back in Albania. They may not know the lie of the land, but they would soon learn. They would also kill. It was now very clear that Makur was in a war with Zander Finn. The thought of this wasn't particularly troubling. He regretted the loss of the men in a purely strategic sense. He knew, or cared, little for their lives. Though he would be sure to be generous to their families back home. He had a benevolent image to maintain. Few men would travel to a foreign land to fight for a man who would abandon their families if things went wrong. In Albania, family came first, money second.

As for his own safety, he had little concern. He'd made sure his wife and children were safely ensconced in a remote cottage on his Aberdeen estate. But this felt ultra-cautious. Almost nobody knew he was from Albania, never mind the boss of a crime family. He was hiding in plain sight and doing it well.

Nonetheless, his sense of caution, which he'd brought from his time in the army, and the study of the great generals of history, told him to be on the move.

Despite the size of the house, Makur made sure he could travel light, and at a moment's notice. The fact that he wasn't already on the road spoke volumes as to how safe he felt.

He was the man from somewhere who did something with green energy. He'd been friendly and generous to his neighbours. He'd hosted parties for his children and their schoolmates. He'd sung songs, played the fool. He'd loaned money to Gavin, his closest neighbour, to enable him to fix his antiquated and leaking roof. He'd even given generously to the church, despite his reservations as to the merits of Presbyterianism.

The fact that Gramoz Makur was a ruthless, brutal criminal mastermind, responsible for the murder and misery of so many, was a taint only visible to God.

But it was time to go to ground, to make sure, to be safe. To plan retaliation from which his enemies could never recover.

Everything he needed would fit into two bags, a laptop case and backpack. Makur took the flash drive from his laptop and slid it into a pocket in his jacket. Carefully, he placed the computer into his the bag, which also contained some paper documents, two chargers and his iPad.

In the backpack, he had some clothes, medication for various ailments he'd picked up over the years, bank cards and a large wad of cash. You could trust cash, and he'd made sure the notes were issued by the Bank of England. If you stayed in Scotland, it was fine. Most Scottish banks issued their own, but he'd noticed how sniffy some traders south of the border were when presented with a 'Scotch' note.

There were only two items left on his desk: his burner phone, and a Glock 19. He'd always liked the weapon. It was compact and powerful, and he had extra ammunition already in the backpack. After all, you couldn't be too careful.

He made sure the phone was off and put it into his pocket. The Glock, he slid into the discreet shoulder holster, more than disguised by the bulky down climbing jacket he was wearing.

Makur heard a call from downstairs. 'Jotir, I'm just coming down.' He noted the familiar voice reply, made one last check of his desk and headed for the old oak staircase. Even from here, he could hear the reassuring tick of the old clock.

As he made his way down the stairs, he could see Jotir standing in the large hall, near the front door, for which he had a key. His trusty lieutenant looked pale, even at this distance. No wonder, reasoned Makur. The man had lost many good friends in the attack by the Paisley mob. And though vengeance burned in his soul, he was better able to hide his true feelings than the lieutenant he had mentored since their army days. However, there was nobody he trusted more.

'Let me wind the clock before we go.' Jotir was framed in the grey light of the open doorway. Gramoz saw him nod in reply and walked down the hall to where the grandfather clock stood.

'Listen, I know how you must feel. I feel it too, don't ever think otherwise. But the good thing is that we are alive. We will mourn those we lost; we will toast their memory. But we must go on, you know that. We will have revenge.'

It was with pleasure that he opened the casement of the old clock once more and reached for the big key. He ran his hand down the walnut veneer. 'For now, old friend, it is goodbye.'

Before he inserted the key into the winding mechanism, he slipped the backpack from his shoulder and left it on the floor beside the computer case. As he began to wind, he heard footsteps approach. 'The car key fob is on the table behind me, Jotir. You drive. I had too much to drink last night, thinking of our fallen comrades.'

The solid click as he wound up the clock was as satisfactory as usual. It was a ritual he enjoyed. But this winding would only last a couple of days at best. Then the clock would fall silent. For some reason, this made him feel unutterably sad. It was like saying goodbye to an old friend.

The first shot hit Makur in the back of the head, propelling him into the clock he loved so much. The next three thudded into his back, making great black holes in his light blue jacket. A single goose feather rose up and then fell slowly to the floor. Soon, like a little boat, it was carried on a gathering pool of dark blood, as the stricken man lay dead, half on the floor, half in the clock. The last swing of the pendulum he so admired hit him in the side of the head. But for Gramoz Makur, time had already stopped.

Three men stood over Jotir now. He was on his knees in the plush hallway, the blood of his master slowly seeping like a pool towards him on the black-and-white tile floor.

'Fuck you!' he shouted. The same words in Tosk, his native tongue, were forming in his head, but before he could give them life, his was gone with two sharp shots to the head and one to the heart.

Jotir's body slumped forward, and soon, as it had for centuries in the far-away Albanian village, his blood mixed with that of Gramoz Makur.

43

Senga Finn pulled herself off Joe Mannion. She could feel her heart pounding in her chest. A film of cooling sweat covered her following her exertions.

They were in a nondescript chain motel in Edinburgh, far from the prying eyes of Paisley and Glasgow. The room was clean and modern, and she preferred it to the squalid hotel that had, hitherto, been the venue for their secret liaisons. But it, thanks to her husband, was gone.

She slumped by Mannion's side, but as she tried to place her head on his heaving chest he pushed her away.

'What's wrong?' she asked, propping herself up on one elbow.

'I can't breathe, that's what. You'll need to give me some space, woman.'

'Oh, I am sorry. I should have remembered I'm fucking an old man.' She rolled to the other side of the bed and grabbed a pack of cigarettes and a lighter.

'You can't smoke in here,' said Mannion.

'Says who?'

'Says me and Premier Inns, that's who.' He grabbed the cigarette packet from her and crushed it in his big hand.

'Why did you do that, you miserable old bastard?'

'Because we came all the way over here so we wouldn't attract attention to ourselves, remember? When you set the fire alarms off, the whole of Edinburgh will be clocking us.'

'Oh, the drama.'

'It's not drama.' He paused. 'Anyway, I need to talk to you about something.'

'Don't tell me you've got crabs.'

'Fuck off! How is it you've such a twisted mind?'

'Spending too much time with arseholes from the East End of Glasgow, likely.'

He grabbed her wrist. 'I'm being serious. We have to talk.'

'Let go, you old bastard.' She struggled from his grip. 'Say what you want to say, but don't grab me like that again!'

'Listen, sorry. But I need to get your attention.'

'Here we go.'

'I can't do this any more.'

'What, fuck me?'

'Exactly.'

'Frightened of your wee wizened wife? I know your balls aren't very big, but I thought they were bigger than that.'

Mannion thought for a moment. 'What do you mean, my balls aren't very big?'

She shrugged. 'I've seen bigger, that's all.'

'No doubt gained from your wide experience of bollock sizes, eh? When you've shagged half the men from here to Paisley, you'll be an expert, I'm sure.'

'Fuck you! If you think I'm going to get all teary-eyed that you and me aren't going to walk off into the sunset, well, think again. I'll soon find some young buck that can go all night, not some broken down old codger.'

'You see, that's just why this has to stop. I don't want to keep you back from enjoying the company of someone your own age.' He pushed himself up in the bed. 'Mind

276

you, don't you think you're being a wee bit optimistic about picking up some "young buck"? I might not be old, but you're no spring chicken either, darling.'

Senga Finn didn't reply. She just lay back in the bed and looked at the ceiling, a blank expression on her face. 'You know what, just you get to fuck. I'm going to stay here another night, go out on the town, pick up some guy, bring him back here and fuck his brains out in this bed.'

'Aye, good luck with that, Senga. Take it from me, you don't look at your best when you've had a drink. So if I was you, I'd stick to orange juice before you try and pick up some guy.' He slid his feet onto the floor. 'Fuck this, I'm having a shower, then I'm going back to Glasgow.'

'Aye, you do that, you withered old cunt.' She bit her lip as she watched him pad across the room to the shower. From behind, he looked like a partially deflated balloon from a children's party – all wrinkled and misshapen. 'By the way, I was faking it – aye, every time!'

'Who cares. I wasn't.' Mannion closed the bathroom door and soon she heard the patter of water from the shower.

Senga shook her head. 'Bastard,' she said under her breath, as she scanned the floor for her clothes.

She noticed the mobile phone sitting on the nightstand on his side of the bed. As the steady drip of water still sounded from the shower, she stretched over and picked it up. Her first thought was to take a picture of herself and send it from Mannion's phone to his wife. She smiled wickedly at this prospect. Senga knew he hadn't set a password on the phone because he'd told her he could never remember it. And, being an older model, she didn't have to worry about Face ID or fingerprint scanners. She knew it wasn't the burner phone he used for 'business', but still, it would be a tool for her revenge. Sure enough, it opened like a dream. The home screen was a picture of his granddaughter.

He was humming in the shower now, so instead of taking the photograph she decided to look through his emails. There seemed to be nothing interesting: the usual come-ons from online companies, and trash, along with the odd anodyne email from his wife. She was about to flick off the emails when one caught her attention.

When Senga opened it, it took her breath away. She dropped the phone on the bed like a hot coal, just as she heard the shower turn off. Quickly, she switched Mannion's phone off and returned it to the nightstand.

Seconds later, the elderly gangster reappeared, wrapped in a large bath towel.

'Just get changed and get to fuck,' said Senga, trying her best to sound casual.

'My pleasure.'

She looked on as he dressed.

As he slipped on his jacket he caught her eye. 'All good things come to an end, Senga. Like you say, you'll soon find somebody else.'

'Oh, I'm heartbroken – not!'

He shrugged. 'It wasn't all bad, eh?'

Senga looked away.

Mannion threw a few items into a holdall, picked up his phone from the nightstand, snapped on his gold watch and left the room. Nothing else passed between them.

As soon as he left, Senga rushed to the toilet and was copiously sick. When she'd emptied the contents of her stomach, she rinsed her mouth. Her hand was trembling so much that some of the water fell onto her bare feet.

Senga leaned on the sink and took deep breaths. Then the tears began to flow.

*

Mannion was halfway along the M8 towards Glasgow when his phone rang. His son had set it up to automatically connect to the car's Bluetooth, so all he had to do was press a button on the steering wheel. It was his wife.

'Hello, dear.'

'Where are you, Joe?'

'Just on the motorway. I had some business in Edinburgh. Glad to be heading back home, to be honest. What's up? You sound tense.'

'Sammy, he's driving me mad with phone calls. He's been trying to get you.'

Mannion realised that he'd left the phone he used for business switched off in the glove box. He knew Sammy Sloane well enough to reckon that, more than likely, something insignificant had happened. Sammy was known to panic at the least thing when his boss wasn't around. 'No worries, I'll drop into the Iron Horse on the way back. Likely the Guinness is off or something. You know what he's like.'

'It sounded urgent, Joey.'

'Ach, I'm sure. I'll see you at about six, okay?'

'Yeah, bye, love. Hope you had a good meeting.'

He clicked off the phone without a reply. Gangster and serial philanderer he may be, but Mannion wasn't immune to bouts of guilt when he'd been unfaithful to his wife. After all, she came as a package with his children and grandchildren, and that was important to him.

He thought back to Senga Finn, spitting fury in the motel room. Well rid, he considered. Sure, she was attractive to look at, but coming events would render what relationship they had impossible. In any case, she had a deeply unattractive side to her personality, and Mannion had more than his fair share of unattractive personalities to deal with.

He looked at the time on the dashboard. With any luck he'd miss the start of the rush hour and be at the Iron horse in just over thirty minutes. He turned on the stereo and cruised in the middle lane to the soothing tones of Frank Sinatra.

*

Senga was dressed now. With still trembling hands, she was dialling on her phone.

First she tried her husband, but his mobile was switched off. Her next thought was to try Chancellor Fabrications, but nobody of consequence was around. She called Donnie Paton's mobile number: at last, an answer.

'Aye, Senga, how can I help you?'

'I need to talk to Zander, and quickly.'

'Haven't seen him, though I know he's out somewhere.'

'Out?'

'Didn't you know? He got huckled for those attacks.'

'No, I didn't.' She mentally cursed the fact that Joe had more than likely known about this but said nothing.

'I might be able to do something.'

Senga bit her lip. She knew the old tale about keeping important things close to her chest. Her time as Paton's boss hadn't gone smoothly; in fact, this was the first conversation they'd had in months. 'No, it's okay, Donnie.

Just do me a favour and get Zander to call me. Tell him it's really important.'

Having finished with Donnie Paton, her next call was to her daughter Gillian.

44

Gillian picked up the phone from the table in the restaurant and stared at the screen. She raised her eyes to her sister. 'It's Mum.' They were together in an Italian restaurant in Glasgow's trendy Merchant City. The lunchtime crowds had gone, and the place was quiet. Still, it was open all day, and her mother's intrusion promised to ruin a nice long lunch.

Sandra grimaced. 'Just when we were relaxing, as well. Fling her a deafy, Gildy.'

Gillian hesitated and then decided to ignore the call. 'You're right. Mum always leaves me on edge these days.'

'Aye, especially since our dear father came back from the dead.' Sandra moved uncomfortably in her seat, her stomach bulging in pregnancy.

'It must be really uncomfortable. You know, with your bump and all.'

'You bet it is, sis. Do yourself a favour: forget having babies. It's bad enough now, and I haven't even got to the difficult bit yet.'

'Huh, you sound like Mum.'

'Oh yeah.' Sandra put the back of one wrist to her forehead and feigned a distraught expression. 'The pain, oh the pain of it. You'll rue the day,' she said, adopting her mother's tones.

'Ha! Just like her.'

'Well, it's not as though I haven't been listening to her for long enough, is it? But, seriously, when I see these guys with the big beer guts, I think, what the fuck? How can you bear being this uncomfortable?'

'I'm sure it's not the same.' Gillian laughed and took another sip of white wine.

'How can it not be? It's like carrying your weekly shop around in a big bag on your stomach.'

'Now you're really beginning to sound like Mum.'

Sandra took in her sister's face. She still had bags under her eyes, and her skin was pale. Otherwise she was much improved when compared to the poor wretch who had lain in the hospital bed after her overdose. 'Can I ask you something?'

As though reading her sister's mind, Gillian replied with an answer before the question had been asked. 'No, I'm not going to do it again.'

'That wasn't my question, Gillian.'

'What, then?'

Sandra lowered her voice. 'All this stuff with the Albanian gangsters. . . . do you think Dad was behind it?'

'No! He was with me at the theatre. We even went to a pub after. These people, you know what they're like.'

'These people?'

'The Albanians, whatever. They're always fighting amongst themselves. Ask Dad, he'll tell you.'

'Yes, I'm sure.'

'You know what it's like for him. He's always the one to blame. He only came back because . . .' Gillian's voice trailed off.

'Yes, why did he come back?'

'He hasn't told you?'

'No. Why would I ask, otherwise?'

Gillian looked round the room. A bored waiter smiled at her. She ignored him. 'It was because Uncle Malky thought we were in danger.'

'*He* certainly was.'

'You know what Malky was like. He never gave up, not like Dad, Sandra.'

'Wow! I might be beginning to sound like Mum, but you're starting to sound like our father! I seem to remember people saying that about Danny.'

'I'm just saying that Dad doesn't want any more trouble. He just wants to keep us safe – get on with things at Chancellor, go straight.'

'And that's why they arrested him?'

'They go for anyone with a past. Dad was the easy option. I gave my statement to our solicitor. He's out, you know that.'

'Yeah, probably off getting pissed.'

'Wouldn't you be?'

'I could murder any drink right now. As soon as I push this sprog out, I'm going to get plastered.'

'Aw, don't call him a sprog!'

'Him? You're confident. Even we don't know. I think it's bad luck.'

'It's a boy, definitely.'

'Mystic Gillian, over here.'

As they laughed at the joke, a waiter appeared at the table.

'Can I offer you ladies something from the dessert menu?'

Sandra gave him a doubtful look. 'Something? Just give me the whole lot.'

The sisters burst into more laughter.

It was impossible. Senga Finn knew she had to do something, but she couldn't get anyone on the phone. Without stopping to shower or even putting on her lipstick, she was dressed and heading for reception.

'I'd like to check out, please,' she said to the fat youth behind the desk.

'Are you sure?'

'What?' The question was sharp.

'Just the gentleman – you know, the one you booked in with – he said you were staying the night.'

'Well, he was wrong, wasn't he?'

A knowing smile spread across the youth's face.

'What's up with your coupon?'

'Nothing.' He shrugged. 'How would you like to pay, cash or card?'

'You mean my friend didn't pay the bill?'

'No, he said you were covering it. The room is in your name, Mrs McGinty.'

'I'll pay by cash.' Senga rummaged in her handbag for her purse. 'How much?'

The receptionist looked at his computer screen. 'Sixty-nine, ninety-five, please.'

Hands still trembling, Senga counted out the money from a roll of ten-pound notes. 'There's seventy quid.'

'Hang on and I'll get your receipt and your change.'

'I don't need a receipt,' she said, as she zipped up her handbag. 'And please, keep the change. Put it towards a membership of Weight Watchers, you cheeky fat bastard!'

With that, Senga Finn turned on her heel and ran out to her car.

Joe Mannion pulled up in his space outside the Iron Horse. There were no markings on the road reserving it or cones to block it off, but everyone in the neighbourhood knew that this was where the 'big man' parked his car.

Before entering the pub, Mannion lit a cigar. He had to puff at it a few times before clouds of grey smoke emerged, fusing with the grey sky above, as spits of rain began to fall.

As he walked through the bar, the usual sight greeted him. Three elderly women were sitting next to the toilet door, and an old man was hammering a tune he couldn't recognise from the badly maintained piano. There were a few worthies slumped against the bar, and a table occupied by three young men who didn't look old enough to be of drinking age.

Mannion sighed. He wasn't particularly bothered about this. After all, he hadn't seen a police officer grace the salubrious surroundings of the Iron Horse since the late nineties. Still, he wanted to draw as little attention to his place of business as he could. 'Hey, Pavel, why the fuck did you serve they boys?'

The Polish barman, who looked perpetually bored, managed to drag his gaze from the horse racing and turned to his boss. 'They deliver a package for Mr Sammy. I think they wait for a reply.'

'Mr Sammy? Is this *Basil Brush* or some fucking thing?'

'Basil who?'

'Never mind.' Mannion looked back at the boys at the table. He didn't know them, and he knew most of the lads that age in the area. 'Cokes, no more alcohol, do you understand?' He bounded up the steep stairs behind the bar to his office.

Mannion was about to berate Sammy Sloane for encouraging underage drinking in his establishment, when a large wooden crate on his desk caught his eye. 'What the fuck is that, Sammy?'

'Fucked if I know, big man. They boys delivered it. Said it's only to be opened by you and they've to bring back an answer.'

'You don't say. So it's not Amazon, then?'

Sammy furrowed his brow. 'No, I don't think so. How, have you ordered anything, like?'

Mannion made his way towards the box on his desk. 'Aye, two toasters and a spice rack.'

'There's your answer, then. I must admit, it had me worried; I tried to get you on the phone, but . . .'

'I'm being sarcastic, you thick bastard! Get a knife and open it up.'

Sammy Sloane bent down and removed something from his boot. In a second, a stiletto blade flashed from its casing and the big man set to work at opening the box. 'Here. I think I'll need a jemmy, big man.'

'Use this.' Mannion reached under his desk and pulled out a short sword. 'Lever the bastard open with it.'

Sloane looked at him, open-mouthed.

'What's wrong? Have you never seen anybody pull a sword out of their desk before? Just get moving!'

Sammy Sloane grabbed the weapon and soon the lid of the box's wooden casing split open. 'Here, it's stuffed with these wee polystyrene balls.'

'Well, pull them out!'

Sloane cupped his hand into the box, then recoiled.

'What's up?'

'There's something wet in there.' He examined his hand,

which was slathered in blood. 'What the fuck?'

'Here, give it to me!' Mannion thrust his hand into the box and grabbed at what felt like a wet dog's coat. He hauled out a severed head, blood dripping from what was left of the neck.

'Oh, you bastard!' said Sammy Sloane, taking two involuntary steps backward.

Mannion held up the head and examined its features. 'Do you recognise him?' He still had a grip of the grotesque object by the ruffle of blood-stained red hair.

'Naw. How, do you?'

Mannion let the head go. It landed with a damp thud on the linoleum, sightless eyes staring up at the ceiling. He delved further into the box and removed a plastic envelope. He opened it and pulled his reading glasses from the breast pocket of his jacket before peering at the printed note.

'The last Albanian. Now, do what we discussed. Everything is in place. G.'

Joe Mannion read on. There was the name and address of a Glasgow restaurant underneath the main message.

'Okay, Sammy. Phone Davie and the boys. They know what to do. Give them this address.' He handed the anonymous note to Sloane. 'Aye, and tell they weans down in the bar that the matter is in hand. Give them a ton for their trouble.'

'What about that?' said Sloane, looking in disgust at the severed head.

'Och, we'll just leave that for the cleaner, eh?'

'Really? Are you sure?'

Mannion shook his head. 'Get the mop and bucket, Sammy. Aye, and make sure it's not stinking of pish this time.'

45

Senga Finn's nerves were frazzled as she arrived in the outskirts of Glasgow. So much for modern communication, she thought. She'd tried everybody, including both of her daughters and Zander. She'd left messages on all of their phones. But nobody had returned her calls.

She banged the steering wheel in frustration as the traffic in front of her slowed to a crawl. What was the point in having a mobile phone if you didn't answer it? Senga screamed in desperation, then thought of a last resort.

*

Amelia Langley was in an unmarked car not far from the pub in Argyle Street. They had a direct line of sight to the door through the straggle of shoppers and office workers making their way home from Glasgow city centre at the end of the day. She looked on as an old man with a walking frame stopped to take a puff of an inhaler.

'Poor old bastard,' said Neil Dickie. 'That's what's in store for us all.'

'If we're lucky,' replied Langley.

'It's a grim prospect.'

Langley checked the time on her phone. 'Finn must be well drunk by now. He's been in there for ages. Are you sure our guys are paying attention at that back door? He's a slippery bastard.'

'He's a hard bastard. Made short work of that pair of arseholes in the bar in Hope Street.'

'Richly deserved, from what the barmaid told us.'

'No doubt.' Dickie placed the radio to his mouth. 'Unit one, any sign of the subject, over?'

'No, sergeant,' came the instant reply.

'We'll give him another fifteen minutes, then we'll have to get somebody in there. I didn't want to do it – you know what an uncanny knack he has of spotting cops.'

'Well, if we're to keep tabs on what he's doing and who he's speaking to, I don't think we've much choice.'

Langley sighed. Why did everything have to be so complicated? She'd had to justify her actions to ACC Green, but she was convinced her superior was holding something back. She had agreed to Finn's release and covert observation all too readily. But, like everything else, Langley just had to do her best. She was too tired and disillusioned to second-guess everybody. Green must do as she saw fit, and she would do the same.

She sat back in her seat and closed her eyes, taking in the so familiar sounds of the city in which she was born. Loud voices, the intermittent rattle of trains from the nearby railway bridge, the squeal of bus brakes, the jarring punctuation of car horns: it was this symphony of Glasgow that lulled her into a much-needed doze.

*

Gillian was feeling more than merry. The wine had gone straight to her head. Unlike the rest of her family, she'd never been a heavy drinker. Her mother, father and siblings made up for that. Not to mention her grandmother, who could drink a sailor on shore-leave under the table. She enjoyed the effects of alcohol to a certain point, but dreaded the hangover that was bound to hit her the next day. Gillian also hated the feeling of losing control, the disorientation that inevitably overtook her if she drank too much.

She remembered being out with her father. With him, she hadn't minded the feeling of vulnerability, basically because she hadn't felt it. That Zander Finn, her father, would keep her safe from just about anything, she was certain.

Gillian smiled as Sandra waddled back from the toilet.

'Everywhere I go now is like climbing Everest. I'm knackered just going to the loo and back,' said Sandra.

'Not too long now,' Gillian replied.

They'd had a great chat, a catch-up. Sandra was sipping soda water and lime, while Gillian drank her wine with rather more gusto. A trickle of late afternoon/early evening customers were beginning to arrive, but their hosts seemed in no hurry to see the sisters leave.

'Why don't we do this much more often?' said Gillian.

Sandra shrugged. 'I guess it's just we've got separate lives – all of us. I mean, what's there to hold us together but Gran?'

'And her egg, beans and chips.'

Sandra laughed. 'You know, I wonder how Dad got so tall on a diet of that when he was growing up.'

'He seems to have done all right.'

Sandra pecked at a bit of biscuit from the big cheese board that sat between them. 'Do you ever think of Danny?'

'Wow, you hit me with that like a rock, sis.'

'I just wondered. It's something none of us ever talk about – or poor Robbie, come to that.'

Gillian gulped back the ache in her throat at the mention of her dead brother's name. 'I still miss him, so much. I mean, I know he could be an arsehole, especially when he was around those mates of his. But when he was on his own – well, he was different.'

'He was just our brother. I miss him too.' Sandra smiled at her sister. 'If you're right and the baby is a boy, I'm going to call him Danny.'

'Aw, that would be so . . .' Gillian hesitated.

'What?'

'Well, I was just wondering what Kevin's family will think of that.'

Sandra's face darkened. 'You still think Joe Mannion has something to do with what happened to Danny, don't you?'

'No – I don't know. Shit, Sandra, does it really matter now? He's gone, Uncle Malky – who next?'

'You can't think like that.'

'But I do.'

'Do you believe for one second that I'd stay with Kevin if I thought his family had anything to do with Danny's death?'

'No, I suppose not.'

'Wow, it's true what they say. Speak of the devil . . .' Sandra nodded towards the front door of the restaurant.

When Gillian turned round to follow her sister's gaze, sure enough, there was the father of her sister's unborn baby, Kevin Mannion, winding his way through tables towards them.

*

Maggie Finn was watching her favourite afternoon quiz show when a knock sounded loudly at the door of her flat. Recently, she'd been plagued by hawkers trying to sell her everything from dishcloths to sunglasses. This time, she was ready for them. From under a cushion on the sofa she produced a short baseball bat. While she had no intention of using it, word would surely get around that the old dear with the leopard-print shoes was not to be messed with or disturbed. She strode purposely from the lounge as another knock echoed down the hall.

Maggie swung the door open with a flourish. 'Right, you bastard!' She brandished the baseball bat, then let it drop at the sight of her daughter-in-law standing forlornly in the close. 'What's up with you? The clap?'

'Listen, I need to come in, Maggie. There's no time to waste.'

Maggie Finn was many things, but a fool she was not. She recognised someone who was really worried when she saw them. 'Come in, Senga. What on earth's wrong with you?'

'We've got to do something. We've got to get a hold of Zander!'

*

Amelia Langley opened her eyes with a start. 'Fuck, how long have I been asleep for?'

DS Dickie looked at his watch. 'Just over twenty minutes, boss. You looked that knackered. I didn't have the heart to wake you.'

'Any sign of our man?'

'No, and he's not dodged out the back either.'

'Right, send one of them in. And tell them to look as inconspicuous as possible.'

Neil Dickie gave the order to unit one. In a couple of minutes, a tall man with a leather jacket appeared at the pub's front door and entered.

'Shit, he looks just like a cop with a leather jacket on. Finn will clock him in two seconds.'

'Relax. He'll be fine. And remember, big Zander's had a few. He likely won't be seeing straight.'

'Oh, you think?'

For Langley, the wait was excruciating. They couldn't contact the officer inside the bar, for fear of breaking his cover. But as the seconds ticked by she began to feel more anxious. 'Does this idiot know what he's doing?'

'Young Milroy? Aye, he's a good lad – quick on the uptake. Keep calm.'

A few more seconds passed. Langley looked at her watch. 'Well, where is he?'

As these words left her lips, Milroy walked out of the bar and looked in their direction. Once he spotted their car, he shrugged his shoulders, holding his arms out in an 'I don't know' gesture.

'Bastard!' shouted Langley. 'Come on, let's get over there.'

The pair left the car, crossing the busy road with care but as rapidly as they could.

Langley was first through the door. This place was a very different prospect to Finn's first port of call. The bar was old-fashioned, populated mainly by older men. It was dark, and a roaring fire added a feeling of claustrophobia rather than comfort. The barman was a silhouette against the bright gantry, the brightest source of light in the room.

Langley flourished her warrant card, engendering a hush akin to that of a Western saloon when the gunslinger arrives.

'Aye, what can I do for you?' said the barman, laconically polishing a pint tumbler.

'There was a man in here. He arrived over two hours ago. Tall, dark hair, with a white streak, just about here.' She pointed to her own head to make the description clearer.

The barman stroked his chin. 'Wait a minute. You know, when you work in here, every bugger kind of looks the same. I'm just counting the minutes until I can go home and get my feet up.'

Langley stepped closer to the bar. 'Don't play the old soldier with me. I'll have my men pull this place apart if you don't co-operate. Are you sure your books are up to date, or are you able to vouch for every item of stock you have on the premises?'

'Okay, hold your horses. I said I was trying to remember, that's all.'

'I hate the fucking polis,' said a voice from the back of the room. Langley looked round to see an elderly man with a white, balding head. He smiled back, revealing a brown, nicotine-stained set of teeth.

'Do yourself a favour, sir,' said Dickie.

'Aye, what would that be?'

'Shut the fuck up, eh?'

Langley looked back at the barman. 'Well?'

'Now you come to mention it, I do remember this guy. Tall, like – late forties, maybe.'

'Yes, that's him.'

'He was feeling a bit squeamish. Your man's had a good few, by the way.'

'Is he in the toilet?'

'No, he went out the fire doors for a breath of fresh air. Must have been about half an hour ago. Bugger never came back. I went out to check, and he was gone.'

'Show me!' said Langley emphatically.

The barman led her and DS Dickie along a short corridor past doors marked out as 'Ladies and Gents'. The third door had the tell-tale metal bar across it and was marked 'Fire Exit' in luminous green letters.

'Open it,' said Langley.

The barman pushed and the door scraped open onto a narrow lane. Langley looked in both directions, then across to the neighbouring building. A fire escape zigzagged its way down its side, punctuated by fire doors similar to the one they had just stepped through on various floors.

'Shite!' exclaimed Neil Dickie.

Langley turned to him, glaring at her detective sergeant angrily. She then turned her attention back to the barman. 'What's in there?'

'Empty – used to be a carpet warehouse, but they've all gone online or out to the likes of Braehead.'

Langley walked to the wall of the opposite building and leaned against it, arms outstretched against the slimy brick. A used condom was floating down a moss-encrusted gutter.

'Fuck!' she said, slapping the wall with both hands in frustration.

46

The barman watched the detectives run up the lane and back into the Glasgow traffic on the main road. DS Dickie just had time to look over his shoulder with a wink before the barman smiled and walked back through the fire doors, securing them from the short corridor. There was a quiet murmur of conversation as he made his way back behind the bar.

'Is that the polis away, Willie?' said the bald man.

'Aye, not in very good humour, neither.'

The toilet door opened and a head popped round it. 'Good work, lads. I wasn't sure you'd pull it off,' said Zander Finn, taking his place back beside his bald friend.

'Zander, I was running away from the cops when your mother was still a lassie.'

'And that's not today or yesterday, Jackie, eh?'

'No, it is not. Anyway, they polis will be away scouting all over Glasgow for you now. This is the last place they'll come back to, son.'

'Aye, let's hope you're right because I've got more drinking to do. Drinks all round, Willie, and keep them coming.'

The tiny bar settled back to business as Willie the barman catered for a sudden rush of customers.

★

The Finn sisters were busy collecting their things together, ready to leave the restaurant. Sandra was tired, so Kevin had agreed to take her home first, then leave Gillian back at her flat. They left a twenty-pound tip for the waiters, who had been friendly, attentive and kind.

When the three of them stepped back into the grey light of Glasgow, Gillian felt disorientated. The same feeling she had whenever she left the cinema on a bright summer's night. It was a sense of dislocation, of things not being quite right. She supposed the wine hadn't helped, but she'd had such a good time. Sandra was always good company. Her sibling's relationship with a Mannion had lessened the time she'd spent with her, even though she liked Kevin.

She watched how attentive he was, as he helped Sandra across the road, fussing over her like an old mother hen. She could see the affection between them, even though Sandra bickered away. But that came from their grand-mother, who Sandra was most like.

Kevin had parked his BMW in a lane off Wilson Street. Crowds of smartly dressed office workers, bearded hipsters, chattering young couples, or just those looking for a change of scene, were making their way to the clubs and bars of the Merchant City. A tall, graceful woman dressed in a well-cut business suit swept past, ordering her phone to make appointments in her diary for the following day. Gillian watched them all as she headed for Kevin's car. She often wondered what motivated people to be part of this rat race; the same thing every day. It was all a constant grind of commuting, office politics, banter and assessments. This was the reason she'd chosen acting. You just never knew what – if anything – would happen next. Former students had gone from the Conservatoire and ended up in Hollywood. Likewise, others had failed to attract work and had either abandoned the stage altogether or toiled away in restaurants, or call centres, waiting to be famous.

Gillian wasn't too bothered about the uncertain nature of the profession she'd chosen. In fact, she was galvanised by the idea of the challenge; of meeting new people and working in new places. She knew, for her, money would never be an object. She reasoned that she was fortunate – she saw herself walking the tightrope with a large safety net beneath her. But hey, the way things were with her family, she reckoned that she more than deserved a break, some compensation for the stress and heartbreak of being one of the notorious Finn clan.

'That's us,' said Kevin, as he pointed the key fob at his car. 'Jump in, ladies.'

Gillian heard the phone ring in her handbag.

'Mum's in one of her needy moods today, that's for sure,' Sandra observed.

'Yeah. I'll wait until I get home and have another glass of wine in my hand before I call her back.'

'That's big of you. I wouldn't bother. I'm afraid her and I have little in common these days.'

'Don't cut her off, Sandra. She'll always be our mum.'

'And she'll always behave like a randy teenager. We haven't spoken in a while.'

Gillian shrugged. There wasn't much she could say in her mother's defence on that score. But nonetheless, she still loved her.

Soon they were back in the rush-hour traffic, heading for Sandra and Kevin's flat.

★

'I'm his mother, not his keeper,' said Maggie Finn, as she and Senga headed along the M8 in Senga's SUV.

'I'm his wife, and I've never known what the fuck he gets up to.'

Maggie looked out of the window wistfully. 'His father was just the same.'

'I remember. Will you try Zander again? I know he just won't pick up for me, anyway.'

'There's no point. If he's off on a guilt trip, he won't speak to anyone apart from the old worthies he enjoys the company of so much.'

'And you're sure he's not in some dive in Paisley?'

'Come on, Senga. He's not going out in Paisley after something like this has happened – or Renfrew, Johnstone or Bridge of Weir. He used to go to some place, but I can't remember where it is. If Malky was here, he'd know.'

'Well, he's not here.'

That Maggie Finn didn't get on with her daughter-in-law was a given. But she always admired the protectiveness she displayed when anything happened to her children. She supposed it was only natural, an instinct most parents could hardly avoid, though she knew a good few exceptions.

She had seen straight away that Senga was worried – frightened, even. So she was doing her best to appear as calm as possible, despite the cold grip on her heart.

'If anything else happens, I'll never forgive myself.' Tears were flowing down Senga's cheeks now.

'You've got to keep it together. We have to find the lassies and Zander, that's all.'

'All? If you could remember where his haunts in Glasgow are, we might stand a chance.'

Maggie stared at her. 'And you know there's something else we have to do.'

'But who can we trust now? I mean . . .'

'We can trust ourselves, Senga! Fuck, I thought you'd been in charge for the last two years.'

'I was kidding myself on. Sure, the money came in, but we know now that everything was a bloody mess – all fucking lies.'

'We all make mistakes. I've made plenty,' said Maggie.

'Huh! That's the first time I've heard that.'

'Well, you're hearing it now. You concentrate on driving. I need to speak to somebody.'

'Who?'

'That's my business. But if they can help, do you have an objection?'

'No.' Senga sounded weary and troubled. The traffic slowed again as they were snarled up in the thousands of cars making their way to and from the city.

*

Gillian Finn said goodbye to her sister and watched as Kevin helped her out of the car, then down the path to the flat they shared. This was Hyndland, the west of Glasgow, and everything was leafy and well kept, save for the odd gang tag on a wall here and there. It was a signal to the affluent that they should always look over their shoulders. After all, they might be rich, but this was Glasgow.

Sandra had invited her up for a glass of wine, but Gillian felt she'd taken up enough of her sister's time, and Kevin seemed anxious to get on.

He returned to the car after a few minutes, a broad smile spread across his face. Gillian tried to picture a young Joe Mannion and reckoned that Kevin was a reasonable facsimile. He was tall, his hair receding – something of which he was very self-conscious. But though they looked the same, Kevin had none of his father's bluster and bullying arrogance. If anything, he was withdrawn and rather shy. She liked these qualities. She had been unhappy that her family were unwilling to give him a chance, just because of who his father was. After all, she was in the same boat. Her recent experience with Kirsty proved that. Gillian hadn't asked to be part of one of Scotland's most notorious crime families, and neither had Kevin. She supposed they had a bond because of it.

Then she thought how different their respective families were. Her father – even her mother, come to that – were determined that their children wouldn't be tainted by the 'family' business. They'd encouraged all four of them to go and make their own lives. The fact that Sandra had struck up a relationship with the son of their father's arch-enemy was another thing entirely. Also, the fact Danny had refused to do anything but join his father wasn't really the fault of their parents. Then she thought of Robbie, and said a silent prayer that he would be okay.

'Want to know a little secret?' Kevin grinned at her.

'As long as it's a good one.'

'Oh, yes. I want to show you something.'

'Don't tell me, it's a pram.'

'Not even close.'

Gillian saw a bead of sweat on Kevin's brow. 'Are you feeling okay? You look hot.'

He cleared his throat. 'Yeah, actually I think I might be

coming down with something. I feel a bit fluey, if you know what I mean.'

'Man flu – you better tell Sandra, though. If you do have anything, it wouldn't be good for her and the baby.'

'Yeah, I will.'

Gillian was sure she could detect nervousness in his smile. After all, she was being trained to portray emotion with a raised brow here and a turned-down mouth there. It was part and parcel of the acting trade. But something told her that Kevin was doing his best to hide his feelings rather than display them.

'Is it our family? I wouldn't blame you if you were getting cold feet, Kevin.'

'No, nothing like that, honestly. Though it's not been easy, you know that. I thought your father was going to set about me when we were at your gran's the other day.'

'He would never do that – well, at least not at my gran's.'

'Thanks, you're really putting my mind at ease.'

'Sorry.' Gillian laughed, and some of the tension seemed to disappear from Kevin's face. 'So, this big secret, what is it?'

'I'm just about to show you.'

Kevin Mannion turned his car onto Great Western Road.

47

At last, Zander Finn was relaxed. The alcohol was having a soothing effect on his soul. Though he knew that tomorrow, along with a hangover, would come even more acute feelings of guilt and shame. It was a process he'd been dealing with for as long as he could remember. He'd fallen into this way of life when his father was murdered. And that murder had shaped him. The will to succeed, to be stronger than anyone else had, in his twenties, driven him to the kind of ruthless actions he'd ordered against the Albanians. But that act had in turn been driven by the murder of his friend Malky Maloney.

It was a cycle of violence, and he was well aware of it. If you were a barber, you cut hair. If you were a lumberjack, you cut down trees. If you were a surgeon, you cut people open. If you were in his line of work . . . well, you did what you had to do to prosper and survive.

But Finn had promised himself something. Now he'd rid himself of the Albanians, and addressed the problems with Joe Mannion, that was it. He was going straight, legitimate. He could do it. With all the threats to his family and friends removed, he would concentrate on building up Chancellor Fabrications. The rest of the crew could go on as normal, but they could do so by themselves; he wanted no part of it.

He remembered the feeling of having no pressure in his life for two years. It had been like being reborn. All he had to do was wake up in the morning, get himself out of the door, and help people. He'd amazed himself how quickly he'd adapted to driving the old people about. He'd made friends with them – well, most of them. Some were more challenging – like his mother, he supposed.

Then he was caught up with the guilt of wondering what would have happened if he hadn't returned, if he had refused to listen to Maloney's pleas to come back to Paisley.

Zander was aware of Jackie asking him a question. 'Sorry, I was miles away.'

'Aye, I could see that.' The old man mashed his gums together. 'You surprise me.'

'In what way?'

'My boys, aye, and their weans too. Never have they phones out of their hands. I've not seen you look at one since you arrived.'

'You know, you're right. I better switch the bloody thing back on and see what I've been missing.' Finn reached into the inside pocket of his jacket and pulled out the smartphone. He realised he hadn't switched it on since being released from custody earlier that morning.

He chatted to his old friend as the phone booted up. As expected, the pings and bleeps of notifications sounded as the mobile came back to life. He ignored them as he listened to the end of a joke.

'And the woman says, "Not with that horse in the room."' They both burst into fits of drunken laughter.

Wiping tears from his eyes, Finn picked up the phone and stared at the screen. He had a lot of phone messages. He dialled the number to retrieve them.

As he listened, his smile disappeared and his face became pale.

'Willie, have you got a motor?'

'Aye, it's in the car park at the St Enoch's Centre. Why do you ask, Zander?'

'Give me the keys!'

'Eh? Come on, big man. You've had a few.'

'Just give me them!' Finn's eyes flashed. 'And don't worry about the car, I'll buy you another one if anything goes wrong.'

'Are you sure? I mean, if you get caught, they'll throw away the key.'

'Just let me worry about that. What's the make and model – the reggie?'

Reluctantly, Willie reached under the bar and fished out a set of car keys. 'It's a pink Mini. "WES" are the last letters on the plate. You can't miss it.'

Finn looked him up and down.

'It's my daughter's motor. She's in Australia.' He shrugged.

Finn grabbed the keys and shot out of the door.

'A pink Mini? Fuck me. How do you manage to get into the bloody thing?' said Jackie.

'Just you keep drinking,' Willie replied.

*

Kevin Mannion pulled up outside a one-storey building on the far south side of Glasgow. It stood alone in some trees, a relatively new construction, though with an unkempt quality about it. Boarded-up windows, sprays of graffiti on the walls and broken glass in the car park adding to the impression.

'Well, what do you think?' said Kevin.

'What is it?' Gillian asked.

'It's an old Chinese restaurant. I picked it up for buttons.' He smiled broadly.

'Oh, great. What are you going to do with it?'

'I know it doesn't look much just now. But it has real potential.'

'It's a bit far out.' Gillian looked out of the car windows at the surrounding area. She could see some distant houses and a factory nearer by. 'It doesn't exactly have a big catchment area, does it? And you're not Chinese.'

'You have no vision. I'm going to turn it into a tech bar.'

'A what?

'A tech bar. You know, with VR headsets, big screens – all the latest stuff. Serve food, coffee – energy drinks. There's a railway station not far away. I'm telling you, it'll be great.'

Gillian bit her lip. 'You don't think that Sandra is going to be able to work in here, do you? Have you any idea how time-consuming having a baby is?'

'I'm not daft! This is for me – us. Something we can make money from, buy a proper house instead of a flat. It'll be our own, not my dad's. You must understand that, Gildy.'

She smiled. 'Yes, I see what you're doing. Just like me, really. Though instead of acting, you're running a pub.'

'Don't call it a pub! Come on, I'll show you inside. I have the keys.'

Gillian was caught up in his obvious enthusiasm for the project. Old-fashioned pubs were closing down all over the place. But this idea seemed to be a good one. Everyone her age loved phones, laptops and tablets – gaming. But not everyone could afford the expensive devices. She supposed that Kevin's idea was a sound one.

Gillian followed him out of the car. She looked at her phone: no signal. 'You'll have to get 5G, there's nothing here.'

'Don't worry. There will be superfast broadband all round.

Gillian shrugged. 'Okay, Mr Tesla, lead on.'

'Who?' Kevin looked confused.

'Never mind. Just show me this great new idea.'

★

Finn was speeding towards his eldest daughter's flat through heavy traffic. It was all he could think to do. Nobody else was answering. He'd called her, but, as expected, there was no reply. Unlike Gillian, Sandra hadn't forgiven him for disappearing. Their relationship was ice cold, despite his attempts to welcome her Mannion boyfriend to the family. *Mannion.*

He was stopped at traffic lights when he heard a car horn sound repeatedly. He looked across at the car in the next lane to his. Two young lads were blowing kisses at him. At first Finn was confused, but then he realised he was driving a pink Mini.

As they pulled away from the lights, he gave them a single finger gesture.

Finn looked at his watch. It was at least another fifteen minutes until he made it to Sandra's. Desperately thinking what to do, he dialled a number.

'Hello, Zander.' Donnie Paton's voice was calm and reassuring. He was back at his desk in Chancellor Fabrications. Though everyone else had left for the evening, he had things to do; things that were best done out of the gaze of secretaries and other colleagues.

'Donnie, I don't have much time. I want you to round everyone up. This is serious. I'll explain.'

Paton listened, and when Finn was finished he nodded. 'Okay, try not to panic, Zan. I'll round up the troops. We're ready, you know that.'

'Okay, thanks, Donnie. I know I can rely on you, buddy.'

Paton heard the call click off. He scrolled down his contacts until he came to the initials 'MG'. He pressed the screen and put the phone back to his ear.

'ACC Green, please.' Within moments, he was connected.

'Well,' said Mary Green at the Organised Crime Unit, 'I didn't think we'd be speaking again so soon, Mr Paton.'

Paton told her about the call he'd received from Finn. 'He's desperate, that's for sure.'

ACC Mary Green thought for a few moments. 'Okay, do as he says. Assemble your merry band of men. Make sure they come armed.'

'What?'

'Just do as I say, Mr Paton.'

'So you're going to spring them when they're tooled up. What about me?'

'You'll wait until they arrive, make an excuse and tell them you have to pop out for a few minutes. Let's say a little job for Mr Finn you can't tell them about. When you're on the road, call me. Then we'll call in the cavalry.'

Paton's face was pale now. 'What about Zander?'

'Well, I think he's about to meet his nemesis, is he not?'

'And you'll just let that happen?'

'Mr Paton, I know how sentimental you are about your criminal associates. But you can be assured of this: the ship is going down, whether you like it or not. If you want to be on that ship – well, stay. If not, and you want a clean break – a new name, a new life – then you'll do as I say.'

'So, people will die. I've known him since he was a boy!'

'How many other boys did you know that have been lying in the ground for years?'

'A few.'

'Also, I want to rid my country of shit like Finn. If, like the other night, one violent criminal chooses to turn on another – well, so be it. Saves me a job and the country a great deal of money. Do you see?'

'Yes.' Paton's tone was one of sad resignation.

'Think, very soon now you'll be free from all this. Oh, have you copied the books, as I asked?'

'I'm doing it now. I had no idea all this would kick off.'

'Belts and braces, then. Leave them in your desk, where I can find them. Just in case we need anything on Zander Finn.' She ended the call.

Paton sighed. He inserted a flash drive in the computer on his desk. The real set of books – the ghost books, as Zander Finn always referred to them – were enough to put him in jail for years for tax evasion and other financial crimes.

Before he could start the computer rolling he heard the buzzer coming from the front door. 'Fuck!' he swore. With a bit of luck one of the boys had heard about Finn's plight and they'd turned up early. If that was the case, they could call round the rest of the crew while he was busy with his clandestine work for ACC Green.

As he left his office to go and answer the door, he wondered what life would be like from now on. He'd wanted to move abroad for years. Now was his chance, and all paid for by the taxpayer, the very people he'd been defrauding for so long. But Donald Paton wasn't sentimental about it. He should have taken over the family when Willie

Finn had died. The man had been a liability. It had been down to Paton that the young Zander Finn was able to run and grow their 'business'. Did he feel guilty for saving his own skin? No. He'd suffered enough.

He hurried down the stairs as fast as his arthritic knees would allow – another reason for living somewhere warm, he considered.

*

Sandra Finn had enjoyed the long lunch with her sister, but she'd become more uncomfortable the longer she'd sat on the restaurant chair. She was glad to be home. All she wanted was a mug of herbal tea and to go for a lie-down.

She filled the kettle and looked out of her kitchen window at the long expanse of communal gardens at the back of the flats. They were well tended by the residents, and she often found herself staring out of this window, letting her mind wander.

She noticed a robin frighten away some starlings. It was a sure sign that winter was on the way. She remembered reading that robins were one of the most violent birds to be found, often fighting each other to death. If they were the size of eagles, there would likely be no other bird in the sky.

The size of eagles.

The words stuck with her.

She waddled to the cupboard, holding her aching back with both hands. She found the herbal teabags and went in search of her favourite china mug. Kevin was obsessively tidy, which sometimes annoyed her. She had to stand on tiptoes to reach the shelf where the mugs were kept.

Just as she managed to hook her fingers around the mug, she was doubled in two by a sharp pain in her stomach, sending the mug smashing to the ground.

Sandra was leaning against the kitchen unit now, agony etched across her face.

'Shit, not now,' she mumbled to herself. When she looked at her feet, she saw a wet pool. Suddenly she felt dizzy and fell to the floor, head spinning. As she landed, her face fell into one of the shards of what remained of her favourite mug.

Desperately, with blood pouring down her cheek, Sandra tried to pull herself to her feet. The fall had twisted her knee, and the slick laminate floor made matters worse.

She flopped back against the kitchen wall, screaming in pain. 'Kevin, where the fuck are you?'

*

Kevin Mannion turned first one key in a large padlock, then another in the door and pushed it open. He searched with one hand and flicked on a switch, bringing some strip lights bursting into life above them.

Gillian looked round. They were standing in a dusty, tiled corridor. The place smelled of decay and rotting food. Gillian screwed up her face in distaste.

'Don't worry, we'll soon get things cleaned up.' He beckoned her forward. 'Come and see the main area.'

They stepped into a room, which, without Kevin doing anything, was quickly illuminated in bright lights. It took a second for Gillian to note that they weren't alone. Three figures stood before them.

'Ah, young Miss Finn,' said Joe Mannion deliberately, as

though he were a foreigner speaking slowly to make sure he got it right.

'What's he doing here?' Gillian turned to Kevin, but he was already edging away down the tiled corridor, a guilty look on his face.

'You promised, Dad. Don't hurt her,' he said earnestly.

'Just you get back to that fat-bellied girl of yours. You did the deal. I bought you this place in return for bringing the charming Gillian here. Done! Now get to fuck.'

Gillian began to shake, as Kevin headed towards the door. He shook his head and shot her a look of apology.

'Sandra will never forgive you, you bastard!' shouted Gillian.

For a moment, the glow of streetlights shone through the opened door as Kevin Mannion disappeared, slamming it shut behind him.

'And who's going to tell your sister what our Kevin did?'

'What?' Gillian spun to face Joe Mannion.

'Och, dear, it pains me to do this, but there's a lot of dosh at stake. Anyway, they tell me you tried to top yourself not that long ago. You can't be that happy with your life.' He said this while puffing clouds of cigar smoke into the fetid air. 'When somebody finds you dead in some dive full of drugs, well, there's only one conclusion.'

'And you think my father will let you get away with this?'

'That's just why you're here. You're about to phone Daddy and tell him that you need him to come and rescue you. You know what a noble guy your father is. He'll come running to save his favourite little daughter.'

'Phone him yourself. I'm not doing it!'

Gillian was grabbed from behind, both arms pulled back painfully. Mannion put his face in hers, as she struggled with the pain. 'You'll do just what I ask you. It's my mate Sammy that has a grip of you, by the way. He's an expert at getting folk to do what he wants them to do. Aren't you, Sammy?'

'Sure am, big man.'

'Fuck you!' Gillian spat in his face and screamed in pain as Sammy Sloane pulled sharply on her twisted arms.

Mannion wiped the spit from his face with a hanky and glared at her. 'Do that one more time and I'll make sure when you're finally dispatched it'll be long and very painful.'

Despite herself, Gillian felt a sob rack her body.

Mannion grabbed her chin and pulled it up so she was looking straight into his eyes. 'That old granny of yours. I'm guessing you like her, aye?'

'What?'

'You see, she's about to take a tumble out of that window of hers – you know, the one on the seventeenth floor.'

'I don't believe you!' Gillian screamed.

'Well, you're here, aren't you? I mean, we did consider trying to lure Zander to come and save her, but I reckoned nobody – not even him – gives a flying fuck about that old tart, right?' He stood up and relit his cigar. 'Grab her phone, Davie.'

A man appeared from behind Mannion. 'Where will I look, big man?'

'Och, maybe she's got it hidden in her hair,' said Mannion. 'You think?'

'In her fucking handbag, you halfwit!'

'Oh aye, right enough.' Davie, a squat, powerful-looking man covered in colourful tattoos, grabbed the bag hanging from Gillian's shoulder. But she was struggling so much he found it impossible to look inside.

'Here,' said Mannion. He handed Davie a long-bladed stiletto knife. 'Cut the straps, for fuck's sake.'

When Davie did as he was asked, the bag fell onto the floor. He picked it up and handed it to Mannion.

The man with the cigar clamped between his teeth rummaged in the young woman's handbag. 'You know, maybe you can answer this question for me. What do you need with a huge bag like this? See, when I was a boy, women had neat wee bags. You could go on holiday for a fortnight with this bloody thing.' He smiled, cigar still between his teeth, as he pulled the mobile phone from the bag. He let the handbag drop at his feet and looked at the screen. 'Now, you be a clever lassie and unlock this.'

'No, I won't do it.'

'Suit yourself. Jim, fetch the buckets of water and that towel.'

'If you want to give me a wash, I'm perfectly clean, thank you.' Gillian screamed again as Sammy Sloane pulled her arms. They felt as though they would either snap or pop out of their sockets at any moment. The pain was excruciating. It was Sammy's trademark.

'Wash you? No, you smell quite sweet enough as it is. I'm going to drown you.'

Gillian screamed.

*

The steel door was heavy. It was locked at a number of points, but Donald Paton had his keys. When he pulled it open, he was surprised to see the man standing on the pavement. He knew him, of course. But somehow, seeing him here at Chancellor, he seemed out of place.

A light drizzle was now falling from the darkening sky over Abercorn Street. 'Come in, come in. I'm afraid it's not a very good time.' Paton showed his new guest into the hallway beside the main office. 'But I'll do my best to help if I can.' He locked the door and was about to take his visitor up to his office when he felt a jarring pain in the small of his back. Before he could turn, strong hands caught him around the neck.

The room began to spin, as his pain and desperation increased. His attacker was muttering something, but not intended for the man he was strangling.

For Donald Paton, everything went black.

48

Zander Finn pulled the Mini up onto the pavement outside Sandra's block of flats.

An old man shook his head at him as he left the car. 'You can't park here,' he shouted. 'You've not got a parking permit.'

'Mind your own business,' said Finn, as he ran for the close door.

'Cheeky bastard,' the man spat, then carried on his slow march down the road.

Finn bounded up the steps and hammered on Sandra's door. 'Open up! I need to speak to you!' He was breathless, his heart pounding.

There was no sound of approaching footsteps in the hall, so he put his ear to the door. It was then he heard a distant cry for help.

'Sandra!' he yelled. When there was no answer, he put his shoulder to the door. It took a few hits to make an impression, by which time his shoulder ached. Wood snapped, but to gain full entry he had no choice other than to kick the door in.

Finn ran into the hallway. He could hear his daughter shouting again, her desperate cry coming from the kitchen.

'Dad,' she said, as she saw her father appear round the kitchen door.

Finn took in the scene with barely disguised horror. His eldest daughter's face was plastered with blood, and she looked pale and frightened. 'Who did this to you?'

'What?' Sandra tried to move.

'Who did this. I want to know now!'

'I'm having a baby, you idiot!'

'What?' Finn looked confused.

'The baby – my waters have broken.'

'Shit!'

'My father: just the man for a crisis. Please, you have to get me to hospital.' Sandra's face was distorted with pain.

'Okay, I'll call an ambulance.' Finn pulled the phone from his pocket.

'Are you still living in the eighties, Dad? I can't wait for an ambulance. You'll have to take me.'

'Right, okay.' Finn stood over her helplessly.

'You'll have to help me up first!'

'Yes, of course.' Finn leaned over his stricken daughter and hauled her to her feet. 'Where's Gillian?'

'What?'

'Gillian – where is she?'

'Home by now – I don't know. Anyway, what can she do?'

'Were you with her this afternoon?' Finn had her arm around his shoulder and was helping Sandra out of the kitchen.

'Fuck, I'm about to have a baby and all you're worried about is where my sister is!' She cried out as she put weight on her twisted knee.

'What's wrong?'

'When I fell, I hurt myself.'

'Here, just stand still.' Finn lifted his daughter in his arms, the blood from her face staining his shirt. 'You didn't used to be this heavy.'

'Cheers, Dad,' said Sandra through gritted teeth.

'Come on, but I need to know about Gillian.'

'We had lunch, what's the problem?' Father and daughter were out on the landing now. Finn staggered, as he took the first step. 'Shit! Don't drop me, Dad.'

'It's okay, trust me. But you need to tell me where Gillian went after lunch.'

A figure appeared at the bottom of the stairs.

'Kevin!' shouted Sandra. 'Where the fuck have you been?'

'You know where I've been. What's wrong, where are you going?' He looked between Sandra and her father as he carried downstairs.

'My dad's taking me to the swing park, what the fuck do you think?'

'Where's your car?' Finn demanded.

'Just a bit down the street. Some wanker has parked a pink Mini in my space.'

'That's mine.'

'You've got a pink Mini? What the fuck is going on? Have they given me the gas and air already.' Sandra looked bewildered.

'Come on, Kevin. You need to get Sandra to the hospital.'

Kevin Mannion looked non-plussed. Here was the man who terrified him, carrying Sandra, his partner, who had blood pouring from a wound on her face. 'What have you done to her?'

'Eh?' said Finn, struggling under the weight of his pregnant daughter as he made for the close door.

'I fell, Kevin. Just do what he says, for fuck's sake!'

Finn carried Sandra down the path and out onto the pavement.

'Your car – where?' said Finn, breathing heavily.

'There, follow me.'

Soon Finn was manhandling his daughter onto the back seat of Kevin's BMW.

'Will I get a towel, or something?' said Kevin.

'If you're worried about me staining your upholstery, we're finished.' Sandra glared at her boyfriend.

'Just get her to hospital, you clown!' Finn leaned into the car. 'You have to tell me about Gillian.'

'Kevin took her home. That's where he's been. Why are you so worried about her, right now of all times?'

'Okay, you relax. You'll be in hospital, soon.' He closed the door. Finn beckoned Kevin behind the car.

'What, Mr Finn?'

Zander grabbed the father of his unborn grandchild by the throat. 'I know what your father is doing. Tell me where my daughter is, or I swear I'll cut your throat right here!'

'She's at the old Chinese on Springpark Road. Not far from St Brandon's.'

'You took her there, didn't you?' Finn tightened his grip on Kevin's throat.

'My father – I had no choice.'

Sandra screamed from the car.

'Get her to hospital. But I swear, if you had any part in any harm coming to my daughter, you won't live to see your baby.' He pushed the younger man away.

★

320

Maggie Finn directed her daughter-in-law along the road in the East End of Glasgow.

'I'd really like to know what we're doing here,' said Senga.

'Trust me. Don't you know this is where your boyfriend does his business?'

'He's not my boyfriend.'

'He was until this morning.'

'Piss off. This isn't important now, is it?'

Senga pulled the car up across the road from the Iron Horse. 'What now?'

'We go in and find this bastard, that's what.'

'Really?'

'Do you want to find Gillian or not? This is where he takes people.'

'How do you know?'

'Trust me, I just know.' Maggie looked her son's estranged wife in the face. 'All the time you thought you were being smart, you were just putting everyone at risk. Joe Mannion is a snake, he always has been.'

'I'm not here to talk about who I do and do not see, Maggie.'

'Come on!' Maggie opened her door and was soon heading across the street.

The bar looked deserted from the outside, but, then again, that was exactly the way it had been designed. Only barred windows, high up on the wall, let out some light to indicate that there was anyone within. The big door was heavy. But Maggie forced it open. She looked around the bar, hands on hips. 'Right, where's Big Joe?'

'Ho-ho, now we're talking,' said the elderly pianist, adjusting his flat cap in order to impress. 'Where did you spring from, honey, eh?'

'I'll spring my toe up your withered arse.' Maggie approached the bar, Senga behind her. 'You, son, where's Joe Mannion?'

Pavel shrugged. 'How should I know? I work for him, he doesn't work for me.'

'Well, you'll not mind if we head up for a look, then, eh?' Maggie tried to make her way behind the bar to access the stair to Mannion's office above.

Two middle-aged women stood. One of them, her thighs thundering under tight jeans, grabbed Maggie by the collar of her jacket and dragged her back. 'If the boy says Mr Mannion isn't in, he isn't in. Got it?'

'Are you his wife?' Maggie turned to Senga with a knowing look.

'Naw, I'm a friend of his. And if you want to keep that wrinkled coupon of yours intact, then you'll fuck off back to wherever you came from.'

'I can't match a big lassie like you,' Maggie replied. 'Here, Senga, we better get going. We'll get no joy here.'

As everyone, including the bruiser who still had a loose grip her collar, turned to face Senga, Maggie twisted from her grip and grabbed a glass bottle of lemonade that was sitting on the bar. In one fluid movement, she crashed it off the head of the woman who'd grabbed her.

'You old bastard!' shouted her friend, and made to grab Maggie.

Maggie smashed the bottle off the bar and was left holding only what was left of it in her hand, as glass splintered onto the linoleum floor. 'If you'd like this in your teeth, then just come ahead, you fat cow.' She flourished the broken bottle in the woman's face by way of a further deterrent.

'I've seen it all now,' Pavel muttered, as he located himself nearer to the TV at the other end of the bar. 'Go up, if you want. You are a mad woman.'

'Thank you, son. Just you make sure that Hardy and Hardy here don't follow us.'

'They wouldn't make it up the stairs, carrying that weight,' he replied, without taking his eyes from the horse racing. 'But you'll be disappointed. There's nobody there.'

'Aye, well, I'll just have a look myself, if you don't mind.

Maggie and Senga made their way behind the bar and took to the steps leading to Joe Mannion's place of business.

49

Zander Finn was back behind the wheel of the pink Mini when his phone rang. He picked it up, hoping to see Gillian's name, but was disappointed. The screen just read 'Private number'. Nonetheless, he decided to answer.

Finn put the phone to his ear. At first the sound on the other end was hard to discern, but soon he thought he could make out the cross between a gasp of breath and a sob. 'Gillian, is that you?'

'No, but you're close, right enough.'

Finn instantly recognised Joe Mannion's voice, as it curled from his phone like a serpent. 'That's your wee lassie you can hear. Do you want to know what we're doing to her?'

'I swear, Joe. You and all your men will go exactly the same way as these Albanian bastards!'

'Typical, eh? You never listen, just want to speak. You just love the sound of your own voice.'

As Finn listened in, he heard a muffled scream.

'Not that you're interested, Zander, but we're water-boarding her – neat, eh?'

'I know where you are and I'm coming for you. This is your last fucking day, Joe Mannion.'

'Oh dear.' Mannion adopted a mocking tone. 'Are you in a bad mood because I've been fucking that tart of a wife of yours, or my son got your other slut daughter up the stick? I just can't make up my mind.'

'I'm coming, and you're dead!'

'Well, don't rely on the cavalry to come and save you. They're otherwise disposed.'

'What do you mean?'

'Your main man – well, since big stupid Malky ended up swinging off the Erskine Bridge – old Paton. He's been firing you into the OCU. Leaky ship, Zander. Nothing worse.'

'You're lying.'

'Give him a call, see if he replies.'

Finn heard another yell.

'Here, have a word with Gillian. Lovely lassie, so she is.'

Finn could hardly make out what his daughter was trying to say. But between desperate gasps for breath, he understood.

'Dad, they're killing me.'

'Gillian!' Finn roared. But the next voice on the phone was Joe Mannion.

'I'm not sure how much more she can take. But I'll make a deal with you. You come over and we do a nice wee swap. Your daughter goes free, and you stay with us. Come alone, mind.'

Finn swallowed hard, desperately thinking of a way out. 'Okay, I'm on my way. But don't you dare lay another finger on her.'

'Good. You know where we are. I'll leave her be for the moment. Any shit and I'll cut her throat myself.'

Finn heard the line go dead. Quickly, he found Donnie Paton's number. He listened to the ring tone until the prompt to leave a voice message sounded loud in his ear.

★

As the barman had promised, Mannion's office was empty. Maggie Finn stared at the big desk, a dark frown spreading across her face.

'I don't know what we're going to achieve here,' said Senga. The thought of the man with whom she had been intimate with was making bile rise in her throat.

'Just look for stuff,' said Maggie.

'Like what?'

'Anything that'll give us a steer as to what this bastard is up to – or where he is.'

The pair went through drawers, filing cabinets and cupboards. But they found nothing to indicate that Joe Mannion was anything other than the respectable owner of the bar downstairs.

Maggie walked across to a drinks cabinet. 'Here, have some, we're going to need it.' She poured two large measures of vodka into glasses and handed one to Senga.

'And who's going to drive?'

'You know, for a lassie that puts it about so much, and was in charge of a criminal gang, you ask the most fucking stupid questions. Drink the bloody thing!'

Senga grabbed the glass and downed the spirit in one gulp. 'Another,' she said.

'We've done what we can do. We have to leave everything – well, leave it to others.'

'Who? This mystery person you were talking to in the car?'

'Yes, and my son.'

'It's a trap, Maggie. You know that. Joe will lure Zander to where he has Gillian and he'll kill him. That's what this is about.'

'People have tried to kill my son before.'

'They succeeded with mine!'

'I know Zander – so should you. And don't underestimate the power of prayer.'

'Really? You're trying to convert me, Maggie? Now's not the time!'

Maggie ignored the comment. 'Right, we can't just stay here. Anyway, Dumb and Dumber down there will soon get the wind back to get up they stairs.' She spotted the shine of metal sticking out from under Joe Mannion's desk. Maggie pulled at it and drew the vicious-looking blade from its cubbyhole.

'It's a sword!'

'Aye, well done, Senga. You should get yourself on one of these quiz shows on the telly. Sharp as a tack, so you are. Come on. If nothing else, I can stick this in one of they fat bastards down in the bar.'

*

Zander Finn drove through the traffic, calculating the chances of rescuing his daughter. Amelia Langley popped into his mind. But in his heart he knew he couldn't trust the police. And knowing Joe Mannion as he did, he would kill Gillian at the first sign of the constabulary.

He had only one choice. He had to give himself up to save his daughter, and to do that he must sacrifice his life. It was stark, but he would rather die than bury another one of his children. In truth, he'd felt despondent for a long time. He'd known what was in store. His flight to London had been as much to do with giving him the space and time to come to terms with what he saw as his inevitable demise as it was to mourn his dead child.

'Live by the sword and die by it.' It was a mantra favoured by Father Giordano. The old priest had been warning him of the consequences of his many sins for longer than he could recall.

Finn was on a less busy road, away from the dual carriage-way, away from the crush of men, women and children in tiny metal boxes, all part of the suicidal race of existence. It was a neat metaphor for life. Everyone was hurtling towards oblivion. It didn't matter what road you were on, or how fast you travelled. The outcome was always the same.

He hadn't far to go. By his reckoning, he was now only a few streets away from saving Gillian.

'One day you will do the right thing. You will redeem yourself. But it may well lead you to eternal damnation.' Father Giordano had said this to him such a long time ago, but it had stuck in his mind. He remembered being insulted by the thought that his confessor, his priest, his spiritual mentor, had not only seen fit to abandon the soul of one of his flock but also to happily taunt him about it.

'And how will you find redemption?' He remembered asking the question so vividly.

'When the time is right, I will know, my son.'

At the time, this reply had troubled Finn. Now he was beginning to realise what the old Italian had meant.

As he turned the corner, he could see the building Joe Mannion had described. For Zander Finn, the time to find redemption and eternal damnation had arrived. And they were one and the same.

50

The chapel was empty, save for the man on his knees before the life-size depiction of Christ on the cross. Father Giordano looked up at this embodiment of sacrifice and pain in exactly the same way he had when he was a boy in Italy so, so long ago. He knew he should feel joy. That Christ had shouldered the sins of the world was his certainty. But he could only ever feel an overwhelming sadness, an undiminishing sense of loss.

'What more could you have done, had you lived?' It was a question he'd asked in many places of worship for many decades. For life was never simple. The world, both spiritual and temporal, was not quite what one expected. And as age, and hopefully wisdom, accumulated, knowledge of what was to come became ever more uncertain. It was as though the boundless faith of youth – his faith – was being tested to destruction. This, so that when the day of judgement came he would be the one who would condemn himself in front of the Lord he so loved, not the reverse.

But was this not the fate of mankind? Surely, he'd come to believe, it was predestined that man, not God, would seal his own fate. The Almighty wasn't keeping score because he didn't have to. The ability to look into the hearts of sinners – and everyone sinned – would suffice.

This plague of realisation that had dawned on him only became more real as the years advanced. Was he a sinner? Most certainly, he was. Had he helped others? Yes, to the best of his ability, he had. But also he had brought others to their end, without mercy. To the young version of himself, this had been right. The older man, though, cried out for the forgiveness he knew he didn't deserve.

Father Giordano genuflected and rose stiffly to his feet. When he left the quiet confines of the church, he was propelled back into the secular world. Many thought that what happened in places of worship was fantasy, but, what passed for reality outside the confines of the church was the real illusion to him. As he stared at the many going about their business under the glow of the streetlights, he could see only players. The drama was of their creation, but the curtain would fall for all, as surely as the darkness had fallen over Paisley this night.

The spire of the church cast a long shadow in the harsh sodium glare. He walked to its peak and turned left, out of the gates and onto a hill on a rise that overlooked much of the town that had been his home for so many years.

He could hear the sirens of the emergency services. A great cloud of smoke hung over the north part of Paisley. It was illuminated by the streetlights, looming like a monster, a devil, slowly morphing in shape and size, as though ready to consume them all.

Head down, the priest began the short walk to his home. But it was the walk to oblivion he had always feared, and it was his next destination. But he knew it was a walk he could only make alone.

★

Maggie Finn was driving, as they crossed over the flyover on the M8 that looked across Paisley.

'That's some fire by the look of things,' said Senga Finn. She had spent the short trip from Glasgow with her head pinned back against the headrest of her own car, as her erstwhile mother-in-law peered into the blinding display of headlights.

Maggie cast a glance to her left. 'That's not just any bloody fire!' She put her foot to the accelerator, jerking Senga back in her seat.

'Be careful! Remember, you're probably over the limit.'

'I don't give a fuck!' Maggie had her face thrust towards the windscreen, as she negotiated her way through the heavy traffic to the nearest exit from the motorway. Soon, she was winding through the dimly lit streets of the town she knew so well. Every street, every pub, every shop – open or boarded up – every school, every empty space where a building had been demolished; everywhere she passed held its own memories. Some were fleeting, a mere moment in time, while others held a greater significance for the woman who would always call Paisley home.

'Exactly where are we going?' said Senga.

'Are you thick? You saw the flames.'

'Do you know, one day you might give me a straight bloody answer. It may have slipped your mind, but I've more to worry about than your stupid riddles.'

Making no reply, Maggie turned the car past Halfords and into Abercorn Street. They didn't travel far up the road until they were stopped at a police cordon. Ahead, blue and red lights twinkled in a haze of smoke.

Maggie wound down her window. She took in the

impossibly young-looking police officer, wearing a hi-vis jacket topped off by a reflective police-issue baseball cap, standing by the line of police tape. 'Hey, son!' She beckoned him towards the car.

'Yes, madam.'

'What's happening?'

'A fire, and it's a big one. If you're trying to get any further, you can forget it.'

'This fire, where is it?'

'They're trying to stop it spreading to other buildings. But at the moment it's contained in one factory unit.'

'What factory unit?'

'Chancellor Fabrications.'

Senga leaned over to talk to the policeman. 'I'm a director! I need to speak to someone.'

'I'm afraid there isn't anyone to talk to at the moment.' The young cop leaned into the car. 'There's nothing but a shell left; the place has been completely gutted. Good thing is, we think everyone had gone home for the evening. So please, try not to worry.'

'Try not to worry? How would you feel if your business was going up in smoke?'

'Not very good, I'm sure.' The policeman looked sheepish. 'But what can you do? I'm sure you're insured. Not that that's any consolation.'

Senga looked at Maggie. 'Well, aren't you going to say anything? Fuck, you ran the place for long enough!'

Maggie shrugged. 'Some things just have their time.' She looked at the policeman. 'Since when did you lot start wearing baseball caps, eh?'

'New issue – from Police Scotland, you know. They're slowly dragging us into the twenty-first century.'

'Aye, well, they should drag you back again. They look bloody awful.'

'Why are you being so calm about all this? How can you be?' asked Senga, as a desperate look spread across her face.

'Because we're being looked after by another power, that's why.'

'Oh, I fucking give up.' Senga held her head in her hands, as the police officer looked on bemused.

*

Finn left the pink Mini at the path that led to the boarded-up Chinese restaurant. A door creaked open, but nobody appeared through it.

Finn approached cautiously. 'Okay, I'm here. Let Gillian out and I'll come in!' He looked round. Mannion had chosen well. This place was just about as isolated as you could get and still be in the city.

'Naw, you come in, then we'll let your wee lassie go.' This was Mannion's voice.

Finn had expected nothing less. He pushed the boarded-up door aside and walked into the darkness. As he peered, waiting for his eyes to adjust, he was aware of movement in front of his face. By instinct, he ducked, but a heavy blow still glanced off his chin.

Like a rugby player in a scrum, Finn doubled down and pushed forward, his hands grasping at shadows. But in a few steps he felt another blow, this time to his back. He dived forward, and this time he was lucky; he caught someone by the legs. A voice grunted in pain as he brought his attacker to the floor.

Finn's eyes were adjusting now. Though it was still

almost pitch black, he could see, feel and smell the man he had by the arm. He began to rain blows down on his exposed back.

Suddenly, everything was illuminated, as neon lights stuttered into life. Finn blinked. He was lying on top of a burly man on a tiled floor. When he looked up, Mannion stood before him, a pistol pointed at his face.

'Fuck's sake, Sammy! You had the element of surprise, darkness, the lot – and you still couldn't do the job, eh?'

'Get this bastard off me!' Sammy Sloane was struggling under Zander Finn's weight.

Mannion gestured with the gun that Finn should release his henchman. 'It's lovely to see you again, Zander. Is it a number fifty-two with fried rice, or just curry sauce and chips?' Mannion laughed at his own joke.

'Where's Gillian?'

'Sammy, drag Mr Finn this way.'

Sloane grabbed Finn by the arm. They stared at each other for a moment, then Finn shrugged. 'You heard your master, poodle boy.' He blew a mock kiss at Sloane.

'Fuck you, Zander. You'll not be blowing kisses shortly, you wanker.' He turned Finn round and applied cable ties, pinning his hands behind his back. For good measure, Sloane took a swing, connecting with the side of Finn's face just under his ear.

The now captive gangster staggered at the force of the blow, fighting to retain his footing. But before he could shake the dizziness he was being pulled along the corridor into a bright room.

'You not feeling so good, Zander?' said Mannion. 'Here's your wee lassie, by the way.'

Finn, his head still spinning, squinted in the direction of

Mannion's gaze. Gillian was tied to a chair, her head bent forward so that her father couldn't see her eyes. 'What have you done to her?'

'Och, the lassie was a wee bit hysterical, so I thought it best we gave her a wee jag to calm her down. She'll be fine.'

'Okay, let her go. That's the deal.'

'Zander, you know me better than that. When's the last time I stuck to a deal? Picture the scene.' Mannion spread his hands as though conjuring up an image from thin air. 'Wee Gillian here goes running off – maybe to her mammy, but more likely to dear old granny, eh?'

'And what's my mother going to do? She's an old woman.'

'Sometimes I forget you're so much younger than me.' Mannion rubbed his chin, as though deep in thought. 'You see, I remember her when she wasn't just an *old woman*.'

'What's this shit?'

'Oh, you know. You don't think for a second that drunken father of yours held things together? Did you never stop to wonder how smoothly everything went when you took over? After all, you were just a boy.'

Finn tried to clear his head by shaking it. 'I was there, remember.'

'Aye. But you know how this game works now. You can't show any kind of weakness, or the wee dogs that do your bidding soon become a pack that'll happily devour you. Who do you think kept everyone in line while you were finding your feet?'

'My mother? Piss off, Joe.'

'Look how quickly things went downhill in the two years you were kicking your heels down in London, eh?'

'Down to my dear wife and her relationship with you, I think.'

Sammy Sloane looked at his boss, mouth gaping in surprise.

'You know, Sammy, you've always reminded me of something, now I can see it.'

'Eh?'

'A cod. You look like a cod. Shut your mouth, you're putting me off my revenge here. Now, where was I?'

'You were telling me what a criminal mastermind my mother is.'

'Oh aye, that's it. You shouldn't underestimate her. I mean, Davie Kelly, old Paton, they'd eat their own granny for breakfast.' He looked over his shoulder. 'Come in, Paulie!' Mannion shouted.

From a side door, a figure emerged.

'Take this young man, for instance.' Mannion was puffing on the stub of a cigar, relighting it in a cloud of smoke with a flaring match. 'While you've been busy clearing all these Albanians out of the way for me, Paulie here has been running Dusky's boys.'

Finn stared at the young man. It didn't take him long to recall when he'd last seen that face. It was in the Tannahill Bar when he and Malky Maloney had met up with Dusky. He'd sent him out to stand in the street.

'Of course, I had the big man in my pocket. But you knew that, didn't you?'

'Yes, that's why he's no longer with us.' Finn stared at him defiantly.

'You know everything, of course.'

Finn snorted in derision.

'I could have left you in London, you know. You were out the way, and what with your stupid wife and Dusky doing my bidding – well, it would have been fine.'

'But?'

'But there was always a risk you'd come back and cause me trouble. You see, I've got a wee thing going – great thing, it is. But we needed they Albanians out the way, which you so kindly attended to. Aye, and I needed to be sure you wouldn't come back to ruin our plans.'

'Oh, and just how did you manage to persuade me back? Because if you think I came up from London at the behest of my wife, you're wrong.'

'Oh no. I mean, you forget I know her – well, in fact.' He smiled and reached into the inside pocket of his jacket. He produced a mobile phone. 'You'll need to give me a second here. Old age doesn't come alone.' He pulled a pair of reading glasses from his breast pocket and started fiddling with the smartphone. 'Ah, here we are.' Joe Mannion held up the phone. Soon a voice echoed in the large empty room.

51

Amelia Langley stood as near to the blaze at Chancellor Fabrications as she could, DS Neil Dickie at her side.

'Well, that's that,' she said with a resigned look.

Dickie screwed up his face against the heat of the blaze. 'You don't think . . .'

'I don't think what?'

'Well, your man, Finn. He might have decided that enough is enough. Do you know what I mean?'

'What?' Langley turned to him with a glare. For some reason this hadn't crossed her mind at all. She felt a most unwanted tug at her heart, an empty feeling in her stomach. 'Don't be ridiculous, Neil. They've torched the place to hide evidence. How long have you been doing this job?'

'Long enough.' He shrugged. 'It was just a thought. I mean, he wasn't exactly full of the joys when he left us, was he?'

'He was his usual self.' Langley hoped she was hiding the feelings she was desperately trying to banish.

A car screeched to a halt behind them.

'Watch out, it's the gaffer,' said Dickie, automatically straightening up.

ACC Mary Green's gold braid reflected the flames, now much diminished, thanks to the attention of the fire brigade.

Her face was stern as she looked up at Langley. 'So, what happened?'

'We're not sure. Obviously, there's been a fire.'

'Top marks, Chief Inspector. I must say, the reason behind your rapid rise in the ranks had eluded me until this moment. Now all is clear.' Green looked at her watch. 'I want you to round up every one of Zander Finn's crew. I'm especially keen to speak to Donald Paton.'

'On what pretext shall we round them up, ma'am?' Langley could barely hide her irritation.

'On the pretext of investigating mass murder of foreign nationals, what do you think? Do you want me to chew your food for you as well?'

'Ma'am, surely it would be better to gather some concrete evidence against them before bringing them in. Right now, we have nothing apart from circumstantial and anecdotal evidence to suggest that the Paisley mob had anything to do with the Albanian deaths. We've already released Finn.'

'Yes, on your advice. And look where that got us.'

'Of course, I'm forgetting *your source*.'

'Just get them rounded up.'

'Finn first, I assume.'

'No, Donald Paton is the priority. Get it done!' Green turned on her heel and was soon back in the passenger seat of her car. The driver executed a quick U-turn and they disappeared back down Abercorn Street.

'I wonder who her source is, then?' said Dickie with a smile.

'Ha! No prizes now, Neil.'

A senior fire officer approached them. His face was slathered in soot and ash from the fire, and he looked exhausted.

'Hard night?' Langley asked sympathetically.

'We had our work cut out trying to stop the fire spreading to other units. These went up a long time ago; there's nothing like enough clearance between buildings.'

'Well, it looks as though you've got it under control now, at least.'

'Yes, that's one of the reasons I wanted to talk to you. You're Langley, right?'

'Yes, that's me.'

'Well, you might want to get a hold of your SOCO team. We've found a body.'

Neil Dickie looked at Amelia Langley with an 'I told you so' expression plastered across his face.

Langley's hand shook as she took the phone from her pocket.

'Are you okay?' asked the fire officer.

'Long day,' she replied. 'A very long day.'

Neil Dickie raised a brow, as his boss called in the SOCO team.

★

At first Zander Finn didn't recognise the voice. Mannion must have noticed his puzzled expression because he walked towards Finn, the smartphone held out in front of him. The recoding was tinny, but perfectly audible.

'So you go down there, persuade your man to come back, and we're both quids in, eh?' This was Mannion's voice, distinctively low and gruff.

For a few moments there was silence, then another voice sounded from the phone. Finn wasn't sure if the echo was in the room or in his head.

'Aye, I'll do it. But it's as we agreed. I want my cut of everything.' The voice of the late Malky Maloney was unmistakable.

'Consider it done. You can do what you do in Paisley. Just leave the big stuff to me and we'll get on fine.'

Mannion clicked off the recording but continued to hold the phone in the air like some kind of trophy. 'Look at your face, eh? Just look at it. This is one of the best days I've had in a long time, that's for sure.'

'It's easy to manipulate voices now.' Finn shrugged, doing his best to look untroubled, though in reality he felt sick to the stomach. 'All you need is some wean that can do it and away you go.'

A flash of irritation passed across Mannion's face. But he soon recovered. 'If you think that, you're mistaken. Malky Maloney was pissed off with your wife, and he was pissed off with you. Accept it. Your best buddy sent you to the wolves.'

'If this shit is true, why did you kill him?'

Mannion thought for a moment before replying. 'You're a fisherman, Zander, I know that much. Out there, with your wee fly and hook, trying to get a fish in all that mud, cold and rain. I've never quite understood it, to be honest.'

'If I had time to write down the things you *never quite understood*, then I'd have nothing else to do.'

'You're not quite getting this, are you? You see, I tried to goad you into getting rid of our Albanian problem before. But instead, you disappeared. Though I knew you wouldn't be away for long. A man like you would have to seek vengeance on the people that killed your son. Problem is, you missed.'

Finn struggled to free himself from Sammy Sloane's grip, but his hands were still firmly pinned behind his back. 'So you're saying you did it? You don't have the balls!' Finn's face was crimson red now, his eyes flashing with hatred.

'My lad's first, actually.'

'Which lad?'

'The father of your new grandchild-to-be: Kevin. It's amazing what even my own family will do for the promise of money, and a shithole like this.' Mannion gestured round the room. 'What a swap, too! Your arsehole of a boy in exchange for a boarded-up Chinese restaurant. He's stupid, of course – like his mother.'

Finn roared at the top of his voice. It was a wordless yell of sheer fury. Though Sloane had his arms pinned back, through the pain and his captor's strength, he moved a few steps towards Mannion.

Mannion nodded.

Finn felt a sharp pain in his neck. His legs gave way and he sagged in Sloane's grip. He was aware of being grabbed by the hair, his head tugged up. The face of Joe Mannion shimmered, then faded to black.

52

Sandra Finn was pushed into the delivery room by an orderly and two harassed-looking nurses. Kevin was holding her hand, but one of the nurses pulled him back.

'You'll need to get scrubbed and kitted out. You're the father, I assume?'

'Yes.'

'Right, come with me.'

They walked down a corridor towards another room. Kevin glanced out of a window that looked over the hospital car park. Under the lights, he could see two figures making their way towards the entrance. He stopped in his tracks.

'Hang on. I've left my camera in the car. I don't want to miss this.'

'You better get a move on!' said the nurse.

Kevin ran back down the corridor. Instead of the main entrance, he paused in front of a fire door. Fearful of alarms, he screwed up his eyes as he pushed it open. Thankfully, there were no bells or whistles. He crept round the corner of the building and stared into the night.

Soon, he was back in his car. He revved the engine and left the hospital's grounds, turning onto the main road with a screech of tyres.

*

Senga Finn and her mother-in-law, Maggie, made their way through the hospital corridors.

'Here, this way,' said Senga, pointing to a sign that read 'Maternity'.

'Are you sure that was the message Zander sent?'

'Yes! For the last time. I'll show it to you, if you want.'

'Fuck, it never rains but it pours. Why the hell do they make these hospitals so big? She'd have been better off having the wean in Paisley.'

'In the RAH? Are you kidding?'

'Nothing wrong with the hospital, nothing at all. Just you have a go trying to administer care to all they junkies and chancers. This will be the first of my family not born in Paisley.'

Senga shook her head as they hurried along.

'What's up with you?'

'I've got to say, you think of the strangest things at such odd times. Here we are, just about to see my first grandchild being born – your great-grandchild. Meanwhile, your son and your youngest grandchild could be dead, for all we know. And all you can think to do is bang on about being born in Paisley!'

Maggie caught Senga's arm. 'You listen to me. Of course I'm worried. But when you get to my age you learn just to deal with what's in front of you. I've told you, it's in good hands. Zander and Gillian will be fine.'

The pair stared at each other for a moment, then pressed on to the maternity ward.

*

Father Giordano was standing with the phone to his ear, listening intently. Only one small lamp illuminated the room – it reflected his gloomy mood.

'You will both meet me in the chapel. We shall pray.'

He listened again, this time impatiently.

'If we lose faith in prayer, then everything is lost. We are merely beasts stumbling around in the darkness.' He glanced round the room, noting the irony of the situation. 'This is what I want. It will be done.'

Call over, he sat down heavily in the leather chair. Giordano felt tired. He knew that age had a lot to do with it; he had flung problems aside as a youth. But now there were other concerns, matters of the heart, not just the soul.

He remembered his mother toiling over the stove. For her, the cooking of food, feeding her family, was a devotion.

'Too many ingredients and the dish is ruined,' he could hear her say, so long ago. 'A pinch of salt, a shake of pepper, can make food sing, or it can make it cry.'

In the gloom, he felt like crying now. He was in no doubt there were far too many ingredients in his life. There had been for a long time. Now it was time to serve the dish he had slaved over for a lifetime: he wasn't sure if it would taste as he wanted it to. Too much salt, perhaps too little pepper; he really didn't know.

'You can't rush,' his mother had said. 'The pot boils when it will.'

Father Giordano knew how this felt. But he was scared that his pot was about to boil over.

53

Zander Finn felt as though he was waking from a drunken sleep. His head was throbbing and his mouth dry. He was disoriented, and it took time to recall recent events. But slowly, horrifically, they returned.

As soon as he tried to move, he realised that he was held fast, arms and legs tied on to the chair upon which he sat. Though he strained at his bonds, they didn't budge.

It was pitch black. At first Finn considered the possibility that Mannion had blinded him. But as his eyes adjusted to the light, he began to make out the shadows of furniture, a bookcase, chairs, and the sheen from a polished table at the head of which he sat. He couldn't be sure where the sliver of light that afforded this paucity of illumination was coming from. It wasn't the curtains, though he could now see their folds. No light escaped from the windows.

Finn could smell money: the sharp, sweet tang of old leather, wood – a musty grandeur. Through the pain in his head, the throbbing behind his eyes, he realised where that smell took him. But it couldn't be.

'Father!' he cried out. 'Father Giordano!'

Movement: the swish of an opening door; a shaft of light; the change in the atmosphere in the room; the sound of footsteps. Then, as had happened in the disused Chinese restaurant, lights blinded him. But as he blinked his sight back, this was not the harsh light of neon bulbs but the gentle glow of lamps.

He tried to focus, as two people walked past him. The click of heels on a wooden floor, the drag of chairs pulled back. Whatever Mannion had stuck in his neck must have been strong. Finn was aware that his full wits had not yet been restored.

'You are comfortable?' The woman's voice was quiet. He recognised the accent.

Finn squinted at her. She was sitting at the other end of the table, right opposite him. Her dark hair was illuminated from behind by the glow of a standard lamp, making it look as though she had a halo – an angel. But Finn was pretty sure that, despite appearances, this was no heavenly body.

To her side, sat the solid figure of Joe Mannion.

'You haven't answered my question, Mr Finn.'

'I'm just dandy. Who the fuck are you, and where's my daughter?'

'Listen to the mouth on this bastard,' said Mannion.

Ignoring both of them, the woman at the head of the table spoke again. 'You are not a man who knows when he's beaten, I think.' The words were soft but precise, showing no sign of emotion.

'I know who your friend is, but who are you?'

'My name is Ginerva. Not that it matters. You are here for only one reason.'

'That is?'

'That we strike a deal.'

Finn made to reply, but she silenced him.

'This is the kind of deal where your choices are limited. In fact, you only have two choices.'

'Aye, we know that one in Scotland too,' said Mannion. He was about to light a cigar, but she stopped him.

'You are not in your stinking pub now, Mr Mannion. There is no smoking in here.'

Finn smiled. 'Where are we?'

'On an island in Loch Lomond, Mr Finn. It does no harm to tell you now. I'd love to show you round, but that would be rather pointless at this stage.' Ginerva smiled.

'Okay, what's the deal?'

'The safety of your daughter, in return for the loyalty of your men.'

'My men? Your friend here tells me he has most of them in his pocket.' He looked across at Mannion.

'That – as with so many things – is wrong, Mr Finn. He may have turned some of your associates, but by no means all.' She clicked her fingers and a man walked through the room. He was dressed in a short jacket and black trousers, the uniform of a waiter. From a silver tray, he served his mistress and then Mannion drinks in sparkling whisky glasses. 'I'm sorry, Mr Finn. I would offer you something but I see you are rather indisposed. I admit I've become rather fond of your malt whisky since I've been here. Rather neglecting my wine, I must say.'

'Okay, so while you pair get pished, you'll have to tell me the rest of what you propose,' said Finn.

'You record a message for those loyal to you. You tell them that their interests are best served by falling in line with me.'

'What about me?' said Mannion, looking slightly taken aback.

Ginerva looked at him balefully, but said nothing.

'And what then?'

'That's quite simple. Then you do what you did before – disappear.'

'Aye, though this time you won't be coming back – get it?' Mannion grinned.

'As you said, not much choice,' said Finn.

Ginerva shrugged. 'No, this is true. But you save your daughter, though she too will have to give undertakings.'

'Where is she?'

'She is safe, that's all you need to know.'

'I want to see her! If not, I'm doing nothing.'

'Mr Finn, there are so many things you don't know. The solid realities of your life are not what you think.'

'Like what?'

'All you must know is that you have a very short time to make your decision.'

'Aye, it's like one of they deals at the furniture shops. Everything must go by Christmas – in this case, you!' Mannion grinned.

One look from Ginerva was enough to shut him up. 'Genuinely, I am sorry for you. But circumstances dictate that my options are limited.'

Zander Finn lowered his head.

*

'That's it, darling. You push with all you've got!' said Maggie Finn over Senga's shoulder.

Sandra fell back, gasping for breath. 'This is not how I imagined it would be. Gran, I don't need any coaching!'

'Take it from one that knows, honey. You keep at the pushing and you'll be fine. Your father was nearly ten pounds.'

'Please shut up,' said Senga to the older woman.

'What is it with you pair? You're not telling me something new. I might be having a baby, but I'm not stupid.' Sandra howled again in her birth pains.

'This is most irregular,' said the midwife. 'Both of you are here to help Sandra. Start helping!'

'I was,' said Maggie indignantly.

'Stating the obvious isn't helping. Now, Sandra, please concentrate on having your baby.'

Senga and Maggie looked at each other, but said nothing.

'Wait, I think we have the head!' said the midwife.

*

'So, that's it. You take your orders from Ginerva and everything will be fine.' As he spoke these words into the mobile phone, Joe Mannion was holding a pistol to Zander Finn's head. 'I'm taking off. I tried, but I failed. I'm sorry.' He looked across the table at the elegant Italian. 'Is that what you wanted?'

'Check it has recorded, Mr Mannion.'

He removed the mobile from in front of Finn's face and opened the recoding app. In moments, Finn's voice could be heard sounding strangely like the short clip of Malky Maloney that Mannion had played in the Chinese restaurant.

'Happy?'

'Yes, I am,' said Ginerva.

'What about my daughter?'

'I will keep my word, Mr Finn.' She nodded to Mannion. Mannion pushed the gun into Finn's temple.

*

'Yes, not long now, Sandra,' said the midwife.

'We're nearly there,' said her mother, as Sandra squeezed her hand.

'*We're* nearly nowhere. It's me that's doing this, Mum.' She pushed again, her face red with exertion.

The midwife smiled. 'You have a baby boy, Sandra!'

Sandra was breathing heavily, hair slathered against her forehead. 'Danny,' she said breathlessly, then fell back.

*

'You have no idea how long I've wanted to do this,' said Joe Mannion.

'Just get on with it, you arsehole. My life was in tatters anyway.' Finn closed his eyes, bracing against oblivion.

There was noise behind the large oak door: thudding footsteps, raised voices, a gunshot.

Mannion looked up the table at Ginerva. 'What the fuck is this?'

She appeared to be unmoved, sitting motionless in her chair like a tailor's dummy.

The door crashed open, revealing two tall men in dark suits with priest's collars.

'Fuck me, I know you're a Roman Catholic, Zander. But you've got to say, this is good service. Puts us Prods to shame, so it does.' He turned the gun on the two men, who appeared unarmed. 'I hope your faith is strong, boys. You might not be as fortunate as our pal, here.'

'Stop!' shouted Ginerva. The colour had drained from her face and she took to her feet, hesitantly.

Between the tall men, a smaller figure appeared, another priest, though an old man with wavy white hair.

Mannion furrowed his brow and looked between this newcomer and Ginerva. 'What the fuck is this? The Vatican Loch Lomond branch?'

'Ginerva, take a seat, please. I will speak in English. It would be rude to converse otherwise when your guests don't have the mother tongue.'

She stood defiantly, her chin tilted in the air.

'Sit!' The old priest's deep voice echoed round the room and the hallway beyond. Ginerva lowered her head and took her seat.

'Father Giordano?' said Finn. He sounded bewildered, because he was. He couldn't reconcile the appearance of his old friend with the predicament in which he now found himself.

Mannion tuned his back on his old enemy to face the priests. 'What do they call you lot, a murder of crows, eh?' He addressed Ginerva without talking to her. 'I'm surprised at you – here's us set to make a fortune across the country and you go all weak at the knees as soon as a priest arrives. Well, not me.' Mannion cocked the gun at the unarmed prelates.

A shot rang out.

Finn instinctively ducked, hitting his head off the polished wood of the table. In the split second between the gun's report and the realisation that he remained unharmed, he heard a groan and beside him on the table fell Joe Mannion. His eyes were wide, face white. He grabbed at Finn desperately.

Joe Mannion's body slid to the floor, leaving a streak of blood and gore across the polished wood. When Finn looked up, Ginerva was still standing with the pistol held out in front of her.

Father Giordano rushed to Mannion's side, muttering a Latin incantation.

Finn looked at him open-mouthed. 'He wasn't one of us, Father. The last rites won't do him any good.'

The old priest finished his mutterings and crossed himself. 'You should know by now, Zander. We are all the creatures of God.' He turned away and addressed his companions. 'Untie this man.'

54

Sandra Finn was in a hospital bed now, cradling her newborn baby. Maggie and Senga were on either side of the bed.

'He's gorgeous, he really is,' said Senga, a fat tear running down her face.

Maggie was busy on her phone.

'Any news?' asked Senga.

Maggie nodded. 'Everything is okay. That's all you need to know, right now.' Maggie Finn widened her eyes in a 'please shut up' expression.

'Are you sure? I need to know.' Senga's tone was more assertive now.

'Yes! Everything – everyone – is fine.'

Sandra looked between them, the tiny child nestled in the crook of her arm. Though she looked drained, she was also radiant. 'Okay, you can tell me what has been going on now. And don't give me any of this "nothing for you to worry about" bullshit. My boyfriend isn't here, and there was clearly something wrong with my father. Why was he asking all these questions about Gillian?'

'Okay,' Maggie replied. 'There's been a wee bit of trouble.'

'You mean between Dad and Kevin? Even when this is happening they can't leave this feud alone?'

'Kevin has nothing to do with this.' Senga stared at Maggie as she said the words. 'And your father and sister are fine, just like your gran says. You're right, there was a problem, but it's been sorted. Hasn't it, Maggie?'

'You tell me the truth, Gran. Don't mollycoddle me just because I've had a baby. I know when you're lying,' said Sandra, a look of desperation on her face.

'Yes! Your mother is right. There was an incident, but it's fine now.'

'Between Dad and Gillian?'

'Listen.' Maggie leaned over her granddaughter and great-grandson. 'You need to concentrate on your baby. I promise, everybody and everything is okay. I swear on your mother's life.'

'Well, that's not much reassurance – you hate each other!'

'We're fine, too.'

The door to the side room opened and the midwife appeared. 'I think we should leave Mum and baby alone now. You can come back any time tomorrow. It's a private room. But Ms Finn and Danny must rest now.'

Maggie and Senga said their goodbyes and were soon walking back along the corridors of the hospital.

'If Zander has done anything to Kevin, she'll never forgive him, Maggie.'

'Are you out of your mind? I know you've just been – well, "intimate" with his father. But the boy betrayed our family. My son and your daughter almost died because of the little shit! But Zander didn't touch him. He's a Mannion; he knows to get on his toes when the going gets tough.'

'And Gillian, what about her?'

'She's a bit shaken, that's all.'

The pair of them walked out through the entrance and stopped in unison, as though they'd hit an invisible wall. Maggie was the first to produce a packet of cigarettes. For a few moments they enjoyed the relaxing power of nicotine before Maggie sighed.

'I knew it! There is something. Tell me, Maggie Finn, or as sure as I stand here I'll beat it out of you.'

'The first time you and I fell out was when you gave me that blouse. Do you remember? You'd just started seeing my Zander. What age were you, eighteen?'

'I remember. And I was nineteen, actually.'

'Turned out you'd lifted it from Arnotts.'

'Oh, for fuck's sake. We're not going through all that again. Don't you think we've got more to talk about?'

'You'll remember our Gwen was working there at the time. They had you on the CCTV footage. Gwen spoke to me about it, and I had her get rid of the tape.'

'All our yesterdays.' Senga shook her head.

'I'm making a point.'

'Which is?'

'No matter what happens between you and Zander, you're still the mother of my grandchildren. I'll always do what I can to help you. You did the right thing when you saw that message from Kevin to his father. Typical of the arrogant prick to leave his phone where you could find it.'

'We'd just split up. I was going to send his wife a picture of my tits from it.'

'Charming.'

'Just as well I looked at it!'

'There is news – bad, depending on your point of view.'

'Fuck! What do you mean, "point of view"?'

'Joe Mannion is dead, Senga.'

Senga took another cigarette from her packet and lit it.

'If it's any consolation, he would have been quite happy to kill your daughter and your husband – estranged or not.'

Senga looked up into the night sky, blowing clouds of smoke into the cold air. 'Do you really think I give a fuck about Joe Mannion?'

Maggie nodded. 'Good. Now come on, you and me need a drink.'

'I'm famished. But there's nowhere open this time of night.'

'That's easy solved. I'll make you some egg, chips and beans.'

*

Four people were sitting in the quiet lounge of the big mansion on the island in the middle of Loch Lomond. They sat in silence, each nursing a drink. Gillian Finn was nestled into her father's side on a leather Chesterfield couch. She looked pale and shaken, but otherwise okay. Her father had his arm round her shoulders, and despite his bumps, bruises, cuts and abrasions, he looked remarkably calm.

On either side of a roaring fire, on chairs that matched the couch, sat Father Giordano and Ginerva. The latter was staring into the flames, shadows playing on her face. Meanwhile Father Giordano gazed into his glass, as though practising the art of divination.

'Are you looking for the future, Father?' asked Finn of the old man.

'No, it's a mortal sin. And who wants to know the future?' he replied. 'If you must know, I've been looking at the present.'

'Just peachy, from where I'm sitting,' said Finn.

'Tell them, Uncle.' Ginerva looked away from the fire, though the flames were still reflected in her dark eyes.

The logs crackled, while outside an owl hooted plaintively.

'Yes, please tell me what the fuck just happened? And why is she calling you uncle?' said Finn.

Father Giordano drained his glass of brandy and, reaching for the decanter, poured himself a large measure. 'It is quite simple: her father was my brother. He died ten years ago.'

'But she's the underboss of the Calabrian Mafia!' Finn looked angry.

'It is true.'

'So all the time you spent lecturing me on my wicked ways, your niece was one of the biggest criminals in Europe.'

Giordano took another drink. 'Yes, this is true, as was her father before her.'

Finn shook his head, while Gillian's expression was hard to read.

'Tell him who the boss is, Uncle.'

The priest looked weary. Somehow the firelight playing against the shadows made him appear even older, exaggerating the shadows and lines on his face. 'It is my fault we are all here. For some, my fault you even exist.'

'Enough of the riddles! I nearly died, so did my daughter. Spit it out!'

'Dad, let him speak,' said Gillian. 'I think I know what he's going to say.'

'Oh, so you've gone all mysterious now. Great!'

'Dad, open your eyes. Look at Ginerva – who does she remind you of?'

'A murdering bastard, that's who.'

Father Giordano smiled at Gillian. 'You remind me of a woman who died many years ago, my child.'

'Your mother, by any chance?' replied Gillian.

'Yes, right first time. She was delicate – like a flower. Just like you. But she was the strongest woman I've ever met.'

'Aye, and he knows your gran,' said Finn.

'Dad, you're so blind.'

Giordano looked up from his drink. His face was a mask, his emotions impossible to read. 'Zander, I told you about the young priest who turned into the cobbled street only to find a car ruined by an explosion.'

'I remember.'

'That young man was me.'

'I had kind of figured that, Father.'

'Father. How many times have you said those words to me? Every time it cuts into my heart like a knife.'

'You should have chosen another profession.' Finn felt his daughter squeeze his arm.

'The man who died in that car was the boss. He ran the town where I grew up, and many other towns besides.'

'He was a Mafioso. I picked that up, too.'

'He was my father.' Giordano stared at Zander Finn. 'Before and after the war in Italy, people starved. They cried out for help, from God – from anyone. My father fed them, he clothed them – he cherished those for whom he was responsible. He made sure their children were warm in their beds. He nurtured his people like a family. He kept us safe – all of us. You cannot imagine how things were then. This modern world is so different, but yet still seeped in sin.'

'But he was a gangster.'

'He was. Alessandro Giordano. He committed many crimes. He stole, killed – but he also saved his own people. The last thing he wanted for his eldest son was the life he led. I became a priest.'

'I sense a but,' said Finn.

'But he died. Murdered by his enemies. Men much like your Joe Mannion, may he rest in peace.'

'May he rest in pieces! What happens to him now – his body, I mean?'

'Why do you ask? You of all men know how these things are handled.'

'Not in front of my daughter!'

'Zander, the time for secrets is over. She must know the truth, as must you.'

Finn shook his head in disbelief. 'I know what you're going to say.'

'You do?'

'You came here to escape what happened to your father.'

'Not directly, but you are right, in the main.'

Ginerva spoke. 'That is true, but it's not the whole story.' She looked at Finn. 'My uncle did complete his training. But not before he and my father killed those who had taken the life of their father. Our codes are strict – not those you would understand. But my father took the burden, while my uncle here travelled to this land to be a man of God.' She looked angrily at Giordano.

'It is what your grandfather wanted,' he said.

'But he wanted something else. Tell them!'

Father Giordano lowered his head. 'He stipulated many things.'

'Mr Finn, I am, as Mr Mannion described, *underboss* of my family.'

'Wait, you can't be saying this.' Finn's face was pale now.

'I am the boss,' said Father Giordano. 'I have been since the day my father was killed in that car. I had no idea my niece was involved with this Mannion. Had I known, I would have put a stop to it all. But then again, everything would have stopped if you had listened to me and left Paisley and stayed away.'

'So it's all my fault!' Finn's voice echoed in the room, and silence reigned for a few moments.

'Tell him the rest, Father,' said Gillian quietly.

The old man appeared to age in front of them. Tears were brimming in his eyes, thick frown lines etched in his forehead, more pronounced. 'There was a young woman. She came to me when she was little more than a child. Her husband beat her, the beatings got worse over the years. My heart ached for her pain. It ached for her.'

'What are you on about now?' Finn drained his glass.

'One night, he battered her half to death. I could take no more.'

'Because you were in love with her,' said Gillian.

'Hold the bus, here. How come I get the feeling that everybody knows what's going on but me.'

'I killed him.'

Finn looked at the old priest, his mind working overtime. 'You killed my father!' He made to get up from his chair, fury etched across his face. But his daughter pulled him back.

Gillian looked at her father, eyes wet with tears. 'Dad, he didn't kill your father, because *he* is your father.'

55

Maggie and Senga Finn arrived back at the seventeenth floor of the Paisley tower block. Maggie kicked off her leopard-print shoes and padded towards the lounge. 'I feel as though I've run a hundred miles today. Come on, time for a drink.'

Senga dutifully followed her. They sat down with a bottle of vodka and one drink became three then four.

'There's more, you know,' said Maggie, her eyes hooded now, the effects of alcohol and tiredness taking their toll.

'More? What makes you think I can take any more tonight?' said Senga.

'True, it'll all become clear soon enough.' Maggie lit another cigarette.

'Like why you phoned a priest when you thought your son was going to be killed and suddenly everything was okay?'

Maggie squinted at her daughter-in-law. 'You're smarter than I thought.' She smiled drunkenly. 'But it's not my place to say.'

They both sat back and drew on their cigarettes.

'You said you were making something to eat, Maggie.'

'Are you still hungry?'

'Aye. I'm sure you know I always get ravenous when I'm stressed.'

'It's a wonder you're not a right fat bastard then.' They both laughed, Senga snorting some of her drink over her jeans.

'By the way, it's like a fucking smokehouse in here. Do you never open a window?'

'Chancellor made them – fitted them, too. They're only supposed to open at the top. In case I decide to top myself. It's the law, apparently.'

'How likely is that, you topping yourself?'

'Impossible. The top window won't open.'

'That's why it's so stuffy in here. I'm sure I can move it.'

The doorbell rang.

'What the fuck now?' Maggie marched off, drunkenly indignant, lurching towards her objective. Two figures were standing in the close when she opened the door.

'I'm Detective Chief Inspector Langley. This is DS Neil Dickie. Can we come in, please, Mrs Finn?'

Maggie shrugged. 'Aye, sure, why not? The more the merrier. We're celebrating.' She put her finger to her mouth in a mock hushing gesture. 'Anyway, what do you want?'

'I have some bad news.'

'Fuck, is there any other kind?' Maggie led them through to the lounge, where Senga was busy lighting yet another cigarette.

Amelia Langley coughed as she entered the room.

'See, I told you this place was like a smokehouse. I'm going to have a go at these windows.' Senga made to stand, then fell onto her chair with a snort of laughter.

'Right, sit yourselves down. What do you have to say?'

Langley and Dickie took a seat on a long sofa. The senior detective cleared her throat. 'You may not be aware, but there was a fire at Chancellor Fabrications earlier this evening. I believe you're a director, Mrs Finn?'

'Aye, I am. And I can't tell a lie. I knew there was a fire. But I was told there was nobody in the building. Anyhow, as you can see, we're celebrating. It's not every day you become a great-grandmother, is it?'

Langley looked at Dickie. 'I'm sorry to say your information was wrong.'

'Bollocks. I heard it from one of the fire officers. We were in Abercorn Street earlier. You cops are always at my family, trying to give us a hard time.'

Langley carried on regardless, as Senga made another attempt to get to her feet. 'There was a body found in the wreckage. We've managed to identify him.'

'Him?' said Maggie.

'Yes. Mr Donald Paton. I believe he ran the business.'

Maggie opened her mouth to speak, but closed it again.

'I know it's a shock, Mrs Finn.'

'Aye, just a wee bit.' She staggered. 'Come on, have a drink with us. We'll raise a glass to a new life and one that's just passed.' Maggie looked at the police officers through the corner of her eyes. 'He'll be sorely missed. I've known the man for forty years.'

Senga had finally got to her feet and was making for the window. 'I never liked the bastard, but I wouldn't have wished that on him.'

'Do you have any idea why he was there, Mrs Finn?'

'Me?' said Senga, pointing to herself. 'If you remember, we spent the whole night at the hospital while my daughter was having her baby. I'm not an executive director – just a title, really, and I get a wee bit of money every year.'

Senga was now on the small ledge, pushing hard at a thin top window. 'Chancellor Fabrications: bloody hopeless, so they are. This fucking thing won't budge.'

'You'll have a drink to wet the baby's head. Come on, officers,' said Maggie.

'Tea or coffee?' said Dickie. 'We're still on duty, Mrs Finn.'

'Aye, of course. You do your job. I'm sorry for Donnie, I really am. Just a shocker.' As she walked from the lounge to the kitchen, a smile broke out across her face. 'Fucking grass,' she said under her breath.

She had just filled the kettle when she heard a scream.

When Maggie hurried back into her lounge, the first thing that hit her was a sudden chill and strong breeze. DS Neil Dickie was staring through a huge hole in the wall where her double-glazed windows had been. He looked back into the room and shook his head.

'She just fell . . . I mean, the whole window gave way.' Langley's mouth was wide in shock.

Maggie Finn collapsed and knocked herself unconscious on the wall.

56

Six months later

London

The street outside the club in south London was almost empty. Kevin Mannion – or Jimmy Dines, as he was now known – wasn't unhappy about that. It was heaving inside his club, Big Joe's. A touching memorial to his father, he thought, without being too obvious. The club was part of Joe Mannion's exit strategy. In case everything went wrong in Glasgow, he had arranged it as an escape route. A ready-made source of money and a great place to launder it; it would be a new start.

Sadly, Joe hadn't lived to take advantage of his forward planning, but his son had. Kevin didn't miss Glasgow, though he still had pangs of guilt about abandoning Sandra and their son. But, as life moved on, he'd met another woman, with whom he was very happy. They had a spacious apartment in Wimbledon and the club was doing really well. Everything was rosy. The ghosts of Glasgow, his family, his enemies and all of his problems, were slowly disappearing.

He stubbed out his cigarette, nodded to the doormen and walked back into the noisy club. It was midweek, cheap drinks, so the place was always rowdy. He passed two young women in an embrace, a young man being helped off the floor by his mates and a middle-aged man staring balefully at the scene. The man looked out of place, but Kevin – Jimmy – paid him little heed. Another man lost in his youth that had long-since escaped forever. He saw their like from time to time: divorced, sad, 'on the scrapheap' guys who had forgotten they had lost their hair and found ten inches round their waist.

He got to his table. It sat on a raised platform that overlooked the dance floor. 'The Royal Box', his regulars called it. Sometimes he would grant the odd favour, let some of the best payers, or anyone with even a hint of celebrity, sit there with him, enjoying free drinks and food. It kept people keen.

Most of the time, though, he liked to be on his own, lord of all he surveyed. It was a great way to attract members of the opposite sex, and that he enjoyed.

He'd been underestimated for most of his life. He knew his father thought little of his potential in any direction, yet here he was. He had reconciled himself to the fact that all this had come from his father's legacy, and if he hadn't disappeared, almost certainly murdered, none of this would have been his.

Did he miss Joe Mannion? No. Did he love the freedom of being his own boss and doing as he pleased? Yes. It was a good trade-off, regardless of the moral conundrum. Kevin had realised that he'd inherited something from his father: the absence of a guilty conscience when it came to getting on. He had consigned his son, his girlfriend, even his mother, to the past. They would remain there, the memory of them fading as he became more and more self-assured, content.

He took a long draw of the cocktail, blinked at the dance floor and spotted a blonde-haired girl in a yellow dress. She was looking directly at him, sitting on his throne. With one finger and a lascivious grin, he beckoned her. Soon she was by his side.

She had long, tanned limbs, big blue eyes and a body to die for. He signalled to the barman to bring her a drink. She smiled.

'Aren't you supposed let me choose what I want?' she shouted above the pulse of the music.

'No, my club, I decide.' He put his hand on her knee. 'What say we have this drink and go upstairs?'

'What's upstairs?' she said with a smile.

'The VIP lounge.'

'Wow, who's up there?'

'Nobody.'

'Oh, I get it, just me and you, right? You're a quick worker.'

'I am. I haven't seen you in before.'

'No, this is my first time. I came here with my friends, but they've all copped off.' She gave the writhing bodies on the dance floor a cursory glance.

'My lucky day.'

'It is!' She kissed his cheek.

'What's your name?'

'Samantha. Yours?'

'Jimmy.'

'Your Scotch, aren't you? All of my friends told me about you here on your stage. King of the world, right?'

'I'm certainly going to be a king tonight.'

The barman arrived with two bright red cocktails in long glasses. Samantha took a sip through a straw.

'Wow, that's so good!' She raised her eyes in delight.

'There's plenty where that came from. Listen, I'll just go to the bog. Then we can go to the VIP suite.'

'The bog? You're funny.'

'And you're posh.'

She watched him walk away from the table and looked around. She slipped a small packet from her bag and pretended to take another sip of her cocktail. She raised the glass to her mouth and slipped the contents of the packet into her drink, swirling the straw round to mix it in. Quickly she swapped drinks and picked up the other glass.

He wasn't gone long, but she noted he'd tidied his thinning hair, brushed it forward.

'Are you ready?'

'Wait, I want to finish our drinks. Let my friends see who I'm with.' Her hand drew his eyes under the table as she drew the hem of her skirt up a few inches to reveal more of her thigh.

'You're a tease.' Kevin discarded the straw, put the glass to his mouth and drained the glass.

'Wow! You're keen.'

'Are you surprised?' He looked her up and down.

Samantha smiled. 'Maybe I'll just take my drink with me.'

Arm in arm, they walked to a door marked 'Private', then up a short winding staircase. The room had thick glass windows, sound-proofed from the noise of the club, though the music was pumped into the space via an array of speakers around the walls. A long couch sat in front of the big window overlooking the revellers below.

'Can they see us?' said Samantha, taking the seat beside him on the couch.

'No. That's the beauty of it. We can fuck in front of the entire place. We can see them, but they can't see us.' Kevin unbuttoned his shirt. Suddenly this room was as hot as Samantha. He placed his hand on her knee and slid it up her thigh.

'Are you okay? You looked a bit flushed.' Samantha pushed his hand away.

Suddenly, Kevin felt his head start to spin, as his heart began to pound. His struggle for breath led to him tearing at his own shirt, not in passion but desperation.

Samantha stood and leaned over him. 'No point struggling, love, you're dying.'

He looked at her through wide, desperate eyes. He tried to speak, but couldn't.

She leaned further forward and whispered in his ear. 'It's your heart. You're having a coronary. Young for that, but it happens.' She drew away, then leaned back into him. 'By the way, greetings from Paisley.'

Calmly, she left the room.

In moments, Kevin Mannion's frenzied writhing stopped and his eyes stared lifelessly through the window over the dancers.

One man dead in a dead man's club.

Epilogue

Langley examined the manila envelope. There was no doubt it was for her: 'PRIVATE' was written above the address in bold capital letters.

She took the paper knife from the mug that held scissors, pens – all manner of things.

At first, when she'd seen the collection of bank statements, she'd sighed. Her first thought was that yet another nutter had sent information of no use to clog up her day. But then something caught her eye.

On closer examination, this was no mere set of bank statements; it was a paper trail, one – judging by its exacting, professional look – prepared by a forensic accountant.

There were two distinct recipients of the totals at the end of each statement. One was nearly sixty thousand pounds, the other larger, over two hundred thousand.

The last page was a summary. As she read on, her mouth gaped open, and her heart began to thud in her chest.

Through a maze of offshore and shell companies, the generosity of the man who had paid these sums into both accounts became obvious: Joe Mannion. In itself, this was no real surprise.

But what rocked her world was the identity of the beneficiaries.

She stared from the window of her office out into the busy general office beyond. Neil Dickie was laughing while chatting to another detective, a mug of tea in his hand. Above, as always, she could feel the looming presence of ACC Mary Green.

But neither of them would be police officers for long.

Langley leaned back in her chair, her breathing rapid, heart still beating fast. Though there was nothing to suggest the identity of the anonymous sender, one name formed on her lips.

'Zander.'

★

I'm back in the room again. The smell is the same, so is the furniture and the company. But, in reality, everything has changed. The old man before me is no longer my priest, my confessor – he is my father.

I watch him as he pours me his wonderful Italian grappa. It's expensive, sweet on the lips, strong on the spirit. He knows I still need fortification. It's been a strange time. I've lost my wife; my children have lost their mother.

But I've gained a father – a whole new family, in fact. The truth is, my whole perception of who I am makes sense now. The way I feel, the truth in my heart, all of the things I've done, the person I've become; it has become clear in its entirety. For we all need to know who we are. We can never really know ourselves until we know the true nature of those with whom we share our lives. Of this I'm sure.

'We will make a better world. At least our little part of it,' he says. He smiles at me, as he has done for all these years.

But how can we make something good come from so much hurt, pain and death?

The two of us: the priest and the gangster; the father, the son, and too many ghosts.

For up-to-the-minute
news and information about
Denzil Meyrick's books
find him here

f DenzilMeyrickAuthor

t LochLomonden